Anytime Anywhere

基本

口語

正式

英會話溝通句典

陳鑫源／編

笛藤出版

本書是《Anytime Anywhere英會話溝通句典 基本·口語·正式》的25K二版，內頁顏色、標題字體都調整得更清晰易讀，方便讀者加強記憶、輕鬆學習，隨時開口溝通無障礙。語言最基本、最普遍的目的，莫過於開口與人說話了，但是當我們要用英語與人互動時，即便學了很久的英語，也常不知該怎麼表達心中所想。英會話溝通的關鍵點其實就在於能否將想表達的意思適切地轉換成英語。以英語為外語的我們，在將母語轉換成英語的過程中，常會東落一點、西落一塊，話到了口邊只剩兩、三個字不成句，最後只好吞了回去。

　　有鑑於這樣的情形，作者陳鑫源先生在書中收編了數千句實用的英會話，本社後續再把固定的「句型」部分獨立出來，為的是強調句型的重要性。英會話與其句型，就如同魚跟釣竿。有了英會話實用句，在用英語溝通時，即能收到立竿見影的成效；而有了固定句型，則可無限創造出適合自己情境的會話句，更能貼切符合個人的需求。

　　在此要感謝席菈為本書編寫中文引導句。引導句表現了每句話所要表達的基本概念，只要從引導句出發，就能輕易延伸出具體的意思，有助於想法的表達，與英會話的學習。這是一本實用的參考書，同時也是一本可提升英會話溝通技巧的學習書，在各位開口說英語，與人交流溝通時，能藉著本書達到讓自己更滿意的表現。

笛藤編輯部

隨時隨地開口英會話　最得體的英語說話術

◆ 【36關鍵主題＋100實際狀況＋4500會話句】

全書36個大主題,都是英會話的關鍵場景,並細分成100多個小項目,涵蓋了各種實際狀況。彙整4500多句會話,教你多種表達方式,隨時隨地都有新的說法可替換,讓你說話不辭窮,溝通無障礙。

◆ 【在對的場合說對的話】

書中會話根據說話場合分為3種:基本說法、日常口語、正式場合。基本說法適用通常的情形,日常口語較隨便、不拘小節,正式場合的用句客氣禮貌,字句較複雜。在用英語溝通之際,視場合和對象使用適當的句子,就能表現得體不失態。

◆ 【固定句型與實用會話句】

本句典以左右對應方式編排,左半邊是會話的固定句型,右半邊則是實用會話句。從固定句型可創造出無數新的句子,符合個人實際遭遇情境。書中有些句子本身即是完整會話句,就不區分為句型跟會話了,可直接整句學起來應用。

◆ 【全天候會話朗讀MP3】

隨書附贈專業美語錄音人員錄製的會話朗讀MP3,時間長達5小時,內容涵蓋書中所有句型與會話句。建議讀者一邊聆聽一邊學習,將美語人士說話的抑揚頓挫吸收進去,當真正開口說英語時,會更有自信,發音與腔調也會更加道地。

建議學習方法：

1. 只想學固定句型的讀者，可以只讀左半邊，由上往下漸次學習。
2. 想從句型紮根，再學會話句的讀者，可以從左邊讀到右邊。
3. 書本搭配MP3一起學習，發音與腔調自然會潛移默化，變得更自然。

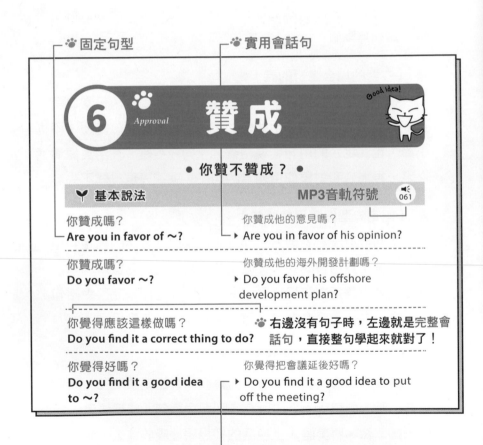

❀ 固定句型　　　　　❀ 實用會話句

Good idea!

6 *Approval*　　**贊成**

● 你贊不贊成？ ●

❣ 基本說法　　　　　　　MP3音軌符號 🔊 061

你贊成嗎？　　　　　　　你贊成他的意見嗎？
Are you in favor of ～?　▸ Are you in favor of his opinion?

你贊成嗎？　　　　　　　你贊成他的海外開發計劃嗎？
Do you favor ～?　　　▸ Do you favor his offshore development plan?

你覺得應該這樣做嗎？　　　❀ 右邊沒有句子時，左邊就是完整會
Do you find it a correct thing to do?　話句，直接整句學起來就對了！

你覺得好嗎？　　　　　　你覺得把會議延後好嗎？
Do you find it a good idea to ～?　▸ Do you find it a good idea to put off the meeting?

❀ 灰色字，可替換成別的字

❀ 黑色字，為主要句型

Contents

1 能力 Ability —————————— 12

- 你會做這些事嗎？ / 12
- 沒問題，我做得到 / 16
- 不好意思，我不會 / 20

2 忠告 Advice —————————— 25

- 你覺得我該怎麼辦？ / 25
- 我勸你這麼做 / 30
- 勸你不要這麼做 / 36

3 同意 Agreement —————————— 42

- 你同意嗎？ / 42
- 我同意你所說的 / 47
- 我同意，可是… / 53
- 我不同意你的說法 / 60
- 我想你才是對的 / 68
- 我們達成協議了 / 72

4 道歉 Apology —————————— 75

- 對不起，很抱歉 / 75
- 沒關係，別在意 / 80
- 不好意思，離開一下 / 84

5 **約會 Appointment** ——————————— 87

● 能約你見面嗎？/ 87

● 要約何時？在哪裡？/ 92

● 約好時間地點 / 98

● 這個時間地點不方便 / 104

● 改變或取消約會 / 107

6 **贊成 Approval** ——————————— 111

● 你贊不贊成？/ 111

● 我贊成 / 116

● 我不贊成 / 123

7 **相信 Belief** ——————————— 129

● 我相信 / 129

● 我不相信 / 132

8 **肯定 Certainty** ——————————— 137

● 你真的確定嗎？/ 137

● 我很肯定 / 142

● 我並不肯定 / 150

★ 最愛的經典名句
★ Q & A

9 **溝通 Communication** ——————————— 161

● 最常用的聊天開場白 / 161

● 引起對方注意 / 165

● 接話的技巧 / 168

● 話鋒一轉，換個話題 / 172

● 結束談話的技巧 / 176

⑩ 比較 Comparison ———————————— 182

● 比較的各種表達 / 182

⑪ 理解 Comprehension ———————————— 187

● 你的意思是…？ / 187

● 你明白我的意思嗎？ / 193

⑫ 恭喜 Congratulations ———————————— 197

● 恭喜你 / 197

⑬ 正確 Correctness ———————————— 200

● 請問這樣是對的嗎？ / 200

● 對，就是這樣 / 203

● 不對，不是這樣 / 206

● 糾正對方 / 209

⑭ 決定 Decision ———————————— 212

● 我已經決定了 / 212

⑮ 再見 Goodbye ———————————— 216

● 再見了 / 216

⑯ 舉例 Exemplification ———————————— 221

● 舉例 / 221

17 祝福 Good Wishes —————————— 225

● 真心祝福你 / 225

● 謝謝你的祝福 / 229

● 在特別的日子裡祝福你 / 231

● 謝謝你特別的祝福 / 234

● 敬你一杯 / 236

18 說閒話 Gossip —————————————— 240

● 說長道短聊八卦 / 240

19 感謝 Gratitude ———————————— 245

● 真的謝謝你 / 245

● 請不用客氣 / 250

20 打招呼 Greetings ———————————— 253

● 跟別人打招呼 / 253

● 親切問候對方 / 257

● 最近過得不錯（不太好）/ 261

21 消息 Information ————————————— 265

● 打聽消息 / 265

● 你知道這件事嗎？/ 269

● 我知道這件事 / 273

● 我不知道這件事 / 277

22 指示 Instruction —————————— 281

- 告訴對方要怎麼做 / 281

23 介紹 Introduction —————————— 285

- 介紹別人認識 / 285
- 自我介紹 / 289
- 對介紹的應答 / 292

24 邀請 Invitation —————————— 296

- 誠摯邀請 / 296
- 接受邀請 / 300
- 拒絕邀請 / 304

25 判斷 Judgment —————————— 308

- 作出判斷 / 308

26 姓名 Name —————————— 313

- 請問貴姓大名 / 313
  ★ 自我介紹篇
  ★ 這時候要怎麼說

27 義務 Obligation —————————— 321

- 我必須這麼做嗎？/ 321
- 你必須這麼做 / 324
- 你沒必要這麼做 / 329
- 你不該這麼做 / 332
- 我必須這麼做 / 335
- 我不該這麼做 / 338

28 提供 Offer ——————————————— 341

- 提供東西給別人 / 341
- 接受提供的東西 / 345
- 謝絕提供的東西 / 349
- 把東西交給對方 / 352
- 提議幫對方做事 / 355
- 接受提供的幫助 / 360
- 謝絕提供的幫助 / 363

29 意見 Opinion ——————————————— 366

- 徵求對方的意見 / 366
- 表示自己的意見 / 370
- 表示自己沒有意見 / 376
- 避免直接發表意見 / 379
- 設法改變對方的意見 / 383

30 許可 Permission ——————————————— 389

- 請求許可 / 389
- 給予許可 / 394
- 拒絕許可 / 398

31 勸說 Persuasion ——————————————— 402

- 設法說服對方 / 402

32 理由 Reason ——————————————— 412

- 說明理由 / 412

㉝ 記憶 Remembrance —————— 417

- 你還記得嗎？ / 417
- 我記得 / 420
- 我想不起來了 / 425
- 提醒對方 / 429

㉞ 複述 Repetition —————— 434

- 請再說一遍 / 434
- 我剛才是說… / 438
- 換一種方式複述 / 441

㉟ 請求 Request —————— 445

- 提出請求 / 445
- 答應請求 / 452
- 拒絕請求 / 455

㊱ 建議 Suggestion —————— 458

- 提出建議 / 458
- 贊成建議 / 465
- 反對建議 / 468

★ 讀書計劃
★ 我的單字卡
★ 我的英會話記憶卡

 Ability

能力

● 你會做這些事嗎？ ●

❤ 基本說法

001

你會嗎？ **Can you ～?**	你會騎腳踏車嗎？ ▸ Can you ride a bike?
你有這種能力嗎？ **Do you have the skill of ～?**	你有開卡車的能力嗎？ ▸ Do you have the skill of driving a truck?
你懂這方面嗎？ **Do you know anything about ～?**	你懂園藝嗎？ ▸ Do you know anything about gardening?
你知道怎麼做嗎？ **Do you know how to ～?**	你知道怎麼烹飪嗎？ ▸ Do you know how to cook?
你認為你會做嗎？ **Do you think you can ～?**	你認為你會打棒球嗎？ ▸ Do you think you can play baseball?
你有這方面的才能嗎？ **Have you got a talent for ～?**	你有繪畫的才能嗎？ ▸ Have you got a talent for painting?
你能做到嗎？ **Will you be able to ～?**	中午前你能把工作完成嗎？ ▸ Will you be able to finish your work by noon?
你會的，不是嗎？ **You can ～, can't you?**	你會背誦這首詩，不是嗎？ ▸ You can recite the poem, can't you?

❀ 日常口語

你行嗎？
Are you any good？

你行嗎？
Are you any good at ～?

你做生意行嗎？
▸ Are you any good at business?

你擅長嗎？
Are you clever at ～?

你擅長數學嗎？
▸ Are you clever at math?

你認為你做得到嗎？
Do you reckon you could ～?

你認為你能贏得比賽嗎？
▸ Do you reckon you could win the game?

你認為你有天賦嗎？
Do you reckon you have the gift of ～?

你認為你有編故事的天賦嗎？
▸ Do you reckon you have the gift of making up stories?

你有本事嗎？
Have you got the know-how for ～?

你有本事打開這個罐頭嗎？
▸ Have you got the know-how for opening the can?

我敢說你不會，對不對？
I bet you can't ～, can you?

我敢說你不會跳水，對不對？
▸ I bet you can't dive, can you?

你會嗎？
Think you can ～?

你會玩牌嗎？
▸ Think you can play cards?

你這方面如何？
What're you like at ～?

你的演說能力如何？
▸ What're you like at public speaking?

♣ 正式場合

你能做到嗎？
Are you able to ～?

你能在10秒鐘內跑完100公尺嗎？
▸ Are you able to cover 100 meters in 10 seconds?

你有能力嗎？
Are you capable of ～?

你有能力畫美麗的圖畫嗎？
▸ Are you capable of painting beautiful pictures?

你這方面擅長嗎？
Are you proficient at ～?

你擅長判斷距離嗎？
▸ Are you proficient at judging distances?

你認為你有能力完成嗎？
Do you consider it within your capacity to ～?

你認為你有能力把故事改編成電影嗎？
▸ Do you consider it within your capacity to adapt the story for the screen?

你覺得你能做到嗎？
Do you feel able to ～?

你覺得你能指揮交響樂團嗎？
▸ Do you feel able to conduct an orchestra?

你有經驗嗎？
Do you have any experience ?

你有經驗嗎？
Do you have any experience of ～?

你有編輯報紙的經驗嗎？
▸ Do you have any experience of editing a newspaper?

你有必備的資歷嗎？
Do you have the qualifications necessary to ～?

你有經營工廠所必備的資歷嗎？
▸ Do you have the qualifications necessary to run a factory?

你覺得你有能力嗎？
Do you think you have the abilities to ～?

你覺得你有能力設計洋裝嗎？
▸ Do you think you have the abilities to design a dress?

你認為你有能力嗎？
Do you think you have the capability to ～?

你認為你有能力主持這次研討會嗎？
▸ Do you think you have the capability to lead the discussion?

你覺得你有能力嗎？
Do you think you are capable of ～?

你覺得你有能力寫詩嗎？
▸ Do you think you are capable of writing poems?

請問你認為你有才能嗎？
Would you say you had the competence for ～?

請問你認為你有理財的才能嗎？
▸ Would you say you had the competence for handling money?

請問你認為你有能力嗎？
Would you say you were able to ～?

請問你認為你有能力管理百貨公司嗎？
▸ Would you say you were able to manage a department store?

● 沒問題，我做得到 ●

❦ 基本說法

004

我能。
I can ~.

我能做到。
▸ I can do it.

我有這種能力。
I have the skill of ~.

我有騎單輪車的能力。
▸ I have the skill of riding a monocycle.

我知道怎麼做。
I know how to ~.

我知道怎麼操作電腦。
▸ I know how to operate a computer.

我略懂。
I know something about ~.

我略懂力學。
▸ I know something about mechanics.

我也許能。
I might be able to ~.

我也許能把它譯成中文。
▸ I might be able to translate it into Chinese.

我想我可以。
I think I can ~.

我想我可以解決這問題。
▸ I think I can solve the problem.

我可以。
I'll be able to ~.

我可以在星期天以前做好這件事。
▸ I'll be able to get it done by Sunday.

對我而言並非難事。
It's not too much a problem for me to ~.

洗碗對我而言並不太難。
▸ It's not too much a problem for me to wash the dishes.

我曾經接受過訓練。
I've had some training in ~.

我受過些烹飪訓練。
▸ I've had some training in cooking.

✿ 日常口語

我很在行。 **I'm pretty good at ～.**	滑水我很在行。 ▸ I'm pretty good at water skiing.

當然能。
Sure.

我剛好會。
There's just a chance I can ～. ▸ 這件事我剛好會做。
There's just a chance I can do it.

是的，沒問題。
Yes, it's a cinch.

是的，小事一樁！
Yes, it's a piece of cake!

是的，這沒什麼。
Yes, it's nothing.

是的，輕而易舉。
Yes, it's quite easy.

是的，沒問題。
Yes, no problem.

♣ 正式場合

我相信我有能力完成。
I believe I have the abilities to ~.

▶ 我相信我有能力舉辦一場派對。
I believe I have the abilities to organize a party.

我認為這是我能力所及。
I consider it within my capacity to ~.

▶ 我認為創辦合資企業是我能力所及的事。
I consider it within my capacity to start a joint venture.

我想這不會太難。
I don't think it would be too difficult to ~.

▶ 照顧你的寵物我想不會太難的。
I don't think it would be too difficult to look after your pet.

我認為不會是大問題。
I don't think that would prove too much a problem to ~.

▶ 我認為集資兩百萬美元不會是大問題。
I don't think that would prove too much a problem to collect 2 million dollars.

我覺得我能。
I feel able to ~.

▶ 我覺得我能游過這條河。
I feel able to swim across the river.

我覺得我能。
I feel capable of ~.

▶ 我覺得我能一個月賺到5萬美元。
I feel capable of earning $50,000 a month.

我有經驗。
I have experience in ~.

▶ 我有語言教學的經驗。
I have experience in teaching languages.

我認為我有能力。
I think I have the capability to ~.

▶ 我認為我有能力經營一家店。
I think I have the capability to run a store.

我認為我有這方面所需能力。
I think I have the competence necessary for ~.

▶ 我認為我有當導遊所需的能力。
I think I have the competence necessary for a tour guide.

我認為我具備所需的資歷。
I'd say I had the qualifications necessary to ～.

我認為我具備經營藥局所需的資歷。
▸ I'd say I had the qualifications necessary to run a drugstore.

我認為我相當熟練。
I'd say I was quite proficient at ～.

我認為我對裁縫方面相當熟練。
▸ I'd say I was quite proficient at tailoring.

我能夠。
I'm able to ～.

我能背誦莎士比亞全部的十四行詩。
▸ I'm able to recite all Shakespeare's Sonnets.

我能夠。
I'm capable of ～.

我能記住大數字。
▸ I'm capable of remembering big numbers.

● 不好意思，我不會 ●

我不能。 **I can't ~.**	我提不起這個箱子。 ▸ I can't lift the box.
我不會做。 **I don't have the skill of ~.**	我不會划獨木舟。 ▸ I don't have the skill of canoeing.
我一無所知。 **I don't know anything about ~.**	我對園藝一無所知。 ▸ I don't know anything about gardening.
我不知道要怎麼做。 **I don't know how I can ~.**	我不知道要怎樣才能把它完成。 ▸ I don't know how I can get it done.
我不知道從哪裡著手。 **I don't know where to begin ~.**	我不知道從哪裡著手數起。 ▸ I don't know where to begin counting them.
我沒辦法做到。 **I won't be able to ~.**	我明天沒辦法到那裡。 ▸ I won't be able to get there tomorrow.
我恐怕不能。 **I'm not sure I can ~.**	這事情我恐怕無法完成。 ▸ I'm not sure I can do it.
我恐怕不知道怎麼做。 **I'm not sure I know how to ~.**	我恐怕不知道怎麼編字典。 ▸ I'm not sure I know how to compile a dictionary.
恐怕我不擅長此事。 **I'm not sure I'm skilled at ~.**	恐怕我不擅長打高爾夫球。 ▸ I'm not sure I'm skilled at playing golf.
我根本辦不到。 **It's just impossible for me to ~.**	我根本沒辦法戒菸。 ▸ It's just impossible for me to quit smoking.

我看我無法做到。
I don't reckon I can ～.

我看我趕不上末班車了。
▶ I don't reckon I can catch the last bus.

我看我一點也不在行。
I don't reckon I'm any good at ～.

我看我對木工一點也不在行。
▶ I don't reckon I'm any good at carpentry.

我看我沒能耐。
I don't reckon I've got the know-how to ～.

我看我沒能耐蓋房子。
▶ I don't reckon I've got the know-how to build a house.

我一竅不通。
I haven't a clue how to ～.

我對譜寫華爾滋是一竅不通。
▶ I haven't a clue how to compose a waltz.

我一點也不會。
I haven't the least idea how to ～.

我一點也不會打橋牌。
▶ I haven't the least idea how to play bridge.

我一竅不通。
I'm hopeless.
我對此一竅不通。
I'm hopeless at ～.

我對數學一竅不通。
▶ I'm hopeless at math.

我不擅長。
I'm no good at ～.

我對跳舞不擅長。
▶ I'm no good at dancing.

我完全不行。
I'm no use.
我完全不行。
I'm no use at ～.

猜謎語我一點都不行。
▶ I'm no use at guessing riddles.

我這方面很差。
I'm pretty bad at ～.

我溜冰溜得很差。
▶ I'm pretty bad at skating.

我根本不行。
I'm useless at ～.

我講故事根本不行。
▸ I'm useless at telling stories.

我不知道怎麼做。
I've got no idea how to ～.

我不知道要怎麼和他聯絡。
▸ I've got no idea how to get into touch with him.

抱歉，沒辦法。
Sorry, can't manage.
抱歉，沒辦法做。
Sorry, can't manage to ～.

對不起，沒辦法找到你要的雜誌。
▸ Sorry, can't manage to find the magazine you want.

我沒辦法做到。
There's no way I can ～.

我沒法找到那個失蹤的男孩。
▸ There's no way I can find the missing boy.

我毫無興趣。
～ just isn't my line.

我對打字毫無興趣。
▸ Typing just isn't my line.

♣ 正式場合

我想我不具備必需的資歷。
I don't believe I have the qualifications necessary to ~.

▸ 我想我不具備當秘書所必需的資歷。
I don't believe I have the qualifications necessary to be a secretary.

我認為我能力不足。
I don't consider it within my capacity to ~.

▸ 我認為我沒能力解決這次紛爭。
I don't consider it within my capacity to settle the dispute.

我覺得我沒這個能力。
I don't feel able to ~.

▸ 我覺得我沒能力游過這條河。
I don't feel able to swim across the river.

我覺得我沒這個能力。
I don't feel capable of ~.

▸ 我覺得我沒演說的能力。
I don't feel capable of making public speech.

我認為我沒有必備能力。
I don't think I have the competence necessary to ~.

▸ 我認為我沒有跟外商談判必備的能力。
I don't think I have the competence necessary to negotiate with a foreign company.

我認為我沒有所需的經驗。
I don't think I have the experience necessary to ~.

▸ 我認為我沒有當會議口譯所需的經驗。
I don't think I have the experience necessary to interpret at a meeting.

我沒有經驗。
I have no experience.
我沒有經驗。
I have no experience in ~.

▸ 我沒有教語言的經驗。
I have no experience in teaching languages.

我認為這對我太難了。
I think it would be too difficult for me to ~.

▸ 我認為我要改變這局面太難了。
I think it would be too difficult for me to change the situation.

我想我是不可能做到的。 **I think that would prove impossible for me to ~.**	▶ I think that would prove impossible for me to pass the exam.
我看我沒有必備的能力。 **I wouldn't say I had the abilities necessary to ~.**	▶ I wouldn't say I had the abilities necessary to manage a department store.
我認為我並不專精。 **I wouldn't say I was proficient at ~.**	▶ I wouldn't say I was proficient at computer programming.
我看這非我能力所及。 **I'd say ~ might be beyond me.**	▶ I'd say running a factory might be beyond me.
我恐怕不能。 **I'm afraid I can't ~.**	▶ I'm afraid I can't cope with those troubles.
這恐怕非我能力所及。 **I'm afraid ~ might be out of my depth.**	▶ I'm afraid organizing a conference might be out of my depth.
我不確定我是否有能力。 **I'm not sure I have the capability of ~.**	▶ I'm not sure I have the capability of designing a modern opera house.
我不確定我能否做到。 **I'm not sure I'm able to ~.**	▶ I'm not sure I'm able to increase our sales in that region.

● 你覺得我該怎麼辦？ ●

❤ 基本說法

🔊 010

你能給我一點忠告嗎？

Can you give me some advice on ～?

對於該怎麼彌補損失的時間，你能給我一點忠告嗎？

▶ Can you give me some advice on how to make up for the time I've lost?

你覺得我應該嗎？

Do you think I should ～?

你覺得我應該改變計劃嗎？

▶ Do you think I should change the plan?

你覺得我該如何？

How do you think I should ～?

你覺得我該如何改時間表？

▶ How do you think I should change the timetable?

你會建議我怎麼做？

How would you advise me to ～?

你會建議我怎麼回覆邀請？

▶ How would you advise me to reply to an invitation?

我想知道你的建議。

I'd like your advice about ～.

我想知道你對我的研究的建議。

▶ I'd like your advice about my research.

我應該嗎？

Ought I to ～?

去美國前我應該複習英語嗎？

▶ Ought I to brush up my English before I go to America?

我應該嗎？

Should I ～?

我應該接受提議嗎？

▶ Should I accept the proposal?

你覺得我能做什麼？

What do you think I can do to ～?

你覺得我能做什麼來幫助他們？

▶ What do you think I can do to help them?

我能做什麼？
What can I do to ～?

我能做些什麼好讓她高興呢？
▸ What can I do to cheer her up?

我應該做什麼？
What should I do to ～?

我該做什麼來解決這個問題呢？
▸ What should I do to solve the problem?

你會建議我做什麼？
What would you advise me to do?

你會建議我做什麼？
What would you advise me to do to ～?

你會建議我做什麼來消除意見分歧？
▸ What would you advise me to do to settle the differences?

你要是處在我的狀況會怎麼辦？
What would you do in my position?

你說我該怎麼辦？
What would you say I should do?

你認為我應該在何時？
When do you think I should ～?

你認為我該什麼時候來？
▸ When do you think I should come?

你認為我應該在何處？
Where do you think I should ～?

你認為我該去哪裡？
▸ Where do you think I should go?

你建議我哪一個？
Which one would you advise me to ～?

你建議我挑選哪一個？
▸ Which one would you advise me to choose?

你會建議我這麼做嗎？
Would you advise me to ～?

你會建議我用信用卡付帳嗎？
▸ Would you advise me to pay the bill with the credit card?

你能給我一點忠告嗎？
Would you give me some advice about ～?

關於我留學的計劃，你能給我忠告嗎？
▸ Would you give me some advice about my plan to study abroad?

❋ 日常口語

你能幫我解決這件事嗎？
Can you help me straighten it out?

你能為我想辦法解決嗎？
Can you straighten me out on ～?

你能為我想辦法解決這件事嗎？
▶ Can you straighten me out on this matter?

幫我解決，好嗎？
Help me sort out ～, will you?

幫我解決問題，好嗎？
▶ Help me sort out my problem, will you?

你如何看待呢？
How do you see ～?

你如何看待我們的思考模式？
▶ How do you see our way of thinking?

你看我能這麼做嗎？
Reckon I can ～?

你看我可以要求加薪嗎？
▶ Reckon I can ask for a pay raise?

你看我應該嗎？
Reckon I should ～?

你看我該向左轉嗎？
▶ Reckon I should turn left?

你看如何呢？
What do you make of ～?

這個建議你看如何？
▶ What do you make of that suggestion?

你看我能怎樣？
What do you reckon I can ～?

你看這件事我能怎麼辦？
▶ What do you reckon I can do about it?

你看我該怎樣？
What do you reckon I should ～?

你看我該怎麼辦？
▶ What do you reckon I should do?

你要是處在我的情況，你會怎麼辦？
What would you do if you were in my shoes?

如果你是我，你會怎麼做？
What would you do if you were me?

27

♣ 正式場合

你能對此提些意見嗎？
Could I ask for some advice about ～?
► 你能對我的研究工作提些意見嗎？
Could I ask for some advice about my research?

請問你對此事有何看法？
Could I ask what your reactions would be to ～?
► 請問你對刪減經費有何看法？
Could I ask what your reactions would be to cutting down expenses?

能否請你提供意見？
Could I have your advice on ～?
► 能否請你對我兒子的教育提供意見？
Could I have your advice on my son's education?

請問這樣是否正確呢？
I'd like to ask whether it is correct to ～?
► 請問參加該公司的保險計劃是否正確？
I'd like to ask whether it is correct to partake in the firm's insurance plan?

我想徵求你的意見。
I'd like to consult you on ～.
► 我想就受邀客人名單來徵求你的意見。
I'd like to consult you on the list of guests to be invited.

我想請你提供意見。
I'd like to have your advice on ～.
► 我想請你對我的作文提供意見。
I'd like to have your advice on my composition.

我想知道你對此的反應。
I was wondering what your reactions would be to ～.
► 我想知道你對我們的提議有什麼反應。
I was wondering what your reactions would be to our proposal.

如果你能給我一些忠告，我會很感激的。
I would appreciate it if you could give me some advice about ～.
► 如果你能在托福考試方面給我一些忠告，我會很感激的。
I would appreciate it if you could give me some advice about the TOEFL test.

如能得到你的建議，我將十分感激。
I would appreciate some advice from you.

我會很感激你提出的建議。
I would appreciate your advice on ～.

我會很感激你對我們的決定提出的建議。
▶ I would appreciate your advice on our decision.

你會建議我採取什麼行動？
What course of action would you advise me to take?

你會建議我怎麼辦？
What would you counsel me to do?

你說該怎麼做呢？
What would you recommend for ～?

你說該怎麼去除我襯衫上的墨水痕跡？
▶ What would you recommend for getting ink stains from my shirt?

你說我該如此嗎？
Would you recommend me to ～?

你說我該接受他的邀請嗎？
▶ Would you recommend me to accept his invitation?

● 我勸你這麼做 ●

你不認為還是這樣好嗎？
Don't you think it might be a good idea to ～?

你不認為還是等一會兒好嗎？
▶ Don't you think it might be a good idea to wait a moment?

我勸你。
I advise you to ～.

我勸你去看醫生。
▶ I advise you to see a doctor.

我說，這對你沒壞處。
I should say ～ would do you no harm.

我說，做一點工作對你沒有壞處。
▶ I should say a little work would do you no harm.

我認為這個意見不錯。
I think it might be a good idea to ～.

我認為現在去游泳的意見不錯。
▶ I think it might be a good idea to go swimming now.

我認為對你有好處。
I think it'll do you good to ～.

我認為每天跑步對你會有好處。
▶ I think it'll do you good to go running every day.

我認為你可以這麼做。
I think you can ～.

我看你可以去曼利海灘換換環境。
▶ I think you can go to Manly Beach for a change.

我認為你可以這麼做。
I think you might ～.

我認為你可以在海灘享受假日。
▶ I think you might enjoy a holiday at the beach.

我認為你應該如此。
I think you ought to ～.

我認為你應該找一間大一點的公寓。
▶ I think you ought to find a bigger flat.

我認為你應該如此。
I think you should ～.

我認為你應該節食。
▶ I think you should go on a diet.

我會…。
I would ～.

我會記下那個人的名字。
▶ I would make a note of that man's name.

如果我是你，我會…。
I'd ～ if I were you.

如果我是你，我會把錢放在保險箱裡。
▶ I'd keep the money in a safe if I were you.

我建議如此。
I'd suggest ～.

我建議你自己去看他。
▶ I'd suggest going to see him yourself.

如果我是你，我會…。
If I were you, I'd ～.

如果我是你，我會拒絕執行他的命令。
▶ If I were you, I'd refuse to carry out his orders.

如果這樣倒也不錯。
It might be an idea if ～.

你如果找一個兼差工作倒也不錯。
▶ It might be an idea if you try to get a part-time job.

這樣比較好。

It might be as well to ～.

你餵小孩牛奶時，先把表面的牛奶撥掉比較好。
▶ It might be as well to cream off the top of the milk before you feed the baby with it.

對你有好處。
It'll do you good to ～.

休息一下對你會有好處的。
▶ It'll do you good to take a rest.

你必須如此。
You have to ～.

如果你聽我的話，就必須少抽菸。
▶ You have to cut down on smoking if you listen to me.

你倒不如這樣。
You might as well ～.

你倒不如把真相告訴她。
▶ You might as well tell her the truth.

你應該如此。
You should ～.

我認為你應該矢志不渝。
▶ You should persist in your ambition, if you ask me.

❀ 日常口語

跟鮑伯斷絕關係。
Break it off with Bob.
＊用祈使句表示直率的勸告。原形動詞開頭，否定時加上Don't或Never。

我看你應該。
I reckon you should ～.

我看你早上應該早點起床。
▶ I reckon you should get up earlier in the morning.

若我處在你的情況，我會…。
I'd ～ if I were in your shoes.

如果我處在你的情況，我會待在那裡。
▶ I'd stay over there if I were in your shoes.

也許是不錯的主意。
It might not be a bad idea to ～.

租車也許是不錯的主意。
▶ It might not be a bad idea to rent a car.

你就這樣做。
Just ～.

你就再試試看。
▶ Just try again.

聽我的話。
Take my advice and ～.

聽我的話，隨他去吧。
▶ Take my advice and leave it as it is.

依我看，你應該如此。
The way I see it, you should ～.

依我看，你應該繼續練習鋼琴。
▶ The way I see it, you should keep up your piano practice.

你為什麼不？
Why don't you ～?

你為什麼不和她談談這件事呢？
▶ Why don't you talk to her about it?

何不？
Why not ～?

何不向你父親求援呢？
▶ Why not go to your father for help?

如果這樣，你可以這麼做。
You can ～ if ～.

如果你不趕時間，可以搭公車去。
▶ You can go by bus if you're not in a hurry.

如果你明白我的意思，你就應該如此。 **You ought to ～ if you get what I mean.**	如果你明白我的意思，你就應該改變飲食。 ▸ You ought to change your diet if you get what I mean.
如果你明白我的意思，你就應該如此。 **You should ～ if you see what I mean.**	如果你明白我的意思，你就該留意這名男子。 ▸ You should keep an eye on the man if you see what I mean.
你最好如此。 **You'd better ～.**	你最好把考卷再檢查一遍。 ▸ You'd better go through your test paper again.

♣ 正式場合

我建議。
I should recommend ~.

我建議早一點去那裡。
▶ I should recommend going there earlier.

我勸你。
I would advise you to ~.

我勸你到夏威夷去住幾星期。
▶ I would advise you to spend a couple of weeks in Hawaii.

若我處在你的立場，我會…。
I would ~ if I were in your place.

若我處在你的立場，我就會改變計劃。
▶ I would change the plan if I were in your place.

如果你聽我的勸告，你就…。
If you follow my recommendations, you'll ~.

如果你聽我的勸，你就接受他的建議。
▶ If you follow my recommendations, you'll accept his proposition.

如果你聽我的勸告，你就…。
If you take my advice, you'll ~.

如果你聽我的勸告，就去從軍。
▶ If you take my advice, you'll join the army.

如果你徵求我的意見，我會…。
If you want my advice, I'd ~.

如果你徵求我的意見，我會寫信到總公司討論這個問題。
▶ If you want my advice, I'd write to the head office about the problem.

這樣比較謹慎。
It would be prudent to ~.

還是把壞天氣考慮在內，這樣比較謹慎。
▶ It would be prudent to allow for the bad weather.

這樣比較明智。
It would be wise to ~.

還是把你的考卷再檢查一遍比較明智。
▶ It would be wise to go over your test paper again.

我的意見是。
My advice would be to ～.

▸ 我的意見是列出參加宴會的客人名單。
My advice would be to draw up a list of the guests for the dinner.

我的看法是。
My reaction would be to ～.

▸ 我的看法是要參加這次演講比賽。
My reaction would be to partake in the speech competition.

你要是不這樣就不明智了。
You would be ill-advised not to ～.

▸ 你要是不反駁她那就不明智了。
You would be ill-advised not to plead against her.

你若不這樣就不明智了。
You would be unwise not to ～.

▸ 你若不辭去委員會工作那就不明智了。
You would be unwise not to resign from the committee.

你最好這樣做。
You would be well advised to ～.

▸ 你最好事先準備。
You would be well advised to prepare in advance.

你最好這樣做。
You would be wise to ～.

▸ 你最好買一台新的電腦。
You would be wise to buy a new computer.

● 勸你不要這麼做 ●

我勸你不要。
I advise you not to ～.

我勸你不要小看他。
▶ I advise you not to look down upon him.

我認為這樣做對你無益。
I don't think it'll do you any good to ～.

我認為你為此自責對你無益。
▶ I don't think it'll do you any good to blame yourself for that.

我認為不好。
I don't think it's a good idea to ～.

我認為你現在賣掉房子不好。
▶ I don't think it's a good idea to sell your house now.

我認為你不該。
I don't think you ought to ～.

我認為你不該放棄當專業歌手的希望。
▶ I don't think you ought to give up all hope of becoming a professional singer.

我認為你不應該。
I don't think you should ～.

我認為你不應該保持沉默。
▶ I don't think you should keep silent.

我勸你不要。
I wouldn't suggest ～.

我勸你沒有特殊原因不要更改時間表。
▶ I wouldn't suggest changing the timetable without any particular reason.

如果我是你，我絕不會如此。
I'd never ～, if I were you.

如果我是你，我絕不會到處閒蕩。
▶ I'd never goof around, if I were you.

如果我是你，我就不會。
If I were you, I wouldn't ～.

如果我是你，我就不會上學遲到。
▶ If I were you, I wouldn't go to school late.

那可能不是好主意。
It might not be a good idea to ～.

你放棄大學的課程可能不是好主意。
▶ It might not be a good idea to give up your college course.

你這樣可不行。	你跟他打官司可不行。
It wouldn't do for you to ～.	▸ It wouldn't do for you to go to law against him.

那對你沒好處。	你為瑪麗傾心沒有好處。
It'll do you no good to ～.	▸ It'll do you no good to fall for Mary.

如果你聽我的，就不應該如此。	如果你聽我的，就不應該放棄經濟學而改讀文學。
You shouldn't ～ if you listen to me.	▸ You shouldn't leave economics to study literature if you listen to me.

🌸 日常口語

017

不要。 **Don't ～.**	如果你想要人幫你，就不要言而無信。 ▸ Don't break your word if you want help.
我看這對你沒好處。 **I don't reckon it'll do you any good to ～.**	我看這種天氣出門對你沒什麼好處。 ▸ I don't reckon it'll do you any good to go out in this weather.
我想那並不好。 **I don't reckon it's a good idea to ～.**	我想熬夜並不好。 ▸ I don't reckon it's a good idea to stay up late at night.
我認為你不應該。 **I don't reckon you should ～.**	我認為你不該計較她的無禮。 ▸ I don't reckon you should care about her rudeness.
若我處在你的情況，我絕不會。 **I'd never ～ if I were in your shoes.**	若我處在你的情況，我絕不會讓她走。 ▸ I'd never let her go if I were in your shoes.
我覺得你不要這樣比較好。 **I'd rather you didn't ～.**	我覺得你不去申請那個職位比較好。 ▸ I'd rather you didn't apply for that position.
如果我處在你的情況，我會三思而後行。 **I'd think twice before I ～ if I were in your shoes.**	如果我處在你的情況，我會三思後再決定怎麼辦。 ▸ I'd think twice before I decide what to do if I were in your shoes.
沒有用。 **It's no good ～.**	抱怨是沒有用的。 ▸ It's no good complaining.
這該由你決定，但我不會…。 **It's up to you but I wouldn't ～.**	這該由你決定，但我不會那樣做。 ▸ It's up to you but I wouldn't do that.

冷靜下來，沒有必要這麼做。
Simmer down, sb., no point of ~.

冷靜下來，凱莉，沒有必要跟他爭論。
▸ Simmer down, Kelly, no point of arguing with him.

聽我的勸告，不要這樣。
Take my advice and don't ~.

聽我的勸告，不要在裡面放鹽。
▸ Take my advice and don't put any salt in it.

依我看，你應該避免。
The way I see it, you should avoid ~.

依我看，你應該避免與她爭吵。
▸ The way I see it, you should avoid quarreling with her.

如果你明白我的意思，你不能如此。
You can't ~ if you see what I mean.

如果你明白我的意思，你不能整天待在家裡。
▸ You can't stay at home all day if you see what I mean.

你不能。
You mustn't ~.

你不能在開車前喝酒。
▸ You mustn't drink before driving.

如果你明白我的意思，你不應該如此。
You shouldn't ~ if you get what I mean.

如果你明白我的意思，你不應該為此責怪你父親。
▸ You shouldn't blame your father for that if you get what I mean.

忠告

♣ 正式場合

🔊 018

我勸你們不要。 **I would advise against ～.**	我勸你們本週末不要舉行派對。 ▸ I would advise against having a party this weekend.
我建議你不要。 **I would recommend you not to ～.**	我建議你上學不要遲到。 ▸ I would recommend you not to go to school late.
若我處在你的狀況，我不會。 **I wouldn't ～, if I were in your position.**	若我處在你的狀況，我不會接受邀請。 ▸ I wouldn't accept the invitation, if I were in your position.
我勸你不要。 **I wouldn't advise you to ～.**	我勸你不要買這台二手相機。 ▸ I wouldn't advise you to buy this used camera.
我建議你不要。 **I wouldn't recommend you to ～.**	我建議你不要那樣對待你的先生。 ▸ I wouldn't recommend you to treat your husband like that.
如果你聽我的勸告，就不要。 **If you follow my recommendations, you won't ～.**	如果你聽從我的勸告，就不要和她聯絡。 ▸ If you follow my recommendations, you won't keep in touch with her.
如果你聽我的勸告，就不要。 **If you take my advice, you won't ～.**	如果你聽我的勸告，就不要把兒子交給你妹妹照顧。 ▸ If you take my advice, you won't commit your son to your sister's care.
如果你徵求我的意見，我認為這樣是不明智的。 **If you want my advice, I think it would be unwise to ～.**	如果你徵求我的意見，我想那樣花錢是不明智的。 ▸ If you want my advice, I think it would be unwise to spend money like that.

40

如果你徵求我的意見，明智的做法就是不要如此。
It would be prudent not to ～ if you ask for my advice.

如果你徵求我的意見，那麼明智的做法就是不要得罪你的上司。
▸ It would be prudent not to displease your higher-ups if you ask for my advice.

我的忠告是：不要如此。
My advice would be, don't ～.

我的忠告是：不要開得太快。
▸ My advice would be, don't drive too fast.

我的看法是，絕對不要如此。
My reaction would be, never ～.

我的看法是，絕對不要投資那項工程。
▸ My reaction would be, never invest in that project.

你這樣就不明智了。
You would be ill-advised to ～.

如果你遲繳房租那就不明智了。
▸ You would be ill-advised to delay payment for rent.

你這樣做是不明智的。
You would be unwise to ～.

如果你把積蓄全部用來購買股票，那是不明智的。
▸ You would be unwise to invest your savings all in stock.

你最好不要這樣。
You would be well advised not to ～.

你最好不要捲入他們的爭吵。
▸ You would be well advised not to get involved in their quarrel.

你最好不要這樣。
You would be wise not to ～.

你最好不要去冒犯他。
▸ You would be wise not to offend him.

 **3** *Agreement* 同 意

● 你同意嗎？ ●

你同意嗎？
Do you agree (that) ～?
你同意嗎？
Do you agree to ～?

你同意我們應該早點出發嗎？
▸ Do you agree (that) we should start early?
你同意我的計劃嗎？
▸ Do you agree to my plan?

你同意我嗎？
Do you agree with me?
你同意我嗎？
Do you agree with me about ～?

你同意我的安排嗎？
▸ Do you agree with me about the arrangement?

你不同意嗎？
Don't you agree?
你不同意嗎？
Don't you agree (that) ～?

你不同意嗎？
Don't you agree to ～?

你不同意我們聚會應該也邀傑克遜嗎？
▸ Don't you agree (that) our party should include Jackson?
你不同意我的建議嗎？
▸ Don't you agree to my suggestion?

你不贊成我嗎？

Don't you agree with me (that) ～?

你不贊成我們應該存錢以備將來所需的說法嗎？
▸ Don't you agree with me (that) we should save money for the future?

你不覺得嗎？
Don't you feel ～?

你不覺得能自己作主很好嗎？
▸ Don't you feel it's good to be your own boss?

你不認為嗎？
Don't you think ～?

你不認為她是個聰明的學生嗎？
▸ Don't you think she's a bright student?

他如此，不是嗎？
He's ～, isn't he?

他很老了，不是嗎？
▸ He's quite old, isn't he?

你不這樣認為嗎？
～, don't you think?

住在鄉村很有趣，你不這樣認為嗎？
▸ It would be interesting to live in the countryside, don't you think?

你說不是嗎？
～, wouldn't you say?

金錢正在失去價值，你說不是嗎？
▸ Money is losing its value, wouldn't you say?

我這麼說不無道理吧？
～, or am I talking nonsense?

污染無法控制，我這麼說不無道理吧？
▸ Pollutions can't be controlled, or am I talking nonsense?

你說不是這樣嗎？
Wouldn't you say so?
你說不是這樣嗎？
Wouldn't you say (that) ～?

你說約翰不是我們最好的朋友嗎？
▸ Wouldn't you say (that) John is our best friend?

你同意我的看法，不是嗎？
You'd agree with me, wouldn't you?

✿ 日常口語

你同意嗎？
All right with you?

你贊同嗎？　　　　　　　你贊同那樣嗎？
Do you go along with ～?　▸ Do you go along with that?

同意嗎？
OK?

你同意嗎？
OK by you?

你同意嗎？
OK with you?

我並非信口開河吧？　　　人們往往想花錢而不是存錢，我並非信口開河吧？

～, or am I speaking through　▸ People tend to spend money rather than
my neck?　　　　　　　save it, or am I speaking through my neck?

對嗎？
Right?

你跟我想的一樣嗎？
Think the same as I do?

是嗎？
Yeah?

♣ 正式場合

請問你是否同意？
Can I ask if you assent to ～?

請問你是否同意他的論點？
▸ Can I ask if you assent to his argument?

請問你是否同意？
Can I ask you if you would give your assent to ～?

請問你是否同意古典音樂更具思想性？
▸ Can I ask you if you would give your assent to the opinion that classical music is more thoughtful?

你同意嗎？
Do you assent to ～?

你同意幫助他嗎？
▸ Do you assent to help him?

我想知道你否同意。
I wonder if you would concur with ～.

我想知道你是否同意金錢不代表幸福。
▸ I wonder if you would concur with the idea that money doesn't mean happiness.

我想知道你是否同意。
I wonder if you would consent to ～.

不知你是否同意布萊克先生的分析。
▸ I wonder if you would consent to Mr. Blake's analysis.

我想請問你是否同意。
I'd like to ask if you would agree with ～.

我想請問你是否同意我的想法。
▸ I'd like to ask if you would agree with my idea.

我想知道你是否同意。
I'd like to know if you would give your consent to ～.

我想知道你是否同意他們的計劃。
▸ I'd like to know if you would give your consent to their plan.

一致通過嗎？
Is ～ agreed?

計劃獲得一致通過了嗎？
▸ Is the plan agreed?

請問你是否同意？
May I ask if you would agree (that) ～?

請問你是否同意我們都應該愛地球？
▸ May I ask if you would agree (that) we all should love the earth?

你接受他的觀點嗎？
Would you accept his view on ～? ▸

你接受他對這個問題的觀點嗎？
Would you accept his view on the issue?

你是否同意？
Would you agree (that) ～?

你是否同意我們總能忘記不愉快之事？
▸ Would you agree (that) we're always able to forget the unpleasant things?

你是否同意？
Would you agree with ～?

你是否同意我剛才說的話？
▸ Would you agree with what I said just now?

你同意嗎？
Would you concur with ～?

你同意這樣的提議嗎？
▸ Would you concur with such a proposal?

你沒有異議，對嗎？
You don't disagree, do you?

你不會有異議，對嗎？
You wouldn't disagree with ～, would you?

你不會對那件事有異議，對嗎？
▸ You wouldn't disagree with that, would you?

你會接受，不是嗎？
You'd accept ～, wouldn't you?

你會接受我的提議，不是嗎？
▸ You'd accept my proposal, wouldn't you?

● 我同意你所説的 ●

❤ 基本說法

你對極了！
How right you are!

那對極了！
How right that is!

千真萬確！
How true!

我也有同樣的想法。
I agree with you altogether.

我不禁也有同樣的想法。
I can't help thinking the same.

我當然同意。
I certainly agree ～.

我當然同意這男孩很聰明。
▶ I certainly agree the boy is intelligent.

我非常同意。
I couldn't agree more.

我很同意你的說法。
I quite agree with you.

我看是如此。
I suppose so.

我也這樣想。
I think so too.

這一點我想你是對的。
I think you're right there.

如果你要這麼說的話。
If you say so.

的確如此！
It certainly is!

噢，沒錯！
Oh, exactly!

我也一樣。
So do I.

這正是我所想的。
That's just what I was thinking.

我也是這麼想的。
That's my feeling, too.

這也是我的意見。
That's my opinion, too.

很對。
That's very true.

的確是這樣！
They certainly are!

確實如此。
True enough.

嗯，你大概是對的。
Well, you're probably right.

你知道這正是我所想的。
You know that's exactly what I think.

🌸 日常口語

我也正是這麼想。
Exactly my thoughts.

絕對正確。
Dead right.

這一點我同意你。
I go along with you there.

這方面我和你一致。
I'm with you there.

的確是這樣！
It sure is!

對。
Right.

對呀！
Right you are!

我和你想的一樣！
Same here!

的確是這樣！
They sure are!

千真萬確。
Too true.

嗯，就是這樣。
Well, that's it.

嗯，就是這麼回事。
Well, that's the thing.

是的。
Yeah.

是的。
Yes.

的確是這樣。
You better believe it.

一點都沒錯！
You can say that again!

你說得對！
You said it!

你說得對。
You're right.

♣ 正式場合
🔊024

（說得）對！（說得）對！
Hear! Hear!
＊開會或眾人討論時，可用這句表示同意。

我完全同意。
I concur absolutely with ～.

我完全同意你的決定。
▶ I concur absolutely with your decision.

我當然同意。
I definitely assent to ～.

我當然同意你的計劃。
▶ I definitely assent to your plan.

我認為沒人會反對。
I don't think anyone would argue with ～.

我認為沒有人會反對她對此事件的解釋。
▶ I don't think anyone would argue with her interpretation of the event.

我認為沒有人會有異議。
I don't think anyone would disagree.

我認為沒人會有異議。
I don't think anyone would dispute (that) ～.
我認為沒人會有異議。
I don't think anyone would dispute with ～.

我們正在消耗太多能源，我想沒人會對這看法有異議。
▶ I don't think anyone would dispute (that) we're using up too much energy.
我認為沒有人會對這點有異議。
▶ I don't think anyone would dispute with that.

我想我完全同意。
I think I entirely agree with ～.

我想我完全同意你的觀點。
▶ I think I entirely agree with your view.

我想我會接受你的觀點。
I think I'd accept your view on ～.

我想我會接受你在這方面的觀點。
▶ I think I'd accept your view on that.

我想我完全接受你的看法。
I think I'd take your point completely.

我想沒人會不同意。
I think nobody would disagree (that) ～.

我想沒人會不同意。
I think nobody would disagree with ～.

人都要誠實，我想沒人不同意這看法。
▸ I think nobody would disagree (that) everyone should be honest.

我想沒人會不同意這一點的。
▸ I think nobody would disagree with that.

我想沒人會有異議。
I think nobody would dissent from ～.

我想沒人會對公司的政策有異議。
▸ I think nobody would dissent from the company's policies.

我贊同你的意見。
I'd like to endorse your opinion.

我的想法和你完全相同。
I'm of exactly the same idea as you.

我正是這麼認為。
My own view precisely.

哦，我完全同意。
Oh, I agree absolutely.

這正是我的意見。
That's just my own opinion.

● 我同意，可是… ●

❤ 基本說法

025

同意，但是？	同意，但是誰能付諸實行呢？
Agreed, but ～?	▸ Agreed, but who can carry it out?

總括來說我同意，但是。	總括來說我同意，但事情沒這麼簡單。
I agree on the whole, but ～.	▸ I agree on the whole, but things are not so easy.

我當然明白你的意思，不過。	我當然明白你的意思，不過瑪麗太年輕沒辦法做到。
I certainly see what you mean, but ～.	▸ I certainly see what you mean, but Mary is too young to do it.

我完全同意，不過。	我完全同意，不過明天可能突然下雨。
I couldn't agree more, but ～.	▸ I couldn't agree more, but there may be a sudden rain tomorrow.

我並不完全同意你。
I don't altogether agree with you.

我知道你說得有道理，但是。	我知道你說得有道理，但不同的人有不同的品味。
I know you have a point there, but ～.	▸ I know you have a point there, but different people have different tastes.

我相當同意你所說的，但是。	我相當同意你所說的，但這世界不再像過去一樣。
I quite agree with what you said, but ～.	▸ I quite agree with what you said, but the world is no longer the same as it was.

我當然明白你的意思，但是。

I surely understand what you said, but we ~.

▸ 我當然明白你的意思，但我們必須把每件事都考慮進去。

▸ I surely understand what you said, but we must take everything into account.

某種程度上說沒錯，但是。

In a way, yes, but ~.

▸ 某種程度上說沒錯，但是沒有錢是很難去旅行的。

▸ In a way, yes, but it's difficult to travel without money.

也許吧，但是？
Maybe, but ~?

▸ 也許吧，但你不認為太遲了嗎？

▸ Maybe, but don't you think it's too late?

這都很好，但是？
That's all very well, but ~?

▸ 這都很好，但是不是有點太會想像了？

▸ That's all very well, but isn't it a bit too imaginative?

這是一種看法，但是。

That's one way of looking at it, but ~.

▸ 這是一種看法，但我們還有別種方式。

▸ That's one way of looking at it, but we have other ways too.

確實如此，不過。

That's quite true, but ~.

▸ 確實如此，不過英語畢竟是世界語言。

▸ That's quite true, but English is after all a world language.

對，不過你不認為這樣嗎？
That's right, but don't you think ~?

▸ 對，不過你不認為太複雜了嗎？

▸ That's right, but don't you think it's too complicated?

你說得很有道理，但是。

There's a lot in what you said, but ~.

▸ 你說得很有道理，但是我們錢不夠。

▸ There's a lot in what you said, but we don't have enough money.

的確，不過另一方面而言。 **True enough, but on the other hand, ~.**	的確，不過另一方面而言這很花時間。 ▸ True enough, but on the other hand, it's time-consuming.
嗯，你說的都是真的，不過。 **Well, what you said is true, but ~.**	嗯，你說的都是真的，不過許多人踢足球踢得很開心。 ▸ Well, what you said is true, but a lot of people have fun playing football.
也許是這樣，不過。 **Yes, perhaps, but ~.**	也許是這樣，不過還有別的問題。 ▸ Yes, perhaps, but there're other problems.
某種程度而言是這樣，不過。 **Yes, to some extent, but ~.**	某程度而言是這樣，但世界不停在變。 ▸ Yes, to some extent, but the world keeps changing.
你也許是對的，不過。 **You're probably right there, but ~.**	你也許是對的，不過這很難付諸實行。 ▸ You're probably right there, but it's hard to put it into practice.

🌸 日常口語　🔊 026

可能是這樣，不過。
Could be, but ～.

可能是這樣，不過他沒有經驗。
▸ Could be, but he's not experienced.

我當然明白這一點，不過。
I can see that, of course, but ～.

我當然明白這點，不過這可能招來麻煩。
▸ I can see that, of course, but it may cause trouble.

這點我大致同意，不過。
I go along with most of that, but ～.

這點我大致同意，但我們根本無法實行。
▸ I go along with most of that, but we simply don't have the means.

我明白你的看法，但是。
I see your point, but ～.

我明白你的看法，但污染仍是一個問題。
▸ I see your point, but pollution is still a problem.

的確如此，但是。
It sure is, but ～.

的確如此，但步行到那裡要花點時間。
▸ It sure is, but it takes time to walk there.

唔，不過？
Mm, but ～?

唔，不過天氣因素你考慮過了嗎？
▸ Mm, but have you thought about the weather?

對，但是。
OK, but ～.

對，但是她只是一個青少年。
▸ OK, but she's only a teenager.

對，不過。
Right, but ～.

對，不過星期天那裡沒人。
▸ Right, but nobody's there on Sunday.

是的，不過。
Yes, but ～.

是的，不過這並不代表一切。
▸ Yes, but that doesn't mean everything.

你說得對，但是。
You're right, but ～.

你說得對，但是物價上漲迅速。
▸ You're right, but the prices are rising quickly.

♣ 正式場合

027

儘管你這麼說，我還是這麼認為。	儘管你這麼說，我認為對這件事我們還是謹慎些好。
Despite all what you said, I think ～.	▶ Despite all what you said, I think we'd better be careful about it.
儘管如此，但是。	儘管如此，但這會破壞一個人的私生活。
Granted, but ～.	▶ Granted, but it's destroying one's private life.
原則上我同意，但是。	原則上我同意，但不管怎麼說我們的感情是存在的。
I agree in principle, but ～.	▶ I agree in principle, but our emotions exist anyway.
某種程度上我同意，但是。	某種程度上我同意，但事情沒那麼容易。
I agree up to a point, but ～.	▶ I agree up to a point, but things are not so easy.
某種程度上我同意，但是。	某種程度上我同意，但是通貨膨脹是不可避免的。
I agree with you to a certain extent, but ～.	▶ I agree with you to a certain extent, but inflation is unavoidable.
你所言我當然大部分同意，不過。	你所言我當然大部分同意，不過那裡的天氣確實很糟。
I certainly accept most of what you said, but ～.	▶ I certainly accept most of what you said, but the weather there is really terrible.
在某種意義上我認同你，但是。	在某種意義上我認同你，但是愛出名是人皆有之的。
I concur with you in a sense, but ～.	▶ I concur with you in a sense, but love of fame is universal.

我接受你的觀點，但是我們不該忘記。

I take your point, but we shouldn't forget ～.

▶ 我接受你的觀點，但是我們不該忘記新聞記者絕不會深入探討任何主題。

▶ I take your point, but we shouldn't forget a reporter never goes deeply into any one subject.

我想我們在這點上意見相同。然而。

I think we're very much in agreement on this. However, ～.

▶ 我想我們在這點上意見相同。然而，電視上的廣告實在太多了。

▶ I think we're very much in agreement on this. However, there're far too many commercials on TV.

我原則上同意，不過。

I'd endorse ～ in principle, but ～.

▶ 我原則上同意你的計劃，不過代溝是無法否認的因素。

▶ I'd endorse your plan in principle, but generation gap is something you can't deny.

我大致上同意，不過。

I'd give my consent to ～ generally, but ～.

▶ 我大致上同意你的意見，不過有時候那裡會非常吵鬧。

▶ I'd give my consent to your opinion generally, but sometimes it could be very noisy there.

也許如此，但從另一方面來看。

That may be so, but on the other hand, ～.

▶ 也許如此，但從另一方面來看，經驗是最好的老師。

▶ That may be so, but on the other hand, experience is the best teacher.

也許那是對的，不過。

That may be true, but ～.

▶ 也許那是對的，不過工業使我們更富裕。

▶ That may be true, but industry is making us wealthier.

你說得很有道理。不過。

你說的很有道理。不過我們還是應該看看它背後的動機。

There's great deal of reason in what you said. Still ～. ▸ There's great deal of reason in what you said. Still we should look at the motives behind it.

你說得有道理，不過就我個人而言，我不至於會。

你說得有道理，不過就我個人而言，我不至於會完全改變我的飲食。

There's some truth in what you said, but personally, I wouldn't go so far as to ～. ▸ There's some truth in what you said, but personally, I wouldn't go so far as to change my diet altogether.

好吧，總體來說我同意你，不過我這麼認為。

好吧，總體來說我同意你，不過我認為還是有失敗的風險。

Well, while I concur with you on the whole, I think ～. ▸ Well, while I concur with you on the whole, I think there's still some risk of failure.

● 我不同意你的説法 ●

❦ 基本說法

028

你真的認為如此？
Do you really think ～?

你真的認為可以接受摩根的看法？
▸ Do you really think Morgan's view is acceptable?

很抱歉，但是你錯了。
Excuse me, but you are wrong.

那樣我無法接受。
I can't accept that.

我不同意。
I can't agree (that) ～.

我不同意電視是可怕的發明的說法。
▸ I can't agree (that) television was a terrible invention.

我極不同意你（的說法）。
I couldn't agree with you less.

我不同意。
I disagree; ～.

我不同意；動手術是危險的。
▸ I disagree; it's dangerous to try an operation.

我不同意。
I don't agree.
我不同意某人。
I don't agree with ～.

我不同意你。
▸ I don't agree with you.

我懷疑某事。
I don't know about ～.

我懷疑這種理論。
▸ I don't know about the theory.

我懷疑是否如此。
I don't know if ～.

我懷疑這是否有用。
▸ I don't know if it'll work.

60

我不這麼認為。
I don't think so.

我認為那是不對的。
I don't think that's right.

我認為這是不合理的。
I don't think that's sensible.

我認為在這點上你是不對的。
I don't think you're right there.

我認為這沒道理。
I think that's not reasonable.

我認為你大錯特錯。
I think you're absolutely wrong.

我認為你搞錯了。
I think you're mistaken.

我不會那麼認為。
I wouldn't go so far as to say that.

我不那麼認為。
I wouldn't say that.

事實上，我認為如此。
In fact, I think ～.

事實上，我認為有中古車總比沒車強。
▸ In fact, I think an old car is better than none.

不，實際上是那方面的問題。
No, actually, it's more a matter of ～.

不，實際上這是人口的問題。
▸ No, actually, it's more a matter of population.

不，這實際上跟那更有關。
No, it's actually more to do with ∼.

不，這實際上跟生活費更有關。
▶ No, it's actually more to do with the cost of living.

並非真的如此。
Not really.

完全不是這麼回事。
That wasn't quite it.

我不是這麼看的。
That's not how I see it.

我看這樣不合適。
That's not the way I see fit.

這顯然是錯的。
That's wrong, surely.

這是你的意見，不是我的。
That's your opinion, not mine.

嗯，事實上。
Well, as a matter of fact, ∼.

嗯，事實上，年輕人太自由了。
▶ Well, as a matter of fact, young people have too much freedom.

❋ 日常口語

029

你在開玩笑吧？
Are you kidding?

不要胡說！
Come off it!

不要說笑了。
Don't make me laugh.

我不能贊同。　　　　　　我不能贊同你的觀點。
I can't go along with ～.　　▸ I can't go along with your view.

我看不出有什麼理由。
I don't see why.

絕不！
Never!

不可能！
No way!

胡說！
Nonsense!

根本不是！
Not at all!

噢，拜託！
Oh, for God's sake!

哦，真是廢話！
Oh, what rubbish!

正好相反。
On the contrary.

完全相反。
Quite the opposite.

當然不。
Surely not.

荒唐。
That's ridiculous.

那是你的想法！
That's what you think!

你不是當真的吧！
You can't be serious!

你不是這個意思吧！
You can't mean that!

你一定是在開玩笑！
You must be joking!

♣ 正式場合

030

請允許我在這件事上跟你意見不同。
I beg to differ with you on this matter.

對不起，但我認為不是如此。
I beg your pardon, but I don't think ~.

▸ 對不起，但我認為你所說的並非事實。
I beg your pardon, but I don't think what you said is true.

我不能贊同你。
I can't say (that) I concur with ~.

▸ 我不能贊同你對這部小說的評價。
I can't say (that) I concur with your assessment of the novel.

我不認為我與你持同樣看法。
I don't think (that) I share your view of ~.

▸ 我不認為在歷史價值問題上我與你持同樣的看法。
I don't think (that) I share your view of historical value.

在此我確實和你意見分歧。
I really have to take issue with you on ~.

▸ 在促銷方法上我確實和你意見分歧。
I really have to take issue with you on the ways to promote sales.

我自己的看法大不相同。
I see things rather differently myself.

恐怕我不能接受你的論點。
I'm afraid I can't accept your argument.

恐怕我的評估與你的不同。
I'm afraid I don't share your evaluation of ~.

▸ 恐怕我對形勢的評估與你的不同。
I'm afraid I don't share your evaluation of the situation.

恐怕我完全不同意。
I'm afraid I entirely disagree with ~.

▸ 恐怕我完全不同意這項安排。
I'm afraid I entirely disagree with this arrangement.

恐怕我有不同的意見。
I'm afraid I have a different opinion.

對此事我恐怕持保留態度。
I'm afraid I have reservations about ~.

▶ 對你的決定我恐怕持保留態度。
I'm afraid I have reservations about your decision.

恐怕我不能同意。
I'm afraid I have to argue with ~.

▶ 恐怕我不能同意你對這次意外的解釋。
I'm afraid I have to argue with your explanation of the accident.

恐怕我不能同意。
I'm afraid I have to dissent from ~.

▶ 恐怕我不能同意你的想法。
I'm afraid I have to dissent from your idea.

這完全無法讓我信服。
I'm not at all convinced by ~.

▶ 你的解釋完全無法讓我信服。
I'm not at all convinced by your explanation.

我完全不相信。
I'm not at all convinced ~.

▶ 我完全不相信這部機器是可靠的。
I'm not at all convinced the machine is reliable.

就我個人而言,我傾向不同意。
Personally, I inclined to disagree with sb. on sth.

▶ 就我個人而言,我傾向不同意你對這問題的意見。
Personally, I inclined to disagree with you on that.

就我個人而言,我寧可同意其他人。
Personally, I'd prefer to agree with ~.

▶ 就我個人而言,我寧可同意克林頓先生的觀點。
Personally, I'd prefer to agree with Mr. Clinton's view.

坦白說,我傾向同意其他人。
To be quite honest, I tend to agree with ~.

▶ 坦白說,我傾向同意克羅夫特的意見。
To be quite honest, I tend to agree with Croft's opinion.

老實說，我比較傾向和你意見相反。
To be quite honest, I'd be more inclined to take the opposite of yours.

嗯，我並不信服。
Well, I'm not convinced.

嗯，我個人意見是這樣。

Well, my own opinion is (that) ～.

嗯，我個人意見是沒有人能在這樣的高溫中存活。

▶ Well, my own opinion is (that) nobody can survive such heat.

● 我想你才是對的 ●

🌱 基本說法 🔊031

哦，也許我錯了。
Oh, maybe I was wrong.

哦，是的，我本來應該記得。
Oh, yes, I should have remembered ～.

▶ 哦，是的，我本來應該記得這個的。
Oh, yes, I should have remembered that.

哦，是的，我本來應該想到。
Oh, yes, I should have thought of ～.

▶ 哦，是的，我本來應該想到這個的。
Oh, yes, I should have thought of that.

哦，是的，你是對的。我當時忘了。
Oh, yes, you're right. I had forgot ～.

▶ 哦，是的，你是對的。我當時忘了這一點。
Oh, yes, you're right. I had forgot that point.

是的，我現在想起來，這樣做是對的。
Yes, now I come to think about it, sb. is right to ～.

▶ 是的，我現在想起來，唐尼辭掉此人是對的。
Yes, now I come to think about it, Donny is right to dismiss the man.

是的，也許這點你是對的。
Yes, perhaps you're right there.

是的，這點我大概錯了。
Yes, probably I'm wrong there.

是的，對不起。我沒想到。
Yes, sorry. I hadn't thought of ～.

▶ 是的，對不起。我沒想到這點。
Yes, sorry. I hadn't thought of that.

是的，對不起。你完全正確。
Yes, sorry. You're quite right.

是的，這點你可能說得有道理。
Yes, you may well have a point there.

是的，你大概是對的。　　　　是的，你決定不去大概是對的。
Yes, you're probably right in ~. ▶ Yes, you're probably right in deciding not to go.

是的，你說得對。我當時真不知道在想什麼。
Yes, you're right. I really don't know what I was thinking of.

❀ 日常口語

好吧，你贏了。
All right, you win.

哦，是的，我真傻！
Oh, yes, how silly of me!

好吧，你是專家。
OK, you're the expert.

對不起，我全搞錯了。
Sorry, I got it all wrong.

對不起，我錯了。
Sorry, my mistake.

對不起，這點上疏忽了。
Sorry, slipped up there.

是的，我真粗心，竟忘了。 **Yes, careless of me to have forgot ～.**	是的，我真粗心，竟忘了那件事。 ▸ Yes, careless of me to have forgot that.
是的，我真傻，竟沒想到。 **Yes, silly of me not to have thought of ～.**	是的，我真傻，竟沒想到那件事。 ▸ Yes, silly of me not to have thought of that.

♣ 正式場合

是的，我必須承認弄錯了。 **Yes, I have to admit I have been in error about ～.** ▸	是的，我必須承認在這點上弄錯了。 Yes, I have to admit I have been in error about that.
是的，我很可能錯了。 **Yes, I may well have been mistaken over ～.** ▸	是的，在這問題上我很可能錯了。 Yes, I may well have been mistaken over this problem.
是的，我得承認我未考慮在內。 **Yes, I must admit I didn't take ～ into consideration.** ▸	是的，我得承認我未將品質考慮在內。 Yes, I must admit I didn't take the quality into consideration.
是的，我一定是搞錯了。 **Yes, I must have mistaken ～ for ～.** ▸	是的，我一定是把這項搞錯為那項了。 Yes, I must have mistaken this for that.
是的，我一定是忽略了。 **Yes, I must have neglected ～.** ▸	是的，我一定是忽略了他的決心。 Yes, I must have neglected his determination.
是的，我完全接受你的論點。 **Yes, I take your point completely.**	
是的，我想我忽略了。 **Yes, I think I have overlooked ～.** ▸	是的，我想我忽略了那點。 Yes, I think I have overlooked that point.
是的，恐怕我的確。 **Yes, I'm afraid I did ～.** ▸	是的，恐怕我的確計算錯誤。 Yes, I'm afraid I did miscalculate.
是，如果考慮到某事，我想你大概是對的。 **Yes, when ～ is considered, I think you're probably right.** ▸	是，如果考慮到時間的話，我想你大概是對的。 Yes, when time is considered, I think you're probably right.

● 我們達成協議了 ●

好，這似乎讓大家都滿意了。
Good, ～ seems to have satisfied everyone.

好，這安排似乎讓大家都滿意了。
▶ Good, the arrangement seems to have satisfied everyone.

好，現在我們似乎是意見一致了。
Good, we seem to be saying the same thing now.

很高興我們終於意見一致了。
I'm glad we've come together at last.

好吧，那麼就這樣同意了。
OK, that's agreed then.

對，我們都同意了。
Right, we all agree then.

那麼我們都同意了，不是嗎？
So we're agreed, aren't we?

那麼我們都同意了，不是嗎？
So we've agreed on ～, haven't we?

那麼我們都同意這樣做了，不是嗎？
▶ So we've agreed on that, haven't we?

那麼，就這樣決定了。
Well, that's settled then.

好了，我們已達成相同意見了。
Well, we've come to the same thing then.

🌸 日常口語

那麼好吧。
All right, then. ~.

那麼好吧，我們六點鐘見面。
▸ All right, then. We'll meet at six.

那麼，大家都高興。
Everybody's pleased about ~, then.

那麼，大家對這決定都高興。
▸ Everybody's pleased about the decision, then.

好，結束了。
Great, that wraps ~ up.

好，我們的討論結束了。
▸ Great, that wraps our discussion up.

看來搞定了。
Looks like ~ is seen after.

看來我們約好了。
▸ Looks like our appointment is seen after.

看來我們已一致同意。
Looks like we've all agreed.
看來我們已一致同意。
Looks like we've all agreed ~.

看來我們已一致同意要去哪裡。
▸ Looks like we've all agreed where to go.

那就這樣了。
So that's that, then.

那麼，我們都滿意了，對吧？
So we're all happy about ~, aren't we?

那麼，我們對這計劃都滿意了，對吧？
▸ So we're all happy about the plan, aren't we?

那我們還爭論什麼呢？
So what are we arguing about?

似乎不錯。
That sounds OK, then.

那就這樣吧。
That's it then.

♣ 正式場合

我很高興我們終於達成協議。
I'm glad (that) we have finally reached an agreement.

那麼，我們似乎都同意。
So, we appear to agree on ～.

那麼，我們似乎都同意增加生產。
▶ So, we appear to agree on the increase of production.

那麼，我們似乎都同意。
So, we seem to agree to ～.

那麼，我們似乎都同意去公園。
▶ So, we seem to agree to go to the park.

那麼基本上我們意見一致了。
So, we're basically in agreement on ～.

那麼基本上在日程方面我們意見一致了。
▶ So, we're basically in agreement on that agenda.

那麼，看來已獲得一致同意了。
That seems to be agreed, then.

那麼，我們一致同意。
We are all agreed, then.
那麼，我們一致同意。
We are all agreed that ～, then.

那麼，我們一致同意延後舊金山之旅。
▶ We are all agreed that we put off the trip to San Francisco, then.

我們似乎已完全一致同意了。
We seem to have come to a complete agreement on ～.

價格方面我們似乎已完全一致同意了。
▶ We seem to have come to a complete agreement on the price.

我們似乎完全一致同意。
We seem to be in complete agreement on ～.

我們似乎完全一致同意接受這項合約。
▶ We seem to be in complete agreement on accepting the contract.

● 對不起，很抱歉 ●

❦ 基本說法 037

對不起。（或：請原諒。）
Excuse me.

請原諒我。
Excuse me for ～.

請原諒我在這裡抽於。
▸ Excuse me for my smoking here.

我真的非常抱歉。
I can't tell you how sorry I am.

我真不知該說什麼才好。
I just don't know what to say.

我真的非常抱歉。
I am really so sorry.

真是非常抱歉。
I am so sorry to ～.

撞到你真是非常抱歉。
▸ I am so sorry to bump into you.

我怕我已經給你帶來太多麻煩。
I'm afraid I've brought you too much trouble.

非常抱歉。我沒注意。
I'm awfully sorry. I didn't realize.

對不起。都是我的錯。
I'm so sorry. It was all my fault.

對不起。
I'm sorry.

對不起。我不是有意傷害你的感情。
I'm sorry. I didn't mean to hurt your feelings.

對不起。 | 對不起，我把它弄丟了。
I'm sorry ～. | ▶ I'm sorry I've lost it.

我非常抱歉。 | 我對此非常抱歉。
I'm terribly sorry about ～. | ▶ I'm terribly sorry about that.

我很抱歉。 | 對你說了這些話，我很抱歉。
I'm very sorry for ～. | ▶ I'm very sorry for what I've said to you.

我真是非常粗心。
It was most careless of me.

這實在不是有意的。
It was really quite unintentional.

這是我的不對。
It was wrong of me.
這是我的不對。 | 錯拿了你的傘，這是我的不對。
It was wrong of me to ～. | ▶ It was wrong of me to pick up your umbrella.

原諒我。（或：對不起。）
Pardon me.
對不起。 | 對不起，我打噴嚏了。
Pardon me for ～. | ▶ Pardon me for sneezing.

請原諒我。 | 請原諒我遲到。
Please excuse my ～. | ▶ Please excuse my coming late.

✿ 日常口語

真是抱歉。
A thousand pardons for ～.

佔用你這麼多時間，真是抱歉。
▸ A thousand pardons for taking up so much of your time.

代我致歉。
Giving my excuses to sb. for ～.

代我向約翰致歉，沒去聽他講課。
▸ Giving my excuses to John for missing his lecture.

我真笨。
How clumsy of me to ～.

我真笨，踩到你的腳。
▸ How clumsy of me to step on your foot.

我實在感到很抱歉。
I really feel bad about ～.

我為此實在感到很抱歉。
▸ I really feel bad about that.

哦，我真笨。
Oh, how silly of me to ～.

哦我真笨，竟把湯灑在你的褲子上了。
▸ Oh, how silly of me to spill the soup on your trousers.

哦，都是我的錯。
Oh, my fault.
哦，是我的錯。
Oh, my fault for ～.

哦，打破玻璃是我的錯。
▸ Oh, my fault for breaking the glass.

對不起！
Sorry!
對不起。
Sorry about ～.

那件事真對不起。
▸ Sorry about that.

對不起。
Sorry for ～.

對不起沒打電話給你。
▸ Sorry for not phoning you.

對不起。
Sorry to ～.

對不起，把你的名片弄丟了。
▸ Sorry to have lost your name card.

♣ 正式場合

我向你道歉。
I apologize for ～.

我為剛才說的話向你道歉。
▶ I apologize for what I said just now.

我實在難以表達我的歉意。
I can't tell you how sorry I am.

我實在難以表達我的歉意。
I can't tell you how sorry I am for ～.

讓你受驚，我實在難以表達我的歉意。
▶ I can't tell you how sorry I am for giving you such a fright.

我請你原諒。
I do beg your pardon.

請你原諒。
I do beg your pardon for ～.

我把事情搞得一團糟，請你原諒。
▶ I do beg your pardon for the mess I've made.

我希望你原諒我。
I hope you will excuse me.

希望你原諒。
I hope you will forgive me for ～.

我誤拆了你的信，希望你原諒。
▶ I hope you will forgive me for opening your letter by mistake.

我希望你原諒我。
I hope you will pardon me for ～.

我希望你原諒我的疏忽大意。
▶ I hope you will pardon me for my negligence.

我必須道歉。
I must apologize.

我必須為此道歉。
I must apologize for ～.

我必須為延誤道歉。
▶ I must apologize for the delay.

我必須為此道歉。
I must make an apology for ～.

我必須為我發脾氣的行為道歉。
▶ I must make an apology for losing my temper.

我必須向你表示最真誠的歉意。
I must offer you my sincerest apologies for ～.

我必須為我對於貴公司所說的話，向你表示最真誠的歉意。
▸ I must offer you my sincerest apologies for what I have said about your company.

我該為此向你道歉。
I owe you an apology for ～.

我該為這次延誤向你道歉。
▸ I owe you an apology for the delay.

我非常抱歉。
I'm extremely sorry.
我非常抱歉。
I'm extremely sorry for ～.
非常抱歉。
I'm extremely sorry to ～.

我為此非常抱歉。
▸ I'm extremely sorry for that.
非常抱歉，你預定的房間還無法提供。
▸ I'm extremely sorry to say the room you reserved isn't available.

我必須向你道歉。
I've got to apologize for ～.

給你造成諸多麻煩，我必須向你道歉。
▸ I've got to apologize for troubling you so much.

謹向你表示最深切的歉意。
May I offer you my profoundest apologies for ～?

給你添麻煩，謹向你表示最深切的歉意。
▸ May I offer you my profoundest apologies for the trouble I have given you?

請接受我的歉意。
Please accept my apologies for ～.

我沒參加你的派對，請接受我的歉意。
▸ Please accept my apologies for not going to your party.

請原諒我。我真的沒有那個意思。
Please forgive me. I really didn't mean that.

請原諒。
Please forgive ～.

請原諒我對你所做的壞事。
▸ Please forgive the wrongs I've done you.

請原諒我。
Please pardon my ～.

請原諒我這麼健忘。
▸ Please pardon my forgetfulness.

● 沒關係，別在意 ●

不要為此感到不安。
Don't let it worry you.

不要為此苦惱。
Don't let that distress you.

不要再去想它了。
Don't think any more about it.

沒關係。
Don't worry about that.

我很了解。
I quite understand.

一點也沒有關係。
It doesn't matter at all.

實在不值一提。
It really isn't worth mentioning.

這不是你的錯。
It's not your fault.

沒什麼。
It's nothing.

別在意。真的沒關係。
Never mind. It doesn't really matter.

這沒關係。
Never mind about that.

不，不會。
No, I haven't been ～.

不，一點也不麻煩。
▸ **No, I haven't been put out at all.**

一點也不會。
Not at all.

請不要這樣。
Please don't be.

請不要再去想了。
Please don't give it another thought.

請別為此過於苛責。
Please don't take it too hard.

請別在意。
Please don't worry.

請不要想了。
Please think nothing of it.

沒有關係。
That's quite all right.

噢，這種事我也發生過。
Well, it's happened to me.

噢，這是常有的事。
Well, it's just one of those things.

❀ 日常口語

算了，別放在心上。
Forget it.

沒有關係。誰都會發生這種事。
It's OK. That can happen to the best of us.

就算了吧。
Let's forget it.

無妨。沒什麼。
No harm.

沒問題。
No problem.

沒什麼。
Not a bit of it.

別在意了。
Not to worry.

請別為此感到不快。
Please don't feel bad about it.

沒有關係。
That's all right.

沒有關係，你欠我一次！
That's OK, you owe me one!

♣ 正式場合

實在沒有必要道歉。
Apologies are really quite unnecessary.

當然。
Certainly.

這實在沒有必要。
It's really not necessary.

這實在是微不足道。
It's really of no importance.

請別自責。
Please don't blame yourself.

完全沒有關係。
That's perfectly all right.

你完全不必在意。
There's no need for you to worry in the least.

不必道歉。
There's no reason to apologize.

不必為這麼微不足道的事道歉。
There's no reason to apologize for such a trifling thing.

● 不好意思，離開一下 ●

Ｙ 基本說法

🔊 043

我可以去洗個手嗎？我馬上回來。
Could I wash my hands? I'll be right back.

不好意思。（我離開一下。）
Excuse me.

不好意思，我馬上回來。
Excuse me a moment.

不好意思，我去看看。　　　　不好意思，我去看看誰打電話來。
Excuse me. I must just see ~. ▶ Excuse me. I must just see who's calling.

不好意思，我一會就回來。
Excuse me. I won't be long.

不好意思，我一下子就回來。
Excuse me. I'll be back in a short while.

不好意思，暫時離開一下。
Excuse me. You have to give me a minute.

🌸 日常口語

別等我了。
Don't wait for me.
＊半路上向同伴表示暫時離開。

等一下。
Hang on a minute.

等一下。
Hold on a second.

我會趕上你的。
I'll catch you up.

等一下。
Just a minute. ～.

等一下。我有電話。
▶ Just a minute. A phone call for me.

不好意思。一下子就回來。
Excuse me. Back in a second.

不好意思。我馬上就回來。
Excuse me. I'll be right back.

不好意思。我馬上就來。
Excuse me. I'll be with you in a second.

不好意思。一會就回來。
Excuse me. Won't be a minute.

等我回來。我不會去很久的。
Wait till I come back. I won't be long.

♣ 正式場合

045

恐怕我得暫時離開。
I'm afraid I must leave you for a little while.

恐怕你得原諒我暫時離開一下。
I'm afraid you'll have to excuse me for a minute or two.

不知能否原諒我暫時離席。
I wonder if I might be excused for a moment.

不知你是否能原諒我暫時離開。
I wonder if you'd excuse me for a moment.

請原諒我暫時告退。
May I be excused for a minute?

請原諒（我離開一下子）。
Will you excuse me, please?

請原諒我暫時告退。
Would you excuse me for a short while, please?

5 Appointment 約會

● 能約你見面嗎？ ●

能和我見面嗎？
Can ～ see me ～?

大衛先生今天能和我見面嗎？
▶ Can Mr. David see me today?

我能來見你嗎？
Could I come to see ～?

今天下午我能來見你嗎？
▶ Could I come to see you this afternoon?

我來找你可以嗎？
Do you mind if I call on ～?

我明天來找你可以嗎？
▶ Do you mind if I call on you tomorrow?

你看那時能和我見面嗎？
Do you think ～ could see me ～?

你看霍布森先生下星期五能和我見面嗎？
▶ Do you think Mr. Hobson could see me next Friday?

你看你能到我這來嗎？
Do you think you could come to my ～?

你看今天下午你能到我辦公室來嗎？
▶ Do you think you could come to my office this afternoon?

我希望能見到。可以嗎？
I hope I can meet ～. All right?

我希望星期天能在傑克家裡見到你。可以嗎？
▶ I hope I can meet you at Jack's home on Sunday. All right?

我希望和你見面。
I hope to see you ～.

我希望下週五在我的辦公室和你見面。
▶ I hope to see you in my office next Friday.

我想前來拜訪。
I'd like to call on ～.

我想這個星期天來拜訪你。
▶ I'd like to call on you this Sunday.

我想順道來訪。
I'd like to drop by ～.

我想今天順便來找你談談你的合約。
▸ I'd like to drop by today to talk over your contract.

我想和你見面。
I'd like to meet you ～.

我想明天和你見面。
▸ I'd like to meet you tomorrow.

我想與你見面。
I'd like to see you ～.

我想上午十點鐘與你見面。
▸ I'd like to see you at ten this morning.

那時造訪你方便嗎？
Will it be convenient if I call on ～?

今晚七點鐘來找你方便嗎？
▸ Will it be convenient if I call on you at seven this evening?

能見我嗎？
Will ～ be able to see me ～?

卡爾先生這星期二能見我嗎？
▸ Will Mr. Karl be able to see me this Tuesday?

有空嗎？
Will ～ be free ～?

下星期五你有空嗎？
▸ Will you be free next Friday?

你有事嗎？
Will you be occupied ～?

今天下午你有事嗎？
▸ Will you be occupied this afternoon?

見你方便嗎？
Would it be convenient to see you ～?

星期一見你方便嗎？
▸ Would it be convenient to see you on Monday?

🌸 日常口語

你有事嗎？
Are you doing anything special ～?

今晚你有事嗎？
▶ Are you doing anything special tonight?

你剛好有事嗎？
Are you doing anything ～, by any chance?

你今天晚上剛好有事嗎？
▶ Are you doing anything this evening, by any chance?

有空嗎？
Are you free ～?

這個星期天有空嗎？
▶ Are you free this coming Sunday?

你有空嗎？
Do you happen to be free ～?

今天晚上你有空嗎？
▶ Do you happen to be free this evening?

你有什麼打算嗎？
Do you have any plans for ～?

這星期天你有什麼打算嗎？
▶ Do you have any plans for this Sunday?

我想我會過來。
I thought I'd drop over for ～.

我想我會過來找你喝一杯。
▶ I thought I'd drop over for a drink.

我們約個時間。
Let's make a date to ～.

我們約個時間去看電影吧。
▶ Let's make a date to see the film.

嗯，你忙嗎？
Uh, are you going to be busy ～?

嗯，你今晚忙嗎？
▶ Uh, are you going to be busy tonight?

唔，我在想…。你要去嗎？
Um, I was thinking of ～. Will you come?

唔，我在想今晚去看電影。你要去嗎？
▶ Um, I was thinking of going to a movie tonight. Will you come?

♣ 正式場合

048

不知道那時見面是否方便。
I wonder if it would be convenient to meet ～.

不知道明天下午見你是否方便。
▸ I wonder if it would be convenient to meet you tomorrow afternoon.

不知能否為我安排時間。
I wonder if ～ could arrange with me about ～.

不知懷斯先生今天能否為我安排開會。
▸ I wonder if Mr. Wise could arrange with me about the meeting today.

不知能否給我時間。
I wonder if ～ could spare me ～.

不知經理明天能否給我半小時的時間。
▸ I wonder if the manager could spare me half an hour tomorrow.

不知能否安排時間。
I wonder if ～ could fit me in ～.

不知眼科醫生下星期五能否安排時間。
▸ I wonder if the oculist could fit me in next Friday.

不知我們能否安排見面。
I wonder if we could make an arrangement to meet ～.

不知我們下週能否找個時間安排見面。
▸ I wonder if we could make an arrangement to meet sometime next week.

我想把約會定在那時。
I'd like an appointment for ～.

我想把約會定在明天下午。
▸ I'd like an appointment for tomorrow afternoon.

我想約個時間見面。
I'd like to fix an appointment with ～.

我想與你約個時間見面。
▸ I'd like to fix an appointment with you.

我希望能約在那時。
I'd like to make an appointment for ～.

我希望能約在下星期一。
▸ I'd like to make an appointment for next Monday.

我想約個時間見面。
I'd like to make an appointment with ～. ▸

我想約個時間和你見面。
I'd like to make an appointment with you.

我可以和你約時間見面嗎？
May I have an appointment with ～?

今晚我可以和你約時間見面嗎？
▸ May I have an appointment with you this evening?

我可以預約嗎？
May I make an appointment?

你可以替我預約嗎？
Would you make an appointment for me?

● 要約何時？在哪裡？ ●

🌱 基本說法　　　🔊 049

什麼時候我能見你？
At what time can I see you?

你明天可以嗎？
Can you make it tomorrow?

可以約見面嗎？　　　　　　可以約七月一日見面嗎？
Could I make it ～?　▸ Could I make it　July 1st?

可以約別的時間嗎？
Could you make it some other time?

你能告訴我什麼時候嗎？　　你能告訴我什麼時候有空嗎？
Could you tell me when ～?　▸ Could you tell me when you'll be free?

你需要見他嗎？　　　　　　你需要今天見他嗎？
Do you need to see him ～?　▸ Do you need to see him today?

你看方便嗎？
Does it suit you?

你看怎麼樣？　　　　　　　你看6點半怎麼樣？
How does ～ sound to you?　▸ How does 6:30 sound to you?

我找對方，還是對方來找我？　我來找你，還是你來找我？
Shall I call for ～ or will ～　▸ Shall I call for you or will you come
come for me?　for me?

我那時來找你好嗎？　　　　我8點左右來找你好嗎？
Shall I come round for ～　▸ Shall I come round for you at about
at about ～?　8 o'clock?

我們約個地方見面好嗎？
Shall we appoint a place to meet ～?

我們今晚約個地方見面好嗎？
▶ Shall we appoint a place to meet this evening?

我們定個日期好嗎？
Shall we fix the date for ～?

我們為這次面試定個日期好嗎？
▶ Shall we fix the date for the interview?

我們在那外面見面好嗎？
Shall we meet outside ～?

我們在廣場外見面好嗎？
▶ Shall we meet outside the square?

我們約定那時，好嗎？
Shall we say ～?

我們約定6點整，好嗎？
▶ Shall we say 6 o'clock sharp?

要是我那時到那裡，行嗎？
Suppose I come to ～?

要是我今晚五點左右到你家，行嗎？
▶ Suppose I come to your house at about five this evening?

那時怎麼樣？
What about ～?

今晚吃過晚飯以後怎麼樣？
▶ What about this evening, after supper?

什麼時候會在？
What time will ～ be in ～?

醫生明天什麼時候會在？
▶ What time will the doctor be in tomorrow?

你要我什麼時候來？
What time would you like me to come?

我什麼時候能見？
When can I see ～?

我什麼時候能見霍爾先生？
▶ When can I see Mr. Hall?

我什麼時候來見？
When shall I see ～?

我什麼時候來見你？
▶ When shall I see you?

我們什麼時候見面？
When shall we meet?

我們什麼地方見面？
Where shall we meet?

可以嗎？
Will ～ be all right?

6點鐘可以嗎？
▸ Will 6 o'clock be all right?

方便嗎？
Will ～ suit ～?

星期天你方便嗎？
▸ Will Sunday suit you?

有空嗎？
Will ～ be free ～?

下星期五你有空嗎？
▸ Will you be free next Friday?

會不會太晚？
Would ～ be too late?

下星期二會不會太晚？
▸ Would next Tuesday be too late?

晚點可以嗎？
Would sometime later be all right with ～?

晚點你可以嗎？
▸ Would sometime later be all right with you?

方便嗎？
Would ～ suit ～?

星期三上午你方便嗎？
▸ Would Wednesday morning suit you?

到我這裡來嗎？
Would ～ come over to me?

你到我這裡來嗎？
▸ Would you come over to me?

比較想約別的時間嗎？
Would ～ prefer some other time?

你比較想約別的時間嗎？
▸ Would you prefer some other time?

不也可以嗎？
Wouldn't ～ be just as good?

三點鐘不也可以嗎？
▸ Wouldn't three o'clock be just as good?

🌸 日常口語 050

好嗎？
All right?

怎麼樣？
How about ～?

下星期怎麼樣？
▸ How about next week?

怎麼樣？
How is ～?

兩點鐘怎麼樣？
▸ How is two o'clock?

行嗎？
Is ～ OK?

五月一日行嗎？
▸ Is May first OK?

那時好嗎？
Is ～ any good?

明天早上好嗎？
▸ Is tomorrow morning any good?

不過，也許那時可以。
Perhaps ～, though.

不過，也許今天下午可以。
▸ Perhaps this afternoon, though.

可以嗎？
Say ～, OK?

今晚7點半吧，可以嗎？
▸ Say 7:30 this evening, OK?

可以嗎？
～, all right?

六點整，可以嗎？
▸ Six o'clock sharp, all right?

這樣可以嗎？
That all right?

老地方？
Usual place?

什麼時間見面最好？
What's the best time to meet?

什麼時候？
When for?

我什麼時候來？
When shall I call?

什麼時候會在？ | 你什麼時候會在？
When will ~ be in? | ▸ When will you be in?

什麼時候來找我？ | 你什麼時候來找我？
When will ~ come for me? | ▸ When will you come for me?

會在哪裡？ | 你會在哪裡？
Where will ~ be? | ▸ Where will you be?

♣ 正式場合

051

能安排時間見面嗎？
Could ～ manage ～?

你能安排星期五見面嗎？
▶ Could you manage Friday?

你看能安排時間處理這事嗎？
Do you think you could arrange for that ～?

你看能安排明天晚上處理這事嗎？
▶ Do you think you could arrange for that tomorrow evening?

你看你能設法到那裡嗎？
Do you think you could manage to be there ～?

你看你能設法六點鐘到那裡嗎？
▶ Do you think you could manage to be there at six?

你看那時見面方便嗎？
Do you think it convenient to meet ～?

你看8點半見面方便嗎？
▶ Do you think it convenient to meet at 8:30?

不知什麼時間最方便？
I don't know what time would be most convenient to ～?

不知什麼時間對你最方便？
▶ I don't know what time would be most convenient to you?

我想知道見面是否方便？
I'd like to know if it is to your convenience to meet ～?

我想知道在我的辦公室見面是否方便？
▶ I'd like to know if it is to your convenience to meet at my office?

你看我們什麼時間見面最合適？
What time do you think would be suitable for us to meet?

那時方便嗎？
Would ～ be convenient?

兩點半方便嗎？
▶ Would half past two be convenient?

那時合適嗎？
Would ～ be suitable for ～?

6點半對你來說合適嗎？
▶ Would 6:30 be suitable for you?

● 約好時間地點 ●

❤ 基本說法

052

什麼時間都行。
Any time will suit me.

| 他那時才回來。 | 他要4點半以後才回來。 |
| **He'll be back ～.** | ▸ He'll be back after 4:30. |

| 他那時有空。 | 他星期二或星期四有空。 |
| **He's available on ～ or ～.** | ▸ He's available on Tuesday or Thursday. |

| 我可以為你抽時間。 | 明天上午我可以為你抽出半小時。 |
| **I can spare you ～.** | ▸ I can spare you half an hour tomorrow morning. |

| 我沒有什麼特別的事。 | 星期五我沒有什麼特別的事。 |
| **I don't have anything particular on ～.** | ▸ I don't have anything particular on Friday. |

| 那麼，我就那時過來。 | 那麼，我就4點半過來。 |
| **I'll be coming over there at ～, then.** | ▸ I'll be coming over there at 4:30, then. |

到時我等你。
I'll be expecting you then.

| 我有空。 | 今天下午我三點鐘有空。 |
| **I'll be free at ～.** | ▸ I'll be free at three this afternoon. |

那時我大概就有空了。
I'll be probably free then.

| 我時間很多。 | 下個月我時間很多。 |
| **I'll be quite free ～.** | ▸ I'll be quite free next month. |

我大約那時到那裡，如果一切順利的話。
I'll be there around ～. All being well that is.

我大約1點半左右到那裡，如果一切順利的話。
▸ I'll be there around 1:30. All being well that is.

我那時在那裡等你。
I'll be waiting for you at ～ in ～.

六點鐘我在辦公室等你。
▸ I'll be waiting for you at six in my office.

我那時去找你。
I'll look out for you at ～.

我四點鐘左右去找你。
▸ I'll look out for you at about four.

我那時在那裡與你見面。
I'll meet you at ～ around ～.

七點左右我在音樂廳與你見面。
▸ I'll meet you at the foyer of the Music Hall around seven.

我們把時間定在那時吧。
Let the time be fixed for ～.

我們把時間定在明天上午10點半吧。
▸ Let the time be fixed for 10:30 tomorrow morning.

我們約定那時吧。
Let's make it ～.

我們約定三點整吧。
▸ Let's make it three o'clock sharp.

我們在那裡見吧。
Let's meet ～.

我們在餐廳見吧。
▸ Let's meet in the restaurant.

對我來說最好是那時。
～ is best for me.

對我來說最好是星期一下午。
▸ Monday afternoon is best for me.

我的辦公時間是。
My office hours are ～ to ～.

我的辦公時間是8點半到中午12點。
▸ My office hours are 8:30 to noon.

好。我記一下。
OK, that's fine. I'll make a note of it.

那好，謝謝你。
That'll be fine, thank you.

那很好。
That'll be quite all right.

那時間（地點）我沒問題。
That's fine with me.

那時對我來說更好。
~ would be better for me.

星期三對我來說更好。
▸ Wednesday would be better for me.

你可以到這裡來。
You can come to ~.

你可以到我家來。
▸ You can come to my house.

如果事情重要你可以這時來。
You can come ~ if it's important.

如果事情重要你可以今天晚上來。
▸ You can come this evening if it's important.

🌸 日常口語 🔊 053

除了那時其他都可以。
Any ～ except ～.

除了星期六這個星期哪一天下午都可以。
▸ Any afternoon this week except Saturday.

哪一天都可以。
Any day ～ will do.

下星期哪一天都可以。
▸ Any day next week will do.

除了那時隨時都可以。
Any time except ～ would be all right.

除了星期一外隨時都可以。
▸ Any time except Monday would be all right.

任何時間都行。
Any time is all right.

什麼時間我都OK。
Any time ～ will be OK with me.

今晚什麼時間我都OK。
▸ Any time this evening will be OK with me.

好極了。
～ would be great.

八點鐘好極了。
▸ Eight o'clock would be great.

好。到時等你。
Fine. I'll be ready.

好。
Fine by me.

我大約6點半來接你。
I'll pick you up about 6:30.

就約那時吧。
Let it be ～.

就約明天下午4點25分吧。
▸ Let it be 4:25 tomorrow afternoon.

和我在那裡見面。
Look for me in ～.

和我在酒館裡見。
▸ Look for me in the bottle shop.

101

那個時間不錯。	星期一不錯。
~ is good.	▸ Monday is good.

好的，我到時過來。	好的，今晚我過來。
OK, I'll be over ~.	▸ OK, I'll be over this evening.

好，到時見了。
OK, I'll see you then.

在那裡見。	火車站見。
See you at ~.	▸ See you at the railway station.

到時候見。
See you then.

如果你沒問題，就約那時。	如果你沒問題，那就約今晚6點鐘。
~, if that's all right with you.	▸ Six o'clock this evening, if that's all right with you.

那就這樣定了。
That's settled then.

好極了。謝謝你。	今天下午好極了。謝謝你。
~ is perfect. Thank you.	▸ This afternoon is perfect. Thank you.

儘量那時左右來。	儘量5點左右來。
Try to come around ~.	▸ Try to come around five.

好的，這樣好極了。
Yes, that's lovely.

好，老地方見。
Yes, usual place.

♣ 正式場合

如果你方便的話，我可以設法那時來。
I could manage to come ~ if that would suit you.

如果你方便的話，我可以設法明天晚上來。
▶ I could manage to come tomorrow night, if that would suit you.

我想我們那時見面最合適。
I think ~ would be most suitable for us to meet.

我想我們下星期二見面最合適。
▶ I think next Tuesday would be most suitable for us to meet.

我看那時很方便。
I think ~ would be convenient.

我看星期五很方便。
▶ I think Friday would be convenient.

我很高興與你那時見面。
I'll be most delighted to meet you at ~.

我很高興在星期一早上8點與你見面。
▶ I'll be most delighted to meet you at eight Monday morning.

我很高興與你那時見面。
I'll be very pleased to see you ~.

我很高興這個星期天下午與你見面。
▶ I'll be very pleased to see you this Sunday afternoon.

我看就那時吧。
On ~ I expect.

我看就星期三吧。
▶ On Wednesday I expect.

只要你方便請隨時過來。
Please come whenever it is to your convenience.

如果你可以的話，那時會比較方便。
~ would be more convenient, if it's all right with you.

如果你可以的話，星期六下午會比較方便。
▶ Saturday afternoon would be more convenient, if it's all right with you.

● 這個時間地點不方便 ●

▼ 基本說法

我抽不出時間。	這個月我抽不出時間。
I couldn't make it ～.	▶ I couldn't make it this month.
在那以前我不會回來。	11點以前我不會回來。
I won't be back till ～.	▶ I won't be back till 11:00.
在那以前我不會有空。	下星期三以前我不會有空。
I won't be free until ～.	▶ I won't be free until next Wednesday.
我恐怕不能來。	下星期一我恐怕不能來。
I'm afraid I can't make it ～.	▶ I'm afraid I can't make it next Monday.
恐怕我不能與你見面。	恐怕我不能在那裡與你見面。
I'm afraid I can't meet you ～.	▶ I'm afraid I can't meet you there.
恐怕我沒有空。	恐怕我星期二沒有空。
I'm afraid I won't be free on ～.	▶ I'm afraid I won't be free on Tuesday.
對不起，我有訪客來。	對不起，今晚我有訪客來。
I'm sorry. I'm expecting some visitors ～.	▶ I'm sorry. I'm expecting some visitors this evening.
抱歉，在那之前我都約滿了。	抱歉，星期一以前我都約滿了。
I'm sorry. I'm fully booked till ～.	▶ I'm sorry. I'm fully booked till Monday.
對不起，我沒有空。	對不起，明早八點到十一點我沒有空。
I'm sorry to say I'm not free ～.	▶ I'm sorry to say I'm not free tomorrow morning from eight to eleven.
在那之前我恐怕沒有空。	星期天以前我恐怕沒有空。
There's nothing before ～, I'm afraid.	▶ There's nothing before Sunday, I'm afraid.

我沒有空。
I'll be filled up ～.

這星期我沒有空。
▸ I'll be filled up this week.

恐怕有點問題。
～ is a bit of a problem, I'm afraid.

星期一恐怕有點問題。
▸ Monday is a bit of a problem, I'm afraid.

恐怕不行。
Not on ～, I'm afraid.

星期二恐怕不行。
▸ Not on Tuesday, I'm afraid.

恐怕有些困難。
～ is difficult, I'm afraid.

星期六恐怕有些困難。
▸ Saturday is difficult, I'm afraid.

對不起，那時也有約了。
Sorry, but that's taken too.

對不起，我必須。
Sorry, I've got to ～.

對不起，今晚我必須當保母。
▸ Sorry, I've got to baby-sit tonight.

恐怕不行。
～ won't do, I'm afraid.

明天恐怕不行。
▸ Tomorrow won't do, I'm afraid.

那裡恐怕太遠了。
～ is too far away, I'm afraid.

西敏寺恐怕太遠了。
▸ Westminster Abbey is too far away, I'm afraid.

♣ 正式場合

057

我看不是合適地點。
I don't think ~ will be a suitable place for the ~.

▶ 我看芝加哥不是開會的合適地點。
I don't think Chicago will be a suitable place for the meeting.

已事先有約。
I have a previous engagement at ~.

▶ 6點半已事先有約。
I have a previous engagement at 6:30.

我看我們那時見面不太合適。
I think ~ is not quite suitable for us to meet.

▶ 我看我們星期六下午見面不太合適。
I think Saturday afternoon is not quite suitable for us to meet.

恐怕我已另有約會。
I'm afraid I'm otherwise engaged ~.

▶ 恐怕明天下午我已另有約會。
I'm afraid I'm otherwise engaged tomorrow afternoon.

對不起，我那時不太方便。
I'm sorry, but ~ won't be so convenient for me.

▶ 對不起，星期五我不太方便。
I'm sorry, but Friday won't be so convenient for me.

對不起，我另有約會。
I'm sorry, I have another appointment ~.

▶ 對不起，這星期天我另有約會。
I'm sorry, I have another appointment this Sunday.

在那以前都沒空。
~ is not available before ~.

▶ 強森先生十月三日以前都沒空。
Mr. Johnson is not available before October 3rd.

喔，我和人有約。對不起。
Well, I've got an appointment with ~. I'm sorry.

▶ 喔，下週日我和瓊斯先生有約。對不起。
Well, I've got an appointment with Mr. Jones next Sunday. I'm sorry.

● 改變或取消約會 ●

🌱 基本說法

我們可以改約晚一點嗎？
Can we make it a little later?

我們改時間見面好嗎？
Could we meet at ～ instead of ～?

我們從明天下午5點改成3點見面好嗎？
▶ Could we meet at three instead of five tomorrow afternoon?

我們延後可以嗎？
Could we put it off to ～?

我們延後到隔天可以嗎？
▶ Could we put it off to the next day?

你可以另約其他時間嗎？
Could you make it some other time?

你看可以抽出時間嗎？
Do you think you could make it sometime ～?

你看下星期五可以抽出時間嗎？
▶ Do you think you could make it sometime next Friday?

我有急事，所以約會只好取消。
I have something urgent ～, so the appointment will have to be canceled.

星期一我有急事，所以約會只好取消。
▶ I have something urgent on Monday, so the appointment will have to be canceled.

萬一我不能赴約，我會再找時間見你。
If by any chance I don't make it, I'll see you sometime ～.

萬一我不能赴約，我下個月會再找時間見你。
▶ If by any chance I don't make it, I'll see you sometime next month.

恐怕我們的約會得改時間了。
I'm afraid we'll have to change our appointment.

對不起，我不能跟你見面了。
I'm sorry, but I won't be able to see you ～.

▸ 對不起，今天下午我不能跟你見面了。
I'm sorry, but I won't be able to see you this afternoon.

很對不起，發生了一件意想不到的事。
I'm terribly sorry, but something unexpected came up.

如果你不介意，我們把聚餐的日子延後吧。
Let's postpone our date for dinner, if you don't mind.

沒有關係，我們可以另約時間。
That's all right, we can make it some other time.

我們得另約時間了。好嗎？
We'll have to make it some other time. Is that all right?

如果你方便的話，最好改約晚一點。
You'd better make it a little later if it's convenient to you.

❀ 日常口語

這件事我只好延後了。
I'll have to take a rain check on that.

發生了點事。我們必須把約會往後延。
Something's come up. We'll have to make our appointment a little later.

對不起，我不能來參加你們的晚會了。
Sorry, but I can't join you for the evening party.

♣ 正式場合

關於約會，不知能否改時間。
**About our appointment for ~,
I wonder if we could change it
from ~ to ~.**

今晚的約會，不知能否從6點改為10點。
▸ About our appointment for tonight,
I wonder if we could change it from
six to ten.

不知我們能否把見面的時間改期。發生了點事。
**I wonder if we could alter the
time of our meeting to ~.
Something's come up.**

不知我們能否把見面的時間改為下星期四。發生了點事。
▸ I wonder if we could alter the time
of our meeting to next Thursday.
Something's come up.

不知你能否改一下時間。
I wonder if you could change the time.

我想把約會的時間改期。
**I'd like to change our
appointment to ~.**

我想把約會的時間改為星期天下午。
▸ I'd like to change our appointment
to Sunday afternoon.

我們的約會恐怕得改時間了。剛發生了件急事。
**I'm afraid our appointment would have to be changed.
Something urgent has just come up.**

很抱歉造成你的不便，但我們得把見面時間延後了。
I'm sorry to inconvenience you, but we have to postpone our meeting.

6 Approval 贊成

● 你贊不贊成？ ●

❦ 基本說法

你贊成嗎？
Are you in favor of ～?

你贊成他的意見嗎？
▸ Are you in favor of his opinion?

你贊成嗎？
Do you favor ～?

你贊成他的海外開發計劃嗎？
▸ Do you favor his offshore development plan?

你覺得應該這樣做嗎？
Do you find it a correct thing to do?

你覺得好嗎？
Do you find it a good idea to ～?

你覺得把會議延後好嗎？
▸ Do you find it a good idea to put off the meeting?

你覺得這有道理嗎？
Do you think it makes sense?

你覺得這行得通嗎？
Do you think it'll work?

你覺得這個主意好嗎？
Do you think it's a sensible idea?

你覺得可以嗎？
Do you think ～ all right?

你覺得這些錄音帶還可以嗎？
▸ Do you think these tapes all right?

111

你看合理嗎？
Is ～ sensible, do you think?

▶ 你看這安排合理嗎？
Is the arrangement sensible, do you think?

你贊成嗎？
Would you favor ～?

▶ 你贊成我的提議嗎？
Would you favor my proposition?

你會贊成，不是嗎？
You would be in favor of ～, wouldn't you?

▶ 你會贊成這個決定的，不是嗎？
You would be in favor of the decision, wouldn't you?

你贊成，不是嗎？
You're in favor of ～, aren't you?

▶ 你贊成這項計劃，不是嗎？
You're in favor of the plan, aren't you?

❋ 日常口語 🔊 062

你贊成嗎？
Are you for ～?

你贊成到加州旅行嗎？
▸ Are you for taking a trip to California?

你看還好嗎？
Do you reckon ～ fine?

你看一切都還好嗎？
▸ Do you reckon everything's fine?

你看可行嗎？
Do you reckon ～ is OK?

你看我的主意可行嗎？
▸ Do you reckon my idea is OK?

可以嗎？
Is ～ all right?

他的決定可以嗎？
▸ Is his decision all right?

現在這樣行嗎？
Is it OK now ?

你看可行嗎？
Reckon it's all right to ～?

你看和瑪姬約會可行嗎？
▸ Reckon it's all right to date Margie?

你會贊成嗎？
Will you back up ～?

你會贊成我的計劃嗎？
▸ Will you back up my plan?

113

♣ 正式場合

能得到你的認可嗎？ **Can I assume (that) ~ meets with your approval?**	此日程表能得到你的認可嗎？ ▸ Can I assume (that) the agenda meets with your approval?
我能否認為得到你的支持？ **Can I take it (that) ~ has your support?**	我能否認為我們的政策得到你的支持？ ▸ Can I take it (that) our policy has your support?
請問你對此有何看法？ **Could I ask about your attitude to ~?**	請問你對智力測驗有何看法？ ▸ Could I ask about your attitude to intelligence tests?
請問你是否贊成？ **Could I ask if you support ~?**	請問你是否贊成早婚？ ▸ Could I ask if you support an early marriage?
你贊成嗎？ **Do you approve?** 你贊成嗎？ **Do you approve of ~?**	你贊成這個新設計嗎？ ▸ Do you approve of the new design?
你認為合理嗎？ **Do you think ~ is reasonable?**	你認為2010年預算合理嗎？ ▸ Do you think the 2010 budget is reasonable?
我想是得到你的贊成了。 **I suppose (that) ~ has your backing.**	我想召開這次會議是得到你的贊成了。 ▸ I suppose (that) the conference has your backing.
我想你不反對吧。 **I take it you are not opposed to ~?**	我想你不反對這個夏天去露營吧。 ▸ I take it you are not opposed to camping this summer?

是否受到認可？
Is ～ acceptable?

新內閣是否受到認可？
▸ Is the new cabinet **acceptable?**

請問你持什麼立場？
May I know your position on ～?

請問你對這問題持什麼立場？
▸ May I know your position on the problem?

你是贊成的，不是嗎？
～ has your approval, hasn't it?

這次採購你是贊成的，不是嗎？
▸ This purchase **has your approval, hasn't it?**

你持什麼看法？
What is your reaction to ～?

對他們的習俗你持什麼看法？
▸ What is your reaction to their customs?

● 我贊成 ●

❤ 基本說法

這正是我心裡想的。
~ is just what I had in mind.

暑期露營正是我心裡想的。
▸ Camping in summer is just what I had in mind.

很好，正應該這樣。
Good, it's the correct thing to do.

你真聰明！
How wise of you!

我看這主意一點都不壞。
I don't think that's a bad idea at all.

我覺得這個主意很好。
I feel that's quite a good idea.

我當然贊成。
I sure favor ~.

我當然贊成你的決定。
▸ I sure favor your decision.

我想我會接受的。
I think I would accept ~.

我想我會接受這個的。
▸ I think I would accept that.

我想我會同意的。
I think I would agree with ~.

我想我會同意這事的。
▸ I think I would agree with that.

我想我會贊同的。
I think I would go along with ~.

我想我會贊同這事的。
▸ I think I would go along with that.

我想這麼做很好。
I think that's quite a good thing to do.

我想這是明智的。
I think that's wise.

我確信你是對的。
I'm sure you're right.

我很滿意你的安排。
I'm very pleased about your arrangement.

我很滿意。
I'm very pleased about ～.

我很滿意你的安排。
▶ I'm very pleased about your arrangement.

我覺得這是合理的想法。
It was a sensible idea, I felt.

喔很好，我非常贊同。
Oh, good, I'm very much in favor of ～.

喔很好，我非常贊同你的提議。
▶ Oh, good, I'm very much in favor of your proposal.

這很合理。
That makes a lot of sense.

我覺得這很合理。
That sounds very sensible to me.

這個主意好極了。
That's an excellent idea.

這正是我的意見。
That's exactly my opinion.

這正是我的看法。
That's just how I see it.

這正是我要說的意思。
That's just what I'm getting at.

這是個很有趣的主意，不是嗎？
That's rather an interesting idea, isn't it?

正應該這樣。
That's the way it should be.

絕對正確。
~ is absolutely right.

這項決定絕對正確。
▸ The decision is absolutely right.

很好。
~ is very good.

這想法很好。
▸ The idea is very good.

你做得很明智。
Very sensible of you.

真是個好主意！
What an excellent idea!

這點你說得有道理。
You have a point there.

好極了。
~ seems just fine.

你的建議好極了。
▸ Your suggestion seems just fine.

這點你說得有些道理。
You've got something there.

❋ 日常口語

好極了！
Excellent!

妙不可言！
Fantastic!

好！
Fine!

做得好！
Good business!

真棒！
Good for you!

好主意！
Good idea!

好極了！
Great!

真是神奇！
How terrific!

對呀！
I'll say!

我完全贊成。
I'm all for that.

這很好。
It's jolly good.

我正需要。
It's just the job.

做得好！
Nice going!

做得好！
Nice work!

好！
OK!

好極了！
Smashing!

聽起來不錯。
Sounds fine.

很好，沒問題。
Suits me fine.

好極了！
Swell!

好極了！
Terrific!

那倒不壞。
That one's not bad.

這聽起來好一點。
That sounds better.

這個主意很好！
That's a great idea!

這個主意不錯！
That's an idea!

這很好。
That's good.

對。
That's it.

這正合我意。
That's just my cup of tea.

這才像話。
That's more like it.

就是這樣。
That's the point.

這就對啦！
That's your sort!

好極了！
Wonderful!

你說對了。
You got it.

好極了。
~ is fine.

你的建議好極了。
▸ Your suggestion is fine.

♣ 正式場合

066

我完全贊成。
~ has my full approval.

我完全贊成早點出發。
▸ An early start **has my full approval.**

我看不出有什麼理由反對。
I can see no reason to disapprove of ~.

我看不出有何理由反對建立電腦中心。
▸ **I can see no reason to disapprove of** establishing a computer center.

我全力推薦。
I can thoroughly recommend ~.

我全力推薦他的新設計。
▸ **I can thoroughly recommend** his new design.

我完全贊成。
I entirely approve of ~.

我完全贊成那種理論。
▸ **I entirely approve of** that theory.

我得說我覺得這很合理。
I must say I find it quite reasonable.

我得說這是恰當的辦法。
I should say ~ is the proper course to take.

我得說改變時間表是恰當的辦法。
▸ **I should say** changing the timetable **is the proper course to take.**

我認為我們可以完全贊成。
I think we can give ~ our full backing.

我認為我們可以完全贊成這項預算。
▸ **I think we can give** the budget **our full backing.**

我肯定支持。
I would certainly give ~ my support.

我肯定支持這項政策。
▸ **I would certainly give** the policy **my support.**

我很願意支持。
I would like to endorse ~.

我很願意支持你的申請。
▸ **I would like to endorse** your application.

● 我不贊成 ●

你真的覺得這合理嗎？
Do you honestly feel that's reasonable?

你認為這是個好主意？
Do you think that's a good idea?

糟透了！
How terrible!

我不能贊成。
I can't favor ～.

我不能贊成你的決定。
▸ I can't favor your decision.

我不贊成。
I don't hold with the idea to ～.

我不贊成和約翰分手。
▸ I don't hold with the idea to break up with John.

我認為那是不對的，真的。
I don't suppose that's right, really.

我看不該那樣做。
I don't think it should have been done like that.

我看這完全不是我們所要的。
I don't think that was quite what we wanted.

我認為這不太好。
I don't think that's very good.

我認為他們不是很贊成。
I don't think ~ was very happy about ~. ▸

我認為納稅人對此不是很贊成。
I don't think the tax payer was very happy about that.

我認為沒有道理。
I don't think ~ makes any sense. ▸

我認為你的計劃沒有道理。
I don't think your plan makes any sense.

我確實不贊成。
I really don't approve of ~.

我確實不贊成他的行為。
▸ I really don't approve of his behavior.

我認為那糟透了！
I think that's dreadful!

我當然不贊成。
I'm certainly not in favor of ~.

我當然不贊成在這種天氣出遊。
▸ I'm certainly not in favor of an outing in this weather.

你知道，我不能確定這是可行的。
I'm not so sure that's practicable, you know.

我不是很贊成。
I'm not very happy about ~.

我不是很贊成我們草率的決定。
▸ I'm not very happy about our rash decision.

我實在不滿意。
I'm really displeased about ~.

我實在不滿意你的粗心大意。
▸ I'm really displeased about your carelessness.

真的一定要嗎？
Is it really necessary to ~?

真的一定要請大衛嗎？
▸ Is it really necessary to treat David?

你認為那真的必要嗎？
Is that really necessary, do you think?

這並不明智。
It isn't sensible to ～.

訂這樣的契約並不明智。
▶ It isn't sensible to make such a contract.

實際上這樣做並不恰當。
It's not a correct thing to do actually.

這是不對的。
It's wrong to ～.

搭公車不買車票是不對的。
▶ It's wrong to travel by bus without paying your fare.

做這種事是可恥的。
That's a base thing to do.

這有點低級，不是嗎？
That's a bit low, isn't it?

這非常不合情理。
That's quite senseless.

這很不對。
That's quite wrong.

這樣有什麼意思？
What's the point of ～?

走這麼長一段路回家有什麼意思？
▶ What's the point of walking such a long distance home?

你不需要這樣。
You don't need to ～.

你不需要整個下午都躺在床上。
▶ You don't need to stay in bed all afternoon.

❋ 日常口語

068

真傻！
How silly!

我絕對不贊成。
I'm dead against ～.

我絕對不贊成借錢。
▸ I'm dead against borrowing money.

這樣是不好的。
No good ～.

抱怨是不好的。
▸ No good complaining.

真是的！
Really!

怎樣能這樣！
Surely not!

這完全錯了。
That's all wrong.

這很傻。
That's silly.

這根本是浪費時間。
That's simply a waste of time.

嗯，我認為那並不高明。
Well, I don't think much of ～.

嗯，我認為這主意並不高明。
▸ Well, I don't think much of the idea.

嗯，不該這麼做的。
Well, that's a rotten thing to do.

為什麼？
What for?

有什麼用呢？
What's the use of ～?

和她爭論有什麼用呢？
▸ What's the use of arguing with her?

♣ 正式場合

069

我當然不能贊成。
I certainly can't give my support to ～.

我當然不能贊成他的觀點。
▶ I certainly can't give my support to his viewpoint.

我看不出有何意義。
I don't quite see the point of ～. ▶

我看不出投資礦業有何意義。
I don't quite see the point of investing money in mining.

我想我不能贊成。
I don't think I can give my support to ～.

我想我不能贊成你辭職。
▶ I don't think I can give my support to your resignation.

我覺得我無法贊成。
I feel I can't give my approval to ～.

我覺得我無法贊成這樣的安排。
▶ I feel I can't give my approval to such an arrangement.

我必須說我不贊成。
I have to say I disapprove of ～. ▶

我必須說我不贊成逃稅。
I have to say I disapprove of tax avoidance.

我必須說我覺得無法接受。
I must say I find it unacceptable.

我實在得表明我不贊成。
I really must register my disapproval of ～.

我實在得表明我不贊成把產量削減20%。
▶ I really must register my disapproval of a 20% reduction in our production.

我想說我很不贊成。
I should like to say how much I disapprove of ～. ▶

我想說我很不贊成採取如此多餘的步驟。
I should like to say how much I disapprove of taking such an unnecessary step.

我想我很難贊成。
I would find it difficult to approve of ～.

我想我很難贊成你的提議。
▶ I would find it difficult to approve of your proposal.

127

這樣恐怕相當不對。	他的缺席恐怕是相當不對的。
I'm afraid ～ is quite wrong.	▶ I'm afraid his absence is quite wrong.
恐怕我不能支持。	恐怕我不能支持你的計劃。
I'm afraid I can't recommend ～.	▶ I'm afraid I can't recommend your plan.
在我看來是相當不合理的。	在我看來你的信仰是相當不合理的。
In my opinion, ～ are quite unreasonable.	▶ In my opinion, your beliefs are quite unreasonable.
我個人覺得也許有點不必要。	我個人覺得這也許有點不必要。
Personally, I feel ～ might be a bit unnecessary.	▶ Personally, I feel that might be a bit unnecessary.
嗯，我絕對不贊成。	嗯，我絕對不贊成在街上踢足球。
Well, I'm definitely opposed to ～.	▶ Well, I'm definitely opposed to playing football on the streets.

相信

● 我相信 ●

❦ 基本說法

🔊 070

我相信。
I believe ～.

　　我相信你說的話。
▶ I believe what you said.

我可以相信。
I can credit ～.

　　我可以相信他對發生的事所作的敘述。
▶ I can credit his account of what happened.

我毫無疑問地相信。
I can easily believe ～.

　　我毫無疑問地相信。
▶ I can easily believe it.

我可以相信。
I can trust ～.

　　我可以相信他的解釋。
▶ I can trust his explanation.

我可以完全相信。
I can well believe ～.

　　我可以完全相信。
▶ I can well believe that.

我不懷疑。
I don't doubt ～.

　　我不懷疑你的話。
▶ I don't doubt your words.

我相信。
I feel confident of ～.

　　我相信他有能力治癒她的疾病。
▶ I feel confident of his ability to cure her disease.

我想是真的。
I think ～ is true.

　　我想你所說的是真的。
▶ I think what you said is true.

我相信。
I'm convinced of ～.

　　我相信他是誠實的。
▶ I'm convinced of his honesty.

這似乎是可信的。
It seems credible.

❋ 日常口語

我相信你的話。
I'll take your word for it.

看來可信。
Looks credible.

似乎可信。
Seems believable.

聽起來像是真的。
Sounds true.

這我相信。
That's my thing.

這我相信。
That's where I am.

♣ 正式場合

我完全相信。
I have complete faith in ～.

我完全相信他說的話。
▶ I have complete faith in what he said.

我完全相信。
I have full confidence (that) ～.

我完全相信他會信守諾言。
▶ I have full confidence (that) he will keep his promise.

我完全相信。
I have full credit in ～.

我完全相信你為人誠實。
▶ I have full credit in your honesty.

我很相信。
I have much belief in ～.

我很相信他的判斷。
▶ I have much belief in his judgment.

我完全信賴。
I have perfect trust in ～.

我完全信賴我的朋友約翰。
▶ I have perfect trust in my friend John.

我相信。
I have the conviction (that) ～.

我相信他講的是實話。
▶ I have the conviction (that) he is telling the truth.

我想我接受。
I think I will accept ～.

我想我接受你所說的話。
▶ I think I will accept what you said.

我認為這是可信的。
I think it's believable.

我相信。
I'm in the belief (that) ～.

我相信他會幫助我。
▶ I'm in the belief (that) he would help me.

我完全相信。
I'm in the full conviction (that) ～.

我完全相信他是誠實的。
▶ I'm in the full conviction (that) he is honest.

● 我不相信 ●

真的嗎？
Did you really?

你以為我會相信這樣的謊話嗎？
Do you think I'd believe a story like that?

別期待我會相信。   別期待我會相信你。
Don't expect me to believe ～. ▸ Don't expect me to believe you.

那怎麼可能呢？
How is that possible?

我不能相信。   我不能相信。
I can't believe ～.   ▸ I can't believe that.

我一點也不相信。   我一點也不相信。
I don't believe a word of ～. ▸ I don't believe a word of it.

不相信。   我不相信你。
I don't believe ～.   ▸ I don't believe you.

我才不相信呢！   我才不相信那呢！
I know better than ～!   ▸ I know better than that!

我不相信。   我不相信。
I refuse to believe ～.   ▸ I refuse to believe that.

我認為這是難以置信的。
I think it's incredible.

真的嗎？
Is that so?

這不可能是真的。
It can't be true.

哪有這麼好的事。
It's too good to be true.

噢，我才不信。
Oh, I wouldn't worry about ～.

噢，我才不信那呢。
▶ Oh, I wouldn't worry about that.

你肯定不是這個意思。
You don't mean that, surely.

你不是當真的，是不是？
You're not serious, are you?

🌸 日常口語

你在跟我開玩笑吧？
Are you kidding me?

別胡扯了。
Come off it: ～

別胡扯了，把實話告訴我！
▸ **Come off it: tell me the truth!**

別開我的玩笑了。
Don't pull my leg.

別胡說八道了！
Don't talk rot!

別扯了！
Get out of it!

去你的，我不信！
Go along (with you)!

我不信你的話。
I don't buy your story.

笨蛋才會相信你的話。
It's fool's trick to trust your words.

我才不信呢！
Never tell me!

別開玩笑了！
No kidding!

哦，去你的，我才不信！
Oh, get away (with you)!

哦，去你的，我才不信！
Oh, get off (with you)!

哦，去你的，我才不信！
Oh, get on (with you)!

聽你胡說！
Says you!

肯定不是！
Surely not!

我可不相信！
Tell me another!

我才不信那鬼話呢。
That story isn't good enough for me.

編得倒有模有樣的。
That's a good one.

我根本不相信。
That's what you say.

真是胡說八道！
What a story!

你一定不是說真的。
You can't be serious.

你一定是在開玩笑。
You must be joking.

你在開玩笑。
You're joking.

你在開玩笑。
You're kidding.

♣ 正式場合

我不相信。
I don't trust ～.

我不相信他的解釋。
▸ I don't trust his explanations.

我覺得這難以置信。
I find that hard to believe.

我不太相信。
I have little confidence in ～.

我不太相信報紙上所言。
▸ I have little confidence in what the newspapers say.

我不太相信。
I have no great belief in ～.

我不太相信我的醫生。
▸ I have no great belief in my doctor.

我不太相信。
I don't have much faith in ～.

我不太相信她說的話。
▸ I don't have much faith in what she says.

我不太相信。
I don't have much trust in ～.

我不太相信他的諾言。
▸ I don't have much trust in his promises.

我絲毫不相信。
I don't have the least faith in ～. ▸

她告訴我的事我絲毫不相信。
I don't have the least faith in what she told me.

我認為這難以置信。
I think it's hard to believe.

你不能期待我相信。
You can't expect me to believe ～.

你不能期待我相信這件事。
▸ You can't expect me to believe that.

8 Certainty 肯定

● 你真的確定嗎？ ●

❤ 基本說法

你肯定嗎？
Are you certain?

你肯定嗎？
Are you certain about ～?
這件事你能肯定嗎？
▸ Are you certain about that?

你肯定嗎？
Are you certain of ～?
你肯定會受歡迎嗎？
▸ Are you certain of a welcome?

你肯定嗎？
Are you certain ～?
你肯定他是誰嗎？
▸ Are you certain who he is?

你確定嗎？
Are you positive about ～?
這事你確定嗎？
▸ Are you positive about that?

你確定嗎？
Are you positive (that) ～?
你確定是午夜嗎？
▸ Are you positive (that) it was midnight?

你確定嗎？
Are you sure?

你確定嗎？
Are you sure about ～?
這件事你能確定嗎？
▸ Are you sure about that?

你確定嗎？
Are you sure of ～?
你確定會受歡迎嗎？
▸ Are you sure of a welcome?

你確定嗎？
Are you sure (that) ～?
你確定他有資格嗎？
▸ Are you sure (that) he's qualified?

你有把握嗎？
Can you be positive about ～?
你對聽到的話有把握嗎？
▸ Can you be positive about what you heard?

你有把握嗎？
Can you be positive (that) ～?
你有把握她會來嗎？
▸ Can you be positive (that) she'll come?

你真的能肯定嗎？
Can you really be certain ～?

你真的能肯定他是誰嗎？
▶ Can you really be certain who he is?

你真的能確信？
Can you really be sure of ～?

你真的能確信他的誠實？
▶ Can you really be sure of his honesty?

肯定嗎？
Definitely?

你確定嗎？
Do you know for certain ～?

你確定他會碰到什麼事嗎？
▶ Do you know for certain what will happen to him?

你確定嗎？
Do you know for sure ～?

你確定他們會贏嗎？
▶ Do you know for sure that they'll win?

你絕對有把握？
You're absolutely certain?

你絕對有把握？
You're absolutely certain about ～?

你絕對有把握他是有罪的？
▶ You're absolutely certain about his guilt?

你很有把握？
You're quite sure?

你很有把握嗎？
You're quite sure ～?

你很有把握他會在這附近露面嗎？
▶ You're quite sure he'll turn up around here?

🌸 日常口語 077

肯定沒問題嗎？
And no mistake?

你肯定？
Do you mean to say ～?

你肯定我們會遇到一場雷雨？
▸ Do you mean to say we're in for a thunder storm?

確定嗎？
For sure?

肯定嗎？
Positive?

真的嗎？
Really?

確定嗎？
Sure?

千真萬確嗎？
Sure as fate ～?

他們是千真萬確不會來了嗎？
▸ Sure as fate they won't come?

你有把握嗎？
You're sure?

♣ 正式場合

你肯定嗎？
Can you say with any certainty (that) ～?

你肯定他會成功嗎？
▶ Can you say with any certainty (that) he will succeed?

你認為無疑嗎？
Do you think you have no doubt of ～?

你認為他無疑的會按時到達嗎？
▶ Do you think you have no doubt of his arrival in time?

你認為你確信這事嗎？
Do you think you're confident (that) ～?

你認為你確信他來自美國？
▶ Do you think you're confident (that) he came from America?

抱歉，不過你真的能肯定嗎？
Pardon me, but are you really certain?

抱歉，不過你真的能肯定嗎？
Pardon me, but are you really certain about ～?

抱歉，不過你對她的能力真有把握嗎？
▶ Pardon me, but are you really certain about her ability?

我想你毫不懷疑吧。
I suppose you have no doubt about ～.

我想你對此毫不懷疑吧。
▶ I suppose you have no doubt about that.

有什麼疑問嗎？
Is there any doubt?

有什麼疑問嗎？
Is there any doubt about ～?

對這事的真實性有什麼疑問嗎？
▶ Is there any doubt about this being true?

還有什麼疑問嗎？
Is there any room for doubt?

還有什麼疑問嗎？
Is there any room for doubt about ～?

這事還有什麼疑問嗎？
▶ Is there any room for doubt about that?

也許我誤解了，不過你有把握嗎？

Perhaps I misunderstood, but are you quite certain ～?

也許我誤解了，不過你有把握該做什麼嗎？

▶ Perhaps I misunderstood, but are you quite certain what to do?

你心裡沒有疑問了嗎？
There's no doubt in your mind?

你心裡沒有疑問了嗎？
There's no doubt in your mind about ～?

對此人的意圖你心裡不存疑慮嗎？

▶ There's no doubt in your mind about the man's intention?

你心裡沒有疑問了嗎？
There's no doubt in your mind ～?

對於他符合這工作的資格你不存疑嗎？

▶ There's no doubt in your mind he's qualified for the job?

● 我很肯定 ●

🌱 基本說法

🔊 079

他一定。
He must be ～.

他一定在廚房裡。
▸ He must be there in the kitchen.

他一定。
He must have ～.

他一定沒趕上六點半的那班火車。
▸ He must have missed the 6:30 train.

他一定會。
He'll certainly ～.

如果你現在不請醫生他一定會死的。
▸ He'll certainly die if you don't get a doctor now.

我可以發誓！
I could have sworn (that) ～!

我可以發誓我看見天上有一架飛碟！
▸ I could have sworn (that) I saw a flying saucer over the sky!

我看沒問題。
I don't see any problem.

我可以向你保證。
I give you my word for it.

我知道將會。
I know ～ will ～.

我知道這部電影將會受歡迎。
▸ I know the film will make a hit.

我完全可以肯定。
I'm absolutely positive.
我完全可以肯定。
I'm absolutely positive about ～.

此事我完全可以肯定。
▸ I'm absolutely positive about that.

我完全可以肯定。
I'm absolutely positive (that) ～.

我完全可以肯定這是商標。
▸ I'm absolutely positive (that) it's the trademark.

我肯定。
I'm certain.
我肯定。
I'm certain about ～.
我肯定他是真誠的。
▸ I'm certain about his sincerity.
我肯定。
I'm certain of ～.
我肯定能成功。
▸ I'm certain of success.
我肯定。
I'm certain (that) ～.
我肯定你會通過這次考試。
▸ I'm certain (that) you'll pass the exam.

我確信。
I'm sure.
我能確信。
I'm sure about ～.
此事我能確信。
▸ I'm sure about that.
我確信。
I'm sure of ～.
我確信今天下午有一場大雨。
▸ I'm sure of a heavy rain this afternoon.
我確信。
I'm sure (that) ～.
我確信他會做得很出色。
▸ I'm sure (that) he'll make a go of it.

一定是這樣。
It can't be otherwise.

一定是的。
It must be.

我肯定。
I have no doubt.
我肯定。
I have no doubt about ～.
此事我可以肯定。
▸ I have no doubt about that.
我肯定。
I have no doubt of ～.
我肯定你有能力。
▸ I have no doubt of your ability.
我肯定。
I have no doubt (that) ～.
我肯定你會在比賽中獲得第一。
▸ I have no doubt (that) you'll come out first in the contest.

毫無疑問。
There's no mistake about it, ~.

毫無疑問，他就是我昨天見到的那個人。
▶ There's no mistake about it, he's the man I saw yesterday.

是的，肯定的。
Yes, definitely.

你可以放心。
You can rest assured ~.

你可以放心我們會把他爭取過來。
▶ You can rest assured we'll win him over.

你可以肯定。
You may be certain (that) ~.

你可以肯定形勢對我們有利。
▶ You may be certain (that) the situation is in our favor.

🌸 日常口語

080

絕對有把握。
Absolutely certain.

絕對有把握。
Absolutely positive.

肯定。
Bet ～.　　我肯定得不到的。
▶ Bet I won't get it.

肯定。
～ for sure.　　他肯定會來。
▶ He'll come for sure.

不會錯的。
～ and no mistake.　　他就是那個賊，不會錯的。
▶ He's the thief and no mistake.

我敢斷定。
I bet.
我敢斷定。
I bet ～.　　我敢斷定他們迷路了。
▶ I bet they've got lost.

我敢拿五塊錢打賭。
I'll bet five dollars (that) ～.　　我敢拿五塊錢打賭他不會來。
▶ I'll bet five dollars (that) he won't come.

我百分之百肯定。
I'm a hundred percent certain.
我百分之百肯定。
I'm a hundred percent certain (that) ～.　　我百分之百肯定他愛上了珍。
▶ I'm a hundred percent certain (that) he's fallen in love with Jane.

肯定。
No doubt ～.　　肯定是的。
▶ No doubt it is.

這不用說是顯而易見的事，不是嗎？
Surely that's obvious, isn't it?

這是毫無疑問的！
That's for sure!

這還用說。
~, you bet.

他們肯定趕不上，這還用說。
▸ They won't make it, you bet.

對。
Yes.

對，真的！
Yes, really!

一定是這樣。
You bet it is.

你可以肯定。
You can be sure.

你可以肯定。
You can be sure about ~.

你可以肯定他們對此很感興趣。
▸ You can be sure about their interest in it.

♣ 正式場合

081

我可以肯定地說。
I can say with certainty (that)
~.

我可以肯定地說，她適合這個職位。
▶ I can say with certainty (that) she is qualified for the position.

我認為我毫無疑問。
I don't think I have any doubt about ~.

我認為我對此事毫無疑問。
▶ I don't think I have any doubt about that.

我認為毫無疑問。
I don't think there can be any doubt of ~.

我認為你的能力是毫無疑問的。
▶ I don't think there can be any doubt of your ability.

我認為毫無疑問。
I don't think there can be any doubt (that) ~.

我認為毫無疑問她會克服困難。
▶ I don't think there can be any doubt (that) she'll overcome the difficulties.

我認為毫無疑問。
I don't think there can be any question of ~.

我認為毫無疑問是他偷了錢。
▶ I don't think there can be any question of his stealing the money.

我得說這是無庸置疑的。
I must say ~ is beyond doubt.

我得說他的誠實是無庸置疑的。
▶ I must say his honesty is beyond doubt.

我想我完全肯定。
I think I'm fully confident of ~.

我想我完全肯定他能成功。
▶ I think I'm fully confident of his success.

我很相信。
I'm quite convinced.

我很相信。
I'm quite convinced of ~.

我很相信她在這方面的經驗。
▶ I'm quite convinced of her experience in it.

我很相信。
I'm quite convinced (that) ~.

我很相信事情會改善。
▶ I'm quite convinced (that) things will improve.

毫無疑問。
It's a certainty (that) ～.

▶ It's a certainty (that) the government will win the next election.

毫無疑問政府會贏得下屆大選。

肯定。
It's definite (that) ～.

▶ It's definite (that) he will win.

他肯定會贏。

我確信。
It's my conviction (that) ～.

▶ It's my conviction (that) the weather will change soon.

我確信不久就要變天了。

肯定。
It's quite certain (that) ～.

▶ It's quite certain (that) the detergent will help clean off the stain.

清潔劑肯定有助於清除這個污點。

我確信如此。
That's my conviction.

毫無疑問。
There can't be any doubt about～.

▶ There can't be any doubt about that.

那是毫無疑問的。

毫無疑問。
There can't be any doubt as to ～.

▶ There can't be any doubt as to who's responsible for the theft.

誰應對此次失竊負責是毫無疑問的。

毫無疑問。
There can't be any doubt (that) ～.

▶ There can't be any doubt (that) our foreign trade is increasing.

毫無疑問我們的外貿正在增加。

無庸置疑。
There can't be any room for doubt about ～.

▶ There can't be any room for doubt about that.

此事無庸置疑。

毫無疑問。
There's no doubt whatsoever about ～.

▶ There's no doubt whatsoever about it.

這是毫無疑問的。

毫無疑問。
There's no question about ～. ▸ There's no question about it.

這是毫無疑問的。

無庸置疑。
There's no room for doubt about ～.

此事無庸置疑。
▸ There's no room for doubt about it.

我不懷疑。
There's very little doubt in my mind.

我不懷疑。
There's very little doubt in my mind about ～.

此事我並不懷疑。
▸ There's very little doubt in my mind about that.

我不懷疑。
There's very little doubt in my mind as to ～.

我不懷疑這是真的。
▸ There's very little doubt in my mind as to this being true.

我不懷疑。
There's very little doubt in my mind (that) ～.

我不懷疑形勢在好轉。
▸ There's very little doubt in my mind (that) the situation is taking a good turn.

● 我並不肯定 ●

❤ 基本說法

082

我不能肯定。
I can't be certain.

我不能肯定。
I can't be sure.

我決定不了。
I can't decide.
我不能決定。 我不能決定什麼時候出發。
I can't decide ~. ▸ **I can't decide** when to start.

我不明白。 我不明白他為什麼這麼晚才回家。
I can't make out ~. ▸ **I can't make out** why he came home so late.

我下不了決心。
I can't make up my mind.
我無法決定。 我無法決定去留。
I can't make up my mind ~. ▸ **I can't make up my mind** whether to go or to stay.

我不能確定。 我不能確定那要花多少時間。
I can't work out ~. ▸ **I can't work out** how much time it will take me.

我無法確定。 我無法確定是在什麼地方弄丟的。
I can't tell ~. ▸ **I can't tell** where it was lost.

我真的無法確定。
I really couldn't tell.

我想是這樣。
I should think I ~.

我想我聽見有聲音。
▸ I should think I heard some noise.

我想可能是…。
I suppose it could be ~.

我想可能是兩點鐘吧。
▸ I suppose it could be two o'clock.

我想那也許是之類的東西。
**I think it was ~
or something like that.**

我想那也許是美國偵探小說之類的東西。
▸ I think it was an American detective story
or something like that.

我無法決定。
I'm in two minds about ~.
我無法決定。
I'm in two minds ~.

我無法決定挑選哪個好。
▸ I'm in two minds about which to choose.
我無法決定把新電視放在哪裡。
▸ I'm in two minds where to put my new TV.

我沒有把握。
I'm not certain about ~.
我沒有把握。
I'm not certain ~.

我對結果沒有把握。
▸ I'm not certain about the result.
我沒有把握是否該把這事告訴你。
▸ I'm not certain if I should tell you this.

我不確定。
I'm not sure about ~.
我不確定。
I'm not sure ~.

對此我不確定。
▸ I'm not sure about that.
我不確定今晚誰會來。
▸ I'm not sure who's coming this evening.

很難說。
It's hard to tell.

我不知道。
I have no idea ~.

我不知道今年夏天要去哪裡。
▸ I have no idea where I'm going this
summer.

也許答案是…。
Perhaps the answer is ~.

也許答案是不要穿它。
▸ Perhaps the answer is not to wear it.

✿ 日常口語

083

難說，這可能是…。
Hard to tell. It could be ～.
　　難說，這可能是一份雜誌的名稱。
▸ Hard to tell. It could be the name of a magazine.

我不能確定。
I can't say for certain.
我不能確定。
I can't say for certain ～.
　　我不能確定該做什麼。
▸ I can't say for certain what to do.

我確實說不出。
I can't say, really, ～.
　　我確實說不出誰做得最好。
▸ I can't say, really, who's done the best.

我覺得腦子裡一團亂。
I feel in such a muddle.

我想不出。
I haven't a clue about ～.
　　我想不出我們該穿什麼。
▸ I haven't a clue about what we should wear.

我不太有把握。
I wouldn't be too sure about ～.
　　這件事我不太有把握。
▸ I wouldn't be too sure about that.

我不太有把握。
I'm not too sure of ～.
　　這件事我不太有把握。
▸ I'm not too sure of it.

咱們聽天由命吧。
Let's leave it to chance.

♣ 正式場合

084

我無法斷言。
I can't say with any certainty about ~.

我不能斷言。
I can't say with any certainty (that) ~.

我無法斷言該公司的未來。
▶ I can't say with any certainty about the company's future.

我不能斷言節食能治療肥胖症。
▶ I can't say with any certainty (that) eating less can be a cure for obesity.

我覺得難下結論。
I find it difficult to come to a conclusion.

我覺得難下結論。
I find it difficult to draw a conclusion on ~.

我覺得此事難下結論。
▶ I find it difficult to draw a conclusion on that.

我有疑問。
I have my doubts about ~.

此事我有疑問。
▶ I have my doubts about that.

我覺得是那樣，不過我可能不是正確的。
I have a feeling (that) ~, but I may not be correct.

我覺得我們走錯了路，不過我可能不是正確的。
▶ I have a feeling (that) we've taken a wrong road, but I may not be correct.

我不知道。
I wonder if ~.

我不知道我能否把錢拿回來。
▶ I wonder if I can get the money back.

我認為還不確定。
I would consider it open to question ~.

我認為競選運動能否成功還不確定。
▶ I would consider it open to question if the campaign will be a success.

我恐怕不能肯定。
I'm afraid I can't be certain about ~.

對此事我恐怕不能肯定。
▶ I'm afraid I can't be certain about that.

恐怕我無法肯定。
I'm afraid I can't be positive about ～.

恐怕我無法肯定汽車爆炸的時間。
▸ I'm afraid I can't be positive about the time when the car exploded.

我看還不確定。
I'm afraid it's questionable if ～.

這項計劃能否被接受，我看還不確定。
▸ I'm afraid it's questionable if the plan will be accepted.

我根本無法確定。
I'm not at all convinced.

我根本無法確定。
I'm not at all convinced about ～.

此事我根本無法確定。
▸ I'm not at all convinced about that.

我根本無法確定。
I'm not at all convinced (that) ～.

我根本無法確定這種食物有益健康。
▸ I'm not at all convinced (that) the food is good for health.

還不能肯定。
It's not yet certain ～.

還不能肯定哪隊將獲勝。
▸ It's not yet certain which team will win.

我心存疑慮。
There's some doubt in my mind.

我心存疑慮。
There's some doubt in my mind about ～.

我對他們的未來心存疑慮。
▸ There's some doubt in my mind about their future.

我心存疑慮。
There's some doubt in my mind if ～.

我對他是否有能力買房子心存疑慮。
▸ There's some doubt in my mind if he can afford to buy the house.

仍然不能完全肯定。
There's yet an element of doubt about ～.

仍然不能完全肯定其可靠性。
▸ There's yet an element of doubt about its reliability.

仍然不能完全肯定。
There's yet an element of doubt (that) ～.

仍然不能完全肯定這種生活節奏會導致精神緊張。
▸ There's yet an element of doubt (that) the pace of life can lead to stress.

154

仍然有些疑問。
There's still some doubt about ～.

仍然有些疑問。
There's still some doubt as to ～.

仍然有些疑問。
There's still some doubt if ～.

此事仍然有些疑問。

▸ There's still some doubt about that.

我們處理此問題的方法仍然有些疑問。

▸ There's still some doubt as to the way we deal with the problem.

我們對於能否控制污染仍然有些疑問。

▸ There's still some doubt if we can control pollutions.

155

最愛的經典名句

記下來，永遠的回味

Tomorrow is another day!
明天又是新的一天
- Gone With the Wind
亂世佳人

這句英語怎麼說？
把它記下來，
拿去問老師吧！

這句英語怎麼說？	這句英語這樣說！
中：隨你便！	英：Suit yourself!
中：	英：
中：	英：
中：	英：
中：	英：
中：	英：
中：	英：
中：	英：

 **Q&A**

這句英語怎麼說？
把它記下來，
拿去問老師吧！

這句英語怎麼說？	這句英語這樣說！
中：隨你便！	英：Suit yourself!
中：	英：
中：	英：
中：	英：
中：	英：
中：	英：
中：	英：
中：	英：

● 最常用的聊天開場白 ●

Ψ 基本說法 085

天氣如此，不是嗎？	天氣很冷，不是嗎？
~ weather, isn't it?	▸ Cold weather, isn't it?
天氣如此，你說不是嗎？	這天氣真討厭，你說不是嗎？
~ weather, don't you think?	▸ Dreadful weather, don't you think?
不好意思，你不是那位嗎？	不好意思，你不是彼得·格林嗎？
Excuse me, aren't you ~?	▸ Excuse me, aren't you Peter Greene?
不好意思請問一下，你是嗎？	不好意思請問一下，你是卡洛斯先生嗎？
Excuse me asking, but are you ~?	▸ Excuse me asking, but are you Mr. Carlos?
不好意思，能告訴我現在幾點嗎？	
Excuse me, but could you tell me the time?	
不好意思，我們是不是見過？	不好意思，我們是否在馬來西亞見過？
Excuse me, didn't we meet in ~?	▸ Excuse me, didn't we meet in Malaysia?
不好意思，你介意我坐在這裡嗎？	
Excuse me, do you mind if I sit here?	
不好意思，你剛好有打火機嗎？	
Excuse me, have you got a light by any chance?	
不好意思，我們是不是在哪見過？	不好意思，我們以前是不是在哪見過？
Excuse me, haven't we met somewhere ~?	▸ Excuse me, haven't we met somewhere before?

161

不好意思，我聽說你是。 **Excuse me, I hear you're ～.**	不好意思，我聽說你是一位音樂家。 ▸ Excuse me, I hear you're a musician.
不是嗎？ **～, isn't it?**	超冷的，不是嗎？ ▸ Freezing, isn't it?
天氣如此。 **～ weather we're having.**	天氣糟透了。 ▸ Horrible weather we're having.
我說，你不是那位嗎？ **I say, aren't you ～?**	我說，你不是約翰·亨利嗎？ ▸ I say, aren't you John Henry?
對不起，我無意聽到，你剛才好像提到某事嗎？ **Sorry, I couldn't help overhearing, did you mention something about ～?**	對不起，我無意聽到，你剛才好像提到了那次事故嗎？ ▸ Sorry, I couldn't help overhearing, did you mention something about the accident?
對不起打擾你了，那是嗎？ **Sorry to interrupt you, is that ～?**	對不起打擾你了，那是印度紅寶石嗎？ ▸ Sorry to interrupt you, is that an Indian ruby?
對不起打擾了，你知道嗎？ **Sorry to trouble you, but do you happen to know ～?**	對不起打擾了，你知道博物館何時開門嗎？ ▸ Sorry to trouble you, but do you happen to know when the museum opens?

🌸 日常口語

你好！
Hello!

嗨！是吧？
Hi! ~, eh?

嗨！好節目，是吧？
▸ Hi! Great show, eh?

嗨！那麼你是那位嗎？
Hi! You're ~, then?

嗨！那麼你是傑克遜先生的祕書嗎？
▸ Hi! You're Mr. Jackson's secretary, then?

欸！我是不是在哪裡看過你？
Say, don't I know you from somewhere?

對不起，我可以看看嗎？
Sorry, but can I have a look at ~?

對不起，我可以看看這份報紙嗎？
▸ Sorry, but can I have a look at the newspaper?

♣ 正式場合

087

不好意思請問一下，你打算這樣嗎？	不好意思請問一下，你打算飛往羅馬嗎？
Do excuse me, please, but are you ～?	▸ Do excuse me, please, but are you flying to Rome?
請原諒我發問，你介意嗎？	請原諒我發問，你介意我開窗嗎？
Forgive me for asking, but do you mind if I ～?	▸ Forgive me for asking, but do you mind if I open the window?
抱歉，你知道嗎？	抱歉，你知道飛機何時到拉斯維加斯嗎？
I beg your pardon, but do you know ～?	▸ I beg your pardon, but do you know when the plane gets to Las Vegas?
希望你不介意我發問，是這樣嗎？	希望你不介意我發問，我們以前在什麼地方見過面嗎？
I hope you don't mind my asking, but ～?	▸ I hope you don't mind my asking, but haven't we met somewhere before?
請原諒我詢問，…？	請原諒我詢問，你不是從紐西蘭來的亨利先生嗎？
Please pardon me for asking, but ～?	▸ Please pardon me for asking, but aren't you Mr. Henry from New Zealand?

● 引起對方注意 ●

088

🌱 基本說法

你知道嗎？
Do you know?

你知道嗎？我剛聽說火車昨晚出軌了。
▶ Do you know? I've just been told (that) the train got derailed last night.

不好意思！
Excuse me!

不好意思，先生。
Excuse me, sir.

嘿。
I say, ~

嘿，哈利，誰打來的電話？
▶ I say, Harry, who's on the telephone?

噢。
Oh, ~

噢，懷特太太，你能為我抽出時間嗎？
▶ Oh, Mrs. White, can you spare me a minute?

對不起。
Sorry, but ~

對不起，那不是你的書嗎？
▶ Sorry, but isn't that your book?

抱歉，打擾你了。
Sorry to bother you, but ~

抱歉，打擾你了，你能載我回家嗎？
▶ Sorry to bother you, but could you give me a lift home?

抱歉，打擾你了，不知道…。

Sorry to trouble you, but I wonder ~.

抱歉，打擾你了，不知道你能不能幫我拿杯飲料。
▶ Sorry to trouble you, but I wonder whether you could get me some drink.

165

❀ 日常口語

哈囉！
Hello there!

喂。
Here, ~.

喂，那個給我。
▶ Here, give that to me.

嘿！你！
Hey! You!

嘿！那邊那位！
Hey! You there!

聽著！
Listen!

看！
Look! ~.

看！你的計程車正在外面等著。
▶ Look! Your taxi's waiting outside.

喂！
Look here!

喂。
Look here, ~

喂，你以為你能騙我嗎？
▶ Look here, do you think you can cheat me?

喂。
See here, ~.

喂，大家。我不想再和你們在一起了。
▶ See here, you guys. I don't want to be with you anymore.

不好意思。
Excuse me, but ~

不好意思，幫我打一份申請單好嗎？
▶ Excuse me, but will you type an application form for me?

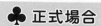 **正式場合**

呃哼，不知我現在能否向你提及？

呃哼，不知我現在能否向你提及這問題？

Ahem, I wonder if I could raise ~ with you now?

▸ Ahem, I wonder if I could raise this problem with you now?

請注意。

Attention, please.

呃，不知我們能否開始？

呃，不知我們能否開始下一個議題？

Er, I wonder if we could move on to ~.

▸ Er, I wonder if we could move on to the next item.

對不起，我可以提醒一下嗎？

不好意思，我可以提醒一下會議將在星期五舉行嗎？

Excuse me, could I just mention (that) ~?

▸ Excuse me, could I just mention (that) the meeting will be held on Friday?

嗯，我想我們現在該開始了。

Hmm, I suppose we should begin now.

請注意。

Let me have your attention, please.

請注意。

May I have your attention, please.

請注意。

Pay attention, please.

● 接話的技巧 ●

🌱 基本說法

🔊 091

談到這方面，我認為。

About ～, I think ～.

談到收入，我認為大多數人都應得到比他們現在得到的更多些。

▶ About income, I think most people deserve more than what they get.

你這麼說很有趣，因為我。

It's interesting you should say so, because I'm ～.

你這麼說很有趣，因為我也盼望在那裡過暑假。

▶ It's interesting you should say so, because I'm looking forward to the summer holiday there.

你會說到那件事還真是奇妙，因為…。

It's strange you should say that, because ～.

你會說到那件事還真是奇妙，因為剛才我自己也在想。

▶ It's strange you should say that, because just now I was thinking of it myself.

談到…。

On the subject of ～.

談到音樂，人們現在喜歡流行音樂而不是古典音樂。

▶ On the subject of music, people nowadays love pop music rather than classical.

談到…。

Speaking of ～, have you ～?

談到電影，你看過《鬥陣俱樂部》嗎？

▶ Speaking of movies, have you seen "Fight Club?"

抱歉打斷一下，我剛才是不是聽到你說？

Sorry to interrupt, but did I hear you say ～?

抱歉打斷一下，我剛才是不是聽到你說快樂書店在大促銷？

▶ Sorry to interrupt, but did I hear you say the Happy Bookstore has a big sale?

談到此事，我知道。 **Talking of ~, I know ~.**	談到誠實，我知道許多人搭車不買票。 ▸ Talking of honesty, I know a lot of people don't pay bus fares.
這使我想起。 **That reminds me of ~.**	這使我想起了我們在西雅圖露營的事情，那時我們的帳篷被吹走了。 ▸ That reminds me of the time we were camping in Seattle and our tent blew away.
回到你剛才談論的話題。 **To go back to what you were saying about ~, I'm ~.**	回到你剛才談論的通貨膨脹，我對價格上漲的情況並不訝異。 ▸ To go back to what you were saying about inflation, I'm not surprised at the way prices have risen.
你剛才提到某人。是啊。 **You mentioned ~ just now. Well, ~.**	你剛才提到了傑克·卡森。是啊，他開車學得很快。 ▸ You mentioned Jack Carson just now. Well, he's very quick at learning how to drive.
你提出了一個很重要的問題，因為…。 **You've brought up an important issue, because ~.**	你提出了一個很重要的問題，因為教育真的很重要。 ▸ You've brought up an important issue, because education is really important.

✿ 日常口語

真有趣你會說到那事。

Funny you should say that. ～. ▸

真有趣你會說到那事。我也正打算買一台藍光播放機。

Funny you should say that. I'm going to buy a Blu-ray Disc player, too.

等等，我們可以繼續談那個問題嗎？

Hang on, can we stick with that point about ～? ▸

等等，我們可以繼續談關於立體主義的那個問題嗎？

Hang on, can we stick with that point about cubism?

對不起插個話，你是不是說？

Sorry to break in, but did I hear you say ～? ▸

對不起插個話，你是不是說街上發生了一件車禍？

Sorry to break in, but did I hear you say there was an accident on the street?

對不起插個話，你說？

Sorry to chip in, but did you say ～? ▸

對不起插個話，你說瑪麗就快來了嗎？

Sorry to chip in, but did you say Mary would come soon?

想不到你會提起這事。

Strange you should bring this up. ～. ▸

想不到你會提起這事。我自己也沒把握。

Strange you should bring this up. I wasn't sure myself.

真巧！我剛…。

What a coincidence! I've just ～. ▸

真巧！我剛聽完那場演唱會回來。

What a coincidence! I've just come back from that concert.

170

♣ 正式場合

093

我認為你剛才提到的問題很重要。

I suppose the problem you raised just now is important, because ～.

▸ 我認為你剛才提到的問題很重要,因為我不想和你爭執。

I suppose the problem you raised just now is important, because I don't argue with you.

請允許我暫時回到你談過的那點。

If I may just go back for a moment to the point you made, I should say ～.

▸ 請允許我暫時回到你談過的那點,我得說政府對此是有責任的。

If I may just go back for a moment to the point you made, I should say the government is responsible for that.

請允許我重提我們剛才討論的問題。

If I might refer back to the problem we were discussing, I think ～.

▸ 請允許我重提我們剛才討論的問題,我想我們應該強調保存我們的自然資源。

If I might refer back to the problem we were discussing, I think we should stress on the conservation of our natural resources.

回到那看法,我這麼認為。

Reverting to sb.'s point about ～, I think ～.

▸ 回到布朗夫人關於金錢的看法,我認為我們永遠不會滿足於我們所獲得的。

Reverting to Mrs. Brown's point about money, I think we are never satisfied with what we earn.

談到那些評論,我這麼認為。

To take up sb.'s remark about ～, I think ～.

▸ 談到傑克遜先生對寫作的評論,我認為簡潔有力是最好的藝術。

To take up Mr. Jackson's remark about writing, I think simplicity is the best art.

既然我們談到這問題,我想請問。

While we're on the subject of ～, may I ask ～?

▸ 既然我們談到錢的問題,我想請問你一個月花多少錢?

While we're on the subject of money, may I ask how much you spend a month?

● 話鋒一轉，換個話題 ●

順便問一下。 **By the way, ～?**	順便問一下，我可以借這本書三週嗎？ ▸ By the way, can I keep the book for three weeks?
不過這與主題無關。 **I ～, but that's beside the question.**	我曾讀過一本書，叫《野性的呼喚》，不過這本與主題無關。 ▸ I once read a book called "The Call Of The Wild", but that's beside the question.
附帶一提。 **Incidentally, ～.**	附帶一提，約翰下星期要回家了。 ▸ Incidentally, John's coming home next week.
暫時打岔一下。 **Just to change the subject for a while, ～?**	暫時打岔一下，你聽說卡門結婚了嗎？ ▸ Just to change the subject for a while, have you heard about Carmen's marriage?
我們換個話題。 **Let's change the subject, and talk about ～.**	我們換一下話題，談談你的工作吧。 ▸ Let's change the subject, and talk about your job.
不過這只是順道一提。 **～, but that's just by the way.**	露西出國了，不過這只是順道一提。 ▸ Lucy has gone abroad, but that's just by the way.
現在我們就別再談這個問題，還是來看看其他事吧。 **Now, let's drop the subject, and have a look at ～.**	現在我們就別再談這個問題，還是來看看明天要做些什麼吧。 ▸ Now, let's drop the subject, and have a look at what we need to do tomorrow.

噢，趁我還沒有忘記。	噢，趁我還沒有忘記，你把信送給史密斯先生了嗎？
Oh, before I forget, ～?	▶ Oh, before I forget, have you sent the letter to Mr. Smith?
噢，我知道我本來想問你什麼了。	噢，我知道我本來想問你什麼了，彼特先生打電話來了嗎？
Oh, I know what I meant to ask you, ～?	▶ Oh, I know what I meant to ask you, has Mr. Pitt telephoned yet?
噢，我知道我想告訴你什麼了。	噢，我知道我想告訴你什麼了，凱西這星期六不會來。
Oh, I know what I meant to tell you, ～.	▶ Oh, I know what I meant to tell you, Cathy isn't coming this Saturday.
噢，趁我還記得。	噢，趁我還記得，傑克遜教授打算今天下午為我們講課。
Oh, while I remember, ～.	▶ Oh, while I remember, Professor Jackson's going to give us a lecture this afternoon.

那麼，我們來談談別的吧。
Well, let's talk about something different.

✿ 日常口語

095

嘿，差點忘了！
Hey, I almost forgot! ~.

嘿，差點忘了！約翰請你打電話給他。
▸ Hey, I almost forgot! John asked you to give him a ring.

噢，我知道有件事我原想告訴你。
Oh, I knew there was something I meant to tell you, ~.

噢，我知道有件事我原想告訴你，我們已接到德比要我們去慶祝聖誕節的邀請。
▸ Oh, I knew there was something I meant to tell you, we've got an invitation from Derby to celebrate the Christmas.

噢，差點忘了！
Oh, it nearly slipped my mind! ~.

噢，差點忘了！丹妮要我把這個給你。
▸ Oh, it nearly slipped my mind! Dannie asked me to give you this.

♣ 正式場合

096

我們可以討論這問題了嗎？
Could we move on now to the problem of ～?

我們可以接著討論運輸問題了嗎？
▸ Could we move on now to the problem of transportations?

我想我們應該接著開始下一個項目。
I think we ought to pass on to the next item.

我們現在是否接著討論這問題。
If we could pass on now to the question of ～.

我們現在是否接著討論合約的問題。
▸ If we could pass on now to the question of the contract.

就一個完全不同的問題，現在我們來談談吧。
On an entirely different matter, now, let's talk about ～.

就一個完全不同的問題，現在我們談談電視的廣告時間吧。
▸ On an entirely different matter, now, let's talk about the advertising time on TV.

議事日程上的下個項目是…。
The next item on the agenda is ～.

議事日程上的下一個項目是婦女洋裝。
▸ The next item on the agenda is women's dress.

那我建議現在接著討論。
Well, I suggest we move on now to ～.

那我建議現在接著討論日程表第五項。
▸ Well, I suggest we move on now to item 5 on the agenda.

那麼我們開始討論這問題吧。
Well, let's turn to the problem of ～.

那麼我們開始討論污染問題吧。
▸ Well, let's turn to the problem of pollutions.

● 結束談話的技巧 ●

097

🌱 基本說法

對不起，我得走了。
Excuse me, I have to take off.

請原諒，我現在真的該上路了。
Excuse me, please, I really ought to be on my way now.

我想我該走了。
I guess I have to go now.

我希望你不介意，不過我真的不能再待了。
I hope you don't mind, but I really mustn't stay any longer.

我真的不能再待了。
I really can't stay any longer.

我真的不喜歡像這樣匆忙離去。
I really hate to rush off like this.

我真的必須離開了。
I really must leave you.

我真的該走了。
I really should be going.

我想我們該動身了。
I think it's about time we made a move.

我不再佔用你的時間了。
I won't take any more of your time.

我最好還是走了吧。
I'd better be going.

我想我最好還是走了。
I'd better be off, I think.

我很想再談一會兒，但是我現在得走了。
I'd like to talk about this some more, but I have to be going now.

請原諒，我現在真的該走了。
If you'll excuse me, I really have to go now.

我現在得掛斷電話了。
I'll have to ring off now.

恐怕我得走了。
I'm afraid I have to leave.

恐怕我得走了。
I'm afraid I have to run along.

恐怕我現在真的必須走了。
I'm afraid I really must be going now.

恐怕我不該再待了。
I'm afraid I ought not to stay any longer.

恐怕我得走了。
I'm afraid I'll have to be going.

恐怕我已佔用了你許多時間了。
I'm afraid I've taken up too much of your time.

那麼，現在我走了。
I'm off now, then.

對不起，不過我得去。
I'm sorry, but I've got to ～.

對不起，不過六點我得去參加會議。
▶ I'm sorry, but I've got to attend a meeting at six.

對不起，現在我得趕快走了。
I'm sorry, I must dash away now.

謝謝你打電話來。
It was nice of you to call.
＊結束電話中的談話。

恐怕我該走了。
It's about time I was going, I'm afraid.

和你談話很愉快。
It's been nice talking with you.

與你談話很有趣，不過我真的該走了。
It's very interesting talking to you, but I really should be off now.

我們該走了。
It's time we were off.

我很喜歡聽。　　　　　　　　　　　我很喜歡聽你談非洲的經歷。
I've enjoyed hearing about ～.　▸ **I've enjoyed hearing about your experience in Africa.**

哦，我沒注意到時間這麼晚了。
Oh, I hadn't realized how late it was.

哦，我現在真的必須走了。
Oh, I really must be off now.

哦，時間不早了。我得走了。
Oh, it's getting late. I have to start.

哦，我該走了。
Oh, it's time for me to go.

不知能否稍後回電給你。
~, I wonder if I could call you back in a few minutes.

有人剛進來，不知能否稍後回電給你。
▸ Someone's just come in, I wonder if I could call you back in a few minutes.

好了，我必須走了。時間不早了。
Well, I must be pushing along now. It's getting late.

好了，我最好還是走囉。
Well, I'd better go and ~.

好了，我最好還是去和布萊德見面。
▸ Well, I'd better go and meet Brad.

好了，我們就到此為止。
Well, let's leave it at that and ~.

好了，我們就到此為止，吃早餐去吧。
▸ Well, let's leave it at that and have our breakfast.

好了，很高興見到你。
Well, nice to have seen you, ~.

好了，莎莉，很高興見到你。
▸ Well, nice to have seen you, Sally.

哦，謝謝你讓我度過愉快的一天。
Well, thank you for a nice day.

好了，謝謝你打電話來。
Well, thank you for calling.
＊結束電話中的談話。

好了，感謝你的幫助。我很高興能與你談話。
Well, thank you for your help. I've enjoyed talking to you.

請你原諒，恐怕我得走了。

請你原諒，恐怕我得走了，看看能否趕上末班車。

Will you excuse me, I'm afraid I have to go and ~.

▸ Will you excuse me, I'm afraid I have to go and see if I can catch the last bus.

請你原諒了。
You'll have to excuse me.

🌸 日常口語

098

得走了。以後再找你。
Gotta go. Check you later.

我不耽誤你了。
I'll let you get back to ～.

我不耽誤你吃晚餐了。
▶ I'll let you get back to your dinner.

我現在得掛斷了。
I've got to hang up now.
＊結束電話中的談話。

對，現在我要走了。
Right, I'm off now.

對不起，我必須上路了。
Sorry, I must be getting on my way.

對不起，我必須走了。
Sorry, I must be running along.

對不起，現在我必須走了。
Sorry, I must be off now.

對不起，我現在得趕快走了。
Sorry, I've got to dash now.

對不起，我現在得趕快走了。
Sorry, I've got to rush now.

謝謝你打電話來。
Thanks for calling.
＊結束電話中的談話。

好了，我想我最好還是走了吧。
Well, better be moving, I suppose.

♣ 正式場合

請你原諒，我現在得離開。
I hope you'll excuse me, but I have to go now, ～.

▶ 請原諒，我現在得離開，有人在等我。
I hope you'll excuse me, but I have to go now, someone is waiting for me.

請你原諒，我想我真的要離開了。
I hope you'll forgive me, but I really think I must be going.

我必須道歉，我恐怕不能再待了。
I must apologize, but I'm afraid I can't stay any longer.

恐怕我們只好談到此為止了。
I'm afraid we shall have to leave it at that.

和你談話很愉快。
It's been a pleasure talking to you.

請原諒，我現在真的得告辭了。
Please excuse me, but I really have to leave now.

請原諒，我現在得告辭了。
Please forgive me, but I have to be going now.

請原諒，我不該再待在這裡了。
Please pardon me, but I shouldn't stay any longer.

10 Comparison 比較

● 比較的各種表達 ●

❦ 基本說法

🔊 100

不再像從前那樣了。
sb. is no longer the same ~ as sb. was ~.

鮑伯不再像十年前那樣是個年輕人了。
▸ Bob is no longer the same young man as he was ten years ago.

一樣快。
A is as fast as B.

開車旅行跟搭火車旅行一樣快。
▸ A car journey is as fast as a train journey.

和…相比。
Compared to ~.

和其他車輛相比，汽車確實很方便。
▸ Compared to other vehicles, cars are really quite convenient.

幾乎不相上下。
A is almost equal to B.

他唱歌幾乎跟麥可‧傑克森不相上下。
▸ He is almost equal to Michael Jackson when he sings.

堪稱第一。
~ rivals the best in ~.

在舞台設計方面他堪稱第一。
▸ He rivals the best in stage designing.

可跟最好的媲美。
~ are comparable to the best.

他的成績可以跟最好的媲美。
▸ His achievements are comparable to the best.

我大致認為A比B更…。
I generally find A more ~ than B.

我大致認為搭飛機比搭船更有趣。
▸ I generally find flying more interesting than going by sea.

如果A跟B相比，後者較輕。
If you compare A with B, the latter is lighter.

▸ 如果你把木材跟塑膠相比，後者較輕。
If you compare wood with plastics, the latter is lighter.

較為…。
It's a bit ~.

▸ 它較慢。
It's bit slower.

這比…更好。
It's better than ~.

▸ 這比那更好。
It's better than that.

這…得多了。
It's much more ~.

▸ 這方便得多了。
It's much more convenient.

也不那麼…。
~ not as ~, either.

▸ 也不那麼重。
It's not as heavy, either.

A比不上B。
A can't compare with B.

▸ 身為悲劇作家，約翰比不上莎士比亞。
John can't compare with Shakespeare as writer of tragedy.

比得上。
A equals B in ~.

▸ 我的車在節能方面比得上你的車。
My car equals yours in economy.

整體說來，更…。
On the whole, sb. is ~er/ more ~.

▸ 整體說來，傑克更聰明。
On the whole, Jack is cleverer.

A和B相比，顯得很…。
A looks quite ~ beside B.

▸ 和你弟比起來你顯得很年輕。
You look quite young beside your brother.

A比不上B。
A isn't a patch on B.

狄納摩隊比不上利物浦隊。
▸ Dynamo isn't a patch on Liverpool.

我不懂你怎麼能相提並論。
I don't see how you can talk about ～ in the same breath.

我不懂你怎麼能把詩和音樂相提並論。
▸ I don't see how you can talk about poetry and music in the same breath.

我想A比B強一點呢。
I think A has the edge on B.

我想絲綢比尼龍強一點呢。
▸ I think silk has the edge on nylon.

A比B略勝一籌。
A is one up on B.

馬汀比大衛略勝一籌。
▸ Martin is one up on David.

A沒有比B好。
There's no way A is better than B.

開車可沒有比走路好。
▸ There's no way driving is better than walking.

你根本無法把A和B相比。
You just can't compare A with B.

你根本無法把夏威夷和阿拉斯加相比。
▸ You just can't compare Hawaii with Alaska.

A當然比不上B。
A is surely not to be compared to B.

論價值，你的項鍊當然比不上她的。
▸ Your necklace is surely not to be compared to hers in value.

♣ 正式場合

🔊 102

實際上論此無人能相提並論。 **Actually no one can parallel ～ in ～.**	實際上論詩歌無人能和他相提並論。 ▸ Actually no one can parallel him in poetry.
大致上，更為…。 **All in all, sb. is more ～ than sb. was ～.**	大致上，他比十年前更有學問了。 ▸ All in all, he is more learned than he was ten years ago.
大致上來說，更好。 **By and large, ～ is better.**	大致上來說，它的品質更好。 ▸ By and large, its quality is better.
我認為A比不上B。 **I consider A to be inferior to B.**	我認為它比不上機器人。 ▸ I consider it to be inferior to robots.
我不認為A有哪裡比B更…。 **I don't consider A to be in any way more ～ than B.**	我不認為釣魚有哪裡比衝浪更有趣。 ▸ I don't consider fishing to be in any way more interesting than surfing.
和B相較，A…。 **In comparison to B, A is ～.**	相較城市生活，鄉村生活寧靜又和平。 ▸ In comparison to city life, life in the country is quiet and peaceful.
A無法等同於B。 **It's impossible to equate A and B.**	財富無法等同於幸福。 ▸ It's impossible to equate wealth and happiness.
大致上更…。 **On balance, ～ is more ～.**	大致上，提摩西的建議更可取。 ▸ On balance, Timothy's suggestion is more acceptable.
A不如B。 **A is less ～ than B.**	紅寶石不如鑽石貴重。 ▸ Ruby is less valuable than diamond.

我認為A的耐久性勝過B。
My assessment is (that) A has an ▶
advantage over B in durability.

我認為尼龍的耐久性勝過棉。
My assessment is (that) nylon has an
advantage over cotton in durability.

我的判斷是A勝過B。
My judgment is (that) A is
superior to B.

我的判斷是芝加哥的經濟勝過洛杉磯。
▶ My judgment is (that) Chicago is
superior to Los Angeles economically.

A跟B兩者完全無法相比。
There's absolutely no
comparison between A and B.

龍蝦跟鰻魚兩者完全無法相比。
▶ There's absolutely no comparison
between lobsters and eels.

A遠比B更…。
A is incomparably more ～
than B.

你的嗓音遠比她的更有魅力。
▶ Your voice is incomparably more
attractive than hers.

● 你的意思是…？ ●

🌱 基本說法　🔊 103

我這樣有誤解你的意思嗎？ **Can I have misunderstood you if I ～?**	我說你不愛都市生活有誤解你的意思嗎？ ▸ Can I have misunderstood you if I say you don't like city life?
你的意思是…？ **Do you intend to say (that) ～?**	你的意思是你不想娶她？ ▸ Do you intend to say (that) you don't want to marry her?
你是說？ **Do you mean ～?**	你是說我不必去辦簽證？ ▸ Do you mean I don't have to get a visa?
這是說？ **Does that mean ～?**	這是說我可以帶二十公斤重的行李而不必付超重費用？ ▸ Does that mean I can take up to twenty kg without paying extra?
如果我的了解沒錯。 **If I understand right, ～.**	如果我的了解沒錯，那麼銀行要到明天才開門。 ▸ If I understand right, the bank won't open till tomorrow.
我不確定我是否理解，意思是…？ **I'm not sure I follow sb. right.** **Does sb. mean (that) ～?**	我不確定我是否理解他的意思。他是不是說雪梨是老年生活的理想地？ ▸ I'm not sure I follow him right. Does he mean (that) Sydney is an ideal place for old people?

不好意思我有點遲鈍，我不確定我是否懂了。這是不是說？

I'm sorry if I'm being a little slow, but I'm not sure I understand. Does this mean ～?

不好意思我有點遲鈍，我不確定我是否懂了。這是不是說我們得十點前到達？

I'm sorry if I'm being a little slow, but I'm not sure I understand. Does this mean we have to be there by ten?

抱歉，我不確定我有沒有聽懂你的意思。你是說？

I'm sorry, I'm not sure I have grasped the point of what you said. Do you mean (that) ～?

抱歉，我不確定我有沒有聽懂你的意思。你是說我得辭職？

I'm sorry, I'm not sure I have grasped the point of what you said. Do you mean (that) I have to quit the job?

所以這麼說對嗎？

So am I right in saying ～?

所以他生病了，這麼說對嗎？

So am I right in saying he is sick?

所以這就是說？

So that means ～?

所以這就是說卡特下星期天不會來了？

So that means Carter isn't coming next Sunday?

所以基本上就是？

So the basic idea is (that) ～?

所以基本上就是現在人大多憤世嫉俗？

So the basic idea is (that) people nowadays are mostly cynical?

所以…？

So ～?

所以我們六點時得在那裡？

So we have to be there at six o'clock?

所以你想說的是？

So what you intend to say is (that) ～?

所以你想說D.C.公司財務方面不可靠？

So what you intend to say is (that) D.C. company is not reliable financially?

🌸 日常口語

104

如果我沒弄錯的話，那你…。

If I see your point right, then you ~.

如果我沒弄錯的話，那你並不覺得她有多好。

▸ If I see your point right, then you don't think much of her.

要是我沒弄錯的話。

If I've got it right, then ~.

要是我沒弄錯的話，那就是你認為他樣樣都行。

▸ If I've got it right, then you think he's capable of everything.

要是我了解得沒錯，那就是說…。

If I've got the picture, then ~.

要是我了解得沒錯，那就是說英國人不善於學習語言。

▸ If I've got the picture, then English people are not good at learning languages.

換句話說，對嗎？

In other words ~. Right?

換句話說我不必用空運郵寄了，對嗎？

▸ In other words I don't have to send it by air mail. Right?

總歸一句話，是嗎？

So what it boils down to is ~. Yeah?

總歸一句話，你想要回你的錢，是嗎？

▸ So what it boils down to is you want your money back. Yeah?

所以你的意思是…，對嗎？

So what you mean is ~. Right?

所以你意思是我該多鍛鍊身體，對嗎？

▸ So what you mean is I should take more exercises. Right?

所以你就是說，對嗎？

So what you're really saying is ~. Right?

那麼你就是說有些商店的確想欺騙顧客，對嗎？

▸ So what you're really saying is some shops do try to cheat people. Right?

抱歉，我不太明白你的意思。你是說？

Sorry, I don't quite catch you. You mean ～?

抱歉，我不太明白你的意思。你是說你買不起？

▸ Sorry, I don't quite catch you. You mean you can't afford to buy it?

抱歉，我不太明白這意思。是不是說？

Sorry, I don't quite see the point. Does it mean ～?

抱歉，我不太明白這意思。是不是說我們都應該彼此相愛？

▸ Sorry, I don't quite see the point. Does it mean we should all love each other?

抱歉，我不太明白你的話。意思是？

Sorry, I'm not quite with what you said. Does it mean ～?

抱歉，我不太明白你的話。意思是班機已經取消了？

▸ Sorry, I'm not quite with what you said. Does it mean the flight has been canceled?

抱歉，關於這點我還是不確定。意思是？

Sorry, I'm still not sure about that point. Does it mean ～?

抱歉，關於這點我還是不確定。意思是這個站應該遷到別的地方去？

▸ Sorry, I'm still not sure about that point. Does it mean the station should be moved to another place?

這是說…，對嗎？

That means ～. Right?

這是說電視正在取代電影，對嗎？

▸ That means television is taking the place of movies. Right?

你是說…，對嗎？

You mean ～. Right?

你是說我犯了一個錯誤，對嗎？

▸ You mean I've made a mistake. Right?

♣ 正式場合

105

我可以弄清楚一件事嗎？ 你這麼認為，是不是？ **Can I get one thing clear? You think ～, don't you?**	我可以弄清楚一件事嗎？你認為大多數理論只是有所根據的揣測，是不是？ ▸ Can I get one thing clear? You think most theories are only educated guesses, don't you?
如果我沒有聽錯的話，你是不是這麼認為？ **If I follow you correctly, then you think ～?**	如果我沒有聽錯的話，你是不是認為草率的決定常常影響到教育與事業？ ▸ If I follow you correctly, then you think a rash decision often affects education and career?
如果我沒有弄錯你的意思的話。 **If I perceive your meaning correctly, then ～.**	如果我沒有弄錯你的意思的話，你認為應該教導孩子們誠實。 ▸ If I perceive your meaning correctly, then you believe children should be taught to be honest.
如果我理解正確的話。 **If I understand you rightly, ～.**	如果我理解正確的話，你打算在這裡待幾個月囉。 ▸ If I understand you rightly, you're going to stay a couple of months here.
我不確定我是否懂你的意思。是不是？ **I'm not certain I've grasped what you meant. Is it (that) ～?**	我不確定我是否懂你的意思。是不是你不滿意你現在的工作？ ▸ I'm not certain I've grasped what you meant. Is it (that) you are not satisfied with your present job?
我只是想搞清楚剛才說的。 **Just to be quite clear about what's just been said, ～.**	我只是想搞懂剛才說的；情形不壞吧。 ▸ Just to be quite clear about what's just been said, the situation is not bad.

那麼，如果我沒弄錯你的意思的話。
So, if I take your point rightly, ～.

那麼，如果我沒弄錯你的意思的話，早婚是不明智的。
▸ So, if I take your point rightly, it's unwise to get married early.

這似乎等於是說。
That seems to be tantamount to saying ～.

這似乎等於是說現代都市交通過於繁忙。
▸ That seems to be tantamount to saying there's too much traffic in modern cities.

這含意似乎是。
The implication seems to be ～.

這含意似乎是我們今年不能休假了。
▸ The implication seems to be we can't have a holiday this year.

我這麼想對嗎？
Would I be correct in supposing ～?

你不想要我走，我這麼想對嗎？
▸ Would I be correct in supposing you don't want me to go?

我這麼說對嗎？
Would I be right in saying ～?

科學讓我們更聰穎，我這麼說對嗎？
▸ Would I be right in saying science is making us wiser?

● 你明白我的意思嗎？ ●

❦ 基本說法

106

你能理解我所說的嗎？
Can you make sense of what I said?

你明白我的意思嗎？
Did you catch my meaning?

你理解我說的意思嗎？
Did you grasp the point of what I said?

你懂我的意思嗎？
Do you follow me?

你明白我的意思嗎？
Do you get me?

你明白我的意思嗎？
Do you get what I mean?

你知道我的意思嗎？
Do you know what I mean?

你明白我的意思嗎？
Do you see my point?

你明白我的意思嗎？
Do you see what I mean?

你明白我的意思嗎？
Do you take me?

你明白我說的話嗎？
Do you understand what I said?

這樣可以了解嗎？
Does that seem to make sense?

你不明白這意思嗎？
Don't you see the point?

如果你明白我的意思。
~, if you see what I mean.

要每天早起，如果你明白我的意思。
▸ Get up early every day, if you see what I mean.

我希望這樣說清楚了。
I hope that's clear.

你覺得這樣清楚嗎？
Is that clear to you?

這很清楚，不是嗎？
That's clear, isn't it?

你懂了，不是嗎？
You got it, didn't you?

✿ 日常口語 107

你明白我的意思了嗎？
Are you with me?

你明白了嗎？
Did you get the picture?

你明白嗎？
Do you see?

瞭嗎？
Get it?

瞭解這意思了嗎？
Got the message yet?

聽清楚了嗎？
Has the penny dropped?

知道我的意思了嗎？
Know what I mean?

知道我說的意思了嗎？
Know what I'm driving at?

知道我的意思了嗎？
Know what I'm getting at?

知道我要說的意思嗎？
Know what I'm trying to say?

明白我的意思嗎？
See what I mean?

你懂我的意思，不是嗎？
You have me, haven't you?

♣ 正式場合

我想你懂我的意思？
Can I say (that) you understand what I mean?

我都說清楚了嗎？
Did I make everything clear?

我這樣說清楚嗎？
Do I make myself clear?

我這樣有說清楚了嗎？
Have I made myself clear?

我不知道我是否說清楚了。
I don't know if I'm making myself clear.

我相信你明白我的意思了？
I trust you understand me?

如果你還有哪裡不清楚的，請提出來。
If there's anything you are still not clear about, please say so.

這樣說還算清楚嗎？
Is that reasonably clear?

如果你明白我的意思。

～, if you take my point.

她太遲鈍所以反應不過來，如果你明白我的意思。

▸ She's bit too slow to respond, if you take my point.

196

● 恭喜你 ●

恭喜。
Congratulations.

恭喜。
Congratulations on ～.

恭喜贏得這場足球賽。
▸ Congratulations on winning the football game.

十分恭喜。
Many, many congratulations on ～.

十分恭喜你們締結良緣。
▸ Many, many congratulations on your marriage.

請代我表示祝賀。
Please send ～ my congratulations.

請代我向他表示祝賀。
▸ Please send him my congratulations.

✿ 日常口語

好極了！
Fantastic!

好一個！ | 好一個鮑伯！
Good old ~! | ▶ Good old Bob!

聽說…，這真是太棒了。 | 聽說你最近升遷了，這真是太棒了。
It was great to hear about ~. | ▶ It was great to hear about your recent promotion.

聽說…，這真是太棒了。 | 聽說你找到一份好工作，真是太棒了。
It was great to hear (that) ~. | ▶ It was great to hear (that) you've got a good job.

好極了！
Super!

好球！ | 好球，亨利！
Nice one, ~! | ▶ Nice one, Henry!

做得好！ | 做得好，柯林！
Well done, ~! | ▶ Well done, Colin!

♣ 正式場合

請允許我向你表示最衷心的祝賀。
Allow me to express my heartiest congratulations.

請允許我表示最熱忱的祝賀。

Allow me to express my warmest congratulations on ~.

請允許我為你們劇團的成功表示最熱忱的祝賀。

▶ Allow me to express my warmest congratulations on the success of your troupe.

我一定要祝賀你。

I must congratulate you on ~.

我一定要祝賀你榮升經理之職。

▶ I must congratulate you on your appointment as a manager.

我想第一個向你表示祝賀。

I'd like to be the first to congratulate you on ~.

我想第一個為你出色的研究表示祝賀。

▶ I'd like to be the first to congratulate you on your excellent research.

讓我向你表示祝賀。

Let me congratulate you on ~.

讓我為你的成就表示祝賀。

▶ Let me congratulate you on your achievement.

請允許我獻上祝賀。

May I offer my congratulations on ~.

請允許我為你的晉升獻上祝賀。

▶ May I offer my congratulations on your promotion.

請接受我衷心的祝賀。
Please accept my sincere congratulations.

請接受我最熱忱的祝賀。

Please accept my warmest congratulations on ~.

請接受我為你們喜結良緣獻上最熱忱的祝賀。

▶ Please accept my warmest congratulations on your marriage.

13 *Correctness* 正確

● 請問這樣是對的嗎？●

🌱 **基本說法**

🔊 112

能否請你告訴我對不對？
Could you please tell me if ~ is correct?

能否請你告訴我這句子對不對？
▶ Could you please tell me if the sentence is correct?

你看對嗎？
Do you think ~ is correct?

你看我的判斷對嗎？
▶ Do you think my judgment is correct?

請問我做對了嗎？
Have I got it right, please?

我想知道我是否弄對了。
I'd like to find out if I've got ~ right.

我想知道我是否把日期弄對了。
▶ I'd like to find out if I've got the date right.

對嗎？
Is it true (that) ~?

在英國來往車輛都靠左行駛，對嗎？
▶ Is it true (that) traffic in Britain keeps left?

請問這對嗎？
Is it correct, please?

請問這對嗎？
Is that right, please?

有錯誤嗎？
Is there any mistake in ~?

我的計劃有錯誤嗎？
▶ Is there any mistake in my plan?

這是對的嗎？
Is this the right thing to ~?

這麼做對嗎？
▶ Is this the right thing to do?

200

✿ 日常口語

我是對的嗎？
Am I right?

有錯誤嗎？
Any mistake?

有錯嗎？
Anything wrong?

有錯嗎？　　　　　　　　　　　這翻譯有錯嗎？
Anything wrong with ～?　　▸ Anything wrong with the translation?

他叫做…，對嗎？　　　　　　　他叫湯姆‧彼特，對嗎？
He's called ～, yes?　　　　▸ He's called Tom Pitt, yes?

他的地址是…，對嗎？　　　　　他的住址是春天街100號，對嗎？
His address is ～, right?　　▸ His address is 100 Spring Street, right?

這對嗎？
Is it OK?

現在是…，對嗎？　　　　　　　現在是早上6點鐘，對嗎？
It's ～, isn't it?　　　　　▸ It's six o'clock in the morning, isn't it?

我做對了，是不是？
I've got it right, haven't I?

對嗎？
That's right?

♣ 正式場合

🔊 114

我這麼認為是對的嗎？

Am I correct in thinking (that) ～?

我認為這是因為她母親太過遷就她所造成的，對嗎？

▶ Am I correct in thinking (that) it's her mother's fault for giving in to her too often?

請問對嗎？

Could I ask if ～ is correct?

請問他算的對嗎？

▶ Could I ask if his calculation is correct?

我想…？

I assume (that) ～?

我想她是無辜的？

▶ I assume (that) she's innocent?

我想弄清楚是否正確。

I'd like to make sure (that) ～ is correct.

我想弄清他們對合約的解釋是否正確。

▶ I'd like to make sure (that) their interpretation of the contract is correct.

這麼說對嗎？

Is it true to say (that) ～?

商人做事應有充分自信，這麼說對嗎？

▶ Is it true to say (that) a businessman should act with perfect self-assurance?

這樣對嗎？

Would it be correct if ～?

我把數字從3改成6，這樣對嗎？

▶ Would it be correct if I change the number from 3 to 6?

這麼說對嗎？

Would it be true to say so?

這是正確的嗎？

Would that be correct?

請告訴我是否正確，好嗎？

Would you mind telling me if ～ is correct?

請告訴我，我的評估是否正確，好嗎？

▶ Would you mind telling me if my estimation is correct?

● 對，就是這樣 ●

🌱 基本說法

一點都沒錯。
Exactly.

我認為沒錯。
I don't think there's anything wrong with ~.

我認為他的發音沒錯。
▸ I don't think there's anything wrong with his pronunciation.

我想你是對的。
I guess you're right.

沒有。沒發現任何錯誤。
No. I didn't find any mistake in ~.

沒有。我沒在他的考卷發現任何錯誤。
▸ No. I didn't find any mistake in his test paper.

不，這沒什麼錯誤。
No, there's nothing wrong with that.

是的，這是對的。
Yes, that's quite correct.

是的，這是對的。
Yes, that's right.

是的，你是對的。
Yes, you're correct in ~.

是的，你這麼說是對的。
▸ Yes, you're correct in saying this.

是的，你很正確。
Yes, you're quite right.

❀ 日常口語

對。
Correct.

看來是這樣。
Kind of looks that way.

沒有錯。
Nothing wrong with ～.

這沒有錯。
▶ Nothing wrong with that.

對。
Right.

一點都沒錯。
Spot on.

完全沒錯。
That's all right.

對。
That's it.

對。
That's OK.

你完全正確。
You're dead right.

♣ 正式場合

絕對正確。
Absolutely.

我得說完全正確。 　　　　我得說你的解釋完全正確。
I should say ～ is perfectly ▸ **I should say your interpretation is**
correct. 　　　　　　　　**perfectly correct.**

我認為絕對正確。 　　　　我認為他所說的絕對正確。
I suppose ～ is absolutely true. ▸ I suppose what he said is absolutely true.

看來你是對的。
It would seem (that) you were right.

正是如此。
Precisely.

這完全正確。
That is perfectly correct.

是的，我可以證實。 　　　　是的，我可以證實他昨天在那裡。
Yes, I can confirm (that) ～. ▸ Yes, I can confirm (that) he was
　　　　　　　　　　　　　　there yesterday.

● 不對，不是這樣 ●

我不認為。
I didn't think ～.

我不認為這孩子聰明。
▸ I didn't think the boy's clever.

我不認為。
I don't think ～.

我不認為他是昨天6點鐘回家的。
▸ I don't think he came home at six yesterday.

我不認為這是正確的。
I don't think ～ is right.

我不認為他的評估正確。
▸ I don't think his assessment is right.

恐怕這是不對的。
I'm afraid it's wrong.

恐怕不太正確。
I'm afraid ～ is not quite right.

你對此人的看法恐怕不太正確。
▸ I'm afraid what you think about the man is not quite right.

我不能肯定你是對的。
I'm not sure you're correct ～.

我不能肯定你在這件事上是對的。
▸ I'm not sure you're correct about that.

不，我不這麼認為。
No, I don't think so.

不，實際上。
No, ～, actually.

不，實際上她考試不及格。
▸ No, she failed the exam, actually.

對不起，這根本不對。
Sorry, that's not at all right.

對不起，這不正確。
Sorry, that's not correct.

❀ 日常口語

不，全錯了。
No, it's all wrong.

不，你錯了。
No, you're wrong.

不，你全弄錯了。
No, you've got it all wrong.

不，你弄錯了。
No, you've ~ wrong.

不，你把我的名字拼錯了。
▶ **No, you've spelled my name wrong.**

胡說。
Nonsense.

胡說。
Rubbish.

這是不對的，是嗎？
~ isn't right, is it?

他們的觀點是不對的，是嗎？
▶ **Their view isn't right, is it?**

事實上你全都搞錯了。
You're all wet, actually.

♣ 正式場合

我認為這點你錯了。
I suppose you're mistaken there.

我想我必須告訴你這不正確。
I think I must tell you (that) ~ is not true.

▸ 我想我必須告訴你他所說的並不正確。
I think I must tell you (that) what he said is not true.

如果我可以這麼說，實際情況並非如此。
If I may say so, it is actually not the case.

如果我可以這麼說，你的消息是不正確的。
If I may say so, the information you have is incorrect.

對不起，但我實在應該指出這是不正確的。
I'm sorry, but I really should point out ~ is not correct.

▸ 對不起，但我實在應該指出，他的評估是不正確的。
I'm sorry, but I really should point out his estimation is not correct.

這麼說似乎是不正確的。
It doesn't seem correct to say (that) ~.

▸ 若說價格不斷上漲，這似乎是不正確的。
It doesn't seem correct to say (that) the prices are rising all the time.

這麼認為也許是不正確的。

It is perhaps incorrect to suppose (that) ~.

▸ 認為更多工業就意味著更多污染，這也許是不正確的。
It is perhaps incorrect to suppose (that) more industry means more pollutions.

● 糾正對方 ●

🌱 基本說法

據我所知。
As far as I know, ～.
▸ As far as I know, she didn't ask for a day off.

據我所知,她並沒有請假。

可是…。
But ～.
▸ But the business has been going down all winter.

可是整個冬天生意一直在下滑。

當然,是這樣的,不是嗎?
Surely, it's ～, isn't it?
▸ Surely, it's the bus which ran into the truck, isn't it?

當然,是公車撞上卡車,不是嗎?

喔,實際上。
Well, actually, ～.
▸ Well, actually, he doesn't always tell the truth.

喔,實際上他不一定說真話。

喔,事實上。
Well, as a matter of fact, ～.
▸ Well, as a matter of fact, she's too young to understand what she did.

喔,事實上她太年輕不明白她做了啥。

喔,事實上。
Well, in fact, ～.
▸ Well, in fact, it was a double room.

喔,事實上那是一間雙人房。

喔,事實上是。
Well, the fact is ～.
▸ Well, the fact is nobody was here yesterday.

喔,事實上昨天沒人在這裡。

🌸 日常口語

等等。
Hang on a minute, it's ∼.

等等，那是他叔叔，不是他爸爸。
▸ Hang on a minute, it's his uncle not his father.

等等。
Hold on a minute, it's ∼.

等等，那只有百分之十五。
▸ Hold on a minute, it's only 15%.

不。
No, ∼.

不，火車9點30分出發。
▸ No, the train leaves at 9:30.

哦不，等一下。
Oh, no, wait a minute, ∼.

哦不，等一下，他已經超過25歲。
▸ Oh, no, wait a minute, he's already past 25.

♣ 正式場合

123

請允許我糾正你說的事。
Allow me to correct one thing you said : ~.
▸ 請允許我糾正你說的事：吸菸有害健康。
Allow me to correct one thing you said : smoking is harmful to health.

我想這麼說可能更確切。
I suppose it might be more correct to say ~.
▸ 我想這麼說可能更確切：嫉妒是人類最富詩意的弱點。
I suppose it might be more correct to say jealousy is the most poetic weakness of human beings.

我認為這麼說可能會更確切。
I think it might be more accurate to say ~.
▸ 我認為如果說這次會議是成功的，可能會更確切。
I think it might be more accurate to say the meeting was a success.

如果我可以糾正你的話，實際上…。
If I may correct you, ~ actually.
▸ 如果我可以糾正你的話，實際上只有三個人去那裡。
If I may correct you, only three people went there actually.

關於這點我恐怕得糾正你。實際上…。
I'm afraid I have to correct you there. Actually ~.
▸ 關於這點我恐怕得糾正你。實際上那次演講是關於人口問題。
I'm afraid I have to correct you there. Actually the lecture was about population.

噢，據我所知。
Well, to my knowledge, ~.
▸ 噢，據我所知，傑克遜並沒有在這次競選中落敗。
Well, to my knowledge, Jackson didn't lose the campaign.

Decision 決定

● 我已經決定了 ●

我認為沒人能阻止我。
I don't think anybody can keep me from ～.

我認為沒人能阻止我和珍結婚。
▶ I don't think anybody can keep me from marrying Jane.

我已決定。
I'm fixed on ～.

我已決定出國度假。
▶ I'm fixed on going abroad for my holiday.

我心意已決。
I'm quite decided.

我已決定不要了。
I've decided against ～.
我已決定了。
I've decided for ～.
我已決定了。
I've decided to ～.

我已決定不賣這棟房子了。
▶ I've decided against selling the house.
我已決定贊成這項工程。
▶ I've decided for the project.
我已決定購買那台腳踏車。
▶ I've decided to buy that bike.

我已下定決心了。
I've made up my mind.
我已下定決心不要了。
I've made up my mind not to ～.

我已下定決心不改變我的行程表了。
▶ I've made up my mind not to change my calendar.

我已決定。
I've set my mind on ～.

我已決定修改這個計劃。
▶ I've set my mind on revising the plan.

沒有什麼能阻止我。
Nothing can stop me from ～.

沒有什麼能阻止我執行我的計劃。
▶ Nothing can stop me from carrying out my plan.

他們已決定。
They've settled on ～.
他們已決定。
They've settled to ～.
他們已決定。
They've settled ～.

他們已決定舉行一場派對。
▶ They've settled on having a party.
他們已決定支持這項建議。
▶ They've settled to support the proposal.
他們已決定到哪裡去露營。
▶ They've settled where to camp.

我們決定。
We decided on ～.

我們決定臥室用藍色油漆。
▶ We decided on blue paint for the bedroom.

我們已同意。
We've agreed on ～.

我們已同意和社會上的惡勢力對抗。
▶ We've agreed on fighting the evil in society.

我們已決定。
We've fixed on ～.

我們已決定明天出發。
▶ We've fixed on starting tomorrow.

❋ 日常口語

125

就這樣了。
And that goes.

就這樣約定了。
It's a go.

我已下定決心了。
My mind is made up.

那就這樣定了。
So that's that.

這使我下定決心。
That decides me.

就這樣決定了。
That settles it.

那成交。
Then it's a deal.

好，我知道要做什麼了。
Well, I know what I'll do.

好，決定了。
Well, that's settled.

♣ 正式場合

🔊 126

我決定。
I'm determined to ～.

我決定付給他一百美元。
▶ I'm determined to pay him 100 dollars.

我決定。
It's my decision to ～.

我決定把我所有的一切都給我的兒子。
▶ It's my decision to give all I have to my son.

我已決定。
I've determined on ～.

我已決定在家裡度假。
▶ I've determined on spending my holiday at home.

我已決定了。
I've made a decision to ～.

我已決定辭職了。
▶ I've made a decision to resign.

我們現在已決定了。
We've arrived at a decision now.

我們已決定。
We've come to a decision (that) ～.

我們已決定會議延期。
▶ We've come to a decision (that) the meeting be postponed.

15 Goodbye 再見

● 再見了 ●

基本說法

別忘了打電話給我。
Don't forget to give me a ring.

再見！
Goodbye!

再見了，如果你來到這，無論如何都要寫封信給我們。
Goodbye and be sure to drop us a line if ever you're in ～.

▶ 再見了，如果你來到倫敦，無論如何都要寫封信給我們。
Goodbye and be sure to drop us a line if ever you're in London.

再見，祝愉快。
Goodbye, and have a good ～.

▶ 再見，旅途愉快。
Goodbye, and have a good journey.

再見了，如果你順道經過我們這裡，記得打電話給我們。
Goodbye and remember to give us a ring if ever you're in our way.

再見了，下次你來這裡時再見。
Goodbye and see you again next time you're here.

再見了，謝謝你為我做的一切。
Goodbye and thank you for all you've done for me.

再見了。很高興見到你。
Goodbye. Nice seeing you.

216

那麼再見了，祝你萬事如意。
Goodbye then, and all the very best.

那麼晚安。
Good night then.

希望能再見到你。旅途愉快。
I hope to see you again. Have a good trip.

希望我們不久能再相聚。現在再見了。
I hope we'll get together again soon. Goodbye for now.

如果你來到這，請來看我。
If you're ever in ～, come and see me.

如果你來芝加哥，請來看我。
▸ If you're ever in Chicago, come and see me.

我會很想念你的。
I'm really going to miss you.

認識你真令人愉快。
It's been really nice knowing you.

希望能再見面。
Let's hope it's au revoir.

記得寫封信給我。
Remember to drop me a line.

如果你來到這裡，記得來看看我。
Remember to look me up if ever you're here.

✿ 日常口語 128

祝你萬事如意。
All the best.

再見了，謝謝你為我做的一切。
Byebye, and thanks for everything.

再見！
Cheerio!

代我向某人問好。　　　　　代我向你女兒問好。
Give my love to ~. ▸ Give my love to your daughter.

祝你好運！
Good luck!
祝好運。　　　　　　　　　祝你全家好運。
Good luck with ~. ▸ Good luck with your family.

祝你度過快樂的一天。
Have a good day.

再見。
I'll be seeing you.

保持聯絡！
Keep in touch!

保重。再見！
Look after yourself. Bye!

期盼不久後再見到你。再見！
Look forward to seeing you again soon. Bye!

順便向某人問好。
Love to ～, by the way.

順便向羅伯問好。
▶ Love to Rob, by the way.

代我向某人問好。
Mention me to ～.

代我向傑克問好。
▶ Mention me to Jack.

代我向某人問好。
Regards to ～.

代我向瑪麗問好。
▶ Regards to Mary.

代我向某人問好。
Say hello to ～ for me.

代我向你叔叔問好。
▶ Say hello to your uncle for me.

再見！
See you!

再見！
See you around!

再見！
See you later!

再見！
See you soon!

再見！
See you ～!

明天見！
▶ See you tomorrow!

代我問好。
Send ～ my best.

代我向約翰問好。
▶ Send John my best.

再見！
So long!

多保重。再見！
Take care. Bye!

♣ 正式場合

希望我們將來能再見面。
I hope we will meet at some future date.

我期盼不久後能再見到你。再見。
I look forward to seeing you again soon. Goodbye.

希望你旅途愉快。再見。
I trust you have a pleasant journey. Goodbye.

我想告別了。
I'd like to say goodbye to ～.

我想向你們大家告別了。
▸ I'd like to say goodbye to you all.

請代我致意。
Please give my best regards to ～.

請代我向你們全家致意。
▸ Please give my best regards to your family.

Plz give an example about...

● 舉例 ●

🌱 基本說法

🔊 130

譬如。 **~, for example, ~.**	譬如，日本製造的相機價錢就很貴。 ▶ Cameras , for example, made in Japan are very expensive.
譬如。 **~, for instance, ~.**	譬如，汽車要消耗大量汽油。 ▶ Cars, for instance, use a lot of petrol.
讓我為你舉個例子。 **Let me give you an example.**	
不僅如此。 **Not only that. ~.**	不僅如此。他的方法也是落伍的。 ▶ Not only that. His methods are antiquated.
像是…。 **~, such as ~.**	片語動詞，像起床、趕上等都很有用的。 ▶ Phrasal verbs, such as get up, catch up with, are very useful.
以此為例。 **Take ~ for instance, ~.**	以現代都市的交通為例，這是一種文明的副作用。 ▶ Take traffic in modern cities for instance, it's one side effect of civilization.
此外。 **What's more, ~.**	此外，你向來以高品質的工作著稱。 ▶ What's more, you've got an excellent reputation for high quality work.
你只需看看。 **You have only to look at ~.**	你只需看看他的日記就知道了。 ▶ You have only to look at his diary.

🌸 日常口語

像…。

像《亂世佳人》、《外星人》之類的片子都是好電影。

~ like ~.

▸ Films **like** Gone with the Wind, E.T., etc., are all good films.

看看…。
Look at ~.

看看美國貿易中心,他們日進斗金。

▸ **Look at** American Trade Center. They're making a fortune.

譬如…。
~. Like ~, for example.

有些人非常有哲理性,譬如德國人就是。

▸ Some people are very philosophical. **Like** the Germans, **for example.**

比方說…。
What about ~.

比方說俱樂部,它在西方國家很流行。

▸ **What about** club. It's popular in western countries.

♣ 正式場合

讓我舉個例子。
Allow me to cite an example.

這方面的一個例子就是。

An example of this would be: ~.

這方面的一個例子就是：1984年我們的出口成長了20%。

▸ An example of this would be: in 1984 our export increased by 20%.

而作為這方面的例證是。

And as evidence of that, ~.

而作為這方面的例證是：人們不再上電影院看好電影了。

▸ And as evidence of that, people don't go to the cinema to see good films any more.

這是根據這點得知。

It follows from that, ~.

這是根據這點得知：婦女有孩子時必須停止工作。

▸ It follows from that, women must stop working when they have children.

讓我舉幾個例子。

Let me cite a few instances: ~.

讓我舉幾個例子：柳丁、香蕉、鳳梨等都是南方水果特產。

▸ Let me cite a few instances: oranges, bananas, pineapples, etc., are all fruit from the south.

讓我舉個例子。

Let me take an example: ~.

讓我舉個例子：工作人員之間的關係複雜得多了。

▸ Let me take an example: staff relations are much more complex.

以此為例。
Take the case of ~.

以電視為例，它對人們有很壞的影響。

▸ Take the case of television, it has a very bad influence on people.

223

就是這方面的例證。
~ is evidence of that.

生產的增加就是這方面的例證。
▸ The increase of production is evidence of that.

為舉例說明，我們來檢視…。
To exemplify ~, let us examine ~.

為舉例說明理論，我們來檢視幾種昆蟲。
▸ To exemplify this theory, let us examine some species of insects.

為舉例說明，讓我們看看…。

To exemplify ~, let us look at ~.

為舉例說明我的意思，讓我們看看我們每年的原油進口。
▸ To exemplify what I mean, let us look at our annual import of crude oil.

為了給你實證，以此為例。
To give you an example of ~, take ~ for instance.

為給你這方面的實證，以現代繪畫為例。
▸ To give you an example of this, take modern painting for instance.

為了闡明，我們來看事例。
To illustrate ~, let us consider the case of ~.

為了闡明我的論點，我們來看梅的事例。
▸ To illustrate my point, let us consider the case of May.

為了使你更清楚，我們來看。
To make it clearer to you, let us have a look at ~.

為了使你更清楚，我們來看看這瓶底。
▸ To make it clearer to you, let us have a look at the bottom of the bottle.

● 真心祝福你 ●

🌱 基本說法

祝萬事如意！
All the best!

祝一切順利。
All the best in ~.
祝你在新的工作崗位上一切順利。
▶ All the best in your new job.

祝一切都好。
All the best with ~.
祝你家人一切都好。
▶ All the best with your family.

祝你萬事如意！
All the very best!

祝成功。
Every success in ~.
祝你事業成功。
▶ Every success in your business.

祝成功。
Every success with ~.
祝你成功。
▶ Every success with you.

希望你事事順心。
I hope everything goes well.

希望你事事順心。
I hope everything goes well with ~.
希望你婚後生活事事順心。
▶ I hope everything goes well with your married life.

希望你能享受遊覽的樂趣！
I hope you enjoy your visit to ~!
希望你能享受遊覽尼加拉瀑布的樂趣！
▶ I hope you enjoy your visit to Niagara Falls!

希望你玩得愉快。
I hope you have a good time.

希望你度過一個愉快的假日。
I hope you have a good holiday.

希望你不久就能恢復過來。
I hope you'll get over it soon.

希望你早日康復。
I hope you'll get well soon.

希望你旅途愉快。
I hope you'll have a nice trip.

希望你的身體趕快好起來。
I hope you'll soon feel better.

祝你成功。
May you succeed.

請致意。
Please give ～ my best wishes.

請向艾略特先生和夫人致意。
▸ Please give Mr. and Mrs. Eliot my best wishes.

請代我問好。
Please remember me to ～.

請代我向你家人問好。
▸ Please remember me to your family.

祝你好運。
The best of luck.

祝順利。
The very best of luck in ～.
祝好運。
The very best of luck with ～.

祝你事業順利。
▸ The very best of luck in your business.
祝你好運。
▸ The very best of luck with you.

❀ 日常口語

祝福你！
Bless you!
＊當對方打噴嚏時就可以說這句。

飛行愉快！
Enjoy your flight!

祝你過得愉快！
Enjoy yourself!

代我問好。
Give my love to ～.

代我向你的孩子們問好。
▶ Give my love to your kids.

祝你順利。
Good luck in ～.
祝好運。
Good luck with ～.

祝你考試順利。
▶ Good luck in the examination.
祝你好運。
▶ Good luck with you.

旅途愉快。
Happy journey.

祝你安全降落。
Happy landing.

祝你過得愉快。
Have a good time.

玩得開心點。
Have fun.

希望你事事順心如意。
Hope things go all right with you.

向⋯問候。
Regards to ～.

向你家人問候。
▶ Regards to your family.

♣ 正式場合

祝你旅途愉快。
I wish you a pleasant journey.

祝你幸福。
I wish you all the happiness in the world.

祝你成功。
I wish you success in ～.
祝你順利成功。
I wish you success with ～.

祝你考試成功。
▸ I wish you success in the examination.
祝你工作順利成功。
▸ I wish you success with your work.

我謹祝你成功。
I'd like to wish you every success in ～.

我謹祝你事業成功。
▸ I'd like to wish you every success in your career.

我謹祝你獲得成功。
May I wish you every success with ～.

我謹祝你新的事業獲得成功。
▸ May I wish you every success with your new venture.

請轉達我最誠摯的祝福。
Please convey my best wishes to ～.

請向奧斯卡教授轉達我最誠摯的祝福。
▸ Please convey my best wishes to Professor Oscar.

請代我致意。
Please give ～ my best regards.

請代我向強森先生致意。
▸ Please give Mr. Johnson my best regards.

請代我致意。
Please give my regards to ～.

請代我向達納先生致意。
▸ Please give my regards to Mr. Dana

請代我致意好嗎？
Would you give ～ my best wishes?

請代我向易普博士致意好嗎？
▸ Would you give Dr. Yip my best wishes?

● 謝謝你的祝福 ●

♥ 基本說法

多謝。
Many thanks.

謝謝你。
Thank you.

非常感謝。
Thank you very much.

✽ 日常口語

多謝啦。
Very many thanks.

謝啦。
Cheers.

謝啦。
Thanks, ~.

謝啦，珍。
▸ Thanks, Jane.

你也是。
You too.

● 在特別的日子裡祝福你 ●

祝你新年快樂。
A happy New Year to you.

祝你聖誕快樂。
A merry Christmas to you.

聖誕快樂，新年快樂！
A merry Christmas and a happy New Year!

祝聖誕快樂，有個快樂的…！　　　祝聖誕快樂，有個快樂的2010年！
A merry Christmas and a 　▸ **A merry Christmas and a happy**
happy ～! 　　　　　　　　　**2010!**

代我表示誠摯祝福。　　　　　　代我向傑克表示新年的誠摯祝福。
Give sb. my best wishes for ～. ▸ **Give Jack my best wishes for the New**
　　　　　　　　　　　　　　　Year.

聖誕快樂！
Have a good Christmas!

結婚週年快樂！
Have a happy anniversary!

生日快樂！
Have a happy birthday!

復活節快樂！
Have a happy Easter!

✿ 日常口語　🔊 139

結婚週年快樂！
Happy anniversary!

生日快樂！
Happy birthday!

聖誕快樂！
Happy Christmas!

復活節快樂！
Happy Easter!

新年快樂！
Happy New Year!
祝新年快樂。　　　　　　　　祝珊蒂新年快樂。
Happy New Year to ～.　▸ Happy New Year to Sandy.

生日快樂！
Many happy returns of the day!

♣ 正式場合

🔊 140

我謹祝你生日快樂。
I'd like to wish you a happy birthday.

我謹祝你生日快樂。
I'd like to wish you many happy returns of the day.

請允我祝你新年快樂。
May I wish you a happy New Year.

請允我祝你生日快樂。
May I wish you many happy returns of the day.

請送上我的聖誕祝福。
Please send my Christmas greetings to ~.

請向史密斯太太送上我的聖誕祝福。
▸ Please send my Christmas greetings to Mrs. Smith.

● 謝謝你特別的祝福 ●

基本說法

謝謝你。祝你復活節快樂！
Thank you. And a happy Easter to you!

謝謝你。也祝你新年快樂！
Thank you. And a happy New Year to you too!

謝謝你。祝你聖誕快樂！
Thank you. And a merry Christmas to you!

謝謝你。我也同樣祝福你！
Thank you. And I wish you the same!

謝謝你。你也一樣！
Thank you. And the same to you!

謝謝你。你也一樣！
Thank you. You too!

日常口語

謝謝。你也一樣！
Thanks. And you too!

謝謝，你也一樣！
Thanks, and that goes double!

謝謝。你也一樣！
Thanks. The same go you!

非常謝謝。你也一樣！
Thanks very much. Same to you!

● 敬你一杯 ●

🌱 基本說法

143

為你的家人乾杯。
And to yours.

祝你好運。
Here's good luck.

祝你們兩人永遠幸福。
Here's to long and productive cheers for you both.

敬你一杯。
Here's to you.

祝你健康。
Here's to your health.

我為⋯乾杯。
I drink to ～.

我為未來乾杯，願它為大家帶來幸福。
▶ I drink to the future; may it bring us all happiness.

我為⋯舉杯。
I raise my glass to ～.

我為這對佳偶舉杯，願他們白頭偕老。
▶ I raise my glass to the happy pair, wishing them a long life together.

我要為此乾杯。
I'll drink to that.

為⋯乾杯。
Let's drink to ～.

為我們永遠的友誼乾杯。
▶ Let's drink to our everlasting friendship.

我們來為…乾杯好嗎？

Shall we propose a toast to ～? ▶ 我們來為老闆的健康乾杯好嗎？

Shall we propose a toast to the health of our boss?

祝你健康！

To your health!

祝你健康。

Your very good health, ～. ▶ 祝妳健康，莫妮卡太太。

Your very good health, Mrs. Monica.

❀ 日常口語

144

乾杯！
Bottoms up!

乾杯！
Cheerio!

乾杯！
Cheers!

乾杯，伙伴。
Cheers, old son.

乾了！
Drink up!

乾杯！
Here's how!

乾杯！
Here's mud in your eye!

乾了！　　　　　　　　　　　　吉米，乾了！
~, the toast! ▸ Jimmy, the toast!

乾杯！
Toast!

♣ 正式場合

145

現在，我想為…乾杯。	現在，我想為我們的好朋友湯姆乾杯。
At this point, I should like to propose a toast to ～.	▶ At this point, I should like to propose a toast to our very good friend, Tom.

我請你們諒解，並請舉杯為…祝福。	我請你們諒解，並請舉杯為他的健康祝福。
I ask you to be understanding, and to raise your glasses to ～.	▶ I ask you to be understanding, and to raise your glasses to his health.

我請你和我一起乾杯。	我請你和我一起為我們的友誼乾杯。
I ask you to join me in a toast to ～.	▶ I ask you to join me in a toast to the friendship between us.

我想請你們舉杯並和我一起乾杯。	我想請你們舉杯，並和我一起為在座所有朋友的健康乾杯。
I'd ask you to raise your glasses and join me in a toast to ～.	▶ I'd ask you to raise your glasses and join me in a toast to the health of all our friends here.

請容我為…乾杯。	請容我為你的成功乾杯。
Let me propose a toast to ～.	▶ Let me propose a toast to your success.

請容我代表某人祝你…。	請容我代表我們的總裁喬丹先生，祝你旅途愉快。
Let me, on behalf of sb., wish you ～.	▶ Let me, on behalf of our president Mr. Jordan, wish you a happy journey.

我很榮幸請你乾杯。	我很榮幸請你為我們的長期合作乾杯。
With great pleasure I ask you to toast ～.	▶ With great pleasure I ask you to toast the long-term cooperation between us.

239

 **Gossip**

說閒話

● 說長道短聊八卦 ●

基本說法

顯然。
Apparently ～.

顯然他失業了。
▸ Apparently he's lost his job.

你聽說過他的近況嗎？
Did you hear the latest about ～?

你聽說過維克的近況嗎？
▸ Did you hear the latest about Vic?

你聽說他的事了嗎？
Did you hear what happened to ～?

你聽說傑克的事了嗎？
▸ Did you hear what happened to Jack?

你知道我剛聽說的事嗎？
Do you know what I've just heard?

你想聽有趣的事情嗎？
Do you want to hear something interesting?

你怎麼知道的？
How do you know that?

我可以告訴你，不過你必須保密。
I can tell you that, but you must keep it to yourself.

我不想在背後議論別人，不過…。
I don't want to talk behind somebody's back, but ～.

我不想在背後議論別人，不過他已變了許多。
▸ I don't want to talk behind somebody's back, but he's changed a lot.

240

我要告訴你一件事，不過別讓人知道是我告訴你的。
I'll tell you something, but don't let on to anybody that I told you.

我告訴你實情，但是不要告訴別人。
I'll tell you what, but don't pass it on to anybody else.

我不是在人身攻擊，不過據說 … 。

I'm not talking personalities, but they say ~.

我不是在人身攻擊，不過據說他這個人不太正經。

▶ I'm not talking personalities, but they say he's not very decent.

我有件事要告訴你，不過你必須保密。
I have something to tell you, but you must keep it from others.

讓我告訴你實情，不過這只能我們兩個人知道。
Let me tell you what, but it's only between ourselves.

當然我不想說閒話，不過你知道嗎？

Now of course I don't want to gossip, but do you know ~?

當然我不想說閒話，不過你知道誰偷了那條金項鍊嗎？

▶ Now of course I don't want to gossip, but do you know who stole the gold necklace?

當然我不想說任何人壞話，不過…

Now of course I don't want to say anything bad about anyone, but ~

當然我不想說任何人壞話，不過你注意到他那奇怪的舉止了嗎？

▶ Now of course I don't want to say anything bad about anyone, but have you noticed his strange manner?

當然這可能不是真的，但…。
Of course it may not be true, but ~.

▶ 當然這可能不是真的，但他確實喝很多。
Of course it may not be true, but he really drinks a lot.

當然這只是蜚短流長。
Of course it's only gossip about ~.

▶ 當然這只是老闆和他老婆的蜚短流長。
Of course it's only gossip about my boss and his wife.

噢，你知道嗎？
Well, do you know (that) ~?

▶ 噢，你知道他是三年前出獄的嗎？
Well, do you know (that) he came off prison three years ago?

噢，你不想知道嗎？
Well, wouldn't you know that?

你是從哪裡聽來的？
Where did you hear that?

❀ 日常口語

好吧，我告訴你這個秘密，不過你一個字也不能對別人說。
All right, I'll tell you the secret, but not a word to anyone.

你知道嗎？
And you know something?

你沒聽說嗎？
Didn't you hear? ~.

你沒聽說嗎？她搬到巴黎去了。
▸ Didn't you hear? She's moved to Paris.

當然你一個字也別透露。
Don't breathe a word of course, but ~.

當然你一個字也別透露，他已經開始酗酒了。
▸ Don't breathe a word of course, but he's taken to heavy drinking.

你猜怎麼了？
Guess what? ~.

你猜怎麼了？約翰結婚了。
▸ Guess what? John's got married.

要是你知道他們的事就好了。
If only you know about them.

這是最高機密，所以你自己知道就行了。
It's a top secret, so keep it under your hat.

這只是聽說，但顯然…。
It's just hearsay, but apparently ~.

只是聽說，但顯然他已離開那女孩了。
▸ It's just hearsay, but apparently he's left the girl.

我最後聽到的消息是…。
The last I heard, ~.

我最後聽到的消息是他已離職了。
▸ The last I heard, he'd quit the job.

243

他們的確說…。
They do say ~.

> 他們的確說他根本不是個正人君子。
> They do say he's not a gentleman at all.

唔，那是他們說的，不過…。
Well, that's what they say, but ~.

> 唔，那是他們說的，不過無風不起浪。
> Well, that's what they say, but there's no smoke without fire.

你知道嗎？
You know something? ~.

> 你知道嗎？湯姆已從國外回來了。
> You know something? Tom has come back from abroad.

你不能把這件事說出去。

You mustn't pass it on, but ~.

> 你不能把這件事說出去，那棟房子裡發生了許多事情。
> You mustn't pass it on, but there's a lot going on in that house.

你絕對不會相信剛才發生的事。
You'll never believe what just happened.

感 謝

● 真的謝謝你 ●

ㄚ 基本說法

非常感謝你。
It was ever so nice of you.

非常感謝你。
It was ever so nice of you to ～. ▸ 非常感謝你支持我們。
It was ever so nice of you to give us support.

真是太謝謝你了。
It's so sweet of you.

真是太謝謝你了。
It's so sweet of you to ～. ▸ 你幫我抬箱子，真是太謝謝你了。
It's so sweet of you to help me lift the box.

多謝。
Many thanks.

多謝。
Many thanks for ～. ▸ 多謝你大駕光臨。
Many thanks for your coming here.

非常感謝。
Much appreciated.

非常感謝。
Much obliged.

謝謝你。
Thank you.

謝謝你。
Thank you for ～, ▸ 謝謝你的光臨。
Thank you for coming.

非常感謝你。
Thank you very much.
非常感謝你。   非常感謝你給我這本書。
Thank you very much for ～. ▸ Thank you very much for the book.

真是非常感謝你。
Thank you very much indeed.
真是非常感謝你。   你幫助我，真是非常感謝。
Thank you very much indeed ▸ Thank you very much indeed for
for ～.   your help.

你真是太好了。
You're just wonderful.

✾ 日常口語

謝謝。
Cheers.

好極了。
Great.

非常感謝你。
Thank you so much.

非常感謝。　　　　　　　　非常感謝你的光臨。
Thank you so much for ～.　▸ Thank you so much for coming.

謝謝。
Thanks.

多謝你。
Thanks a lot.

多謝你。　　　　　　　　　多謝你告訴我。
Thanks a lot for ～.　▸ Thanks a lot for what you've told me.

超感謝你。
Thanks a million.

超感謝你。　　　　　　　　超感謝你給我這封信。
Thanks a million for ～.　▸ Thanks a million for the letter.

非常感謝。
Thanks very much.

非常感謝。　　　　　　　　非常感謝你的邀請。
Thanks very much for ～.　▸ Thanks very much for your invitation.

♣ 正式場合

我無以銘謝。
I can never thank you enough.
對此我無以銘謝。
I can never thank you enough for ～.

對你的慷慨大度我無以銘謝。
▸ I can never thank you enough for your generosity.

我真的很感謝。
I do appreciate ～.

我真的很感謝你的及時幫助。
▸ I do appreciate your timely help.

我真是感激不盡。
I really can't thank you enough.
對此我真是感激不盡。
I really can't thank you enough for ～.

對你的邀請我真是感激不盡。
▸ I really can't thank you enough for the invitation.

我真不知怎樣謝你才好。
I really don't know how I can thank you enough.

我謹表示我的謝意。
I should like to express my appreciation.

我謹表示我的感謝。
I should like to express my gratitude for ～.

對你的好意我謹表示我的感謝。
▸ I should like to express my gratitude for your kindness.

我謹表示我深切的謝意。
I should like to say how grateful I am.
我謹表示我深切的謝意。
I should like to say how grateful I am for ～.

我謹對他提供的消息表示深切的謝意。
▸ I should like to say how grateful I am for his information.

我非常感謝你。
I'm much obliged to you.

我真的非常感謝你。
I'm really very grateful to you for ~.

我真的非常感謝你的勸告。
▸ **I'm really very grateful to you for** your advice.

真是太感謝你了。
It's very good of you ~.

你給我這本書真是太感謝了。
▸ **It's very good of you** to give me the book.

你想得真周到。
It's most thoughtful of you.

非常感謝你。
It's very kind of you.

非常感謝你。
Thank you so much for ~.

非常感謝你的盛情款待。
▸ **Thank you so much for** your hospitality.

真是太感謝你了。
That was extremely good of you.

你真能體諒人。
You are most understanding.

你幫了我一個大忙。
You are very helpful.

你真好。
You are very kind.

你想得真周到。
You are very thoughtful.

● 請不用客氣 ●

願為你效勞。
At your service.

我很高興你喜歡。
I'm very glad you enjoyed it.

我很樂意。
It's a pleasure.

我很樂意。
My pleasure.

不麻煩。
No bother at all.

沒什麼。
No trouble at all.

別客氣。
Not at all.

請不用客氣。
Please don't mention it.

我很樂意。
Pleasure was all mine.

不客氣。
You are welcome.

❁ 日常口語

隨時為你效勞。
Any time.
＊非常口語的用法。

應該的。
Sure.

這沒什麼。
That's all right.

這沒什麼。
That's OK.

沒什麼。
Think nothing of it.

是啊，這沒什麼。
Yeah, it's all right.

應該的。
You bet.

♣ 正式場合

153

很高興能幫助你。
Delighted I was able to help.

很高興能對你有所幫助。
Delighted to have been of some help.

我很高興為你效勞。
I was glad to be of some service.

我很高興能為你效勞。
I'm glad to have been of some service.

這實在微不足道，我只是盡力而為。
It was the least I could do.
＊當對方遇到很大麻煩，或以前曾幫你很大的忙時。

很高興能對你有所幫助。
It's a pleasure to have been of some assistance.

我敢肯定，如果你處在我的立場，一定也會這麼做的。
You would have done the same in my position, I'm sure.

252

打招呼

● 跟別人打招呼 ●

❧ 基本說法 🔊 154

很高興在這裡見到你。
Glad to meet you here.

很高興又見到你。
Good to see you again.

好久不見了。
Haven't seen you for some time.

真高興又見到了你。
How nice to see you again.

見到你真高興。
How very nice to meet you.

你能來我很高興。
I'm so glad you could come.

很高興又見到你。
Pleased to meet you again.

真沒想到會遇見你！
This is a pleasant surprise!

真沒想到會遇見你！真是意外！
What a pleasant surprise!

沒想到你會來，真是太好了！
What an unexpected pleasure!

❋ 日常口語

啊。我正想找你。
Ah, ～. Just the person I wanted to see. ▸

啊，杰。我正想找你。
Ah, Jay. Just the person I wanted to see.

和你巧遇真幸運。
Bumping into you like that was a bit of luck.

真想不到會在這裡遇見你。
Fancy seeing you here.

哎呀，你們能來真是太好了。
Gee, it's nice to have you here in ～.

哎呀，你們能來波士頓真是太好了。
▸ Gee, it's nice to have you here in Boston.

你好，夥計。
Good day, mate.
＊澳洲流行用語。

好久不見了。
Haven't run into you for ages.

好久不見了。
Haven't seen you for ages.

你好，老朋友！
Hello, old chap!

你好，真巧啊！
Hello there, what a coincidence!

你好，老兄！真高興在這裡見到你。
Hi, buddy! Good to see you here.

254

你好。
Hi there, ～.

你好，保羅。
▸ Hi there, Paul.

你好，我親愛的朋友！
Howdy, my dear friends!
＊Howdy是How do you do？的簡略說法，也是美國蠻流行的招呼語。

世界真小，又見面了。
Small world, isn't it?

好久不見了。
It's been a long time.

我正要找你。
Just the man I was looking for.

好久不見了！
Long time no see!

還是這麼忙啊。
Still as busy as ever I see.

我正要找你。
The very person I was after.

嗨，看誰來了！
Well, look who's here!

今天什麼風把你吹來啦？
What brings you here today?

喂！
What ho!

♣ 正式場合

你好！
Good afternoon!
＊下午見面時用。

你好！
Good evening!
＊晚上見面時用。

你好！
Good morning!
＊早上見面時用。

你好嗎？
How are you?

很高興有機會在這裡與你見面。
I'm glad to have had the opportunity to meet you here.

夫人。
Madam.

先生。
Sir.

● 親切問候對方 ●

❤ 基本說法　　　🔊 157

你好點了嗎？
Are you better?

你現在覺得好點了嗎？
Are you feeling better now?

你好嗎？
Are you well?

你過得怎麼樣？
How are things going with you?

你身體怎麼樣？
How are you?

你過得怎麼樣？
How are you doing?

你過得怎麼樣？
How are you keeping?

家裡一切都好嗎？
How is everything at home?

你過得怎麼樣？　　　　　　　你週末過得怎麼樣？
How was your ～? 　　　▸ How was your weekend?

最近在忙什麼？
What are you doing these days?

❀ 日常口語

近來怎樣？
Anything new?

你好嗎？
How are things with you?

你過得怎麼樣？
How are you making out?

近來如何？
How goes it?

你近來如何？
How goes it with you?

你近來怎麼樣？
How goes the world with you?

日子過得怎樣？
How's it going?

一切都好嗎？
How's everything?

家裡一切都好嗎？
How's everything at home?

生活過得好嗎？
How's life?

你過得怎麼樣？
How's life treating you?

你過得怎麼樣？
How's life with you?

狀況不錯吧，嗯？
In good shape, are you?

你近來在忙些什麼？
What are you up to these days?

近來怎樣？
What gives?

近來怎樣？
What's cooking?

近來怎麼樣？
What's happening?

近況怎樣？
What's new?

你近況怎樣？
What's new with you?

近來好嗎？
What's the good news?

近來好嗎？
What's the good word?

近況怎麼樣？
What's the latest?

近況怎麼樣？
What's the news?

你好嗎？
What's with you?

♣ 正式場合

我想你一切都好吧？
I hope all goes well with you?

我想你過得不錯吧！
I trust you're keeping well!

● 最近過得不錯（不太好）●

很好，謝謝你。
All right, thank you.

很好，謝謝你。
I'm fine, thank you.

好多了，謝謝你。
Much better, thank you.

不太好，真的。
Not very good really.

很好，謝謝你。
Pretty good, thank you.

很好，謝謝你。
Quite well, thank you.

很好，謝謝你。
Very well, thank you.

嗯，不怎麼好。不過比以前好點了。
Well, not too good yet. Better than I was though.

好極了。好得不能再好了。
Wonderful. Things couldn't be better.

✿ 日常口語

馬馬虎虎。
Bearing up, bearing up.

還過得去。
Can't complain.

沒有那麼好，不過還不壞。
Could be better, but not bad.

還算好，謝謝。
Fair to middling, thanks.

很好，謝謝。
Fine, just fine.

過得很好。
Getting along splendidly.

很好。你呢？
Great. You?

我快樂得不得了。
I'm full of the joys of spring.

我過得很棒。
I'm just great.

我過得幸福美滿，謝謝。
I'm on top of the world, thanks.

過得去吧。
Mustn't grumble.

沒什麼可抱怨的。
No complaints.

不，不怎麼好。
No, nothing much.

不怎麼樣。
Not too much.

哦，老樣子。
Oh, the usual rounds.

還不錯，謝謝。
OK, thanks.

相當不錯，謝謝。
Pretty fair, thanks.

很好。
Really fine.

和以前一樣。
Same as ever.

馬馬虎虎，謝謝。
Soso, thanks.

還活著，一點也不好。
Still alive-just not at all well.

勉勉強強，謝謝。
Surviving, thanks.

♣ 正式場合

我過得極好，謝謝你。
I'm extremely well, thank you.

我很健康，謝謝你。
I'm in excellent health, thank you.

我確實過得很好，謝謝你。
I'm very well indeed, thank you.

21 Information 消息

● 打聽消息 ●

你能告訴我相關情況嗎？
Can you tell me something about ～?

你能告訴我這方面的情況嗎？
▶ Can you tell me something about it?

請你告訴我好嗎？
Can you tell me ～, please?

請你告訴我這條河的名字好嗎？
▶ Can you tell me the name of the river, please?

誰能告訴我？
Could anyone tell me?
有人能告訴我嗎？
Could anyone tell me ～?

有人能告訴我剛才誰在這裡嗎？
▶ Could anyone tell me who was here a moment ago?

你能再多告訴我一些嗎？
Could you tell me some more about ～?

你能再多告訴我一些情況嗎？
▶ Could you tell me some more about it?

你能不能告訴我？
Could you tell me ～?

你能不能告訴我你住哪裡？
▶ Could you tell me where you live?

你知道嗎？
Do you know ～?

你知道他們住在哪裡嗎？
▶ Do you know where they live?

對不起，你知道嗎？
Excuse me, do you happen to know ～?

對不起，你知道他們怎麼開始爭吵的嗎？
▶ Excuse me, do you happen to know how they started quarreling?

我想知道更多。 **I'd like to know more about ~.**	我想知道新產品的更多情形。 ▸ I'd like to know more about the new product.
我想知道。 **I'd like to know ~.**	我想知道飛機何時起飛。 ▸ I'd like to know when the plane takes off.
另外我還想知道的是…。 **Something else I'd like to know is ~.**	另外我還想知道的是誰家被偷了。 ▸ Something else I'd like to know is whose house was broken into.
對不起老纏著你，但是你能告訴我嗎？ **Sorry to keep after you, but could you tell me ~?**	對不起老纏著你，但是你能告訴我誰應對此負責嗎？ ▸ Sorry to keep after you, but could you tell me who's responsible for it?
對不起打擾你了。 **Sorry to trouble you, but will ~?**	對不起打擾你了，明天他會來這裡嗎？ ▸ Sorry to trouble you, but will he come here tomorrow?
你能告訴我嗎？ **Would you mind telling me ~?**	你能告訴我那輛車怎麼撞上燈柱的嗎？ ▸ Would you mind telling me how the car struck the lamp post?

🌸 日常口語

你知道嗎？
Any clue?

你知道嗎？
Any clue ～?

你知道發生什麼事了嗎？
▸ **Any clue** what's happened?

你知道嗎？
Got any idea?

你知道嗎？
Got any idea ～?

你知道公車誤點的原因嗎？
▸ **Got any idea** why the bus is late?

你知道嗎？
Happen to know ～?

你知道他的名字嗎？
▸ **Happen to know** his name?

你知道嗎？
～, do you know?

你知道他要出國嗎？
▸ Is he going abroad, do you know?

出什麼事了？
What is to pay?

發生什麼事了？
What went on?

出什麼事了？
What's up?

♣ 正式場合

請問？
Could I ask ～?
能否向你請教？
Could I ask you about ～?

請問誰負責這件事？
▶ Could I ask who is in charge of the matter?
能否向你請教這次事故的情況？
▶ Could I ask you about the accident?

如果你不介意我詢問的話。

～, if you don't mind my asking?

如果你不介意我詢問的話，你是在銀行上班嗎？
▶ Do you work in a bank, if you don't mind my asking?

我希望你不介意我問這個問題，我想知道…。
I hope you don't mind my asking, but I'd like to know ～.

我希望你不介意我問這個問題，我想知道下星期你要去哪裡。
▶ I hope you don't mind my asking, but I'd like to know where you're going next week.

我想知道。
I should be interested to know ～. ▶

我想知道事實真相。
I should be interested to know the fact.

不知能否請教你。
I wonder if I could ask ～.

不知能否請教你為什麼這麼做。
▶ I wonder if I could ask why you did it.

不知你能否告訴我。
I wonder if you could tell me ～. ▶

不知你能否告訴我往紐約的火車何時開。
I wonder if you could tell me when the train for New York leaves.

不知你可否告訴我。
I wonder whether you'd mind telling me ～.

不知你可否告訴我你是做什麼工作的。
▶ I wonder whether you'd mind telling me what line of work you are in.

我不知道你能否幫個忙，我想知道…。
I was wondering whether you could help me. I'd like to know ～.

我不知道你能否幫個忙，我想知道你是靠什麼謀生的。
▶ I was wondering whether you could help me. I'd like to know what you do for a living.

● 你知道這件事嗎？ ●

有人告訴你嗎？
Did someone tell you?

有人告訴你嗎？
Did someone tell you about ～? ▶ Did someone tell you about the robbery yesterday?

有人告訴你昨天的搶劫案了嗎？

有人告訴你這消息了嗎？
Did someone tell you the news?

你聽說…的事了嗎？　　　　　你聽說肯的事了嗎？
Did you hear what happened ▶ Did you hear what happened to
to ～? Ken?

你知道嗎？　　　　　　　　你知道最近在伊朗發生的劫機事件嗎？
Did you know about ～? ▶ Did you know about the recent hijacking in Iran?

你知道嗎？　　　　　　　　你知道我們該怎麼做才能成為記者嗎？
Did you know ～? ▶ Did you know what we should do to become a reporter?

你不知道嗎？　　　　　　　你不知道我明年要去紐約嗎？
Didn't you know ～? ▶ Didn't you know I'm going to New York next year?

你知道嗎？　　　　　　　　你知道今晚的電視節目嗎？
Do you happen to know ▶ Do you happen to know anything
anything about ～? about the TV program for tonight?

你知道嗎？　　　　　　　　你知道這個百萬富翁的事嗎？
Do you know about ～? ▶ Do you know about the millionaire?

269

你知道嗎？
Do you know anything about ~?
你知道埃及的歷史嗎？
▶ Do you know anything about the history of Egypt?

你知道嗎？
Do you know ~?
你知道這房子是誰的嗎？
▶ Do you know who owns the house?

你知道嗎？
Do you realize (that) ~?
你知道她遇到麻煩了嗎？
▶ Do you realize (that) she was in trouble?

有人告訴你了嗎？
Has somebody told you?
有人告訴你了嗎？
Has somebody told you about ~?
有人告訴你他們離婚了嗎？
▶ Has somebody told you about their divorce?
有人告訴過你嗎？
Has somebody told you (that) ~ ?
有人告訴你那列火車因濃霧延誤了嗎？
▶ Has somebody told you (that) the train's delayed by the heavy fog?

你聽過嗎？
Have you heard about ~?
你聽過亞當和夏娃的故事嗎？
▶ Have you heard about the story of Adam and Eve?

你聽說了嗎？
Have you heard (that) ~?
你聽說他們被解僱了嗎？
▶ Have you heard (that) they've been dismissed?

你知道的，不是嗎？
You know ~, don't you?
你知道這事的，不是嗎？
▶ You know that, don't you?
你知道的，不是嗎？
You know about ~, don't you?
你知道我們的目標，不是嗎？
▶ You know about our goals, don't you?

🌸 日常口語

你知道嗎？
Have you got any idea ～?

你知道這塔有多高嗎？
▸ Have you got any idea how high the tower is?

你知道嗎？
Have you got any idea about ～?

你知道雲端運算嗎？
▸ Have you got any idea about cloud computing?

聽說了嗎？
Heard about ～?

聽說這電影了嗎？
▸ Heard about the film?

知道嗎？
Know anything about ～?

知道「存在主義」嗎？
▸ Know anything about the Existentialism?

知道嗎？
Know ～?

知道這男人對他妻子發飆嗎？
▸ Know the man's mad at his wife?

♣ 正式場合

你知道嗎？
Are you aware of ～?

你知道你的兒子正誤入歧途嗎？
▶ Are you aware of your son's falling into evil ways?

你知道嗎？
Are you aware (that) ～?

你知道你踩到我的腳了嗎？
▶ Are you aware (that) you're stepping on my foot?

你知道嗎？
Are you conscious of ～?

你知道該做什麼嗎？
▶ Are you conscious of what you must do?

你知道嗎？
Are you conscious (that) ～?

你知道他不贊成此事嗎？
▶ Are you conscious (that) he is not in favor of that?

你可以告訴我相關訊息嗎？
Could you give me any information about ～?

你可以告訴我這項新發明的訊息嗎？
▶ Could you give me any information about the new invention, please?

你可以告訴我相關知識嗎？
Could you give me any information on ～?

你可以告訴我操縱這台機器的知識嗎？
▶ Could you give me any information on how to operate the machine?

不知你是否瞭解？
I wonder if you realize (that) ～?

不知你是否瞭解這公司需要幫助？
▶ I wonder if you realize (that) the company needs help?

不知你能否告訴我那些事。
I wonder whether you could let me know something about ～.

不知你能否告訴我諾貝爾獎的二三事。
▶ I wonder whether you could let me know something about Nobel Prize.

● 我知道這件事 ●

基本說法

169

我想。
I gather ～.

我想沒有人進過那座城堡。
▶ I gather nobody has entered that castle.

我聽說。
I hear ～.

我聽說亨利先生打算辭職。
▶ I hear Mr. Henry is going to resign.

我已聽說。
I've been told about ～.
我已聽說。
I've been told (that) ～.

我已聽說了那次劫機事件。
▶ I've been told about the hijacking.
我已聽說這種汽車以其性能著稱。
▶ I've been told (that) this car is
famous for its performance.

已經有人告訴我了。
Somebody has told me about ～.

已經有人告訴我這件事了。
▶ Somebody has told me about that.

有人告訴我。
Somebody told me (that) ～.

有人告訴我里昂先生很會開玩笑。
▶ Somebody told me (that) Mr. Leon
is very good at making jokes.

是的，我的確知道。
Yes, I do know ～.
是的，我的確知道。
Yes, I do know about ～.

是的，我的確知道他要跟誰結婚。
▶ Yes, I do know whom he's going to marry.
是的，我的確知道這次事故。
▶ Yes, I do know about the accident.

是的，我已聽說了。
Yes, I've heard about ～.
是的，我已聽說了。
Yes, I've heard (that) ～.

是的，我已聽說這消息了。
▶ Yes, I've heard about the news.
是的，我已聽說他要來了。
▶ Yes, I've heard (that) he's coming.

🌸 日常口語

你猜怎麼了。
Guess what: ~.

你猜怎麼了，他們昨天在街上打起來。
▸ **Guess what: they fell into fight in the street yesterday.**

你知道。
~, you know?

你知道，大部分夫妻吵架是為了錢。
▸ **Most married people fall out over money, you know?**

是這麼說的。
So ~ said.

傑弗瑞是這麼說的。
▸ **So Jeffrey said.**

是這麼說的。
So ~ were saying.

他們是這麼說的。
▸ **So they were saying.**

我是這麼聽說的。
That's what I heard.

他們說。
They say ~.

他們說三隻小鳥從鳥巢裡掉出來了。
▸ **They say three baby birds fell out of the nest.**

我知道，這還用你告訴我。
You're telling me.

♣ 正式場合 🔊 171

就我所知。
For all I know, ~.
　　就我所知，他可能已經去法國了。
▶ For all I know, he may have left for France.

我完全清楚。
I am fully aware of ~.
　　我完全清楚這事。
▶ I am fully aware of that.

我很清楚。
I am quite aware (that) ~.
　　我很清楚有一百名旅客在事故中喪生。
▶ I am quite aware (that) a hundred passengers were killed in the accident.

我很清楚。
I'm quite conscious of ~.
我很清楚。
I'm quite conscious (that) ~.
　　我很清楚他的誠實。
▶ I'm quite conscious of his honesty.
　　我很清楚我們正面臨強烈的反對。
▶ I'm quite conscious (that) we are facing a strong opposition.

我有充分的根據知道。
I have it on good authority (that) ~.
　　我有充分的根據知道他在這筆交易中賺了一萬美元。
▶ I have it on good authority (that) he's made ten thousand dollars on the deal.

我聽說。
I'm told ~.
　　我聽說這種小巴士能靠很少的汽油走很長的路。
▶ I'm told this minibus can go far on very little petrol.

看來。
It appears (that) ~.
　　看來他不喜歡固定的工作時間。
▶ It appears (that) he doesn't like fixed working hours.

看來。
It would appear (that) ~.
　　看來他的意圖是幫助窮人。
▶ It would appear (that) his intention was to help the poor.

275

我所得到的消息是…。 | 我所得到的訊息是他們打算離婚。

My information is ～.

▸ My information is they're going to divorce.

我也是這麼想。但還是謝謝你把這件事告訴我。

So I gather. But thank you for telling me this.

我所了解的也是如此。但還是謝謝你把這件事告訴我。

So I understand. But thank you for telling me this.

我也是這麼聽說。但還是謝謝你把這件事告訴我。

So I'm told. But thank you for telling me this.

是的，我的確了解。 | 是的，我的確了解到許多人在這次事故中喪生。

Yes, I did realize ～.

▸ Yes, I did realize many people were killed in the accident.

是的，我很感謝你的消息。

Yes, I do appreciate your information.

● 我不知道這件事 ●

那方面恐怕我無法幫助你。（那方面我不清楚）
I'm afraid I can't help you there.

我恐怕無法告訴你。
I'm afraid I can't tell you.

我恐怕不清楚。
I'm afraid I couldn't say ～.

我恐怕不清楚他有律師資格。
▶ I'm afraid I couldn't say he's qualified as a lawyer.

我恐怕不知道。
I'm afraid I don't know.

我恐怕不知道。
I'm afraid I've no idea ～.

恐怕我不知道在這天氣出航是否安全。
▶ I'm afraid I've no idea if it is safe to sail in this weather.

我不知道這件事。
I'm quite in the dark about it.

很抱歉我一無所知。
I'm sorry I don't know anything about ～.

很抱歉這件事我一無所知。
▶ I'm sorry I don't know anything about that.

很抱歉，我一無所知。
I'm sorry I know nothing about ～.

很抱歉，他們爭吵的事我一無所知。
▶ I'm sorry I know nothing about their quarrel.

這事我現在才知道。
That's news to me.

❀ 日常口語

別問我；我不知道。
Don't ask me.

別問我。 | 別問我是誰把電燈關掉的。
Don't ask me ~. | ▶ **Don't ask me** who turned off the light.

不知道。
Don't know.

一點也不知道。
Haven't a clue.

我沒辦法告訴你。
I couldn't tell you.

我沒辦法告訴你。 | 我沒辦法告訴你這事是什麼引起的。
I couldn't tell you ~. | ▶ **I couldn't tell you** what caused that.

我一點也不知道。 | 我一點也不知道這件訴訟案的事。
I don't know the first thing about ~. | ▶ **I don't know the first thing about** the lawsuit.

我一點也不知道。 | 這個交通問題我一點也不知道。
I haven't got a clue about ~. | ▶ **I haven't got a clue about** the traffic problem.

我一點也不知道。 | 我一點也不知道要怎麼發動摩托車。
I haven't got a clue ~. | ▶ **I haven't got a clue** how to start a motorcycle.

我一點也不知道。 | 我一點也不知道她的罪行。
I haven't the faintest idea about ~. | ▶ **I haven't the faintest idea about** her crimes.

我一點也不知道。
I haven't the foggiest.

我壓根不知道。
I haven't the remotest idea ～. ▸ 我壓根不知道他是誰。
I haven't the remotest idea who he is.

我壓根什麼也不知道。
I haven't got the slightest idea.

我要知道就好了。
I wish I knew.

我要是全知道就好了。
I wish I knew all about ～. ▸ 這件事我要是全知道就好了。
I wish I knew all about this matter.

我根本不知道。
I'm blest if I know.

我真的不知道。
Search me.

對不起，我真的不知道。
Sorry, I really don't know.

對不起，不知道。
Sorry, no idea.
對不起，不知道。 對不起，不知道是誰唆使他騙人的。
Sorry, no idea ～. ▸ Sorry, no idea who put him up to cheating.

♣ 正式場合

我得承認，我知之甚少。
I have to admit I know very little about ～.

▸ 我得承認，她的婚姻生活我知之甚少。
I have to admit I know very little about her married life.

我得承認我知道得不多。
I have to say (that) ～ is not something I know very much about.

▸ 我得承認我對立體主義知道得不多。
I have to say (that) cubism is not something I know very much about.

恐怕我還沒有收到消息。
I'm afraid I haven't obtained that information.

對不起，我無法回答你的詢問。
I'm sorry. I'm not able to help you with your enquiry.

很遺憾，我並不瞭解。
I'm sorry to say I didn't realize ～.

▸ 很遺憾，我並不瞭解此事。
I'm sorry to say I didn't realize that.

很遺憾，我所知甚微。
I'm sorry to say I don't know much about ～.

▸ 很遺憾，我對那部電影所知甚微。
I'm sorry to say I don't know much about that movie.

遺憾的是，我不知道。
Unfortunately I wasn't aware of ～.

▸ 遺憾的是，我不知道此事。
Unfortunately I wasn't aware of that.

22 *Instruction* 指示

● 告訴對方要怎麼做 ●

175

這個完成之後你就…。
After you've done that, you~. ▶ 這個完成之後，你就換檔。
After you've done that, you shift gears.

首先你…。
First of all you ~. ▶ 首先你把想買的東西列個清單。
First of all you make a list of what you want to buy.

你先…，然後…。
First you ~, then you ~. ▶ 你先在孔裡投一枚硬幣，然後再撥號。
First you deposit a coin in a slot, then you dial the number.

你得先…。
First you have to ~. ▶ 你得先打一通電話。
First you have to make a phone call.

就像這樣：先…，然後…。
It's like this: first you ~, and then ~. ▶ 像這樣：先打蛋，然後慢慢拌入麵粉。
It's like this: first you beat the eggs, and then mix in the flour gradually.

讓我教你。先…，然後…。
Let me show you. First you ~, then ~. ▶ 讓我教你。你先洗頭髮，然後用溫熱的清水沖洗兩次。
Let me show you. First you wash your hair, then rinse it twice with clean warm water.

你得做的第一件事是…。
The first thing you have to do is ~. ▶ 你得做的第一件事是加滿油箱。
The first thing you have to do is top up the tank with oil.

接下來你要做的是…。
The next thing you do is ~.

▸ 接下來你要做的是捲起褲管讓傷口露出。
▸ The next thing you do is peel back your trouser leg to expose the wound.

你就這麼做。

This is how you do it: you ~.

你就這麼做：你撕下標籤，把它寄給製造商，這樣他們就會退回一部分錢。

▸ This is how you do it: you peel the label off and send it to the makers, then they will send some of your money back.

對，小心不要…。
Yes, and be careful not to ~.

對，小心不要碰到電線。
▸ Yes, and be careful not to touch the wire.

對了，然後別忘了。
Yes, and then don't forget to ~.

對了，然後別忘了放進一杯牛奶。
▸ Yes, and then don't forget to put in a glass of milk.

你這麼辦。
You do it like this: you ~.

你這麼辦：你左手持釣竿，用右手捲線。

▸ You do it like this: you hold the fishing rod with your left hand, reel in your line with your right hand.

❀ 日常口語

176

這很容易，你⋯。
It's quite easy. You ~.

這很容易。你開收音機，然後聽音樂。
▸ It's quite easy. You turn on the radio, and listen to music.

看，你只要⋯。
Look, all you do is ~.

看，你只要按那個按鈕就可以用了。
▸ Look, all you do is press that button and it's ready to use.

一定要記住。
Make sure you remember ~.

一定要記住先在孔裡投幾個硬幣。
▸ Make sure you remember to put some coins in the slot first.

看好。

Watch. You ~.

看好。你要往這個方向捲底片，不是從另一邊。
▸ Watch. You slide the film in this way round, not the other way round.

♣ 正式場合

第一步是…。
The first step is ~.

▶ 第一步是與我們的外國顧客聯絡。
The first step is to contact our foreign customers.

應採取下列步驟。

The following procedure should be adopted: ~.

▶ 應採取下列步驟：輕按兩邊，取下電池蓋，插入電池，然後蓋上蓋子。
The following procedure should be adopted: remove battery holder by pressing lightly on both sides, insert the battery and refit the holder.

這項工作應按下列步驟進行：……
The job should be done according to the following procedure: …

整個過程應按下列步驟進行：……
The process should be carried out according to the following procedure: …

這件事按下述方法進行：……
This is done as follows: …

您可按以下所述操作。

You can proceed as follows: ~.

▶ 您可按以下所述操作：按著按鈕④，同時按下按鈕③調整正確時間。
You can proceed as follows: keep button ④ pressed and adjust the correct time with button ③.

介 紹

● 介紹別人認識 ●

❦ 基本說法

🔊 178

順便問一下,你們彼此認識嗎?	順便問一下,你們彼此認識嗎?這位是約翰布朗,這位是蘇珊史密斯。
By the way, do you know each other?	▸ By the way, do you know each other? John Brown, Susan Smith.
我把你介紹給某人了嗎?	大衛,我把你介紹給寶琳斯特雷特太太了嗎?
A, have I introduced you to B?	▸ David, have I introduced you to Mrs. Pauline Strait?
你認識嗎? **A, do you know B?**	傑克,你認識卡爾彼特先生嗎? ▸ Jack, do you know Mr. Carl Pitt?
你見過嗎? **A, have you met B?**	瑪麗,你見過納森馬爾庫姆嗎? ▸ Mary, have you met Nathan Malcolm?
我希望你見見。 **A, I want you to meet B.**	林德先生,我希望你見見史丹王先生。 ▸ Mr. Lynd, I want you to meet Mr. Stan Wang.
我想要你見見。 **A, I'd like you to meet B.**	羅伯先生,我想要你見見好萊塢著名影星,希拉羅達。 ▸ Mr. Rob, I'd like you to meet Sheila Rhoda, famous film star in Hollywood.
這位是。 **This is ～.**	這位是尼可拉斯尼米茲,D.C.公司經理。 ▸ This is Nicholas Nimitz, manager of D.C. Company.

✿ 日常口語

見見⋯吧。
Meet ～.

見見我的兄弟渥克吧。
▸ Meet my brother Walker.

瞧，有人來了！

瞧，約翰來了！約翰，這是湯姆；湯姆，這是約翰。

Look, here's ～!

▸ Look, here's John! John—Tom, Tom—John.

哦，A來了，見見B吧。
Oh, here's A. A, meet B.

哦，大衛來了。大衛，來見見馬克。
▸ Oh, here's David. David, meet Mark.

哦瞧，A來了，見見B吧。
Oh look, A's here.
A, come and meet B.

哦瞧，溫蒂來了。溫蒂，來見見羅傑。
▸ Oh look, Wendy's here. Wendy, come and meet Roger.

♣ 正式場合

容我介紹。

容我介紹世界野生動物協會主席，珍妮辛普森太太。

Allow me to introduce ～.

▶ Allow me to introduce Mrs. Jenny Sampson, Chairman of World Wild Life.

我願介紹。

我願向各位介紹我們的主任西德尼卡森先生。

I'd like to introduce ～.

▶ I'd like to introduce our director Mr. Sidney Carson.

我很榮幸介紹。

我很榮幸向你們介紹蘇珊金女士，她將替我們上歷史課。

I'm honored to present ～.

▶ I'm honored to present Ms. Susan King, who will give us a lecture on history.

我很高興介紹。

很高興向你們介紹羅伯特卡爾森先生，他今天將和我們談談世界經濟問題。

I'm very pleased to present ～.

▶ I'm very pleased to present Mr. Robert Carlson, who will talk with us today about world economy.

我很高興向你們介紹。

我很高興向你們介紹通用電氣公司副經理，史丹利楊先生。

It is with great pleasure that I introduce to you ～.

▶ It is with great pleasure that I introduce to you Mr. Stanley Yang, Assistant Manager of General Electric.

請允許我介紹。

請允許我介紹卡內基基金會主席，約翰格蘭特先生。

Please let me introduce ～.

▶ Please let me introduce President of the Carnegie Foundation, Mr. John Grant.

請容我介紹。

May I introduce ～?

請容我介紹卡內基基金會主席，埃德加湯普森先生。

▶ May I introduce Mr. Edgar Thompson, Chairman of the Carnegie Foundation?

請容我介紹一下。

May I present ～?

請容我介紹一下通用電氣公司副經理，史丹利楊先生。

▶ May I present Mr. Stanley Yang, Assistant Manager of General Electric?

請允許我介紹。

Perhaps I could introduce ～.

請允許我介紹華盛頓大學榮譽教授萊克柯爾比先生。

▶ Perhaps I could introduce Mr. Lake Kirby, an emeritus professor form Washington University.

● 自我介紹 ●

♈ 基本說法

181

對不起。我相信我們還沒有見過面。我是…。
Excuse me. I don't believe we've met before. I'm ~.

▶ 對不起。我相信我們還沒有見過面。我是埃德加斯諾。
Excuse me. I don't believe we've met before. I'm Edgar Snow.

對不起。我是…。
Excuse me. I'm ~.

▶ 對不起。我是劍橋來的史蒂芬懷特。
Excuse me. I'm Steven White from Cambridge.

喂？我是…。（電話中）
Hello? ~ speaking.

▶ 喂？我是艾略特維克多。
Hello? Eliot Victor speaking.

喂？我的名字叫…。（電話中）
Hello? My name's ~.

▶ 喂？我的名字叫湯瑪斯普萊爾。
Hello? My name's Thomas Prior.

喂？我是…。（電話中）
Hello? This is ~ speaking.

▶ 喂？我是傑克遜爾文。
Hello? This is Jackson Irving speaking.

你好。我想我們還沒見過面。我的名字叫…。
How do you do? I don't think we've met. My name's ~.

▶ 你好。我想我們還沒有見過面。我的名字叫史蒂芬懷特。
How do you do? I don't think we've met. My name's Steven White.

你好。我是…。
How do you do? I'm ~.

▶ 你好。我是約翰韋斯特。
How do you do? I'm John West.

你好。我的名字叫…。
How do you do? My name's ~.

▶ 你好。我的名字叫查理斯福特。
How do you do? My name's Charles Ford.

✿ 日常口語

你好！我是…。
Hello! I'm ~.

你好！我是西德尼卡森。
▸ Hello! I'm Sidney Carson.

你好！
Hello! ~.

你好！艾薩克李文斯頓。
▸ Hello! Isaac Livingstone.

喂？我是…。（電話中）
Hello? This is ~.

喂！我是德克斯特艾默森。
▸ Hello! This is Dexter Emerson.

喂？我是…。（電話中）
Hello? ~ here.

喂？我是托尼。
▸ Hello? Tony here.

你好！我是…。
Hi! I'm ~.

你好！我是莫里斯濟慈。
▸ Hi! I'm Morris Keats.

♣ 正式場合

183

請容我自我介紹。

Allow me to introduce myself: ~.

請允許我自我介紹。
May I introduce myself: ~.

請讓我自我介紹。

Please let me introduce myself: ~.

請容我自我介紹：我是葛林公司的工程師，珍妮海伍德。

▶ Allow me to introduce myself: Jenny Heywood, an engineer from Green.

請允許我自我介紹：唐納德爾文。

▶ May I introduce myself: Donald Ervin.

請讓我自我介紹：我是英語系主任大衛艾默里。

▶ Please let me introduce myself: David Emory, director of the English Department.

● 對介紹的應答 ●

❦ 基本說法

🔊 184

很高興認識你。
Happy to know you.

你好。
How do you do?

久仰，久仰。
I have often heard about you.

我一直想見你。
I have often wanted to meet you.

久仰大名。
I know you very well by reputation.

我很高興見到你。
I'm glad to meet you.

我很高興見到你。
I'm pleased to meet you.

久仰，久仰。
I've heard so much about you.

有人常談起你。
~ has often talked about you.

楚門先生常談起你。
▶ Mr. Truman has often talked about you.

不，實際上我沒見過。你好。
No, I don't actually. How do you do?

不，我想不認識。很高興…。　　　不，我想不認識。很高興見到你。
No, I don't think I do. Pleased　▸ No, I don't think I do. Pleased to
to ～.　　　　　　　　　　　　　meet you.

不，我想我不曾見過。很高興見到你。
No, I don't think I have. Well pleased to meet you.

不，我想我不認識。你好。
No, I don't think so. How do you do?

是的，我想我認識。
Yes, I think I do.

是的，我想我曾見過。
Yes, I think I have.

是的，我想我們彼此認識，不是嗎？
Yes, I think we do, don't we?

是的，我想我們彼此見過，不是嗎？
Yes, I think we have, haven't we?

293

✿ 日常口語

很高興見到你。
Glad to meet you.

你好！
Hi!

很高興見到你。
Nice meeting you.

很高興見到你。
Nice to meet you.

哦，你好！
Oh, hello!

♣ 正式場合

很高興和您見面。
I'm delighted to meet you.

很榮幸和您見面。
I'm honored to meet you.

我很高興有機會和您見面。
I'm very glad to have the opportunity to meet you.

很高興和您見面。
I'm very happy to meet you.

我很高興能認識您。
I'm very pleased to make your acquaintance.

很高興見到您。
It's a pleasure to meet you.

很榮幸認識您。　　　　　　　　很榮幸認識您，湯普森先生。
It's a privilege to know you, ～. ▶ It's a privilege to know you, Mr. Thompson.

Invitation

邀 請

● 誠摯邀請 ●

🌱 基本說法

187

希望你能來。
～, we'd like you to come.

貝蒂和我本週末辦派對，希望你能來。
▶ Betty and I will throw a party this weekend, we'd like you to come.

你能過來跟我們一起嗎？
Can you come over and join us?

務必和我一起。
Do join me for ～.

務必和我一起喝杯咖啡。
▶ Do join me for a coffee.

我很希望你來。
I'd very much like you to come to ～.

我很希望你來參加我們的聚餐。
▶ I'd very much like you to come to our dinner party.

如果你來，請務必來看我。
If ever you're in ～, please do look me up.

如果你來芝加哥，請務必來看我。
▶ If ever you're in Chicago, please do look me up.

我們…好嗎？
Shall we ～?

我們在這家餐廳喝一杯好嗎？
▶ Shall we have a drink at this restaurant?

如果你能來，我們會很高興。
We'll be glad if you can come to ～.

如果你能來參加會議，我們會很高興。
▶ We'll be glad if you can come to attend our meeting.

我希望你能來。
～. I hope you make it.

週日我們準備舉行舞會。我希望你能來。
▶ We're having a dance on Sunday. I hope you make it.

你要一起來嗎？
～. Will you join us?

這週末我們要辦派對。你要一起來嗎？
▸ We're having a party this weekend. Will you join us?

你不要嗎？
Won't you ～?

你不要跟我一起來嗎？
▸ Won't you come with me?

你能不能？
Would you be able to ～?

今晚你能不能順便來我們家聊聊？
▸ Would you be able to drop in on us for a chat this evening?

你願意嗎？
Would you like to ～?

你願意來參加我們的婚禮嗎？
▸ Would you like to attend our wedding?

你會來，不是嗎？
You will come to ～, won't you?

你會來和我們共進晚餐的，不是嗎？
▸ You will come to have dinner with us, won't you?

你能來的，不是嗎？
You'll be able to come, won't you?

❀ 日常口語 🔊 188

來⋯吧。
Come and ~.
　　下星期五來看我吧。
▸ Come and see me next Friday.

過來⋯。
Come on over to ~.
　　你過來試一下。
▸ Come on over to have a try.

你想一起來嗎？
Do you fancy coming along?

如果你沒事，過來坐坐。
Drop by ~ if you've nothing on.
　　如果你沒事，明天找個時間過來坐坐。
▸ Drop by sometime tomorrow if you've nothing on.

我們去⋯吧。
Let's go for ~.
　　我們去吃冰淇淋吧。
▸ Let's go for an ice cream.

想來嗎？
Like to come to ~?
　　想來參加我們的化裝舞會嗎？
▸ Like to come to our fancy dress party?

如果你不忙，就留下來。
Stay for ~, unless you're busy.
　　如果你不忙，就留下來吃晚餐吧。
▸ Stay for dinner, unless you're busy.

想和我們一起嗎？
Want to join us for ~?
　　想和我們一起去烤肉嗎？
▸ Want to join us for a barbecue?

這樣如何？
What about ~?
　　來見見我太太如何？
▸ What about meeting my wife?

你為何不和我們一起呢？
Why don't you come ~ with us?
　　你為何不和我們一起度假呢？
▸ Why don't you come on a holiday with us?

你一定要和我們一起。
You must join us for ~.
　　你一定要和我們一起吃午餐。
▸ You must join us for lunch.

♣ 正式場合

189

可否請你光臨？
Could we have the honor of your presence ～?

▸ 可否請你光臨本次會議？
Could we have the honor of your presence at the meeting?

不知你是否願意。
I was wondering if you'd care to ～.

▸ 不知你是否願意下星期來我們家作客。
I was wondering if you'd care to visit us next week.

如果可以的話，我們想請你…。
If you could manage, we'd like you to ～.

▸ 如果可以的話，我們想請你參加星期四上午舉行的演講比賽。
If you could manage, we'd like you to attend our speech contest on Thursday morning.

我們有這榮幸請你一起嗎？
May we have the pleasure of your company at ～?

▸ 我們有這榮幸請你一起共進晚餐嗎？
May we have the pleasure of your company at dinner?

也許你願意吧？
Perhaps you'd care to ～?

▸ 也許你願意跟我們一起去看電影吧？
Perhaps you'd care to go to the movies with us?

如果你能，我們會很高興的。
We should be so pleased if you could ～.

▸ 如果你能來我們會很高興的。
We should be so pleased if you could come.

我們冒昧邀請你。
We thought you might like to ～.

▸ 我們冒昧邀請你參加我們的排練。
We thought you might like to participate in our rehearsal.

如蒙光臨，不勝榮幸之至。
Would you honor us with a visit?

● 接受邀請 ●

❤ 基本說法
🔊 190

我很願意。謝謝你。
I do very much. Thank you.

我很願意。謝謝你。
I would very much. Thank you.

我很樂意。
I'd enjoy that very much.

再好不過了。
I'd like nothing better.

我很願意。
I'd like that very much.

我會晚點到，行嗎？
I'll be a little late, is that OK?

很高興。
It would be very nice to ～.

很高興參加你們的婚禮。
▸ It would be very nice to attend your wedding ceremony.

哦，你用不著這麼客氣的。
Oh, you shouldn't have.

謝謝你。我很願意。
Thank you. I'd like to very much.

這個主意聽起來很棒。
That sounds a very good idea.

那太好了。
That would be very nice.

那太好了。
That would be wonderful.

多謝你的好意。
That's very nice of you.

哦，好的，如果不會太麻煩的話，我願意來。
Well, yes, I'd like to, if it's not too much trouble.

噢好的，那太好了。
Why yes, that'll be very nice.

好的。
With pleasure.

好的，我會的。謝謝你。
Yes, I do. Thank you.

好的，我會來的。這是再好不過的事了。
Yes, I will. I'd like nothing better than to ～.

好的，我會來的。和你父母見面是再好不過的事了。
▸ Yes, I will. I'd like nothing better than to meet your parents.

好的，我很想來。謝謝你。
Yes, I'd like to. Thank you.

好的，如果你要我來的話。
Yes, if you want me to.

好的，如果你要我來的話。
Yes, if you'd like me to.

✳ 日常口語

那好吧!
All right then!

我不會拒絕的！
I won't say no!

我很樂意與你們一起。　　　　　我很樂意與你們一起共進午餐。
I'd love to join you for ~.　　▶ I'd love to join you for lunch.

我很樂意！
I'd love to very much!

那好，我會來的。
I'll see you, then.

我接受你這個邀請。
I'll take you up on that.

我願意！多謝。
I'm on! Thanks a lot.

好極了。
Lovely.

好的，如果你堅持。
OK, if you insist.

聽起來不錯/很棒。
Sounds good / great.

哈，好極了！
Well, good for you!

當然可以！
You certainly can!

♣ 正式場合

如果能和你們一起，我們會非常高興。

It would give us great pleasure to ~ with you. ▸

如果能和你們一起歡度感恩節，我們會非常高興。

It would give us great pleasure to enjoy Thanksgiving with you.

非常榮幸。謝謝你。

That would be very pleasant. Thank you.

那將使我們榮幸之至。

That would give us the greatest of pleasure.

真是非常感謝你了。

That's really very kind of you.

我們很高興接受你的邀請。

We'd be much delighted to accept your invitation.

我們很想和你們一起。

We'd very much like to ~ with you. ▸

我們很想和你們一起共進晚餐。

We'd very much like to have dinner with you.

真是個令人高興的主意，謝謝你。

What a delightful idea, thank you.

榮幸之至。

With the greatest of pleasure.

● 拒絕邀請 ●

🌱 基本說法

我希望我能，但是…。
I wish I could, but ～.

我希望能接受邀請，但莉莎今晚要來。
▸ I wish I could, but Lisa is coming this evening.

我還是不去了。
I'd better not.

我想來，但是…。
I'd like to, but ～.

我想來，但是我的先生不會同意的。
▸ I'd like to, but my husband wouldn't like it.

我還是不去了。
I'd rather not.

我恐怕不能來了。不過我還是要謝謝你。
I'm afraid I can't. But thank you all the same.

我恐怕不能。
I'm afraid I can't ～.

我恐怕明天不能來了。
▸ I'm afraid I can't come tomorrow.

我恐怕已經有約了。不過還是要謝謝你。
I'm afraid I'm already booked up for ～. But thank you just the same.

下星期天我恐怕已經有約了。不過還是要謝謝你。
▸ I'm afraid I'm already booked up for next Sunday. But thank you just the same.

對不起，我不能來。
I'm sorry, I can't.

我很抱歉，我想我來不了。
I'm terribly sorry, but I don't think I can make it ～.

我很抱歉，我想那天我來不了。
▸ I'm terribly sorry, but I don't think I can make it that day.

非常感謝你，不過我已答應別人。
Thank you very much, but I've already promised to ～.

非常感謝你，不過我已答應今晚要和基辛格見面了。
▶ Thank you very much, but I've already promised to meet Kissinger this evening.

謝謝你邀請我，不過我…。
Thank you very much for asking me, but I ～.

謝謝你邀請我，不過我覺得很累了。
▶ Thank you very much for asking me, but I feel rather tired.

這真的沒有必要。
That's really not necessary.

謝謝你，不過我…。
That's very nice of you, but I ～.

謝謝你，不過我必須複習準備考試。
▶ That's very nice of you, but I have to review for an exam.

✿ 日常口語

當然不了。
Certainly not.

我想去，可是…。
I'd love to, but ～.

我想去，可是我爸爸要來看我。
▶ I'd love to, but my father's going to call at me.

不，我不去了。
No, I don't.

不，我不會去。
No, I wouldn't.

不，謝謝。
No, thanks.

哦，可惜！
Oh, shame! ～.

哦，可惜！我明天有約。
▶ Oh, shame! I have a date tomorrow.

哦，真可惜！
Oh, what a pity! ～.

哦，真可惜！我要去參加一個派對。
▶ Oh, what a pity! I'm going to a party.

對不起，我不能來。不過還是謝謝你。
Sorry, I can't. But thanks anyway.

♣ 正式場合

我雖然很想去，但恐怕我沒空。
Much as I should like to. I'm afraid I won't be free ～.

▶ 我雖然很想去，但恐怕下週日我沒空。
Much as I should like to. I'm afraid I won't be free next Sunday.

很遺憾，我不能。
Greatly to my regret, I wouldn't be able to ～.

▶ 很遺憾，週六我不能參加你們的派對。
Greatly to my regret. I wouldn't be able to attend your party this Saturday.

很遺憾我有事。不過還是謝謝你想到了我。
I regret to say that ～. However, thank you for thinking of me.

▶ 很遺憾，那天晚上我另有約會。不過還是謝謝你想到了我。
I regret to say that I have a previous engagement that evening. However, thank you for thinking of me.

很遺憾，我必須…。不過，我很感謝你邀請我。
Regrettably, I'm obliged to ～. But thank you very much of inviting me.

▶ 很遺憾，那天我必須主持一個開幕典禮。不過，我很感謝你邀請我。
Regrettably, I'm obliged to conduct an opening ceremony that day. But thank you very much of inviting me.

謝謝你，但因為…，所以我不能來。
That's very kind of you, but owing to ～, I won't be able to come to ～.

▶ 謝謝你，但因為我已先有約，所以不能來見你的朋友。
That's very kind of you, but owing to a prior appointment, I won't be able to come to meet your friend.

真不湊巧，那天我得…。
Unfortunately, I'll have to ～ that day.

▶ 真不湊巧，那天我得出席一個會議。
Unfortunately, I'll have to attend a conference that day.

判斷

● 作出判斷 ●

☘ 基本說法

🔊 196

他可能。
He may be ~.

他可能是對的。
▸ He may be right.

他也許。
He's perhaps ~.

他也許是對的。
▸ He's perhaps right.

他大概。
He's probably ~.

他大概已聽說這消息了。
▸ He's probably been told about the news.

我覺得好像。
I feel as if ~.

我覺得好像要下雨了。
▸ I feel as if it were going to rain.

在我看來。
I feel (that) ~.

在我看來這計劃還不錯。
▸ I feel (that) the plan was good.

我想。
I guess ~.

我想你是對的。
▸ I guess you're right.

我斷定。
I judge ~.

我斷定他40歲左右。
▸ I judge him to be about 40.

我想。
I should guess ~.

我想他的年齡在30歲左右。
▸ I should guess his age at about 30.

我想一定。
I think ~ must've ~.

我想他們一定很早就走了。
▸ I think they must've left early.

可能。
It may ~.

傍晚以前可能下雨。
▸ It may rain before evening.

一定是。
It must be ~.

一定是到了鋼琴演奏的時候。
▶ It must be about time for playing the piano.

看來。
It seems ~.

看來這沒問題。
▶ It seems all right.

看來可能。
It seems likely (that) ~.

看來他們可能是迷路了。
▶ It seems likely (that) they've got lost.

看來。
It seems (that) ~.

看來你在撒謊。
▶ It seems (that) you were lying.

不大可能。
It's unlikely (that) ~.

這隻鳥不大可能活下來了。
▶ It's unlikely (that) the bird will survive.

從這判斷，一定是。
Judging by ~, sb. must be ~.

從他的口音判斷，他一定是南方人。
▶ Judging by his accent, he must be from the South.

從這判斷，似乎。
Judging from ~, sb. seems to ~.

從母親來信判斷，她似乎覺得好多了。
▶ Judging from her letters, Mother seems to be feeling a lot better.

我看應該。
That ought to be ~, I think.

我看那魚應該夠三個人吃的。
▶ That ought to be enough fish for three people, I think.

我想那是。
That would be ~, I think.

我想那是1976年。
▶ That would be 1976, I think.

可能。
~ might ~.

只要我們小心操縱，這機器就可能運轉。
▶ The machine might work if we handle it carefully.

一定有。
There must be ～.

這個鐘一定有什麼地方壞了。
▸ There must be something wrong with the clock.

很可能。
There's a good chance ～.

他很可能失敗。
▸ There's a good chance he will fail.

我想應該。
～ should ～, I think.

我想他們現在應該到那裡了。
▸ They should be there by now, I think.

根據判斷。
To judge by ～.

根據地址判斷，這房子離市中心很遠。
▸ To judge by the address, the house is a long way from the downtown.

你好像不…。
You don't seem to ～.

你今天好像不太高興。
▸ You don't seem to be quite yourself today.

🌸 日常口語

可能。
~ can have been ~.
他可能被濃霧所耽誤了。
▸ He can have been delayed by fog.

我說。
~, I say.
我說，他會很激動的。
▸ He'll be thrilled, I say.

我預估。
I figure ~.
我預估她不久就會回來。
▸ I figure she'll be back soon.

我料想。
I imagine ~.
我料想他六點鐘以前會完成這項工作。
▸ I imagine he'll have finished the job by six o'clock.

這聽起來。
It sounds ~.
這聽起來挺不錯。
▸ It sounds quite all right.

看起來。
Looks like ~.
今天看起來是個晴天。
▸ Looks like a fine day today.

聽起來不錯。
Sounds all right.

這並不太壞。
That isn't too bad.

差不多是這樣。
That's about it.

看來是這樣。
That's how it looks.

他們很可能。
They'll very likely ~.
他們很可能會坐車來。
▸ They'll very likely come by car.

♣ 正式場合

我看不太可能。
I would consider it unlikely (that) ～.

> 我看今年長裙不太可能會過時。
> I would consider it unlikely (that) long skirts will go out this year.

我估計。
I would estimate ～.

> 我估計這花園的面積有1000平方公尺。
> I would estimate the size of the garden at 1000 square meters.

很可能。
It seems probable (that) ～.

> 我們很可能會遇到一些預想外的麻煩。
> It seems probable (that) we might encounter some unexpected troubles.

看來完全不可能。
It seems totally out of the question (that) ～.

> 看來會議完全不可能成功了。
> It seems totally out of the question (that) the meeting will be a success.

看來。
It would seem (that) ～.

> 看來你對這計劃並不滿意。
> It would seem (that) you were not pleased with the plan.

大概。
It's probable (that) ～.

> 他大概不回英國了。
> It's probable (that) he won't return to England.

我的判斷是。
My judgment is (that) ～.

> 我的判斷是，在這種天氣飛行很危險。
> My judgment is (that) it's dangerous to fly in this weather.

看來。
There seems to be ～.

> 看來拒絕毫無意義。
> There seems to be no point in refusing.

26 Name 姓名

● 請問貴姓大名 ●

🌱 基本說法 🔊199

請告訴我你的姓名好嗎？
Can you tell me your name, please?

我想你是…，對嗎？
I believe you're ～, aren't you?

我想你是傑克遜先生，對嗎？
▶ I believe you're Mr. Jackson, aren't you?

你的名字是不是？
Is your name ～?

你的名字是不是愛德華貝斯特？
▶ Is your name Edward Best?

你打算幫…取什麼名字？
What are you going to call ～?

你打算幫這個孩子取什麼名字？
▶ What are you going to call the baby?

你剛才說那名字叫什麼來著？
What did you say the name was?

你姓什麼？
What's your family name?

你的全名是什麼？
What's your full name?

請問你的姓名？
What's your name, please, ～?

請問你的姓名，先生？
▶ What's your name, please, sir?

請問訂位姓名？
Who's the booking for, please, ～?

請問訂位姓名，先生？
▶ Who's the booking for, please, sir?

✿ 日常口語 🔊 200

你叫？
Are you called ～?

你叫迪克？
▸ Are you called Dick?

你的朋友都叫你？
Do your friends call you ～?

你的朋友都叫你鮑勃嗎？
▸ Do your friends call you Bob?

你的父母都叫你什麼？
What do your parents call you?

♣ 正式場合

告訴我您的姓名好嗎？
Could you give me your name, please, ～?

請告訴我您的姓名好嗎，先生？
▸ Could you give me your name, please, sir?

您好。
How do you do? ～.
＊這是一種間接詢問對方姓名的方式。

您好。我是班哈德森。
▸ How do you do? I'm Ben Hudson.

對不起打擾了，您怎麼稱呼？
I'm sorry to disturb you, ～, but what's your name?

對不起打擾了，先生，您怎麼稱呼？
▸ I'm sorry to disturb you, sir, but what's your name?

請問貴姓大名？
May I have your name?

請問貴姓大名？
May I know your name?

您就是…吧？
～, I presume?

您就是亞當斯先生吧？
▸ Mr. Adams, I presume?

請問貴姓？（電話中）
Who shall I say, ～?

請問貴姓，先生？
▸ Who shall I say, sir?

請問貴姓大名？
Would you give me your name?

自我介紹篇

想一段精彩的自我介紹吧！

名字，暱稱 ⎯⎯⎯⎯⎯⎯⎯⎯⎯⎯⎯⎯⎯⎯⎯⎯⎯⎯⎯⎯⎯⎯⎯⎯⎯⎯⎯

擅長的事情 ⎯⎯⎯⎯⎯⎯⎯⎯⎯⎯⎯⎯⎯⎯⎯⎯⎯⎯⎯⎯⎯⎯⎯⎯⎯⎯⎯

⎯⎯⎯⎯⎯⎯⎯⎯⎯⎯⎯⎯⎯⎯⎯⎯⎯⎯⎯⎯⎯⎯⎯⎯⎯⎯⎯⎯⎯⎯⎯⎯⎯⎯⎯⎯⎯⎯

平時的休閒 ⎯⎯⎯⎯⎯⎯⎯⎯⎯⎯⎯⎯⎯⎯⎯⎯⎯⎯⎯⎯⎯⎯⎯⎯⎯⎯⎯

⎯⎯⎯⎯⎯⎯⎯⎯⎯⎯⎯⎯⎯⎯⎯⎯⎯⎯⎯⎯⎯⎯⎯⎯⎯⎯⎯⎯⎯⎯⎯⎯⎯⎯⎯⎯⎯⎯

最喜歡的電影 ⎯⎯⎯⎯⎯⎯⎯⎯⎯⎯⎯⎯⎯⎯⎯⎯⎯⎯⎯⎯⎯⎯⎯⎯⎯

⎯⎯⎯⎯⎯⎯⎯⎯⎯⎯⎯⎯⎯⎯⎯⎯⎯⎯⎯⎯⎯⎯⎯⎯⎯⎯⎯⎯⎯⎯⎯⎯⎯⎯⎯⎯⎯⎯

最值得驕傲的事 ⎯⎯⎯⎯⎯⎯⎯⎯⎯⎯⎯⎯⎯⎯⎯⎯⎯⎯⎯⎯⎯⎯⎯⎯

⎯⎯⎯⎯⎯⎯⎯⎯⎯⎯⎯⎯⎯⎯⎯⎯⎯⎯⎯⎯⎯⎯⎯⎯⎯⎯⎯⎯⎯⎯⎯⎯⎯⎯⎯⎯⎯⎯

做過最呆的事 ⎯⎯⎯⎯⎯⎯⎯⎯⎯⎯⎯⎯⎯⎯⎯⎯⎯⎯⎯⎯⎯⎯⎯⎯⎯

⎯⎯⎯⎯⎯⎯⎯⎯⎯⎯⎯⎯⎯⎯⎯⎯⎯⎯⎯⎯⎯⎯⎯⎯⎯⎯⎯⎯⎯⎯⎯⎯⎯⎯⎯⎯⎯⎯

Yes! We can!

My name is ...

My favorite ... is ...

I believe ...

I can ...

這時候要怎麼說？

模擬劇場

下面6個生活常遇到的情境，
現在先想好如何回答，到時就不會詞窮囉！

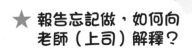

★ **報告忘記做，如何向
老師（上司）解釋？**

有條理的向對方說明自己未
能達成目標（報告未作、遲
到..）的原因（見9、11、
32章），請對方理解原諒。
（見4、35章）

★ **朋友生日，
我想用英語祝福！**

對不同朋友祝福有不同
說法，可以依適合的情
況預先想好祝賀說詞。
（見12、17、19章）

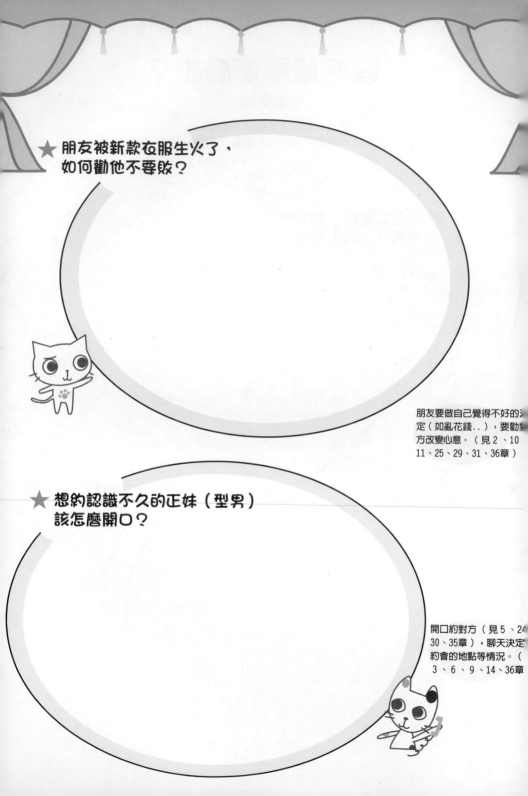

★ 朋友被新款衣服生火了，
　如何勸他不要敗？

朋友要做自己覺得不好的決
定（如亂花錢..），要勸對
方改變心意。（見 2 、10 、
11、25、29、31、36章）

★ 想約認識不久的正妹（型男）
　該怎麼開口？

開口約對方（見 5 、24、
30、35章），聊天決定
約會的地點等情況。（見
3 、6 、9 、14、36章）

★ 和外國朋友吃飯時
   如何介紹菜色跟給建議呢？

建議他吃什麼菜（見
2、28、29、36章）
或預告對方那道菜可
能不合外國人口味。
（見25、31章）

★ 跟外國人聊天時先說些什麼？

剛頭時先說些什麼？打招呼？
聊八卦？溝通意見？先想好一
個有趣的話題吧！（見9、18
、20、23、26、34章）

Hey! Apple!

Hey! Orange!

27 Obligation 義務

● 我必須這麼做嗎？ ●

🌱 基本說法

🔊 202

我需要這樣做嗎？ **Am I expected to ～?**	我需要重複一遍嗎？ ▶ Am I expected to repeat it?
我是不是應該？ **Am I supposed to ～?**	我是不是應該去看看卡羅琳？ ▶ Am I supposed to get over and see Caroline?
我是不是得這樣做？ **Do I have to ～?**	我是不是得改掉我的壞習慣？ ▶ Do I have to do away with my bad habits?
我真的需要嗎？ **Do I really need to ～?**	我真的需要把它抄下來嗎？ ▶ Do I really need to copy it?
我應該這樣做，是不是？ **I ought to ～, oughtn't I?**	我應該預先告訴他，是不是？ ▶ I ought to tell him beforehand, oughtn't I?
我該這樣做，是不是？ **I should ～, shouldn't I?**	我該退出競賽，是不是？ ▶ I should drop out of the competition, shouldn't I?
我需要這樣做嗎？ **Need I ～?**	我需要為這付錢嗎？ ▶ Need I pay for it?
我該嗎？ **Ought I to ～?**	我該去嗎？ ▶ Ought I to go?
我是不是該？ **Should I ～?**	我是不是該把桌子往後挪？ ▶ Should I move the table back?

 日常口語

是不是該我去？	是不是該我去報告這次事故？
Am I the one that's got to ～?	▸ Am I the one that's got to give a report about the accident?

我一定得這樣嗎？
Have I got to?
我一定得這樣做嗎？ 　　　　　　我一定得把選票投進這箱子嗎？
Have I got to ～? 　　　　▸ Have I got to put my voting paper in the box?

我想我得？	我想我得等新室友來？
I suppose I've got to ～?	▸ I suppose I've got to wait for the new roommate?

我必須嗎？	我必須作筆記嗎？
Must I ～?	▸ Must I take notes?

我不能嗎？	我不能進來嗎？
Mustn't I ～?	▸ Mustn't I come in?

♣ 正式場合

我們是不是得這樣？
Are we required to ～?

我們是不是今天就得制訂出計劃來？
▸ Are we required to work out a plan today?

我們是不是有義務？
Are we under any obligation to ～?

我們是不是有義務支持這家公司？
▸ Are we under any obligation to support the company?

我們不是非得這麼做不可嗎？
Aren't we obliged to ～?

我們不是非得研究合約細節不可嗎？
▸ Aren't we obliged to study the details of the contract?

你認為我們需要嗎？
Do you think we are required to ～?

你認為我們需要繳所得稅嗎？
▸ Do you think we are required to pay income taxes?

我們是不是必須？
Is it compulsory for us to ～?

我們是不是必須放棄假期？
▸ Is it compulsory for us to put away our holiday?

我們有沒有必要？
Is it necessary for us to ～?

我們有沒有必要調查這件事？
▸ Is it necessary for us to look into the matter?

我們有義務嗎？
Is it obligatory on us to ～?

我們有義務幫助窮人嗎？
▸ Is it obligatory on us to help the poor?

我們有義務嗎？
Is it our duty to ～?

我們有義務遵從他的要求嗎？
▸ Is it our duty to comply with his requests?

我們是不是需要？
Is there any need for us to ～?

我們是不是需要辦簽證？
▸ Is there any need for us to get a visa?

這不是義務的嗎？
Isn't ～ obligatory?

拜訪喬治先生不是義務的嗎？
▸ Isn't a visit to Mr. George obligatory?

● 你必須這麼做 ●

▼ 基本說法

205

我想你不能不做。
I don't think you can avoid ~.

我想你不能不把真相告訴他。
▸ I don't think you can avoid telling him the truth.

我看你得這樣做。
I think you have to ~.

我看你得在今天完成這項工作。
▸ I think you have to finish the job today.

我看你需要。
I think you need to ~.

我看你需要向幾所大學提出申請。
▸ I think you need to apply to several colleges.

我看你應該。
I think you ought to ~.

我看你應該放掉這條狗。
▸ I think you ought to let go of the dog.

我看你應該。
I think you should ~.

我看你應該按兵不動。
▸ I think you should stay where you are.

我看你要。
I think you're expected to ~.

我看你要改正自己的錯誤。
▸ I think you're expected to correct your own mistakes.

我看你得。
I think you're meant to ~.

我看你得排隊。
▸ I think you're meant to queue.

恐怕你不能不這樣做。
I'm afraid you can't avoid ~.

恐怕你不能不到機場替他送行。
▸ I'm afraid you can't avoid seeing him off at the airport.

恐怕你必須。
I'm afraid you must ~.

恐怕你必須洗掉這污漬。
▸ I'm afraid you must wash out this stain.

恐怕你得。
I'm afraid you'll have to ~.

恐怕你得容忍他的壞脾氣。
▶ I'm afraid you'll have to put up with his bad temper.

恐怕你必須。
I'm afraid you're supposed to ~.

恐怕你必須償還你妻子的債務。
▶ I'm afraid you're supposed to pay your wife's debt.

你得這樣做。
You are to ~.

你明天得主持會議。
▶ You are to chair the meeting tomorrow.

❀ 日常口語

我看你沒法逃避。
I don't see how you can get off ~.

我看你沒法逃避送兒子上學的義務。
▶ I don't see how you can get off your duty to send your son to school.

我看你躲不了。
I don't see how you can get let off ~.

我看你躲不了洗碗盤的工作。
▶ I don't see how you can get let off doing the dishes.

我看你逃不過。
I don't see how you can slip out of ~.

我看你逃不過要寫份關於此事的報告。
▶ I don't see how you can slip out of writing a report about that.

恐怕你逃避不了。
I'm afraid you can't get away with ~.

恐怕你逃避不了得去做菜。
▶ I'm afraid you can't get away with cooking.

恐怕你躲不過。
I'm afraid you can't get out of ~.

恐怕你躲不過做家事。
▶ I'm afraid you can't get out of your housework.

恐怕你不能就這樣不做。
I'm afraid you can't just not ~.

恐怕你不能就這樣不拿走這垃圾。
▶ I'm afraid you can't just not take away this rubbish.

恐怕你得這樣做。
I'm afraid you've got to.
恐怕你得。
I'm afraid you've got to ~.

恐怕你得罵他一頓。
▶ I'm afraid you've got to jack him up.

當然你必須這麼做。
Sure you must.
當然你必須。
Sure you must ~.

當然你必須把它換掉。
▶ Sure you must change it.

♣ 正式場合

實際上，你有義務。
Actually, it is your duty to ～.
▶ 實際上你有義務通知他董事會的決定。
Actually, it is your duty to inform him of the board's decision.

我認為這是義務。
I think ～ is obligatory.
▶ 我認為遵守法規是必須履行的義務。
I think abiding by the law is obligatory.

我認為這是非做不可的。
I think it is compulsory.
我認為這是非做不可的。
I think it is compulsory to ～.
▶ 我認為檢查這棟房子是非做不可的。
I think it is compulsory to look over the house.

我認為這是有必要的。
I think it is necessary.
我認為你有必要。
I think it is necessary for you to ～.
▶ 我認為你有必要向警察報備這件竊案。
I think it Is necessary for you to report the theft to the police.

我認為你有義務。
I think it is obligatory on you to ～.
▶ 我認為你有義務保護你的家人。
I think it is obligatory on you to protect your family.

恐怕你有必要。
I'm afraid there's need for you to ～.
▶ 恐怕你有必要送學術參考資料給他們。
I'm afraid there's need for you to send them some academic references.

恐怕你有義務。
I'm afraid you have an obligation to ～.
▶ 恐怕你有義務幫助舉辦一次音樂會。
I'm afraid you have an obligation to promote a concert.

恐怕你必須。
I'm afraid you're obliged to ～.
▶ 恐怕你必須寫下這些指令。
I'm afraid you're obliged to copy down these instructions.

恐怕你需要。
I'm afraid you're required to ～. ▸

恐怕你需要重寫你的論文。
I'm afraid you're required to rewrite your paper.

恐怕你有義務。
I'm afraid you're under an obligation.

恐怕你有義務。
I'm afraid you're under an obligation to ～.

恐怕你有義務打電話給莉塔。
▸ I'm afraid you're under an obligation to call Rita.

● 你沒必要這麼做 ●

我讓你自己決定。
I leave it up to you.

我讓你自己決定。
I leave it up to you ～.

我讓你自己決定什麼時候訂船票。
▸ **I leave it up to you** when to book a passage.

這由你決定。
It's for you to decide.

由你決定。
It's for you to decide ～.

是走是留由你決定。
▸ **It's for you to decide** whether to go or to stay.

沒有必要。
There's no need to ～.

沒有必要掩飾你的錯誤。
▸ **There's no need to** cover up your mistakes.

你沒有理由這麼做。
There's no reason why you should ～.

你沒有理由拉倒那個籬笆。
▸ **There's no reason why you should** pull down that fence.

你沒必要。
You don't have to ～.

你沒必要這麼做。
▸ **You don't have to** do that.

你不需要。
You don't need to ～.

你不需要每天拖地板。
▸ **You don't need to** mop the floor every day.

你不需要。
You're not expected to ～.

你今晚不需要當保姆。
▸ **You're not expected to** baby-sit this evening.

不懂你為什麼要這樣。
Can't see why you should ～.

不懂你為什麼要這麼做。
▶ Can't see why you should do that.

不懂你為什麼必須這樣。
Don't see why you shouldn't stop ～.

不懂你為什麼必須每天把書本帶回家。
▶ Don't see why you shouldn't stop carrying the books home every day.

由你決定。
It's up to you.
由你決定。
It's up to you to decide.

你不一定要。
You haven't got to ～.

你不一定要重寫這段文章。
▶ You haven't got to rewrite the passage.

♣ 正式場合

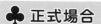

210

我認為你沒有必要。
I don't think it's necessary for you to ~. ▸

我認為你沒有必要向他妥協。
I don't think it's necessary for you to compromise with him.

我認為你不必。
I don't think it's your duty to ~. ▸

我認為你不必減少開支。
I don't think it's your duty to cut down on expenses.

由你決定。
I leave it in your hands ~. ▸

等不等由你決定。
I leave it in your hands whether to wait or not.

我讓你決定。
I leave the decision in your hands.

我認為你不一定要。
I shouldn't see ~ as something you have to do. ▸

我認為你不一定要早上6點起床。
I shouldn't see getting up at 6 a.m. as something you have to do.

● 你不該這麼做 ●

❤ 基本說法

我看你不應該。
I don't think you ought to.

我看你不應該。
I don't think you ought to ～.

我看你不應該燒毀那間小屋。
▸ I don't think you ought to burn down that shed.

我看你不應該。
I don't think you should.

我看你不應該。
I don't think you should ～.

我看你不應該把東西到處亂扔。
▸ I don't think you should litter things about.

這裡不准抽菸。
Smoking is not allowed here.

你務必不要。
There's need for you not to ～.

你務必不要辭退他。
▸ There's need for you not to dismiss him.

你不該。
You oughtn't to ～.

你不該把電話丟掉。
▸ You oughtn't to throw out the phone.

你不該。
You shouldn't ～.

你不該脫掉帽子。
▸ You shouldn't take off your hat.

❀ 日常口語

看在上帝份上，別…。
For goodness sake, don't ~.

看在上帝份上，別開得這麼快。
▸ For goodness sake, don't drive so fast.

慢著！
Hold it!

別去碰！
Leave ~ alone!

別去碰它！
▸ Leave it alone!

停下！
Stop!

千萬別…。
Whatever you do, don't ~.

千萬別把這帽子脫掉。
▸ Whatever you do, don't pull off this cap.

你不能。
You can't ~.

你不能那麼做。
▸ You can't do that.

你不准。
You mustn't ~.

你不准停止奔跑。
▸ You mustn't stop running.

你最好不要。
You'd better not ~.

你最好不要上學遲到。
▸ You'd better not go to school late.

你不可以。
You're not meant to ~.

你不可以伸出你的手。
▸ You're not meant to hold out your hand.

你不可以。
You're not supposed to ~.

你不可以參加這個派對。
▸ You're not supposed to join the party.

你不准。
You're not to ~.

你不准把貓帶進來。
▸ You're not to bring in your cat.

♣ 正式場合

我認為你不能。
I think you are required not to ~.

> 我認為你不能對你的弟弟失去耐心。
> I think you are required not to lose patience with your brother.

我認為你不能。
I think you are under an obligation not to ~.

> 我認為你不能拒絕他的提議。
> I think you are under an obligation not to turn down his offer.

恐怕你不能。
I'm afraid you are obliged not to ~.

> 恐怕你不能反對這項決定。
> I'm afraid you are obliged not to protest against the decision.

恐怕你有義務不這麼做。
I'm afraid you have an obligation not to ~.

> 恐怕你有義務不能把這秘密洩露出去。
> I'm afraid you have an obligation not to let out the secret.

你絕對不准。
On no account must you ~.

> 你絕對不准把貨物走私進入這個國家。
> On no account must you smuggle things into the country.

你應當等到那時為止。
You owe it to wait until ~.

> 你應當等到我們見過全部候選人為止。
> You owe it to wait until we've seen all the candidates.

● 我必須這麼做 ●

❦ 基本說法

214

我必須。
I have to ~.

我必須親自去寄這封信。
▸ I have to mail the letter myself.

我必須。
I must ~.

我必須回他電話。
▸ I must call him back.

我需要。
I need to ~.

我需要把它譯成英語。
▸ I need to translate it into English.

我應該。
I ought to ~.

我應該打電話給她。
▸ I ought to give her a ring.

我應該。
I should ~.

我應該早點起床。
▸ I should get up earlier.

我最好。
I'd better ~.

我最好把它記下來。
▸ I'd better jot it down.

我必須。
I'm supposed to ~.

我必須五點鐘到那裡。
▸ I'm supposed to be there at five.

✿ 日常口語

對不起，最好還是。 **Sorry, better ~.**	對不起，最好還是取消。 ▸ Sorry, better cancel it.
對不起，我不得不這樣做。 **Sorry, can't avoid ~.**	對不起，我不得不6點鐘就叫醒他。 ▸ Sorry, can't avoid waking him up at six.
對不起，我必須。 **Sorry, got to ~.**	對不起，我必須趕6點30分的火車。 ▸ Sorry, got to catch the 6:30 train.
對不起，我必須。 **Sorry, must ~.**	對不起，我必須改變計劃。 ▸ Sorry, must change the plan.

♣ 正式場合

🔊 216

我必須。
I am obliged to ～.

我必須提出辭呈。
▸ I am obliged to offer my resignation.

我認為我們有責任。
I believe the onus is upon us to ～.

我認為我們有責任否決這項工程。
▸ I believe the onus is upon us to vote down the project.

我覺得我絕對有必要。
I feel it is absolutely necessary for me to ～.

我覺得我絕對有必要提醒他今天的會議。
▸ I feel it is absolutely necessary for me to remind him of the meeting today.

我覺得這是我的義務。
I feel it is my duty.

我覺得我有義務。
I feel it is my duty to ～.

我覺得我有義務幫助那個小孩。
▸ I feel it is my duty to help the kid.

我有義務。
I have an obligation to ～.

我有義務把真相告訴你。
▸ I have an obligation to tell you the truth.

除此之外我別無選擇。
I have no alternative but to ～.

除了放棄我別無選擇。
▸ I have no alternative but to give it up.

我認為這是我們的責任。
I think it's incumbent upon us to ～.

我認為支持他是我們的責任。
▸ I think it's incumbent upon us to support him.

除此之外似乎沒有別的選擇。
There appears to be no alternative to ～.

除了提高價格之外似乎沒有別的選擇。
▸ There appears to be no alternative to the increase of prices.

我們必須。
We are committed to ～.

我們必須照此行動。
▸ We are committed to act on it.

● 我不該這麼做 ●

🌱 基本說法

217

不，我不能。
No, I can't.

不，我不能。 　　　　　　　　　　不，我不能讓他的計劃失敗。
No, I can't ～. ▸ No, I can't possibly blow up his plan.

不，我不能。
No, I couldn't.

不，我不能。 　　　　　　　　　　不，我不能兩個都拿。
No, I couldn't ～. ▸ No, I couldn't take both of them.

不，我絕不能。
No, I mustn't.

不，我絕不能。 　　　　　　　　　　不，我上課絕不能遲到。
No, I mustn't ～. ▸ No, I mustn't be late for class.

不，我不應該。
No, I oughtn't to.

不，我不應該。 　　　　　　　　　　不，我不應該接受這個提議。
No, I oughtn't to ～. ▸ No, I oughtn't to accept the offer.

不，我不應該。
No, I shouldn't.

不，我不應該。 　　　　　　　　　　不，我不應該對他說謊。
No, I shouldn't ～. ▸ No, I shouldn't tell him a lie.

不，我最好不要。 　　　　　　　　　　不，我最好不要反對他的建議。
No, I'd better not ～. ▸ No, I'd better not object to his proposal.

不，我不可以。 　　　　　　　　　　不，我不可以在這裡說英語。
No, I'm not supposed to ～. ▸ No, I'm not supposed to speak
English here.

❀ 日常口語 🔊 218

最好不要這樣。
Better not.
最好不要。 最好不要在草地上走。
Better not ~. ▶ Better not walk on the grass.

不，不能。 不，現在不能離開他。
No, can't ~. ▶ No, can't leave him now.

不行！
No way!

對不起，不能。 對不起，不能把真相告訴你。
Sorry, mustn't ~. ▶ Sorry, mustn't tell you the truth.

義務

♣ 正式場合

我覺得我有義務不這樣。
I feel it is my duty not to.

我覺得我有義務不這樣。　　　我覺得我有義務不透露姓名。
I feel it is my duty not to ～. ▸ I feel it is my duty not to reveal the name.

我覺得我不能這樣。
I feel obliged not to.

我覺得我不能這樣。　　　我覺得我不能讓他操勞過度。
I feel obliged not to ～. ▸ I feel obliged not to work him too much.

我有義務不這樣。
I have an obligation not to.

我有義務不這樣。　　　我有義務對此不予置評。
I have an obligation not to ～. ▸ I have an obligation not to comment on it.

我不能。　　　我不能讓她失望。
I'm committed not to ～. ▸ I'm committed not to let her down.

我不能。　　　我不能拒絕他們的建議。
I'm obliged not to ～. ▸ I'm obliged not to reject their proposal.

我不可以這樣。
It would be wrong of me.

我不可以這樣。　　　我不可以欺騙梅勒。
It would be wrong of me to ～. ▸ It would be wrong of me to cheat Mailer.

28 *Offer* 提供

● 提供東西給別人 ●

Ψ 基本說法
🔊 220

你要不要？
Can I get you ～?

你要不要飲料？
▸ Can I get you a drink?

給你好嗎？
Can I give you ～?

給你一件小小的紀念品，好嗎？
▸ Can I give you a small souvenir?

給你好嗎？
Can I offer you ～?

給你一份小小的禮物，好嗎？
▸ Can I offer you a little gift?

請吃點東西。
Help yourself to ～.

請吃點蘋果派。
▸ Help yourself to this apple pie.

這是我的一點小意思。
Here's a little something from me.

這是我的一點心意。
Here's a little token of my affection.

請收下。
Please take it.

這是我的一點小意思，希望你喜歡。
This is a small something for you. I hope you like it.

我能給你弄點什麼？
What can I get you?

你要吃什麼？
What will you have?

如何？
What would you say to ～?

吃塊喉糖如何？
▸ What would you say to a cough sweet?

你怎麼不喝（吃）？
Why don't you have ～?

你怎麼不喝點酒？
▸ Why don't you have some wine?

你要喝一杯嗎？
Will you have a drink?

你不吃嗎？
Won't you have some ～?

你不吃點巧克力嗎？
▸ Won't you have some chocolate?

你想吃嗎？
Would you like some ～?

你想吃點柳丁嗎？
▸ Would you like some oranges?

✿ 日常口語

想來點嗎？
Fancy some ～?

想來點魚子醬嗎？
▸ Fancy some caviar?

來一杯嗎？
A glass of ～?

來一杯酒嗎？
▸ A glass of wine?

你自己拿吧。
Grab yourself ～.

你自己拿些餅乾吧。
▸ Grab yourself some cookies.

抽（吃/喝）。
Have ～.

抽支菸。
▸ Have a cigarette.

怎麼樣？
How about ～?

來杯可口可樂怎麼樣？
▸ How about a Coke?

我有個驚喜要給你。
～, I have a surprise for you.

珍，我有個驚喜要給你。
▸ Jane, I have a surprise for you.

想喝（吃）嗎？
Like ～?

想喝杯啤酒嗎？
▸ Like a beer?

想喝（吃）嗎？
Want ～?

想喝一杯嗎？
▸ Want a cuppa?

要喝（吃）什麼？
What's it to be, ～?

大衛，要喝什麼？
▸ What's it to be, David?

你喝（吃）什麼？
What's yours, ～?

約翰，你喝什麼？
▸ What's yours, John?

♣ 正式場合

請允許我。
Allow me to ～.

請允許我給您再斟上一杯。
▸ Allow me to refill your cup.

給您好嗎？
Could I offer you ～?

給您一些讀物好嗎？
▸ Could I offer you something to read?

請務必吃（喝）。
Do have ～.

請務必吃點蘑菇。
▸ Do have some mushrooms.

我看給您吧。
I suspect you might find ～ helpful.

我看給您來杯飲料吧。
▸ I suspect you might find a drink helpful.

不知我是否可以給您。
I wonder if I might give you ～.

不知我是否可以給您一串項鍊。
▸ I wonder if I might give you a necklace.

如果您接受，我會非常高興。
I'd be much delighted if you would accept ～.

如果您接受這份小禮物，我會非常高興。
▸ I'd be much delighted if you would accept this little present.

去拿給您好嗎？
May I fetch you ～?

再去拿杯飲料給您好嗎？
▸ May I fetch you another drink?

請允許我贈送這個給您，向您聊表謝意。
May I give you this? A small way of saying thank you.

您想喝（吃）嗎？
Would you care for ～?

您想喝可口可樂嗎？
▸ Would you care for a Coke?

● 接受提供的東西 ●

❦ 基本說法

我想這是最好不過的了。
I can think of nothing better.

好的。
I don't mind if I do.

好的。
I wouldn't say no.

如果你願意,我會非常高興。
I'd be so pleased if you would.

好的,我很想要。
I'd like it very much, please.

如果你願意。
If you would, please.

這會非常有用的。
It'll be most useful.

這正是我想要的。
It's exactly what I wanted.

這正好是我一直想要的。
It's just the very thing I have been wanting.

哦,你真是太好了!
Oh, you're just wonderful!

謝謝你。
Thank you.

謝謝你,我要的。
Thank you, I will.

謝謝你,我要的。
Thank you. I would.

非常謝謝你,不過你真的用不著這樣做的。
Thank you so much, but you really shouldn't have done that.

那真是幫了大忙。
That would be a great help.

那太好了。
That would be very nice.

好的。
Yes, please.

🌸 日常口語

好極了。
Great.

我想要一點。
I'd love some.

真是好極了。
It's just lovely.

哦，棒呆了！
Oh, breathtaking!

唔，好的。
Oh, please.

哦，太棒了！
Oh, terrific!

謝謝。
Thanks.

超謝謝你。
Thanks an awful lot.

當然囉。
You bet.

♣ 正式場合

如果你願意，我會非常高興的。
I'd be most delighted if you would.

哦，非常謝謝你。
Oh, that was extremely good of you.

非常感謝你。
Thank you so much.

那太好了。
That'd be most delightful.

非常感謝你。
That's very kind of you.

很高興。
With pleasure.

十分高興。
With the greatest of pleasure.

● 謝絕提供的東西 ●

我還是不要吧，謝謝你。
I'd better not, thank you.

恐怕我不能，不過還是謝謝你。
I'm afraid I can't, but thank you just the same.

不，真的不用了，謝謝你。
No, I really won't, thank you.

不，謝謝你。
No, thank you.

不，謝謝你，我不要。
No, thank you, I won't.

不，非常謝謝你。
No, thank you very much.

我不要，謝謝你。
Not for me, thank you.

✿ 日常口語

不用了，謝謝。
I won't, thanks.

如果對你來說都一樣，我就不要了吧。
If it's all the same to you, I won't.
＊意指如果對方不介意的話，就要拒絕對方的好意。

不，謝謝。
No, thanks.

不，謝謝，這次不要。
No, thanks, not this time.

我不要，謝謝。
Not for me, thanks.

這次不要，謝謝。
Not this time, thanks.

謝謝，不過不用了。
Thanks all the same, but I won't.

正式場合

🔊 228

如果您不介意，我還是不要吧。
I'd prefer not, if you don't mind.

那就不必了。
That won't be necessary.

謝謝您，不過不用了。
That's very kind of you, but I'd prefer not.

● 把東西交給對方 ●

❤ 基本說法

給你。
~ for you.

給你一本書。
▸ A book for you.

這些是你要的東西。
Here are ~ you need.

這些是你要的報告。
▸ Here are the reports you need.

給你。
Here you are.

這是。
Here's ~.

這是蘇珊給你的信。
▸ Here's Susan's letter to you.

我要你收下這個。
I want you to take this.

我想給你。
I'd like to give you ~.

我想給你這枚胸針。
▸ I'd like to give you this brooch.

我希望你收下。
I'd like you to have ~.

我希望你收下這雙鞋。
▸ I'd like you to have this pair of shoes.

請收下。
Please take it.

是給你的。
~ is for you.

這金牌是給你的。
▸ The gold medal is for you.

你要的東西。
~ you need.

你要的電影票。
▸ The movie tickets you need.

這是你要的東西。
This is ~ you asked for.

這是你要的那本書。
▸ This is the book you asked for.

🌸 日常口語 🔊 230

給你。
Here.

拿去吧。
Here you go.

要嗎？
Need ～?

要這水壺嗎？
▸ **Need** the kettle?

這是給你的。
That's for you.

給你。
There.

要嗎？
Want ～?

要這把扳手嗎？
▸ **Want** the spanner?

你的。
Your ～.

你的帽子，傑克。
▸ **Your** cap, Jack.

♣ 正式場合

請容我向您獻上。

請容我向您獻上本公司的一點小小心意，感謝您二十年來的服務。

Allow me to present you with this, ~.

▶ Allow me to present you with this, a small token of the company's appreciation for your twenty years' service.

我很高興向您頒發。

我很高興向您頒發您經過四年研究而取得的碩士證書。

I have great pleasure in presenting you with ~.

▶ I have great pleasure in presenting you with the MA certificate you earn with four years' research.

我謹向您獻上。

我謹向您獻上一點心意，感謝您的幫助。

I'd like to present you with ~.

▶ I'd like to present you with this small token of our appreciation for your help.

我想請您接受。

想請您接受這份小禮，感謝您的合作。

I'd like you to accept ~.

▶ I'd like you to accept this small present as our gratitude for your cooperation.

我很高興向您頒發。

很高興向您頒發您當之無愧的葛萊美獎。

It was with great pleasure that I present you with ~.

▶ It was with great pleasure that I present you with this Grammy Award you fully deserve.

請收下這個，就當作是紀念。

請收下這個，就當是紀念我們的友誼。

Please accept this as a souvenir for ~.

▶ Please accept this as a souvenir for our friendship.

● 提議幫對方做事 ●

我能幫忙嗎？
Can I be of help?

我幫你好嗎？
Can I give you a hand with ～?　▸ Can I give you a hand with the dishes?

我可以幫忙嗎？
Can I help?
我可以幫你嗎？
Can I help you?
我可以幫你嗎？
Can I help you with ～?　我可以幫你做這件事嗎？
▸ Can I help you with that?

如果你願意，我可以。
If you like, I could ～.　如果你願意，我可以為你做一套衣服。
▸ If you like, I could make you a suit.

如果你要的話，我可以。
If you want, I could ～.　如果你要的話，我可以幫你把它加熱。
▸ If you want, I could heat it up for you.

我會替你帶來。
I'll bring you ～.　我會替你帶一些花來。
▸ I'll bring you some flowers.

我幫你。
I'll give you a hand with ～.　我幫你洗碗盤。
▸ I'll give you a hand with the dishes.

我能幫你什麼忙嗎？
Is there anything I can do for you?

我能不能做點什麼？
Is there anything I can do to ～?　打掃房間時我能不能做點什麼？
▸ Is there anything I can do to clean the room?

355

讓我幫你。
Let me ～ for you.

讓我幫你完成。
▸ Let me do it for you.

我來幫你。
Let me help you (to) ～.

我來幫你打掃房間。
▸ Let me help you (to) clean the room.

要是我能幫忙就告訴我。
Let me know if I can help.

我幫你好嗎？
Shall I help you ～?

我幫你鋪床好嗎？
▸ Shall I help you make the bed?

我這樣做好嗎？
Shall I ～?

我開車送你回去好嗎？
▸ Shall I run you back in the car?

我能幫忙做點什麼？
What can I do to help?
我能幫忙做點什麼嗎？
What can I do to help ～?

準備晚餐時我能幫忙做點什麼嗎？
▸ What can I do to help prepare the dinner?

你需要幫忙嗎？
Would you like any help?
需不需要幫忙？
Would you like any help to ～?

需不需要幫忙掃掃地？
▸ Would you like any help to sweep the floor?

你要不要我去做？
Would you like me to ～?

你要不要我去準備一些咖啡？
▸ Would you like me to fix some coffee?

❀ 日常口語

幫你好嗎？
Any point in ～ for you?

我幫你粉刷房間好嗎？
▸ Any point in my painting the room for you?

我能幫忙做點什麼？
Anything I can do to help?

我能幫忙嗎？
Can I help out?

嘿，我來幫你。
Here, I'll ～ for you.

嘿，我來幫你洗。
▸ Here, I'll wash it for you.

嘿，讓我幫你吧。
Here, let me help you.

我幫你做怎麼樣？
How about me ～ for you?

我幫你寫信怎麼樣？
▸ How about me writing the letter for you?

什麼時候你遇到麻煩，就打電話給我。
Just call me whenever you're in trouble.

如果你需要幫助，就告訴我。
Just let me know if you need any help.

要幫忙嗎？
Need a hand, ～?

要幫忙嗎，湯姆？
▸ Need a hand, Tom?

要幫忙嗎？
Need a hand to ～?

要幫忙移開這只箱子嗎？
▸ Need a hand to remove the box?

要幫忙嗎？
Want some help?

要幫忙嗎？
Want some help to ～?

要幫忙推嗎？
▸ Want some help to push it?

你何不讓我幫忙呢？
Why don't you let me help?

看來你需要些幫助。
You look like you could do with some help.

看來你需要人幫忙。
You look like you need some help to ～.

看來你需要人幫忙移動這張桌子。
▸ You look like you need some help to move the table.

♣ 正式場合

讓我來吧。
Allow me.

我是不是可以幫助您？
Am I allowed to help you?

如果我們能有所幫助的話，請即刻告訴我們。
If we can be of any assistance, please do not hesitate to tell us.

我是不是可以幫點忙？
May I be of any assistance?

我可以幫忙嗎？
May I be of any help?

我幫您好嗎？
May I ~ for you?

我幫您拿這只箱子好嗎？
▸ **May I take the case for you?**

我可以幫忙嗎？
Might I help at all?

也許我能有所幫助？
Perhaps I could assist in some way?

● 接受提供的幫助 ●

♈ 基本說法

如果你確定這麼做不麻煩的話。
If you're sure it's no trouble for you to do it.

好，（需要幫忙的話）我會告訴你的。
OK, I will.

你真好，謝謝你。
That's nice of you, thank you.

那太好了。
That's very kind.

你真是太好了，謝謝你。
That's very kind of you, thank you.

好的，我真希望如此。
Yes, I hope so.

好的。
Yes, please.

好的，如果不會太麻煩的話。
Yes, please, if it's not too much trouble.

好的，如果你確定不會麻煩的話。
Yes, please, if you're sure it's no trouble for you.

🌸 日常口語

噢耶！
Cheers!

太棒了！
Great!

我正需要呢！
Just what I needed!

我正需要你幫忙呢！
Just what I needed to have your help!

太好了！
Lovely!

哦，你肯幫忙？謝啦。
Oh, would you? Thanks.

謝啦。
Thanks.

你幫了我一個大忙。多謝了。
That'd be a big help. Thanks a lot.

♣ 正式場合

237

如果您能幫助我，我會非常高興。
I'd be most delighted if you could help me.

我很高興得到您的幫助。
I'd be most delighted to have your help.

我會非常感激您的幫助。
I'd be most grateful for your help.

謝謝您。我很感激。
Thank you. I'd appreciate it.

真是太感謝您了。
That's extremely good of you to ~.

您幫我收拾這些桌子，真是太感謝了。
▶ That's extremely good of you to help me clear the tables.

您想得真周到。
You are most thoughtful.

● 謝絕提供的幫助 ●

我想不必了，謝謝你。
I don't think so, thank you.

不，不用費心了。我自己做得到。
No, don't bother. I can do it myself.

不，不用費心了，真的。
No, don't bother, really.

不，沒關係，我做得到。
No, it's all right, I can manage.

不，沒關係，真的。
No, it's all right, really.

暫時還不用，謝謝你。
Not at the moment, thank you.

請不用費心了。
Please don't bother.

請不必為這件事費心。
Please don't bother about it.

感謝你的提議。
Thank you for offering.

非常感謝，不過…。　　　　　　非常感謝，不過我在等我太太來。
That's very kind of you, but ～. ▸ That's very kind of you, but I'm
　　　　　　　　　　　　　　　　expecting my wife.

❀ 日常口語

不用擔心。我能應付。
Don't worry. I can handle it.

這主意很好，但我可以…。　　這主意很好，但我可在回家的路上寄出。
Nice thought, but I can ~.　▸ Nice thought, but I can post it on my way home.

不，不用擔心。
No, don't worry.

不，沒關係。不用為我擔心。
No, it's all right. Don't worry about me.

不，沒關係；這事不用擔心。
No, it's OK; don't worry about that.

不，沒關係，謝謝。
No, it's all right, thanks.

不，沒關係，謝謝。
No, it's OK, thanks.

不，謝謝。我沒問題。
No, thanks. It's OK with me.

多謝，不過我還OK。
Thanks a lot, but I'm OK.

♣ 正式場合

恐怕我不能接受您的好意。
I'm afraid I can't accept your kindness to help.

恐怕我沒有立場接受您的幫助。
I'm afraid I'm not in a position to accept your offer of help.

我很感激您的好意，但我相信
… 。

I'm most grateful for your offer.
But I believe ～.

我很感激您的好意，但是我相信我兒子
會來接我的。

I'm most grateful for your offer. But I
believe my son will come to fetch me.

謝謝您的好意，不過我可以。

It's extremely kind of you to
offer, but I can ～.

謝謝您的好意，不過我可以叫計程車。

▸ It's extremely kind of you to offer,
but I can call a taxi.

請不用費心了。
Please don't trouble.
請不要為此費心。
Please don't trouble about it.
請您不要為此費心。
Please don't trouble yourself about it.

您想得真周到，不過我想我能應付。
That's most thoughtful of you, but I think I can manage.

29 *Opinion* 意見

● 徵求對方的意見 ●

🌱 基本說法

🔊 241

你覺得怎麼樣？
How do you like ～?
你覺得在這裡工作怎麼樣？
▸ How do you like working here?

你覺得怎麼樣？
What are your feelings about ～?
你覺得在德國的生活怎麼樣？
▸ What are your feelings about life in Germany?

你有什麼看法？
What are your views on ～?
你對形勢有什麼看法？
▸ What are your views on the situation?

你覺得怎麼樣？
What do you feel about ～?
你覺得在這裡工作怎麼樣？
▸ What do you feel about working here?

你覺得如何？
What do you think about ～?
你覺得波特的演講如何？
▸ What do you think about Potter's lecture?

你覺得怎麼樣？
What do you think of ～?
你覺得你的新工作怎麼樣？
▸ What do you think of your new job?

你有什麼看法？
What's your opinion of ～?
你對你的鄰居有什麼看法？
▸ What's your opinion of your neighbors?

你持什麼觀點？
What's your stand on ～?
你對這次事件持什麼觀點？
▸ What's your stand on the event?

你有什麼見解？
What's your view?

✿ 日常口語 🔊 242

如何？
How about ～?

那個如何？
▸ How about that?

你覺得如何？
How do you feel about ～?

在電視上接受採訪你覺得如何？
▸ How do you feel about being interviewed on TV?

你覺得怎麼樣？
How do you find things over ～?

你覺得這筆買賣怎麼樣？
▸ How do you find things over the bargain?

你對這類事件有何看法？
How do you see things like this?

我覺得不怎麼樣，你呢？
I don't think much of ～, do you?

我覺得當一個上班族不怎麼樣，你呢？
▸ I don't think much of being an office worker, do you?

你覺得不錯吧？
That all right with you, ～?

你覺得不錯吧，海倫？
▸ That all right with you, Helen?

很討厭的，不是嗎？
～ are pretty awful, aren't they?

增加稅收是很討厭的，不是嗎？
▸ The tax increases are awful, aren't they?

怎麼樣？
What about ～?

他的新發明怎麼樣？
▸ What about his new invention?

你怎麼看？
What do you make of ～?

這個你怎麼看？
▸ What do you make of it?

你有何看法？
What do you reckon about ～?

你對物價上漲有何看法？
▸ What do you reckon about price increases?

你說怎麼樣？
What do you say?

♣ 正式場合

請問你對此有何看法？
Could I have your opinion on ～?
▸ 請問你對該公司的名聲有何看法？
Could I have your opinion on the company's reputation?

我能不能知道你的看法？
Could I know your standpoint on ～?
▸ 我能否知道你對最近一次竊案的看法？
Could I know your standpoint on the recent burglary?

你有什麼評論嗎？
Do you have any comments on ～?
▸ 你對這節目有什麼評論嗎？
Do you have any comments on this program?

你有什麼意見嗎？
Do you have any opinion on ～?
▸ 你對我的法國之旅有什麼意見嗎？
Do you have any opinion on my trip in France?

你有什麼特殊的見解？
Do you have any particular views on ～?
▸ 對該公司的財務危機你有何特殊見解？
Do you have any particular views on the company's financial disaster?

你認為這有什麼好處嗎？
Do you see any advantage of ～?
▸ 你認為接受它有什麼好處嗎？
Do you see any advantage of accepting it?

你對此有何反應？
How would you react to ～?
▸ 你對提出抗議有何反應？
How would you react to putting up a protest?

我很高興聽聽你對此的見解。
I'd be grateful to have your view on ～.
▸ 我很高興聽聽你對這次事件的見解。
I'd be grateful to have your view on the event.

我想知道你的看法。
I'd like to have your opinion on ～.

　　我想知道你對1995世博的看法。
▸ I'd like to have your opinion on the 1995 world Expo.

能否請教你的反應？
May I know your reaction to ～? ▸

　　能否請教你對喬丹先生的政策的反應？
May I know your reaction to Mr. Jordan's policy?

你有什麼看法？
What is your position on ～?

　　你對他的反對有什麼看法？
▸ What is your position on his opposition?

你說怎麼樣？
What would you say to ～?

　　和陌生人同住一間房，你說怎麼樣？
▸ What would you say to sharing your bedroom with a stranger?

● 表示自己的意見 ●

🌱 基本說法

244

就我來說，我認為。
As far as I'm concerned, I think ～.

▸ 就我來說，我認為運動對你有好處。
As far as I'm concerned, I think sport is good for you.

在我看來。

As I see it, ～.

▸ 在我看來，與人們接觸在現代生活中是很重要的。
As I see it, meeting people is very important in modern life.

你不同意嗎？
Don't you agree (that) ～?

▸ 你不同意這很可能是世界上最好的嗎？
Don't you agree (that) it's probably the best in the world?

你不認為嗎？
Don't you think ～?

▸ 你不認為開快車很危險嗎？
Don't you think driving fast is dangerous?

依我看。
From my point of view, ～.

▸ 依我看，世界上沒有十全十美的東西。
From my point of view, nothing in this world is perfect.

我不禁認為。
I can't help thinking (that) ～.

▸ 我不禁認為教育應向大眾開放。
I can't help thinking (that) education should be free for all.

我認為。
I think ～.

▸ 我認為電視上暴力太多。
I think there's too much violence on TV.

我真想說。
I'd just like to say ～.

▸ 我真想說年輕人太自由了。
I'd just like to say young people have too much freedom.

依我來看。
In my opinion, ～.

依我來看，這沒什麼了不起。
▸ In my opinion, it doesn't amount to very much.

在我看來。
In my view, ～.

在我看來，我們都有秘密。
▸ In my view, we all have secrets.

看來。
It seems to me (that) ～.

看來他們可以靠畫畫賺得額外收入。
▸ It seems to me (that) they can earn extra money by painting.

我個人認為。
Personally, I believe ～.

我個人認為酗酒仍是一個大問題。
▸ Personally, I believe alcoholism is still a big problem.

我個人覺得。
Personally, I feel ～.

我個人覺得這是基於充分的思考。
▸ Personally, I feel it's based on sound thinking.

我個人認為可以。
Personally, I see it fit to ～.

我個人認為可以邀請他。
▸ Personally, I see it fit to invite him.

我的看法是。
The point is ～.

我的看法是世界正在進步。
▸ The point is the world is improving.

依我看。
To my way of thinking, ～.

依我看，教師薪水不高。
▸ To my way of thinking, teachers are not well paid.

噢，我必須說。
Well, I must say ～.

噢，我必須說電視只是消耗精力的一種消極方式。
▸ Well, I must say television's just a passive way of letting off steam.

噢，顯然⋯。

Well, obviously ～.

噢，顯然他不應該把它賣掉。

▸ Well, obviously he shouldn't have sold it.

實際的情況是⋯。

What's really happening is (that) ～.

實際的情況是湯姆愛上珍妮。

▸ What's really happening is (that) Tom falls in love with Jenny.

你不認為嗎？

Wouldn't you say (that) ～?

你不認為女人的職責是在家庭嗎？

▸ Wouldn't you say (that) a woman's place is at home?

❀ 日常口語
245

依我看來。
From where I stand, ～.

依我看來，了解外語要比講外語容易些。
▸ From where I stand, it is easier to understand a foreign language than to speak it.

我看。
I'd say ～.

我看你現在非常悲觀。
▸ I'd say you're being very pessimistic.

如果你問我，我認為。
If you ask me, I think ～.

如果你問我，我認為那是困難的。
▸ If you ask me, I think it's difficult.

這沒有道理。
It makes no sense.

沒什麼。
Not much.

依我看。
The way I see it, ～.

依我看，那是我們肯定能做的事。
▸ The way I see it, that's something we definitely could do.

依我看來。
To my mind, ～.

依我看來，慢跑對健康有益。
▸ To my mind, jogging is good for health.

我所想的是。
What I reckon is, ～.

我所想的是，她不太可能會來。
▸ What I reckon is, she isn't likely to come.

你知道我怎麼想？我想…。
You know what I think? I think ～.

你知道我怎麼想？我想在街上跑步是不會愉快的。
▸ You know what I think? I think it wouldn't be nice to go running in the streets.

♣ 正式場合

我認為。
I consider ~.

我認為沒人能不受廣告的影響。
▶ I consider nobody can avoid being influenced by advertisement.

我覺得我該這麼說。
I feel I ought to say that ~.

我覺得我該說它們不會污染空氣。
▶ I feel I ought to say that they don't pollute the air.

我認為。
I feel ~.

我認為總得有人做這事。
▶ I feel someone will have to do it.

我認為。

I hold the opinion (that) ~.

我認為我們現在存的錢過了10年或許就毫無價值了。
▶ I hold the opinion (that) money we save now might be worthless in 10 years' time.

我認為。
I maintain (that) ~.

我認為電視對人有很不好的影響。
▶ I maintain (that) TV has a very bad influence on people.

我想指出。
I'd like to point out (that) ~.

我想指出，我以父母為榮。
▶ I'd like to point out (that) I am proud of my parents.

如果我可以這麼說的話。

If I may say so, ~.

如果我可以這麼說的話，這不是可以開玩笑的事。
▶ If I may say so, this is not something to joke about.

我深信。
I'm convinced (that) ~.

我深信每個人都應該要友善。
▶ I'm convinced (that) everyone should be kind.

我的意見是…。
I'm of the opinion (that) ～.

我的意見是道路改善會降低事故發生率。
▸ I'm of the opinion (that) better roads would decrease the accident rate.

我經過深思熟慮的意見是…。

It's my considered opinion (that) ～.

我經過深思熟慮的意見是，工業正使我們越來越富裕。
▸ It's my considered opinion (that) industry is making us wealthier.

我的看法是…。

It's my feeling (that) ～.

我的看法是，通貨膨脹是對生活水平的一大威脅。
▸ It's my feeling (that) inflation is a great threat to living standards.

我對這件事的見解是…。
My own view of the matter is ～.

我對這事的見解是，沒人能從中獲利。
▸ My own view of the matter is nobody can make any profit out of it.

我對這問題的態度是…。
My position on this problem is (that) ～.

我對這問題的態度是我們不能坐視不管。
▸ My position on this problem is (that) we can't just sit by.

我個人認為。
Personally, I consider ～.

我個人認為他可以有自己的主張。
▸ Personally, I consider he's entitled to his own opinion.

坦白說。
To be quite frank, ～.

坦白說，人人都只對流行音樂感興趣。
▸ To be quite frank, nobody's interested in anything but pop music.

老實說吧。
To be perfectly honest, ～.

老實說吧，污染在現代是不可避免的。
▸ To be perfectly honest, pollution is unavoidable in modern times.

據我所知。
To my knowledge, ～.

據我所知，他們已削減了開支。
▸ To my knowledge, they have cut down on expenses.

● 表示自己沒有意見 ●

❤ 基本說法

247

恐怕我說不上來。
I couldn't say, I'm afraid.

我說不上來，這恐怕不是我能了解的。
I couldn't say, I'm afraid it's beyond me.

對此我的確沒有什麼可說的。
I really don't have anything to say about ~.
▸ 對他們的建議，我的確沒什麼可說的。
I really don't have anything to say about their suggestion.

我的確沒有什麼意見。
I really don't have any opinion about ~.
▸ 我的確對此沒有什麼意見。
I really don't have any opinion about that.

我的確不知道說什麼。
I really don't know what to say.

恐怕這其實跟我沒有太大關係。
It doesn't really affect me, I'm afraid.

恐怕這對我來說確實無關緊要。
It doesn't really matter to me, I'm afraid.

沒有什麼可說的。
I have nothing to say about ~.
▸ 我對這次事件沒有什麼可說的。
I have nothing to say about the event.

我不知道。
I don't know.

這對我沒啥差別。
It makes no odds to me.
這對我沒啥差別。 　　　　到哪裡去我都沒啥差別。
It makes no odds to me ～. ▸ It makes no odds to me where to go.

我跟你一樣不清楚。
Your guess is as good as mine.

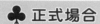

♣ 正式場合

我說不上有什麼特殊的見解。
I can't say I have any particular views on ～.

▸ 對這問題我說不上有什麼特殊的見解。
I can't say I have any particular views on the question.

我並不持有任何特殊立場。
I don't hold any particular position on ～.

▸ 對那項工程我並不持有任何特殊立場。
I don't hold any particular position on that project.

恐怕這事我考慮得不多。
It is not something I've considered a great deal, I'm afraid.

● 避免直接發表意見 ●

你這樣認為嗎？
Do you think so?

我還沒有明確的想法。
I can't say anything definite yet.

我想這要看你的觀點了。
I suppose it depends on your point of view.

我得好好想想。
I'd have to think about it.

對此我寧願不發表任何意見。
I'd prefer not to say anything about ～.

對他遇到的麻煩我寧願不發表任何意見。
▶ I'd prefer not to say anything about his trouble.

對此我寧願不發表任何意見。
I'd rather not say anything about ～.

對此我寧願不發表任何意見。
▶ I'd rather not say anything about that.

關於此事我得去問…。
I'll have to ask ～ about that.

關於此事我得去問我的同事。
▶ I'll have to ask my colleagues about that.

很抱歉我無法回答這個問題。
I'm sorry I can't answer the question.

是嗎？
Is it?

很難說。
It's difficult to say.

很難說 ～。
It's hard to say ～.

很難說她的女兒是否該移民到義大利。
▶ It's hard to say if her daughter should immigrate into Italy.

不予置評。
No comment.

真的嗎？
Really?

這該由你來說了。
That'll be for you to decide.

這不是我能說的。
That's more than what I can say.

這是個有趣的想法，不過這不是我說了就算數。
That's an interesting idea, but it's not for me to say.

你最好問…那個問題，而不是問我。
You'd better ask ～ that question, not me.

你最好問董事會那個問題，而不是問我。
▶ You'd better ask the board that question, not me.

🌸 日常口語

說不上來，真的。
Can't say, really.

可能是吧。
Could be.

我不想說什麼。
I'm not saying.

要看情形了。
It all depends.

恐怕這不是我能知道的。
Not my department, I'm afraid.

也許。
Perhaps.

我回答不了！
Search me!

這是你的意見，是嗎？
That's your opinion, is it?

噢，我真的不知道。
Well, I don't know really.

噢，我不知道。
Well, I don't know ~.

噢，我不知道他會怎麼樣。
▶ Well, I don't know what'll become of him.

噢，這倒是個難題。
Well, now you're asking.

噢，這問題可把我難倒了。
Well, that's a good question.

♣ 正式場合

此刻我無法回答這個問題。
I can't give the answer to that at the moment.

我想我無話可說。
I don't think I have anything to say on ~.

▶

我想對他的舉止我無話可說。
I don't think I have anything to say on his manners.

如果您不介意，我倒希望不發表意見。
I'd rather not commit myself on ~, if you don't mind.

▶

如果您不介意，我倒希望不對此事發表意見。
I'd rather not commit myself on that, if you don't mind.

恐怕我不能加以評論。
I'm afraid I can't comment on ~.

▶

恐怕我不能對此問題加以評論。
I'm afraid I can't comment on the issue.

恐怕這事您得問…。
I'm afraid you'd have to ask ~ about that.

▶

恐怕這事您得問多布森先生。
I'm afraid you'd have to ask Mr. Dobson about that.

我無法發表任何意見。
I'm not in a position to say anything about ~.

▶

我無法就這次罷工發表任何意見。
I'm not in a position to say anything about the strike.

很抱歉，我無法評判。
I'm sorry I'm no judge of ~.

▶

很抱歉，對最近發生的事我無法評判。
I'm sorry I'm no judge of the recent happenings.

很難立即發表意見。
It's difficult to give an opinion right away.

● 設法改變對方的意見 ●

❧ 基本說法

但是你不認為嗎？ **But don't you think ～?**	但是你不認為他很快會恢復健康嗎？ ▸ But don't you think he'll recover soon?
我想這在一定程度上是對的，但是…。 **I guess that's partly true, but ～.**	我想這在一定程度上是對的，但是輿論可能會變。 ▸ I guess that's partly true, but public opinion may change.
我想你可以這麼說，但是…。 **I guess you could say that, but ～.**	我想你可以這麼說，但誰也不准超速。 ▸ I guess you could say that, but nobody is allowed to pass the speed limit.
我明白你的意思，不過…。 **I see what you mean, but ～.**	我明白你的意思，不過他的粗心大意可能沒那麼嚴重。 ▸ I see what you mean, but his carelessness may not be so serious.
我不確定你是否同意，不過…。 **I'm not sure if you agree, but ～.**	我不確定你是否同意，不過電腦正在改變我們的生活。 ▸ I'm not sure if you agree, but computers are changing our life.
也許吧，但是你不認為嗎？ **May be, but don't you think (that) ～?**	也許吧，但你不認為這種藥有副作用嗎？ ▸ May be, but don't you think (that) the medicine has side effects?
當然不是，我是說…。 **Surely not, I mean ～.**	當然不是，我是說多數謀殺都有計劃。 ▸ Surely not, I mean most murders are planned.

這或多或少是對的，不過⋯。

That's more or less true, but ～. ▸

這或多或少是對的，但我們可做廣告。

That's more or less true, but we can put up an advertisement.

不錯，你的話有點道理，但是⋯？

Well, you have a point there, but ～?

不錯，你的話有點道理，但是誰應對這次失竊負責呢？

▸ Well, you have a point there, but who's responsible for the theft?

是的，不過從另一方面看。

Yes, but another way of looking at it would be (that) ～. ▸

是的，不過從另一方面看，你也可能還來不及享受你的積蓄就一命嗚呼了。

Yes, but another way of looking at it would be (that) you might die before you can enjoy your savings.

是的，但是你真的認為嗎？

Yes, but do you really think ～? ▸

是的，但是你真的認為你買得起嗎？

Yes, but do you really think you can afford it?

是的，但是會不會如此呢？

Yes, but is it possible (that) ～? ▸

是的，但是你的女朋友會不會因為你抽菸而離開你呢？

Yes, but is it possible (that) your girl friend leaves you because you smoke?

是的，但是這不也是事實嗎？

Yes, but isn't it also true (that) ～?

是的，但是顧客不喜歡付高價，這不也是事實嗎？

▸ Yes, but isn't it also true (that) customers do not like to pay such high prices?

是的，但另一方面。

Yes, but on the other hand ～. ▸

是的，但另一方面，出口也可能下跌。

Yes, but on the other hand exports might fall.

是的，但是顯然你不相信。

Yes, but surely you don't believe ～.

是的，但是顯然你不相信男人比女人更常生病。

▸ Yes, but surely you don't believe men are ill more often than women.

是的，但是你沒有抓住重點。

Yes, but you didn't get the main point, ～.

是的，但是你沒有抓住重點，他們的產品都過時了。

▸ Yes, but you didn't get the main point, their products are out of date.

是的，這很正確，但是…。
Yes, that's quite true, but ～.

是的，這很正確，但是人人都有權投票。

▸ Yes, that's quite true, but everybody has the right to vote.

🌸 日常口語

你是開玩笑嗎？
Are you kidding?

但是你從這方面來看。
But look at it like this, ～.

但你從這方面來看，老闆也有許多難題。
▸ But look at it like this, a boss also has a lot of problems.

等一下。那麼說還為時過早呢。
Hang on. It's too early to say that yet.

不，但是你看，他並非那麼一無是處。
No, but look, he wasn't that worthless.

哦，得了吧。
Oh, come on. ～.

哦，得了吧。他實際上並沒那麼糟。
▸ Oh, come on. He wasn't so bad actually.

嗯，你這樣想想看。

Well, think of it this way, ～.

嗯，你這樣想想看，富人不一定比窮人更加幸福。

▸ Well, think of it this way, rich people may not be happier than poor people.

你當然不會是這個意思吧？
You can't mean that, surely?

你真的不認為嗎？
You don't really think ～?

你真的不認為多數人都是善良的嗎？
▸ You don't really think most people are good?

♣ 正式場合 🔊 255

但是如果我們從另一方面考慮。 **But if we look at it in another light, ～.**	但是如果我們從另一方面考慮,企業管理也並不容易。 ▸ But if we look at it in another light, business management is not easy.
但是從另一角度看,你也可以說。 **But seen from another angle, one might say ～.**	但是從另一角度看,你也可以說學習英語很費時。 ▸ But seen from another angle, one might say learning English takes time.
但是還有其他因素要考慮。例如…。 **But there are other considerations. For example, ～.**	但是還有其他因素要考慮。例如,地底下只有這麼多石油。 ▸ But there are other considerations. For example, there is only so much oil in the earth.
當然我尊重你的意見。但…。 **I respect your opinion, of course. However, ～.**	當然我尊重你的意見。但權力使人腐化。 ▸ I respect your opinion, of course. However, power tends to corrupt.
考慮到…,我不知道這觀點是否還正確。 **I wonder if that view is justified in the light of ～.**	考慮到可能到來的暴風雪,我不知道這觀點是否還正確。 ▸ I wonder if that view is justified in the light of a possible snowstorm.
我不知道你是否把一切都考慮進去了。例如…。 **I wonder if you have taken everything into consideration. For instance, ～.**	我不知道你是否把一切都考慮進去了。例如壞天氣對飛行員就是棘手的問題。 ▸ I wonder if you have taken everything into consideration. For instance, bad weather is a problem for pilots.

顯然你不認為可以…。 **Surely you don't think it's possible to ～.**	顯然你不認為可以忽略那一點。 ▸ Surely you don't think it's possible to overlook that point.
毫無疑問，但是…？ **There's no doubt whatsoever, but ～?**	毫無疑問，但是誰願意貫徹執行呢？ ▸ There's no doubt whatsoever, but who would be willing to carry it out?
噢，我認為別人可能會說…。 **Well, I think others might say ～.**	噢，我認為別人可能會說一個家庭有許多項支出。 ▸ Well, I think others might say a family has a lot of expenses.
是的，但是如果我們從全局來看。 **Yes, but if we look at the whole picture, ～.**	是的，但是如果我們從全局來看，形勢未必如此激勵人心。 ▸ Yes, but if we look at the whole picture, the situation may not be so encouraging.

30 *Permission* 許可

● 請求許可 ●

❦ 基本說法

🔊 256

大家不反對吧？
Anybody mind if I ～?

我擔任這個職務大家不反對吧？
▸ Anybody mind if I take the position?

我可以嗎？
Can I ～, please?

我可以看看嗎？
▸ Can I have a look at it, please?

我可以嗎？
Could I ～?

我可以把窗戶打開嗎？
▸ Could I open the window?

你不介意吧？
Do you mind if I ～?

我把燈關掉你不介意吧？
▸ Do you mind if I turn off the light?

你看我可以嗎？
Do you think I could ～?

你看我可以見見這位電影明星嗎？
▸ Do you think I could meet the movie star?

我可以嗎？
I can ～, can't I?

我拿這個可以嗎？
▸ I can have this one, can't I?

我想我要。
I thought I'd ～.

我想我要用這本辭典。
▸ I thought I'd use the dictionary.

我在想不知道可不可以。
I was wondering if I could ～.

我在想不知道可不可以和她見面。
▸ I was wondering if I could meet her.

不知道我是否可以？
I wonder whether I could possibly ～?

不知道我是否可以把它拿走？
▸ I wonder whether I could possibly take it away?

389

如果可以，我想。
I'll ~ if I may.

如果可以，我想把我的名字寫在上面。
▸ I'll put my name on it if I may.

我們能不能？
Is there any way we could ~?

我們能不能在這裡露營？
▸ Is there any way we could camp here?

我們能不能？
What are our chances of ~?

我們能不能觀看你們排練？
▸ What are our chances of sitting in on your rehearsal?

你允許我這樣做嗎？
Will you allow me to ~?

你允許我把車停在這兒嗎？
▸ Will you allow me to park here?

讓我這樣做，好嗎？
Will you let me ~?

讓我現在就辦理登記手續，好嗎？
▸ Will you let me check in now?

我這樣做可以嗎？
Would it be all right if I ~?

我坐在這裡可以嗎？
▸ Would it be all right if I sit here?

可以嗎？
Would it be possible to ~?

可以讓我進來嗎？
▸ Would it be possible to let me in?

我這樣做你不介意吧？
Would you mind if I ~?

我在這裡抽菸，你不介意吧？
▸ Would you mind if I smoke here?

你不介意我這樣做吧？
Would you mind my ~?

你不介意我在這裡抽菸吧？
▸ Would you mind my smoking here?

讓我這樣做，好嗎？
You'll let me ~, won't you?

讓我借這本書，好嗎？
▸ You'll let me borrow the book, won't you?

✿ 日常口語

我可以嗎？
All right if I ～?

我可以和洛斯先生說話嗎？
▸ All right if I speak to Mr. Ross?

可以嗎？
All right to ～?

可以和洛斯先生說話嗎？
▸ All right to speak to Mr. Ross?

有可能嗎？
Any chance of ～?

有可能見見這位教授嗎？
▸ Any chance of meeting the professor?

我可以嗎？
Have I got the go-ahead to ～?

我可以把火熄掉嗎？
▸ Have I got the go-ahead to put out the fire?

讓我這樣做，好嗎？
Let me ～, would you?

給我這張照片，好嗎？
▸ Let me have the photo, would you?

你不介意我這樣做吧？
Mind if I ～?

我把這張床搬到樓上去，你不介意吧？
▸ Mind if I move the bed upstairs?

你不介意我這樣做吧？
Mind my ～?

你不介意我把椅子挪開吧？
▸ Mind my moving the chair aside?

我這樣做行嗎？
OK if I ～?

我明天來找你行嗎？
▸ OK if I call on you tomorrow?

行嗎？
OK to ～?

用一下你的電話行嗎？
▸ OK to use your phone?

♣ 正式場合

允許我這樣做嗎？
Am I allowed to ～?

允許我提一個建議嗎？
▸ Am I allowed to make a suggestion?

我可以得到您的允許嗎？
Do I have your permission?
您允許我這樣做嗎？
Do I have your permission to ～?

您允許我在這裡讀書嗎？
▸ Do I have your permission to study here?

您反對嗎？
Do you have any objection?
我這樣做您反對嗎？
Do you have any objection if I ～?

我休假一天，您反對嗎？
▸ Do you have any objection if I have a day off?

我這樣做您反對嗎？
Do you have any objection to my ～?

我休假一天，您反對嗎？
▸ Do you have any objection to my having a day off?

我希望您不介意，我可以這樣做嗎？
I hope you don't mind, but wouldn't it be possible for me to ～?

我希望您不介意，我可以在這裡打報告嗎？
▸ I hope you don't mind, but wouldn't it be possible for me to type a report here?

我希望您不介意我這樣做。
I hope you don't mind my ～.

我希望您不介意我在這裡吃午餐。
▸ I hope you don't mind my eating lunch here.

如果允許的話，我想這樣做。
I should like to ～, if I may.

如果允許的話，我想在這裡打個電話。
▸ I should like to make a phone call here, if I may.

如果您不反對，我想這樣做。
I should like to ～, if you don't see any objection. ▸ 如果您不反對，我想在這裡畫圖。
I should like to draw pictures here , if you don't see any objection.

如果您不反對，我想這樣做。
I should like to ～, if you don't have any objection. ▸ 如果您不反對的話，我想在這裡拍照。
I should like to take pictures here, if you don't have any objection.

如果您允許，我想這樣做。
I should like to ～, if you'll allow me. ▸ 如果您允許，我想在這裡休息一下。
I should like to take a rest here, if you'll allow me.

可以嗎？
Is it possible to ～? ▸ 可以半價買您的汽車嗎？
Is it possible to buy your car at half price?

有人反對嗎？
Is there any objection if ～? ▸ 我們現在離開，有人反對嗎？
Is there any objection if we leave now?

可以嗎？
May I ～? ▸ 借用一下你的筆可以嗎？
May I borrow your pen?

我們想獲得許可這樣做。
We'd like permission to ～. ▸ 我們想獲得許可在義大利再住一個月。
We'd like permission to stay in Italy for another month.

如果您允許，我想這樣做。
With your permission, I should like to ～. ▸ 如果您允許，我想申請轉學。
With your permission, I should like to put in for a transfer.

允許我這樣做嗎？
Would I be allowed to ～? ▸ 允許我宣佈選舉結果嗎？
Would I be allowed to declare the result of the election?

我能這樣做嗎？
Would I be in a position to ～? ▸ 我能對此發表意見嗎？
Would I be in a position to express my opinion on this?

● 給予許可 ●

❤ 基本說法

如你所願。
As you wish.

當然可以。
By all means, ～.　　　　　　當然可以，拿去吧。
▸ By all means, do take it.

我不在乎，就隨你了。
I don't mind, just as you like.

我不介意你這樣做。
I don't mind your ～.　　　　　我不介意你開收音機。
▸ I don't mind your turning on the radio.

如果你願意。
If you like.

一點兒也不。請吧。
Not at all. Please do.

當然可以。
Of course.

當然不反對。
Of course not.

是的，你當然可以。
Yes, certainly you can.

是的，我想可以。
Yes, I guess so.

歡迎你這樣做。
You're welcome to ～.　　　　歡迎你使用電話。
▸ You're welcome to use the phone.

394

行。
All right.

隨你怎麼樣都行！
Anything goes!

隨你便。
Feel free.

隨你去做。
Feel free to do that.

好啊。
Fine.

去吧！（或：說吧！）
Go ahead!

去吧！你想做什麼就做什麼。
Go ahead and do what you like.

你當然可以。 　　　　　你要秤一下當然可以。
It's OK if you ~. ▸ It's OK if you weigh it.

沒有什麼不可以的。
No reason why not.

你沒有什麼不應該的。
No reason why you shouldn't.
你沒有理由不這樣做。 　　　你沒有理由不娶她。
No reason why you shouldn't ~. ▸ No reason why you shouldn't marry her.

行！
OK by me!

隨你便。
Suit yourself.

當然可以。
Sure.

當然可以。
Sure can.

沒有關係。
That's all right.

好啊。
That's fine.

沒問題。
That's OK.

當然！
To be sure!

是的，你當然可以。
Yes, of course you can.

是的，你當然可以這樣做。 是的，你當然可以換。
Yes, of course you can ～. ▶ Yes, of course you can change it.

好啊，有何不可？
Yes, why not?

你就這麼做吧。
You do just that.

♣ 正式場合

我認為沒什麼好反對。
I can see no objection to ~.

▸ 我認為你的請求沒什麼好反對。
I can see no objection to what you asked for.

我認為沒什麼不可以。
I can't see any reason why you shouldn't ~.

▸ 你申請出國留學我認為沒什麼不可以。
I can't see any reason why you shouldn't apply to study abroad.

我不覺得有什麼不可以。
I don't find any objection to ~.

▸ 我不覺得你來聽課有什麼不可以。
I don't find any objection to your attending the lecture.

這似乎完全可以接受。
That seems perfectly acceptable.

這很妥當。
That's quite in order.

似乎無可非議。
There seems to be no objection to ~.

▸ 你要接受邀請似乎無可非議。
There seems to be no objection to your accepting the invitation.

似乎沒什麼不可以。
There seems to be no reason why you shouldn't ~.

▸ 你要把它剪短似乎沒什麼不可以。
There seems to be no reason why you shouldn't cut it short.

是的，你真的可以。
Yes, indeed you may ~.

▸ 是的，你真的可以留著它。
Yes, indeed you may keep it.

你想要的話，可以。
You may ~, if you like.

▸ 你想要的話，可以抽菸。
You may smoke, if you like.

● 拒絕許可 ●

❦ 基本說法

262

我真的不認為你該這麼做。
I don't really think you should ~.

我真的不認為你該收下這個禮物。
▸ I don't really think you should take this gift.

我寧願你不這樣做。
I'd rather you didn't.

恐怕我不能答應你。
I'm afraid I can't let you.
恐怕我不能讓你這樣做。
I'm afraid I can't let you ~.

恐怕我不能讓你駕駛這輛卡車。
▸ I'm afraid I can't let you drive the truck.

恐怕你不能這樣做。
I'm afraid it's not possible for you to ~.

恐怕你不能接管這項工作。
▸ I'm afraid it's not possible for you to take over the job.

恐怕這真的不行。
I'm afraid that's not really possible.

恐怕你不能這樣做。
I'm afraid you can't ~.

恐怕你不能單獨去那裡。
▸ I'm afraid you can't go there alone.

對不起，但這是不可能的。
I'm sorry, but that's not possible.

對不起，我不能讓你這樣做。
I'm sorry, I'm not supposed to let you ~.

對不起，我不能讓你參加這次派對。
▸ I'm sorry, I'm not supposed to let you attend the party.

對不起。這是不允許的。
I'm sorry. That's not allowed.

對不起，你不能。
I'm sorry, you can't.
對不起，你們不能這樣做。
I'm sorry, you can't ~.

對不起，你們不能在這裡舉行派對。
▶ I'm sorry, you can't have a party here.

對不起。你不准這樣做。
I'm sorry, you're not allowed to ~.

對不起。你不准在此停車。
▶ I'm sorry, you're not allowed to park your car here.

這是不允許的。
It's not allowed to ~.

隨地吐痰是不允許的。
▶ It's not allowed to spit everywhere.

不，恐怕不行。
No, I'm afraid not.

噢，如果你這麼做，你會…。
Well, if you did that, you'll ~.

噢，如果你這麼做，你會妨礙鄰居的。
▶ Well, if you did that, you'll disturb your neighbors.

你真的不可以這樣做。
You're not really supposed to ~.

你真的不可以把這首歌的音調升高。
▶ You're not really supposed to pitch the song up.

❖ 日常口語

我實在不能。
I can't possibly ~.

我實在不能把我的照相機借給你。
▶ I can't possibly lend you my camera.

我是願意的，但是…。
I'd like to, but ~.

我是願意的，但是我的太太不願意。
▶ I'd like to, but my wife wouldn't.

不，這不行。
No, that's just not on.

不，你不能。
No, you can't.

恐怕不行。
No way, I'm afraid.

當然不可以。
Of course not.

哦，不，這不行。
Oh, no, that will never do.

恐怕不可能。
Out of the question, I'm afraid.

對不起，不可能。
Sorry, no way.

對不起，不可能。
Sorry, out of the question.

對不起，那不行。
Sorry, it's not on.

恐怕不行。
That's not on, I'm afraid.

♣ 正式場合

264

恐怕我不能允許你這樣做。	恐怕我不能允許你打開這個保險箱。
I'm afraid I can't give you permission to ～.	▸ I'm afraid I can't give you permission to open the safe.

這麼做恐怕違反規定。	這麼做恐怕是違反規定的。
I'm afraid it's against the regulations to ～.	▸ I'm afraid it's against the regulations to do that.

恐怕誰都不可以。	恐怕誰也不可以改變他的工作時間。
I'm afraid nobody is allowed to ～.	▸ I'm afraid nobody is allowed to change his working hours.

恐怕我們不能允許。	恐怕我們不能允許此事。
I'm afraid we can't permit ～.	▸ I'm afraid we can't permit that.

恐怕我們無權這樣做。	恐怕我們無權延後日期。
I'm afraid we don't have the authority to ～.	▸ I'm afraid we don't have the authority to postpone the date.

恐怕我們無權讓你這樣做。	恐怕我們無權讓你參加這次競賽。
I'm afraid we don't have the authority to allow you to ～.	▸ I'm afraid we don't have the authority to allow you to enter the competition.

恐怕我不能讓你這樣做。	恐怕我不能讓你辭職。
I'm afraid you can't have my permission to ～.	▸ I'm afraid you can't have my permission to resign.

Persuasion

勸 說

● 設法説服對方 ●

🌱 基本說法

265

你真的確定不能嗎？

Are you really sure you can't ~?

你真的確定不能替我把那個紅色的挑選出來嗎？

▸ Are you really sure you can't pick out the red one for me?

你確定你應該這樣嗎？

Are you sure you ought to ~?

你確定你應該在開車時喝酒嗎？

▸ Are you sure you ought to drink when you're driving?

老實說，你可以…。

Be honest, you'll ~.

老實說，你可以從中賺一大筆錢呢。

▸ Be honest, you'll make a fortune out of it.

但是點點滴滴都有用處的，不是嗎？

But every little helps, doesn't it?

但是值得冒這個險嗎？

But is it worth the risk?

但是假如這樣，那你怎麼想呢？

But supposing ~, what do you think then?

但是假如湯姆愛茱蒂，那你怎麼想呢？

▸ But supposing Tom loves Judy, what do you think then?

但這該怎麼辦呢？

But what about ~?

但要是遇到一場大雨，該怎麼辦呢？

▸ But what about being caught in a heavy rain?

就這麼做吧。
Do ～.

就讓我試試吧。
▸ Do let me have a try.

你看你能這麼做嗎？
Do you think you could ～?

你看你能慢一點嗎？
▸ Do you think you could go a little slower?

我就是不懂，我們為什麼不呢。
I just don't see why we shouldn't ～.

我就是不懂，我們為什麼不試一下呢。
▸ I just don't see why we shouldn't have a try.

我真的認為你還是這樣做好。
I really think you'd do well to ～.

我真的認為你還是為孩子們編個故事好。
▸ I really think you'd do well to make up a story for the children.

這麼做不會有壞處。
It wouldn't hurt to ～.

跟他們交朋友不會有壞處。
▸ It wouldn't hurt to make friends with them.

如果我們不能這麼做，那太可惜了。
It's a pity if we can't ～.

如果我們不能在這點上互相讓步，那太可惜了。
▸ It's a pity if we can't compromise on it.

我從來沒有請求過你任何事情，所以這次拜託了。
I've never asked you anything, so please.

我們還是明智點吧。誰也不會失去什麼。
Let's be sensible. Nobody will lose anything.

哦，我可以向你保證。
Oh, I can assure you I'm ～.

哦，我可以向你保證，我這個工程師有能力作出判斷。
▸ Oh, I can assure you I'm a good enough engineer to judge that.

403

也許你應該這麼做。
Perhaps you should ~.

也許你應該在決定前考慮一下。
▸ Perhaps you should think before you decide.

請讓我這麼做。
Please let me ~.

請讓我把理由告訴你。
▸ Please let me tell you the reason.

別忘了。
Remember ~.

別忘了，目前要找另一個工作並不容易。
▸ Remember it's difficult to get another job at the moment.

想必你打算這麼做。
Surely you're going to ~.

想必你打算讓它那樣了。
▸ Surely you're going to leave it like that.

他們說這可能會⋯。
They say it can be ~.

他們說這可能會很危險。
▸ They say it can be dangerous.

要是那樣怎麼辦呢？
What if ~?

要是樓梯塌下來怎麼辦呢？
▸ What if the stairs collapse?

你何不這麼做呢？
Why don't you ~?

你何不聽從道理呢？
▸ Why don't you listen to reason?

請你讓我這麼做吧？
Won't you ~, please?

請你讓我看一看吧？
▸ Won't you let me have a look, please?

你一定得這麼做。沒有你就不一樣了。
You must ~. It won't be the same without you.

你一定得來參加聚會。你不來，這聚會就不一樣了。
▸ You must come to the party. It won't be the same without you.

你並不想那樣的，是嗎？
You wouldn't like that, would you?

404

你知道，你得這樣做的。
You'll have to ~, you know.

你知道，你得在這上面花許多錢的。
▸ You'll have to spend quite a lot on it, you know.

如果你不這樣，我會不高興的。
You'll hurt my feelings, if you don't ~.

如果你不多吃一點，我會不高興的。
▸ You'll hurt my feelings, if you don't have some more.

你要謹慎而行。
You're taking no chances.

🌸 日常口語

來吧。
Come on, ~.

來吧，露意莎，拿去。
▸ Come on, Louisa, take it.

別這樣！
Don't be like that!

看在老天的份上，別這樣吧。
Don't for goodness' sake.

別忘了這件事。
Don't forget ~.

別忘了，你不會一直在這裡的。
▸ Don't forget you won't be here all the time.

別讓那件事阻止了你！
Don't let that stop you!

來吧！
Go on!

你這樣是行不通的。
It'll get you nowhere.

就為了我吧！
Just for me!

就這一次吧！
Just this once!

就聽我一次吧，好嗎？
Listen to me just once, OK?

就算是為了我也不行嗎？
Not even for me?

哦，得了吧。

Oh come, ~.

哦，得了吧，我的孩子。爭吵一點意思都沒有的。

▸ Oh come, my boy. There's no point in arguing.

哦，得了吧。我敢肯定你不會想這樣的。

Oh, come on, I'm sure you wouldn't like ~.

哦，得了吧。我敢肯定你不會想被解僱而丟掉一份薪水優渥的工作。

▸ Oh, come on, I'm sure you wouldn't like being fired from a well-paid job.

拜託！
Please!

別開玩笑了，拜託。
Seriously, oh come.

你不會讓我失望的，對嗎？
You're not going to let me down. Are you?

♣ 正式場合

你確定不要嗎？
Are you quite sure you won't ～?
▸ Are you quite sure you won't reconsider the proposal?

你確定不重新考慮這個提議了嗎？

你確定一切都考慮過了？
Are you quite sure you've taken everything into consideration?

但這肯定是為了我們自己的利益。
But surely it's in our own interest to ～.
▸ But surely it's in our own interest to change the plan.

但是改變計劃肯定是為了我們自己的利益。

但是你一定明白，這是為了你自己的利益。
But surely you can see (that) it would be in your interest to ～.
▸ But surely you can see (that) it would be in your interest to save money.

但是你一定明白，儲蓄是為了你自己的利益。

我能不能讓你相信？
Can I persuade you (that) ～?
▸ Can I persuade you (that) he is reliable?

我能不能讓你相信他是可靠的？

我不能說服你嗎？
Can't I persuade you to ～?
▸ Can't I persuade you to buy the car?

我不能說服你買這輛車嗎？

你能否聽勸呢？
Could you be persuaded to～?
▸ Could you be persuaded to wait until you get a report on the project?

你能否聽我的勸告，等到拿到企劃的報告書再說？

我要怎樣才能說服你呢？ **How can I persuade you to ～?**	我要怎樣才能說服你接受這個提議呢？ ▸ How can I persuade you to accept the offer?
我的確不這麼認為。 **I don't really think ～.**	我的確不認為這會有效果，因為沒有人對它感興趣。 ▸ I don't really think that would work because nobody is interested in it.
我不是要勸你接受，不過…。 **I don't want to talk you into accepting it, but ～.**	我不是要勸你接受，不過這真的很方便。 ▸ I don't want to talk you into accepting it, but it's really convenient.
我真的不這麼認為，因為…。 **I really don't think so, because ～.**	我真的不這麼認為，因為泰德不誠實。 ▸ I really don't think so, because Ted is not honest.
我真心認為這會很可惜。 **I really think it would be a pity if ～.**	我真心認為如果我們不接受他的勸告會很可惜。 ▸ I really think it would be a pity if we didn't take his advice.
我明白你的意思，但是如果這樣呢？ **I see what you mean, but if ～?**	我明白你的意思，但是如果發生了一件交通事故呢？ ▸ I see what you mean, but if there should be a traffic accident?
哦，是的，但是你沒有抓住重點。 **Oh yes, but you didn't get the main point. ～.**	哦，是的，但是你沒有抓住重點。他們的產品都過時了。 ▸ Oh yes, but you didn't get the main point.Their products are out of date.

最好的辦法無疑是這麼做。
Surely the best course of action would be to ~. ▶

最好的辦法無疑是和你的律師擬定協議。
Surely the best course of action would be to draw up an agreement with your lawyer.

最明智的辦法無疑是這麼做。
Surely the most sensible thing would be to ~. ▶

最明智的辦法無疑是去看醫生。
Surely the most sensible thing would be to consult a doctor.

這可能是不錯的，但是我們必須全面考慮。
That might be OK, but we must take everything into account.

這是個好主意，但是…。
That's a good idea, but ~. ▶

這是個好主意，但是這裡的情況不同。
That's a good idea, but things are different here.

這從理論上來說是可以的，但實際上未必行得通。
That's all right in theory, but in practice it may not work.

是沒錯，但是如果…。

是沒錯，但是如果明天下雨的話，我們就只能待在家裡了。

That's true, but if ~. ▶

That's true, but if it rains tomorrow, we can only stay at home.

毫無疑問，但是…？
There's no doubt whatsoever, but ~? ▶

毫無疑問，但是誰願意呢？
There's no doubt whatsoever, but who would be willing to?

你似乎不明白。
What you don't seem to understand is (that) ~.

你似乎不明白法官的決定未必對你有利。
▸ What you don't seem to understand is (that) the judge's decision may not go in your favor.

是的，但是你必須承認。
Yes, but you must admit ~.

是的，但你必須承認他們的能力有限。
▸ Yes, but you must admit there's a limit to what they can do.

你似乎沒有發現到。
You don't seem to realize (that) ~.

你似乎沒有發現到還有更多牽連在裡面。
▸ You don't seem to realize (that) there's more involved.

你是對的，但是你必須瞭解到。
You're right, but you've got to realize (that) ~.

你是對的，但是你必須瞭解到，雞蛋價格在春天通常是下跌的。
▸ You're right, but you've got to realize (that) egg prices usually go down in the spring.

理由

Reason

● 説明理由 ●

☙ 基本說法

🔊 268

因為。 **~ due to ~.**	因為交通繁忙，所有的公車都誤點了。 ▸ All the buses were late **due to** heavy traffic.
因為。 **As ~.**	因為他病了，我們只好取消西湖之旅。 ▸ **As** she is ill, we have to cancel our trip to West Lake.
因為。 **Because of ~.**	因為生病，他只好整天躺在床上。 ▸ **Because of** his illness, he has to stay in bed all day.
但是確實。 **But surely, ~.**	但是確實，汽車仍然很貴。 ▸ **But surely,** cars are still quite expensive.
但是問題是。 **But the point is ~.**	但是問題是大多數公司都賺錢。 ▸ **But the point is** most companies make profits.
以便。 **~ so as to ~.**	他跑得很快以便趕上末班車。 ▸ He ran quickly **so as to** catch the last bus.
所以。 **~, and that's why ~.**	我沒有這卷錄音帶，所以我想拷貝一份。 ▸ I don't have this tape, **and that's why** I'd like to make a copy of it.

這樣就⋯。	我會告訴你發生了什麼事，這樣你就可以自己判斷了。
～ so that ～.	▸ I'll tell you what's happened so that you can judge for yourself.
這是因為。	這是因為我不喜歡固定的工作時間。
It's because ～.	▸ It's because I don't like fixed working hours.
讓我解釋一下。你知道的⋯。	讓我解釋一下。你知道，物價一直在漲。
Let me explain. You see, ～.	▸ Let me explain. You see, the prices are rising all the time.
因為。	因為這場大雨，我們大家渾身都濕透了。
Owing to ～.	▸ Owing to the heavy rain, all of us were soaked to the skin.
原因是。	我缺席的原因是我病了。
The reason for ～ was that ～.	▸ The reason for my absence was that I was ill.
原因是。	原因是許多人喜歡說雙關語。
The reason was that ～.	▸ The reason was that a lot of people like to make puns.
原因是。	他沒買這本書的原因是缺錢。
The reason why ～.	▸ The reason why he didn't buy the book was lack of money.
噢，因為。	噢，因為他不太有經驗。
Well, because ～.	▸ Well, because he's not very experienced.

✿ 日常口語

不過他的確完全正確。
But surely he's dead right: ~.

不過他的確完全正確：這個老師很嚴肅。
▶ But surely he's dead right: the teacher is serious.

說得有道理。你知道的。
sb.'s got a point. You know, ~.

弗雷德說得有道理。你知道的，他得進行一次健康檢查。
▶ Fred's got a point. You know, he has to have a check-up.

我來告訴你為什麼。你知道的。
I'll tell you why. You see, ~.

我來告訴你為什麼。你知道的，鮑勃已經好幾天沒來了。
▶ I'll tell you why. You see, Bob hasn't come for days.

是這樣的，你知道。
It's like this, you see, ~.

是這樣的，你知道，油箱裡沒多少汽油。
▶ It's like this, you see, there isn't much petrol left in the tank.

噢，問題在於⋯。
Well, the thing is, ~.

噢，問題在於檔案遺失了。
▶ Well, the thing is, the file is missing.

♣ 正式場合 🔊 270

由於。
By reason of ～.
▸ 由於年輕這孩子免受處罰。
▸ By reason of his youth the boy escaped punishment.

辯解的理由是。

sb.'s justification for sth. was that ～.
▸ 柯林為自己偷竊辯解的理由是他的家人正在挨餓。
▸ Collin's justification for stealing was that his family were starving.

我相信這麼說是完全有道理的。
I believe sb. is fully justified in saying (that) ～.
▸ 我相信，約翰說通貨膨脹在西方國家十分普遍是完全有道理的。
▸ I believe John is fully justified in saying (that) inflation is common in the West countries.

我想下述理由是對的。
I think sb. is right for the following reason: ～.
▸ 我認為貝蒂的下述理由是對的：看電視便宜，而且不必大老遠到電影院去。
▸ I think Betty is right for the following reason: it's cheap watching TV, and you don't have to go a long way to a cinema.

我認為這證明了⋯。
I think ～ warrants ～.
▸ 我認為這個結果證明了他努力帶動產業改革是對的。
▸ I think the result warrants his effort to bring about changes in industry.

我認為事實上有個很好的理由可說明⋯。
I think there's actually a good case for ～.
▸ 我認為，事實上有個很好的理由可說明減少進口是正確的。
▸ I think there's actually a good case for cutting down on imports.

如果我能解釋的話。

If I could explain: ~.

如果我能解釋的話：用於投資的錢已經花完了。

▶ If I could explain: the money for the investment has run out.

有充分的理由說明…。

sb. has ample justification for sth.

馬汀有充分的理由說明他所做的是對的。

▶ Martin has ample justification for what he did.

由於。

On account of ~.

由於通貨膨脹，貨幣正在貶值。

▶ On account of inflation, money is lowering its value.

這就是我的理由。

~, and that's my reason for ~.

這星期五楊教授要來，而這就是我把會議延後到下星期的理由。

▶ Professor Young is coming this Friday, and that's my reason for postponing our meeting till next week.

根本原因是…。

The basic reason is that ~.

根本原因是很難用外語進行精采的演講。

▶ The basic reason is that it's difficult to give a good speech in a foreign language.

33 Remembrance 記憶

● 你還記得嗎？ ●

❦ 基本說法 🔊 271

你想得起來嗎？ **Can you bring to mind ～?**	你想得起來那孩子的姓名嗎？ ▸ Can you bring to mind the name of the child?
你還記得嗎？ **Can you call up ～?**	你還記得我們一起工作的日子嗎？ ▸ Can you call up the days when we worked together?
你還記得嗎？ **Can you recall ～?**	你還記得你的學生時代嗎？ ▸ Can you recall your schooldays?
你記得嗎？ **Do you remember ～?**	你記得他的名字嗎？ ▸ Do you remember his name?
不知你是否還記得？ **I wonder if you remember ～?**	不知你是否還記得它？ ▸ I wonder if you remember it?
也許你已經忘了？ **Perhaps you've forgot ～?**	也許你已忘了她對你說的那些輕蔑的話？ ▸ Perhaps you've forgot her scornful remarks about you?
你沒有忘記吧，對不對？ **You haven't forgot ～, have you?**	你沒有忘記艾咪吧，對不對？ ▸ You haven't forgot Amy, have you?
你記得，對不對？ **You remember ～, don't you?**	你記得我的名字，對不對？ ▸ You remember my name, don't you?

417

✿ 日常口語 🔊 272

你記不得了？
Can't you remember?

你記不得了嗎？
Can't you remember ～?

你記不得他們什麼時候結婚了嗎？
▸ Can't you remember when they got married?

你想不起那段回憶了嗎？
Can't you summon up the memory of ～?

你想不起你們結婚旅行的回憶了嗎？
▸ Can't you summon up the memory of your wedding trip?

你是不是忘了？
Have you forgot ～?

你是不是忘了你初次探望我父母的事了？
▸ Have you forgot your first visit to my parents?

記得嗎？
Remember ～?

記得我們昨天遇到的那個女孩嗎？
▸ Remember that girl we met yesterday?

你一定還記得吧。
Surely you remember ～.

你一定還記得他是什麼時候走的吧。
▸ Surely you remember when he left.

你不可能忘記吧。
You can't have forgot about ～.

你不可能忘記這麼大一筆債務吧。
▸ You can't have forgot about such a large debt.

你一定記得吧。
You must remember ～.

你一定記得她對我們有多好吧。
▸ You must remember her kindness to us.

♣ 正式場合

請問你記得嗎？	請問你記得他的電話號碼嗎？
Could I ask if you remember ～? ▸	Could I ask if you remember his telephone number?
你也許記得吧？	你也許記得他在會議上提出的建議吧？
Do you by any chance remember ～?	▸ Do you by any chance remember what he suggested at the meeting?
你記得嗎？	你記得他們的售貨條件嗎？
Do you happen to remember ～?	▸ Do you happen to remember their sales terms?
你還想得起來嗎？	那次會議你還想得起來嗎？
Do you have any recall of ～?	▸ Do you have any recall of the meeting?
你想你還沒忘記嗎？	你想你還沒忘記兩個月前遇見她的事嗎？
Do you think you haven't forgot ～?	▸ Do you think you haven't forgot meeting her two months ago?
不知你是否記得？	不知你是否記得，他們是怎麼做的？
I was wondering whether you remember ～?	▸ I was wondering whether you remember how they made it?
我想知道你能否想起。	我想知道你能否想起那次事故的詳情。
I'd like to know if you could recall ～.	▸ I'd like to know if you could recall the details of the accident.
請你告訴我你是否還記得好嗎？	請你告訴我你是否還記得寄信給他的事好嗎？
Would you mind telling me if you still remember ～?	▸ Would you mind telling me if you still remember sending him a letter?

● 我記得 ●

❣ 基本說法
🔊 274

就我所能回想起來的。
As far as I can recollect, ~.

就我所能回想起的，他10點鐘才回家。
▸ As far as I can recollect, he wasn't home until 10 o'clock.

就我所能記得的。
As far as I could remember, ~.

就我所能記得的，他是1960年代芝加哥的市長。
▸ As far as I could remember, he was Mayor of Chicago in the 1960's.

就我所能回想起來的。
As far as I recall, ~.

就我所能回想起來的，那裡本來只種了兩棵樹。
▸ As far as I recall, only two trees were planted there.

我還記得。
I can recall ~.

我還記得這個人的容貌。
▸ I can recall the man's features.

我記得。
I remember ~.

我記得沒有人進過這座城堡。
▸ I remember nobody's ever entered the castle.

我尤其記得。
I remember especially ~.

我尤其記得她研讀歷史的方法。
▸ I remember especially the way she studied history.

我記得很清楚。
I remember quite clearly.
我記得很清楚。
I remember quite clearly ~.

我記得很清楚她當時不在那裡。
▸ I remember quite clearly she was not there at that time.

我會永遠記住的。
I'll always remember.

我會永遠記得。
I'll always remember ~.

我會永遠記得你的忠告。
▶ I'll always remember your advice.

我永遠不會忘記。
I'll never forget.

我永遠不會忘記。
I'll never forget about ~.

我永遠不會忘記此事。
▶ I'll never forget about that.

不，我還沒忘記。
No, I haven't forgot ~.

不，我還沒忘記他的住址。
▶ No, I haven't forgot his address.

讓人回想起。
~ calls up ~.

教堂的鐘聲讓我回想起結婚的那一天。
▶ The church bell calls up my wedding day.

是的，我記得。
Yes, I remember.

🌸 日常口語

現在我想起來了！
I can see it now !

我知道了。
I know: ～.

我知道了：我把我的皮夾放枕頭下了。
▸ I know: I left my wallet under the pillow.

現在我漸漸想起來了。

It's coming back to me now: ～.

現在我漸漸想起來了：門鈴響的時候正是12點半。
▸ It's coming back to me now: it was 12:30 when the doorbell rang.

這件事我正好記在腦海裡。
I've got it right in my mind.

我現在回想起來。

Now I think about it, ～.

我現在回想起來，當我去拜訪她時她正在煮飯。
▸ Now I think about it, she was cooking when I called on her.

我記得。
What I can remember is ～.

我記得當時房裡沒有人。
▸ What I can remember is nobody was in the room at that time.

是的，這仍在我的記憶裡。
Yes, it's still in my mind.

♣ 正式場合

就我所記得的。

As I can recall, ～.

就我所記得的，亞力克西斯先生當時負責這個業務。

▶ As I can recall, Mr. Alexis was in charge of the business.

我記得。

As I remember it, ～.

我記得有三個人在那次暴動中被捕。

▶ As I remember it, three men were arrested in the riot.

我清楚地記得。

I distinctly recollect ～.

我清楚地記得他直到7點鐘才回家。

▶ I distinctly recollect he wasn't home until 7 o'clock.

我稍微記得。

I have some recollection of ～.

我稍微記得他們的爭吵。

▶ I have some recollection of their quarrel.

我似乎記得。

I seem to remember ～.

我似乎記得發生衝突時他在場。

▶ I seem to remember he was present during the conflict.

如果我記得沒錯的話。

If I remember correctly, ～.

如果我記得沒錯的話，這次會議在六月二日舉行。

▶ If I remember correctly, the meeting was called for June 2.

如果我沒記錯。

If I'm not mistaken, ～.

如果我沒記錯，盒子裡本來沒有東西。

▶ If I'm not mistaken, there was nothing in the box.

如果我沒記錯的話。

If my memory serves me right, ～.

如果我沒記錯的話，那顆失蹤的寶石是在那店主手裡。

▶ It my memory serves me right, the missing jewel was in the hands of that shopkeeper.

我記得。
It is within my recollection (that) ~.

我記得這房子是賣給一個外國人的。
▶ It is within my recollection (that) the house was sold to a foreigner.

就我記憶所及。
To the best of my memory, ~.

就我記憶所及，他開了張200元的支票。
▶ To the best of my memory, he wrote a check for $200.

我永遠不會忘記。
What I shall never forget is ~.

我永遠不會忘記你的慷慨。
▶ What I shall never forget is your generosity.

● 我想不起來了 ●

🌱 基本說法

我想不起來了。
I can't bring ～ to mind.

我想不起日期了。
▶ I can't bring the date to mind.

我想不起來。
I can't recall to mind ～.

我想不起來以前在哪裡見過她。
▶ I can't recall to mind where I have seen her before.

我記不得了。
I can't remember.
我不記得。
I can't remember ～.

我不記得見過這輛車。
▶ I can't remember having seen the car.

我想不起來了。
I couldn't recollect ～.

我想不起遊覽歐洲的全部細節了。
▶ I couldn't recollect all the details of my visit in Europe.

我記不得了。
I couldn't remember ～.

他的計劃我什麼也記不得了。
▶ I couldn't remember anything about his plan.

我想不起來。
I don't recall ～.

我想不起來曾經見過他。
▶ I don't recall meeting him.

我想不起來。
I don't recollect ～.

我想不起來怎樣開船了。
▶ I don't recollect how to sail a boat.

我不記得。
I don't remember.
我不記得。
I don't remember ～.

我不記得曾和這位陌生人說過話。
▶ I don't remember talking to the stranger.

恐怕我現在忘了。
I'm afraid I forget it now.

對不起，我完全忘了。
I'm sorry, I've completely forgot.

對不起，我完全忘了。
I'm sorry, I've completely forgot ～.

　　　　對不起，我完全忘了在哪裡找到它的。
▶ I'm sorry, I've completely forgot where I found it.

這件事我都忘光了。
I've forgot all about it.

恐怕我忘了。
I've forgot I'm afraid.

❀ 日常口語

278

我不記得。
I can't place ~.

我不記得他了。
▸ I can't place him.

我就是想不起。
I just can't call ~ to mind.

我就是想不起他的長相。
▸ I just can't call his face to mind.

我剛好忘了。
It just slips my memory.

忘了。
It's gone.

我忘得精光。
It's gone clean out of my mind.

我把它給忘了。
It's slipped my mind.

對不起，我什麼都想不起來了。
Sorry, my mind's gone blank.

就是想不起來。
~ just won't come to mind.

就是想不起來那個標題。
▸ The title just won't come to mind.

♣ 正式場合

我似乎想不起來。
I can't seem to bring to mind ~.
　　我似乎想不起來這地方的名稱。
▶ I can't seem to bring to mind the name of the place.

我完全不記得。
I had no recollection at all of ~.
　　我完全不記得我的童年。
▶ I had no recollection at all of my childhood.

我不記得了。
I have no memory of ~.
　　我不記得確切的話了。
▶ I have no memory of the exact words.

我得承認我忘了。
I must confess (that) I have forgot.

我似乎忘了。
I seem to have forgot.
我似乎忘了。
I seem to have forgot ~.
　　我似乎忘了她告訴我的話。
▶ I seem to have forgot what she told me.

我恐怕想不起來了。
I'm afraid I have no remembrance of ~.
　　我恐怕想不起我們在一起的時光了。
▶ I'm afraid I have no remembrance of our days together.

恐怕我一時想不起來。
I'm afraid that escapes me for the moment.

● 提醒對方 ●

我可以提醒你嗎？
Could I remind you to ～?
我可以提醒你嗎？
Could I remind you ～?

我可以提醒你寫報告嗎？
▸ Could I remind you to write a report?
我可以提醒你喬治先生正在外面等嗎？
▸ Could I remind you Mr. George is waiting outside?

我可以提醒你嗎？
Could I remind you of ～?

我可以提醒你今天你得參加一個會議嗎？
▸ Could I remind you of the meeting you have to attend today?

我想你應該已經做了，不過…。
I expect you've already done it, but ～.

我想你應該已經打過電話了，不過經理要你今天下午打電話給他。
▸ I expect you've already done it, but the manager asked you to give him a ring this afternoon.

我想你剛才有說過。
I think you said ～.

我想你剛才有說過要打個長途電話。
▸ I think you said you were going to make a long-distance call.

不知你記不記得。
I wonder if you remember ～.

不知你記不記得我的生日。
▸ I wonder if you remember my birthday.

我想提醒你。
I'd like to remind you about ～.

我想提醒你今晚有約會。
▸ I'd like to remind you about your date this evening.

我想提醒你。
I'd like to remind you (that) ～.

我想提醒你演講6點鐘開始。
▸ I'd like to remind you (that) the lecture is at 6 o'clock.

請別忘了。
Please don't forget to ～.

請別忘了關燈。
▸ Please don't forget to turn off the light.

請你記得好嗎？
Will you please remember to ～?
▸ Will you please remember to answer the letter?
請你記得回覆這封信好嗎？

你沒有忘記吧，是不是？
You haven't forgot about ～, have you?
▸ You haven't forgot about the party this evening, have you?
你沒有忘記今晚的派對吧，是不是？

你沒有忘記吧，是不是？
You haven't forgot to ～, have you?
▸ You haven't forgot to pay the rent, have you?
你沒有忘記付房租吧，是不是？

你會記得的，是嗎？
You will remember to ～, won't you?
▸ You will remember to pay him a visit, won't you?
你會記得去拜訪他一次的，是嗎？

你不會忘記的，對不對？
You won't forget about ～, will you?
▸ You won't forget about it, will you?
你不會忘記這件事的，對不對？

你不會忘記的，對不對？
You won't forget to ～, will you?
▸ You won't forget to tip the driver, will you?
你不會忘記給駕駛小費的，對不對？

❋ 日常口語

別忘了。
Don't forget about ～.

別忘了。
Don't forget to ～.

別忘了學習。
▸ Don't forget about your study.

別忘了幫我買本日曆。
▸ Don't forget to buy me a calendar.

嘿。
Hey, ～.

嘿，你的手提箱。
▸ Hey, your suitcase.

記得。
Remember about ～.

記得。
Remember to ～.

記得這件事。
▸ Remember about that.

記得寄這封信。
▸ Remember to post the letter.

怎麼樣呢？
What about ～?

你下星期的旅行怎麼樣呢？
▸ What about your trip next week?

你準備這麼做，對不對？
You're going to ～, aren't you?

你準備送她一份禮物，對不對？
▸ You're going to give her a gift, aren't you?

♣ 正式場合

不好意思，我想我應該提醒你。
Excuse me, I think I should remind you (that) ～.

不好意思，我想我應該提醒你，你要趕2點半開往紐約的那班列車。
▶ Excuse me, I think I should remind you (that) you're going to catch the 2:30 train for New York.

我希望你不介意我提醒你。
I hope you won't mind my reminding you about ～.
我希望你不介意我提醒你。
I hope you won't mind my reminding you to ～.

我希望你不介意我提醒你和蘇菲的約會。
▶ I hope you won't mind my reminding you about your appointment with Sophie.
我希望你不介意我提醒你寫信給李先生。
▶ I hope you won't mind my reminding you to write a letter to Mr. Lee.

我一定得提醒你。
I must just remind you to ～.

我一定得提醒你把保險箱鎖上。
▶ I must just remind you to lock the safe.

我應該要提醒你。
I ought to remind you about ～.

我應該要提醒你有關我們協議的事。
▶ I ought to remind you about our agreement.

我想你記得吧？
I take it (that) you remember to ～?

我想你記得要趕6點半的火車吧？
▶ I take it (that) you remember to catch the 6:30 train?

如果你記得。
If you recall, ～.

如果你記得，我們三年前在巴黎見過。
▶ If you recall, we met in Paris three years ago.

恐怕我得提醒你。
I'm afraid I have to remind you (that) ～.

恐怕我得提醒你房租已經到期了。
▶ I'm afraid I have to remind you (that) the rent is due.

我想你一定記得。
I'm sure you've remembered, but ～.

我想你一定記得，今天是海倫的生日。
▸ I'm sure you've remembered, but today's Helen's birthday.

我可以提醒你嗎？
May I remind you to ～?

我可以提醒你為我寫一份履歷表嗎？
▸ May I remind you to write a resume for me?

也許我有義務提醒你。
Perhaps it's my duty to remind you (that) ～.

也許我有義務提醒你末班車10點半開。
▸ Perhaps it's my duty to remind you (that) the last bus leaves at 10:30.

Repetition

複述

Pardon me?

● 請再說一遍 ●

❤ 基本說法

🔊 283

請重複一次可以嗎？　　　　　　請重複一次那句話可以嗎？
Could you repeat ～, please? ▸ Could you repeat that, please?

能不能請你再說一遍？　　　　　能不能請你把那件事再說一遍？
Could you say ～ again, please? ▸ Could you say that again, please?

我恐怕沒聽見。　　　　　　　　我恐怕沒聽見那句話。
I'm afraid I didn't hear ～. ▸ I'm afraid I didn't hear that.

我恐怕沒聽清楚你說的話。
I'm afraid I didn't quite hear what you said.

對不起，你說什麼？
I'm sorry?

對不起，但是我沒聽見。　　　　對不起，但是我沒聽見那件事。
I'm sorry, but I didn't catch ～. ▸ I'm sorry, but I didn't catch that.

對不起，但是我沒聽清楚你說什麼。
I'm sorry, but I didn't quite catch what you were saying.

對不起，我聽不見你說的話。
I'm sorry. I couldn't hear what you said.

對不起，我沒聽見。
I'm sorry. I didn't hear ~.

對不起，我沒聽見那句話。
▶ I'm sorry, I didn't hear that.

對不起，我沒聽見你說的話。
I'm sorry. I didn't quite hear what you said.

對不起，你說什麼？
I'm sorry. What did you say?

對不起，那是什麼？
I'm sorry. What was that?

對不起，再說一遍那是什麼？
I'm sorry. What was ~ again?

對不起，再說一遍他的名字叫什麼？
▶ I'm sorry, what was his name again?

對不起，你說什麼？
I'm sorry. ~ did you say?

對不起，你說什麼時候？
▶ I'm sorry, when did you say?

對不起，你說什麼？
Pardon me?

請再講一遍。
Please say it again.

請再說一遍，那是什麼？
What was ~ again, please?

請再說一遍，地址是什麼？
▶ What was the address again, please?

請重複你剛說的話好嗎？
Would you repeat what you said, please?

日常口語

284

抱歉，你說什麼？
Beg pardon?

再說一遍行嗎？
Come again?

我沒聽清楚。你再說一遍行嗎？
I didn't hear you. Could you come back?

你說什麼？
Pardon?

請再說一遍。
Say that again, please.

對不起，但是我沒聽見。
Sorry, but I missed ～.

對不起，但是我沒聽見那句話。
▸ Sorry, but I missed that.

對不起，我完全沒聽到。
Sorry, I didn't get any of ～.

對不起，我完全沒聽到那件事。
▸ Sorry, I didn't get any of that.

抱歉？
Sorry? ～?

抱歉？紐約嗎？
▸ Sorry? New York?

抱歉，你說什麼？
Sorry, what did you say?

那是什麼？再說一遍。
What was that again?

你說的是什麼？
What was that you said?

♣ 正式場合

你說什麼？
I beg your pardon?

不知你是否介意再說一遍？
I wonder if you'd mind repeating ～?

不知你是否介意把號碼再說一遍？
▸ I wonder if you'd mind repeating the number?

對不起，能否請你再說一遍？
I'm sorry, could I ask you to repeat ～, please?

對不起，能否請你把那個字再說一遍？
▸ I'm sorry, could I ask you to repeat that word, please?

對不起，請你重複可以嗎？
I'm sorry, could you possibly repeat ～, please?

對不起，請你重複可以嗎？
▸ I'm sorry, could you possibly repeat it, please?

對不起，能否請你再說一遍？
I'm sorry, would it be possible for you to repeat ～, please?

對不起，能否請你把那句再說一遍？
▸ I'm sorry, would it be possible for you to repeat that sentence, please?

對不起，請你再說一遍好嗎？
I'm sorry, would you mind repeating ～, please?

對不起，那件事請你再說一遍好嗎？
▸ I'm sorry, would you mind repeating that, please?

對不起，請你再說一遍好嗎？
I'm sorry, would you mind saying it again?

請重述。
Please be good enough to reiterate ～.

請重述你的觀點。
▸ Please be good enough to reiterate your point.

● 我剛才是說… ●

基本說法

286

我是說。
I said, ～

我是說：「你能不能收音機開小聲點？」
▸ I said, "Could you turn the radio down a bit?"

我剛才是問。
I was just asking ～.

我剛才是問你什麼時候動身。
▸ I was just asking when you're leaving.

我剛才是說。
I was just remarking ～.

我剛才是說他病了。
▸ I was just remarking he is ill.

我剛才是說。
I was just saying ～.

我剛才是說傑克森要到今天晚上才有空。
▸ I was just saying Jackson won't be free till this evening.

我剛才是想知道。
I was just wondering ～.

我剛才是想知道誰將是本屆會議主席。
▸ I was just wondering who will be Chairman of this conference.

✿ 日常口語

你聾了嗎？我是說。
Are you deaf? I said ～.

你聾了嗎？我是說我喜歡你。
▸ Are you deaf? I said I like you.

我剛才說的是。
What I said was, ～.

我剛才說的是，景色美極了。
▸ What I said was, it's a terrific view.

♣ 正式場合

我剛才是問為什麼會這樣。 **I was just enquiring why ~.**	我剛才是問，政府為什麼無法停止戰爭。 ▸ I was just enquiring why the governments are unable to stop the war.
我剛才是表示這樣的看法。 **I was just expressing the view (that) ~.**	我剛才是表示這樣的看法：我們正失去對世界人口的控制力。 ▸ I was just expressing the view (that) we are losing control of the world population.
我剛才是建議這麼做。 **I was just making the suggestion (that) ~.**	我剛才是建議設立委員會調查此事故。 ▸ I was just making the suggestion (that) a committee be set up to investigate into the accident.
我剛才只是指出此事。 **I was merely pointing out (that) ~.**	我只是指出，汙染源就是人類。 ▸ I was merely pointing out (that) the source of pollution is human beings.
我剛才只是如此主張。 **I was merely putting forward the opinion (that) ~.**	我剛才只是主張，我們應該外出用餐以節省時間。 ▸ I was merely putting forward the opinion (that) we should dine out to save time.
我剛才只是說明這個事實。 **I was merely stating the fact (that) ~.**	我剛才只是說明這個事實：音樂家基本上都是特別的人。 ▸ I was merely stating the fact (that) musicians are basically special people.
我只是想知道。 **I was merely wondering ~.**	我只是想知道他住在哪裡。 ▸ I was merely wondering where he lives.

● 換一種方式複述 ●

🌱 基本說法

或者更確切地說。

~, or rather, ~.

美國人，或者更確切地說，非洲裔美國人擅長於爵士音樂。

▶ Americans, or rather, Afro-Americans are good at jazz music.

而那就是說。
And that means ~.

而那就是說，生活就是一場戰役。

▶ And that means life is a battle.

這基本上全是…的問題。
Basically, it's all a question of ~.

這基本上全是教養的問題。

▶ Basically, it's all a question of upbringing.

或者說得更確切些。

~, or better, ~.

醫生通常都有點愛管閒事，或者說得更確切些，有點愛打聽人家隱私。

▶ Doctors are usually a bit nosy, or better, a bit inquisitive.

換句話說。
In other words, ~.

換句話說，這不帶有疾病。

▶ In other words, it's carrying no diseases.

讓我換一種說法。
Let me put it another way, ~.

讓我換個說法，教育是進步不可或缺的。

▶ Let me put it another way, education is essential for progress.

我的意思是說…。

~, by which I mean, ~.

生活就像運動，我的意思是說，生活是劇烈的競爭。

▶ Life is like sport, by which I mean, it's hard competitive business.

這樣說吧。
Look at it this way. ~.

這樣說吧：工業化程度越高污染越嚴重。

▶ Look at it this way. The more industrialization you have, the more pollution there is.

或者也可以說。
Or you could say ～.

或者也可以說，歷史經常重演。
▸ Or you could say history repeats itself.

也就是說。
That's to say, ～.

也就是說，慢跑可以治療心臟病。
▸ That's to say, jogging can be a cure for heart troubles.

換句話說。
To put it another way, ～.

換句話說，在海邊度假對教師有益。
▸ To put it another way, seaside holidays are good for teachers.

我的意思是說。

What I mean is, ～.

我的意思是說，線上遊戲只受到年輕人的喜愛。
▸ What I mean is, online games are popular only with young people.

我剛才的意思是。
What I meant was, ～.

我剛的意思是，巴西咖啡品質通常很好。
▸ What I meant was, coffee from Brazil is usually of good quality.

我所說的意思是。
What I'm suggesting is ～.

我所說的意思是，人類的本性難移。
▸ What I'm suggesting is human nature does not change.

❀ 日常口語

我的意思不過是。	我的意思不過是,不要為了芝麻小事而大驚小怪。
All I'm suggesting is ~.	▸ All I'm suggesting is don't fuss about trifles.
我想說的不過是。	我想說的不過是,他很慷慨大方。
All I'm trying to say is, ~.	▸ All I'm trying to say is, he's generous.
我是說。	我是說我們的潛能受到身體的限制。
I mean ~.	▸ I mean there are physical limits to our potential.
我想說的是。	我想說的是,這不值得買。
What I'm driving at is, ~.	▸ What I'm driving at is, it's not worth buying.
我想說的是。	我想說的是,人口是無法控制的。
What I'm getting at is, ~.	▸ What I'm getting at is, population can't be controlled.
我想說的是。	我想說的是,我愛你。
What I'm trying to say is, ~.	▸ What I'm trying to say is, I love you.

♣ 正式場合

如果我可以換個說法。
If I can re-express that, I ～.

▸ 如果可以換個說法，我認為書越來越貴。
If I can re-express that, I think books are becoming more and more expensive.

如果我可以把我剛說的話重新整理。
If I can rephrase what I've just said, I ～.

▸ 如果我可以把我剛說的話重新整理，我認為我們的資源是不能再生的。
If I can rephrase what I've just said, I think our resources are not renewable.

如果可以重述我的觀點，我認為這麼說比較清楚。
If I could restate my point, I think it would be more accurate to say ～.

▸ 如果可以重述我的觀點，我認為這麼說比較清楚，自然是永恆的。
If I could restate my point, I think it would be more accurate to say Nature is permanent.

也許我這麼說更清楚。

Perhaps I could make that clearer by saying ～.

▸ 也許我這麼說更清楚：老一輩的人普遍來說都是保守的。
Perhaps I could make that clearer by saying the older generation are generally conservative.

也許這麼說會更清楚。
Perhaps it would be clearer to say ～.

▸ 也許這麼說更清楚：工人要求提高工資。
Perhaps it would be clearer to say workers are demanding for higher wages.

我所說的重點是。

The point I'm making is (that) ～.

▸ 我所說的重點是，現在的父母往往過分溺愛自己的孩子。
The point I'm making is (that) modern parents tend to be indulgent to their children.

35 *Request* 請 求

● 提出請求 ●

🌱 基本說法
292

可以嗎？
Can you ～?
▸ 可以載我一程嗎？
▸ Can you give me a lift?

你能不能幫我？
Can you help me?

你能不能幫我？
Can you oblige me with ～?
▸ 你能不能借一把雨傘給我？
▸ Can you oblige me with an umbrella?

能不能請你？
Could I ask you to ～?
▸ 能不能請你寫封信給他？
▸ Could I ask you to write him a letter?

我可以嗎？
Could I ～?
▸ 我可以借用一下你的眼鏡嗎？
▸ Could I borrow your spectacles?

你可以嗎？
Could you ～?
▸ 你可以把碎玻璃打掃乾淨嗎？
▸ Could you clean up the broken glass?

請你給我…可以嗎？
Could you spare me ～, please?
▸ 請你給我點鹽可以嗎？
▸ Could you spare me some salt, please?

請問你介意我這樣做嗎？
Do you mind if I ～, please?
▸ 請問你介意我搭你的車嗎？
▸ Do you mind if I get a lift in your car, please?

你看你能這樣做嗎？
Do you think you could possibly ～?
▸ 你看你能把車往前開一點嗎？
▸ Do you think you could possibly move your car forward a bit?

445

請你幫我好嗎？
Get me ～, will you please?

請你幫我找些喝的好嗎？
▶ Get me some drink, will you please?

如果你這樣做，我會很感激。
I'd be very grateful if you'd ～.

如果你明天6點半叫醒我，我會很感激。
▶ I'd be very grateful if you'd get me up at 6:30 tomorrow.

我想要…，麻煩了。
I'd like ～, please.

我想要來根菸，麻煩了。
▶ I'd like some cigarettes, please.

有機會可以嗎？
Is there any chance of ～?

有機會可以去聽你的講課嗎？
▶ Is there any chance of attending your lecture?

請你幫個忙好嗎？
May I ask a favor of you?

可以和你私下說話嗎？
May I have a word with you?

麻煩你這樣做好嗎？
May I trouble you to ～?

麻煩你把椅子移開一點好嗎？
▶ May I trouble you to move your chair a bit?

請幫我做這件事。
Please oblige me by ～.

請幫我抬這個箱子。
▶ Please oblige me by lifting the box.

對不起打擾你，你有嗎？
Sorry to trouble you, but do you have ～?

對不起打擾你，你有信封嗎？
▶ Sorry to trouble you, but do you have an envelope?

請你幫我，好嗎？
Will you please ～ for me?

請你替我解開這個結，好嗎？
▶ Will you please untie the knot for me?

請替我，可以嗎？
Would you be able to ～ for me, please?

請替我買棵聖誕樹，可以嗎？
▸ Would you be able to buy a Christmas tree for me, please?

你可以幫我個忙嗎？
Would you do me a favor?

你可以幫我做件事嗎？
Would you do me a good turn?

你可以幫我做件事嗎？
Would you do me a good turn by ～?

你可以幫我裝飾這棵聖誕樹嗎？
▸ Would you do me a good turn by dressing the Christmas tree?

請你這麼做好嗎？
Would you like to ～, please?

請你關掉收音機好嗎？
▸ Would you like to turn off the radio, please?

請你幫我好嗎？
Would you mind ～ for me, please?

請你幫我兌換這張十元鈔票好嗎？
▸ Would you mind changing this ten-dollar note for me, please?

你可以嗎？
You could possibly ～?

你可以讓我過夜嗎？
▸ You could possibly put me up for the night?

你能不能借我？
You couldn't lend me ～, could you?

你能不能借我一百塊錢？
▸ You couldn't lend me a hundred dollars, could you?

你或許能幫我吧？
You might help me with ～?

你或許能幫我搬這張桌子吧？
▸ You might help me with the desk?

❀ 日常口語

可以嗎？	可以用一下你的電話嗎？
Any chance of ～?	▸ Any chance of using your telephone?
行行好。	行行好跟我說實話。
Be kind enough to ～.	▸ Be kind enough to tell me the truth.
幫幫忙。	幫幫忙把窗戶關上。
Do me a favor and ～.	▸ Do me a favor and close the window.
別這樣，好嗎？	別發出聲響，好嗎？
Don't ～, will you?	▸ Don't make any noise, will you?
你也許有吧？	你也許有點糖吧？
Have you got ～, by any chance?	▸ Have you got some sugar, by any chance?
嘿，我這邊沒了。	嘿，我這邊沒水了。
Hey, I'm out of ～.	▸ Hey, I'm out of water.
如何？	給我來杯咖啡如何？
How about ～?	▸ How about some coffee?
幫我行嗎？	幫我打一份行嗎？
Mind ～ for me?	▸ Mind typing it for me?
你有沒有？	你有沒有牛奶？
You don't have ～, do you?	▸ You don't have any milk, do you?
你能不能？	你能不能幫我買一張票？
You couldn't ～, could you?	▸ You couldn't get me a ticket, could you?
你有沒有？	你有沒有腳踏車？
You haven't got ～, have you?	▸ You haven't got a bike, have you?

♣ 正式場合

你能不能？
Could you possibly ～?

你能不能接管這家工廠？
▶ Could you possibly take over the factory?

你認為可以嗎？
Do you think it would be possible to ～?

你認為可以幫我加薪嗎？
▶ Do you think it would be possible to give me a pay raise?

我真是難以啟齒，你看能不能？
I don't quite know how to ask you, but do you think I could possibly ～?

我真是難以啟齒，你看這房子我能不能借住一年？
▶ I don't quite know how to ask you, but do you think I could possibly use this house for a year?

我希望我這麼問你不會介意，我想知道是否有可能？
I hope you don't mind my asking, but I wonder if it might be at all possible for me to ～?

我希望我這麼問你不會介意，我想知道是否有可能與你同住這間房？
▶ I hope you don't mind my asking, but I wonder if it might be at all possible for me to share the room with you?

如果你幫忙，我會非常高興。
I should be pleased if you would ～.

如果你幫我做工作，我會非常高興。
▶ I should be pleased if you would help me with my work.

不知你能否。
I wonder if you could ～.

不知你能否幫助我。
▶ I wonder if you could help me.

不知你是否介意我。
I wonder if you'd mind my ～.

不知你是否介意我使用你的筆電。
▶ I wonder if you'd mind my using your notebook.

如果你能，我會非常感謝。
I'd appreciate it if you could ～.

如果你能借我一千元，我會非常感謝。
▶ I'd appreciate it if you could loan me a thousand dollars.

如果你能，我將感激不盡。
I'll regard it as a favor if you could ～.

若你能來我們的派對，我將感激不盡。
▸ I'll regard it as a favor if you could attend our party.

我真不知道怎麼說才好，你看你能嗎？
I'm not quite sure how to put this, but do you think you could possibly ～?

我真不知道怎麼說才好，你看你能改一下日期嗎？
▸ I'm not quite sure how to put this, but do you think you could possibly change the date?

對不起麻煩你了，你可以嗎？
I'm sorry to trouble you, but could you ～?

對不起麻煩你了，明天晚上你可以打電話給我嗎？
▸ I'm sorry to trouble you, but could you give me a ring tomorrow evening?

如果你們能，那就大大地幫了我的忙了。
It would help me a great deal if you could ～.

如果你們都能準時上課，那就大大地幫了我的忙了。
▸ It would help me a great deal if you could all be punctual to class.

我能否有此榮幸？
May I have the honor of ～?

我能否有此榮幸聽你講課？
▸ May I have the honor of attending your lecture?

我是否可以？
May I have the pleasure of ～?

我是否可以穿這件洋裝？
▸ May I have the pleasure of wearing the dress?

如果你能，我們將非常感謝。
We should be most grateful, if you could possibly ～.

如果你能主持會議，我們將非常感謝。
▸ We should be most grateful, if you could possibly chair the meeting.

你能不能？
Would it be possible for you to ～?

你能不能去調查一下這次暴動？
▶ Would it be possible for you to investigate the riot?

能不能？
Would there be any possibility of ～?

能不能討論一下日程安排？
▶ Would there be any possibility of discussing the agenda?

能不能請你？
Would you be so kind as to ～?

能不能請你說明一下這個理論？
▶ Would you be so kind as to explain the theory?

請你這麼做，好嗎？
Would you mind ～, please?

請你把這一段全部抄下來，好嗎？
▶ Would you mind copying out this paragraph, please?

● 答應請求 ●

❦ 基本說法

我看沒問題。
I don't see any problem.

我要是能做，我會做的。
I would if could.

我很樂意。
I'd be glad to. / I'd love to.

這對我而言不會麻煩。
It'll be no bother to me.

不，我一點也不介意。
No, I don't mind in the least.

一點也不麻煩。
That's no trouble at all.

好吧，如果我辦得到的話。
Well, if I can.

好吧，要是那樣，可以。
Well, in that case, all right.

好吧，我想是可以的。
Well, OK, I suppose so.

願意效勞。
Willingly.

好的，我答應。
Yes, I promise.

✿日常口語

296

請便，別客氣。
Be my guest.

當然可以。
By all means.

好啊，當然可以。
Do, by all means.

放心吧。我會的。
Don't worry. I will.

我會試試看。是什麼事？
I'll try. What's the matter?

說吧。
Just name it.

行。
OK.

當然可以！
Sure!

好啊！是什麼事？
Sure! What is it?

當然可以！
Sure thing!

噢，當然可以！
Why, of course!

好啊。
Will do.

♣ 正式場合

當然可以。
I most certainly can.

我很樂意。
I'd be delighted to.

如果我辦得到的話，我很樂意幫忙。
I'd be delighted to help, if I can.

我將盡力而為，先生。
I'll do my best, sir.

非常樂意。
With great pleasure.

好的，我想那沒問題。
Yes. I think that would be all right.

好的，我是早就勸告過你的。
Yes. I've already advised you to.

好的，我是早就建議過你的。
Yes, I've already recommended you to.

好的，我是早就跟你說過了的。
Yes, I've already told you to.

● 拒絕請求 ●

我很願意，但是我沒有。
I'd like to, but I don't ～.

我很願意，但是我身上沒有帶零錢。
▸ I'd like to, but I don't have any change on me.

對不起，不過我現在正好在用。
I'm sorry, but I'm using it right now.

對不起我不能。
I'm sorry I can't.

對不起我不能答應你的請求。
I'm sorry I can't oblige you.

很對不起，不過我從來不把它借給任何人。
I'm very sorry, but I never lend it to anyone.

不，恐怕我不能。
No, I'm afraid I can't.

不，恐怕我不能幫你。
No, I'm afraid I can't help you.

✿ 日常口語

真不知我怎麼能。
Can't really see how I can ～.

真不知我怎麼能把它給你。
▸ Can't really see how I can give it to you.

當然不行！
Certainly not!

我當然不願意！
I certainly will not!

不行，為什麼要這樣。
No, can't see it.

不行。
Not a chance.

對不起，不行。
Sorry, can't be done.

對不起，我實在沒辦法。
Sorry, can't be helped.

對不起，夥伴，不行。
Sorry, old chap, nothing doing.

對不起，不行。
Sorry, out of the question.

當然不行！
Sure not!

♣ 正式場合

🔊 300

很遺憾，我不能幫助你。
I regret (that) I can't help you.

我想答應，不過偏偏辦不到。
I'd like to say yes, but that's just impossible.

如果你不介意，我倒不想這樣。
I'd rather not if you don't mind.

我真的想幫助你，可是我自己也身無分文了。
I'd really like to help you out, but I'm broke myself.

不，在那方面我對你恐怕沒有多大幫助。
No, I'm afraid I can't be very much help to you there.

噢，我真不知說什麼好。你明白，我一直都在使用它。
Well, I don't really know what to say. You see, I've been using it.

噢，我不知說什麼好了。問題是，我不能少了它。
Well, I don't quite know what to say. The point is, I can't spare it.

建議

Suggestion

● 提出建議 ●

🌱 基本說法

🔊 301

你看怎麼樣？
Do you think it would be an idea to ～?

你看把這艘船命名為『海豚號』怎麼樣？
▸ Do you think it would be an idea to name the Ship Dolphin?

你不認為這是個好主意嗎？
Don't you think it might be a good idea to ～?

你不認為領養孩子是個好主意嗎？
▸ Don't you think it might be a good idea to foster a child?

你想過嗎？
Have you ever thought of ～?

你想過今晚外出吃飯嗎？
▸ Have you ever thought of dining out this evening?

你覺得怎麼樣？
How would you like to ～?

你覺得去溜冰怎麼樣？
▸ How would you like to go skating?

我想這是個很棒的主意。
I think it'd be a great idea to ～.

我想，打一局網球是個很棒的主意。
▸ I think it'd be a great idea to have a round of tennis.

我想你可能會想要吧。
I thought you might like to ～.

我想，你可能會想要春天去露營度假吧。
▸ I thought you might like to have a camping holiday in the spring.

如果你方便的話，我…。
If it's all right with you, I'll ～.

如果你方便的話，我明天打電話給你。
▸ If it's all right with you, I'll give you a call tomorrow.

這會是個好主意。
It might be a good idea to ～.

把它放在保險箱裡會是個好主意。
▸ It might be a good idea to put it in a safe.

你還是這樣的好。
It will be just as well for you to ～.

你還是少說為妙。
▸ It will be just as well for you to save your breath.

這樣做要好得多。
It'd be much better to ～.

把會議延到星期五要好得多。
▸ It'd be much better to put off the meeting till Friday.

你還是這樣的好。
It'll be a good idea for you to ～.

你還是有空就休息的好。
▸ It'll be a good idea for you to have a rest while you can.

也許你應該。
Maybe you ought to ～.

也許你應該辭掉這工作。
▸ Maybe you ought to quit the job.

有個建議是。
One idea would be to ～.

有個建議就是做廣告。
▸ One idea would be to put up an advertisement.

我們這樣好嗎？
Shall we ～?

我們去散散步好嗎？
▸ Shall we go for a walk?

我們不妨。
We may as well ～.

我們不妨買個新平底鍋。
▸ We may as well buy a new frying pan.

我們可以。
We might ～.

我們可以待在原地不動。
▸ We might stay where we are.

我們最好。
We'd better ～.

我們最好現在就去。
▸ We'd better go now.

你看怎麼樣？
What do you think of ～?

你看到機場為他送行怎麼樣？
▸ What do you think of seeing him off at the airport?

你覺得怎麼樣？
What would you say to ～?

你覺得到鄉間旅行怎麼樣？
▸ What would you say to a trip to the countryside?

這樣不是比較好嗎？
Would it be better to ～?

現在關店停業不是比較好嗎？
▸ Would it be better to put up the shutter now?

不是很好嗎？
Wouldn't it be an idea to ～?

預先訂位不是很好嗎？
▸ Wouldn't it be an idea to make a reservation in advance?

不是比較好嗎？
Wouldn't you be better off ～?

你穿T恤不是比較好嗎？
▸ Wouldn't you be better off with a T-shirt?

你總可以。
You could always ～.

你總可以坐飛機旅行。
▸ You could always travel by air.

你不妨。
You might as well ～.

你不妨趁他現在在這裡去看看他。
▸ You might as well see him now he is here.

❀ 日常口語

換掉它。
Change it.
＊用祈使句表示建議。

那麼，想嗎？ | 那麼，想喝一杯嗎？
Fancy ～, then? | ▸ Fancy a drink, then?

想嗎？ | 想打一場網球嗎？
Feel like ～? | ▸ Feel like a game of tennis?

這樣好不好？ | 這樣好不好：放手讓他去做，然後看看結果如何？
How about ～? | ▸ How about giving him a free hand and see how it will turn out?

這個主意如何。 | 我們改到海邊過暑假，這個主意如何。
How about this idea: ～. | ▸ How about this idea: we have our summer vacation on the beach instead.

你覺得怎麼樣？ | 你覺得去雪山旅行怎麼樣？
How does ～ strike you? | ▸ How does a trip to Snow Mountain strike you?

我知道了！我們這麼做吧。 | 我知道了！我們先幫冰箱除霜吧。
I know! Let's ～. | ▸ I know! Let's defrost the fridge first.

我知道我們可以怎麼做。 | 我知道我們可以怎麼做：叫計程車吧。
I know what we can do: let's ～. | ▸ I know what we can do: let's call a taxi.

我告訴你該怎麼辦。 | 我告訴你該怎辦：喝杯水把這藥吞下去。
I tell you what: ～. | ▸ I tell you what: take a cup of water to rinse the medicine down.

你聽我說，我們何不～呢？
I'll tell you what-why don't we ～?

▸ 你聽我說，我們何不搬到湖區呢？
▸ I'll tell you what-why don't we move to the Lake District?

我有個很棒的主意。

I've got a fantastic idea: ～.

▸ 我有個很棒的主意：我們邀請市長先生參加我們的婚禮。
▸ I've got a fantastic idea: we'll ask Mr. Mayor to attend our wedding ceremony.

我這個主意真的不錯。

I've got this really good idea: ～.

▸ 我這個主意真的不錯：我要租一輛汽車，然後直接開到那裡。
▸ I've got this really good idea: I'll rent a car and drive straight there.

我們這麼做吧。
Let's ～.

▸ 我們來幫他們一下吧。
▸ Let's give them a hand.

我們這麼做，好嗎？
Let's ～, shall we?

▸ 我們來聽聽這張CD，好嗎？
▸ Let's listen to the CD, shall we?

假如這樣呢？
Suppose ～?

▸ 假如我預先訂好座位呢？
▸ Suppose I reserve seats in advance?

我們總可以。
We could always ～.

▸ 我們總可以叫輛計程車在市區逛逛。
▸ We could always call a taxi to go about the city.

我們何不呢？
Why don't we ～?

▸ 我們何不洗個熱水澡提提神呢？
▸ Why don't we freshen up with a hot bath?

那你何不這麼做？
Why not ～, then?

▸ 那你何不將約會延到星期一？
▸ Why not put off your date till Monday, then?

♣ 正式場合

303

能不能？ **Could it be that ～?**	我們能否為資優兒童建所特殊學校？ ▸ Could it be that we set up a special school for gifted children?
那麼，你是否考慮過？ **Have you considered ～, then?**	那麼，你是否考慮過留言給她？ ▸ Have you considered leaving a message to her, then?
我想提個建議。 **I should like to put forward a suggestion: let's ～.**	我想提個建議：我們來討論住屋問題。 ▸ I should like to put forward a suggestion: let's discuss the housing question.
不知你是否考慮過？ **I was wondering if you'd ever thought of ～?**	不知你是否考慮過取消這次會議？ ▸ I was wondering if you'd ever thought of canceling the conference?
不知道你是否想？ **I wonder whether you'd like to ～?**	不知週六晚上你是否想去爵士俱樂部？ ▸ I wonder whether you'd like to go to a jazz-club Saturday night?
我想建議。 **I'd like to suggest (that) ～.**	我想建議你參加我們的俱樂部。 ▸ I'd like to suggest (that) you join our club.
我建議。 **I'd propose ～.**	我建議你寫一份關於這次事件的報告。 ▸ I'd propose you write a report about the event.
如果我可以提出建議的話。 **If I may make a suggestion, ～.**	如果我可以提出建議的話，那麼給學生舉些這方面的例子吧。 ▸ If I may make a suggestion, give the students some examples of this.

可不可以建議？
May I suggest ～?

可不可以建議在他的祕書那裡留言？
▸ May I suggest leaving a message with his secretary?

也許你願意吧？
Perhaps you'd care to ～?

也許你願意把這棟房子賣給建設公司吧？
▸ Perhaps you'd care to sell the house to a building firm?

你願意嗎？
Would you care to ～?

你願意把文章再寫長一點嗎？
▸ Would you care to lengthen your article out a little?

你想嗎？
Would you like to ～?

你想在和平餐廳吃午餐嗎？
▸ Would you like to have lunch at the Peace Restaurant?

你也許想吧！
You might like to ～!

你也許想抄下這篇文章吧！
▸ You might like to copy this article!

● 贊成建議 ●

🌱 基本說法
304

好，我就拿這個。
All right, I'll have it.

好，如果這會讓你高興的話。
All right, if that will make you happy.

我都可以。
I don't mind.

我很想這樣。
I'd like that very much.

這也許就是我要做的。
Maybe that's what I'll do.

這聽起來像是個好主意。
That sounds like a good idea.

那太好了。
That would be very nice.

真是好主意。
That's a good idea.

對，我想這個主意不錯。
Yes, I think it's a lovely idea.

對，這主意真是好極了。
Yes, that'll be just fine.

❀ 日常口語

任何時間我都可以。
Any time will suit me.

我一定這麼做。
Believe I will.

好，我們走吧。
Good enough, let's go.

這個主意好！
I'd like that!

這個主意好極了。
I'd like that very much.

你這麼說正合我意。
Now you're talking.

哦，好。你要怎樣都可以。
Oh, OK. Anything you want.

這對我來說正好。
That suits me all right.

我OK。
That'll be OK by me.

太棒了。
That's great.

這正合我意。
That's just my cup of tea.

你說的都行。
Whatever you say.

♣ 正式場合

對。我看這是個絕佳的提議！
Yes. I think that's an excellent proposal!

對。我認為你的建議是可取的。
Yes. I think your suggestion is acceptable.

對。我認為應該這麼做。
Yes. I think that's the proper course to take.

● 反對建議 ●

▼ 基本說法

307

我想我不要，不過還是謝謝你。
I don't think I will, but thank you all the same.

我想，但是我沒時間。
I'd like that, but I can't afford the time.

事實上我不太感興趣。
I'm not quite keen, actually.

我想這倒是個主意，但…。
It's an idea, I suppose, but ～.

我想這倒是個主意，但可能很花錢。
▶ It's an idea, I suppose, but it may cost a lot of money.

不，別麻煩了。
No, don't bother.

不，我不這樣認為。
No, I don't think so.

不，我們改去衝浪吧。
No, let's go surfing for a change.

真的不行。我不想那樣。
No, really. I'm not in the mood for it.

如果你不介意的話，我倒不想那樣。
I'd rather not if you don't mind.

✳ 日常口語

不行。
Can't be done.

別再跟我說這件事了。
I wouldn't hear of it.

我倒希望你不要這樣。
I'd rather you wouldn't.

不可能。
Impossible.

不行！
No!

不行（不可能）！
No way!

一點也不想。
Not a bit.

♣ 正式場合

我很遺憾我不能接受你的建議。
I regret to say I can't accept your suggestion.

你的建議恐怕是不可取的。
I'm afraid your proposal is not acceptable.

那也許會很愉快，不過我可能沒有足夠的時間。
That would be very pleasant, but I may not have enough time.

讀書計劃

選擇自己的學習方式打√，一步一腳印確實做到

✓ 打電話時用英文和朋友聊天	早上起床英聽練習15分鐘	睡前跟mp3同步口語練習10分鐘	走路時用英會話自言自語
每天練習__句句型造句	洗澡時練習自我介紹	上廁所時背____個單字	等人時背____個單字
打掃的時候用英文碎碎念	把不會的句子記錄下來	把英文歌詞融入英會話	
用英會話句型寫3句日記	一天背10句會話句型！	晚上回家時英聽練習15分鐘	週末和朋友用英文練習對話
在公園大聲唸英會話句子	meow	用英文聊LINE	用英文和朋友玩桌遊
在Facebook上用英文留言	用英文寫網誌	早上搭車時背__個單字	練習____則英文笑話
（自己設定）	（自己設定）	（自己設定）	（自己設定）
（自己設定）	（自己設定）	（自己設定）	

comprehension
n.
理解

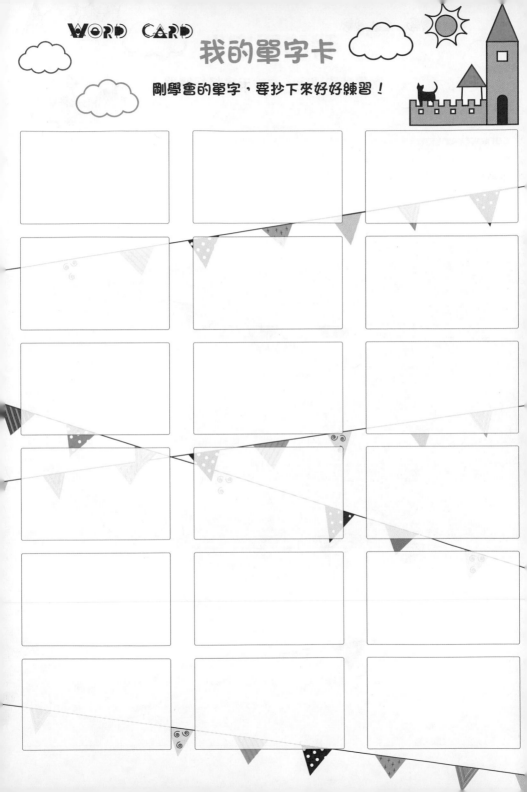

WORD CARD

我的單字卡

剛學會的單字，要抄下來好好練習！

comprehension

n.

理解

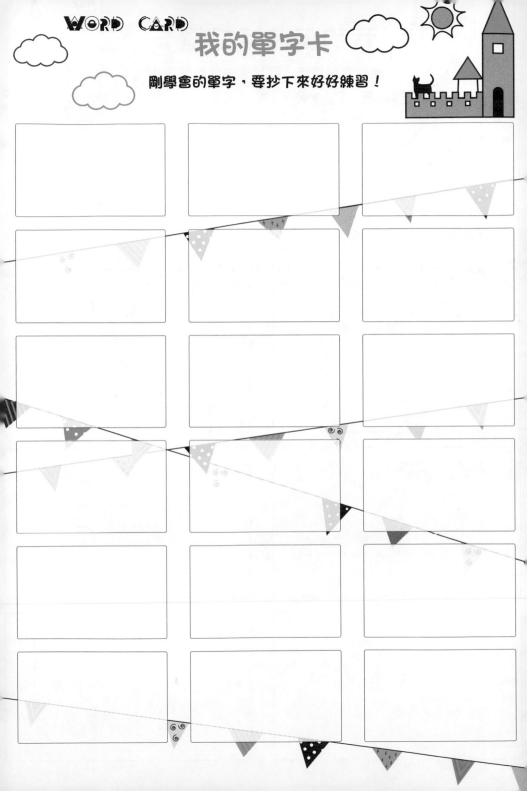

我的英會話記憶卡

剛學會的會話，要抄下來好好練習！

SENTENCE CARD

* will you be able to ...?
  你能做到嗎？

* Will you be able to Finish your
  work by noon?
  中午前你能把工作完成嗎？

我的英會話記憶卡

剛學會的會話，要抄下來好好練習！

SENTENCE CARD

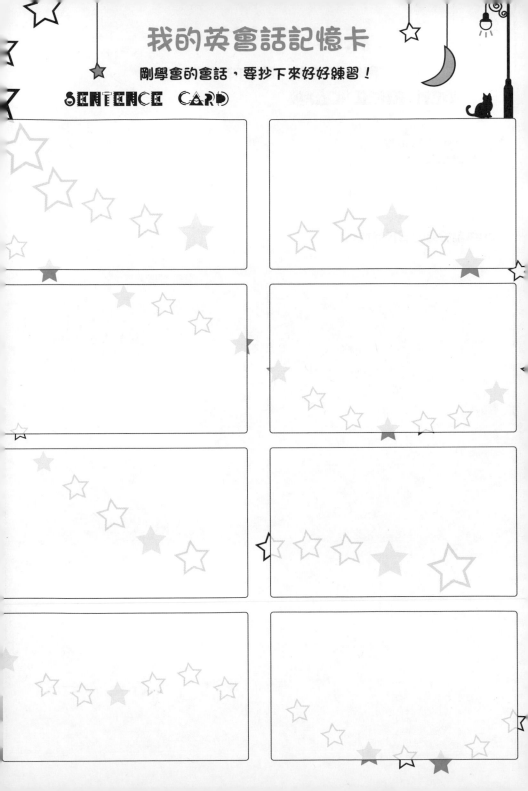

我的英會話記憶卡

剛學會的會話，要抄下來好好練習！

SENTENCE CARD

* will you be able to ...?
你能做到嗎？

* Will you be able to finish your
 work by noon?
中午前你能把工作完成嗎？

我的英會話記憶卡

剛學會的會話，要抄下來好好練習！

SENTENCE CARD

國家圖書館出版品預行編目(CIP)資料

新版Anytime Anywhere英會話溝通句典 / 陳鑫源編.
-- 2版. -- 臺北市：笛藤, 2018.01
　　面；　公分
ISBN 978-957-710-714-5(25K平裝附光碟片)
1.英語 2.會話 3.句法

805.188　　　　　　　　　　　　107000616

Anytime
Anywhere

英會話
溝通句典　附MP3

2018年1月23日 2版 第1刷　定價380元

著　　　者	陳鑫源
引　導　句	席菈
編　　　輯	伍曉玥
封 面 設 計	王舒玗
插　　　畫	徐一巧
內 頁 設 計	葉艾青、王舒玗
總　編　輯	賴巧凌
發　行　所	笛藤出版圖書有限公司
發　行　人	林建仲
地　　　址	台北市中正區重慶南路三段1號3樓之1
電　　　話	(02)2358-3891
傳　　　真	(02)2358-3902
總　經　銷	聯合發行股份有限公司
地　　　址	新北市新店區寶橋路235巷6弄6號2樓
電　　　話	(02)2917-8022・(02)2917-8042
製　版　廠	造極彩色印刷製版股份有限公司
地　　　址	新北市中和區中山路2段340巷36號
電　　　話	(02)2240-0333・(02)2248-3904
郵 撥 帳 戶	八方出版股份有限公司
郵 撥 帳 號	19809050